Regency Surrender: Rebellious Debutantes

ANNIE BURROWS

MILLS & BOON

First Published in Great Britain 2019
By Mills & Boon, an imprint of HarperCollinsPublishers
1 London Bridge Street, London, SE1 9GF

REGENCY SURRENDER: REBELLIOUS DEBUTANTES © 2019 Harlequin Books S.A.

Lord Havelock's List © 2014 Annie Burrows
Portrait of a Scandal © 2014 Annie Burrows

ISBN: 978-0-263-26793-8

52-0219

MIX
Paper from
responsible sources
FSC® C007454

This book is produced from independently certified FSC™ paper
to ensure responsible forest management.

For more information visit: www.harpercollins.co.uk/green

Printed and bound in Great Britain
by CPI Group (UK) Ltd. Croydon, CRO 4YY

LORD HAVELOCK'S
LIST

My lovely new editor Pippa - such a pleasure to work with.

Chapter One

December 1814

'Ho, there, Chepstow! Need some advice.'

Lord Chepstow, who'd been sauntering across the lobby of his club, paused, recognised Lord Havelock and grinned.

'From me?' He shook his head ruefully. 'Lord, you must be in the suds to want *my* advice.'

'I am,' said Lord Havelock bluntly. Then glanced meaningfully in the direction of the club's servant, who'd stepped forward to take his coat and hat.

Chepstow's grin faded. 'Need to find somewhere quiet, to talk in private?'

'Yes,' said Lord Havelock, feeling a great weight rolling off his shoulders. Not that he had much hope that Chepstow, of all men, would come up with any fresh ideas. But at least he was willing to listen.

As soon as they'd passed through the door to the library—the one room almost sure to be deserted at this, or any other, time of the day—he said it.

Out loud.

'Got to get married.'

'Good grief.' Chepstow's jaw dropped. 'Would never have thought you the type to get some girl into trouble. Not one you feel you have to marry, at any rate.'

Havelock clenched his fists in automatic repudiation of such a slur on his honour, causing Chepstow to raise his own hands in a placatory gesture.

'Now I come to think of it…' Chepstow said, carefully moving a few feet out of his range, 'sort of thing could happen to anyone.'

'Not me,' Havelock insisted. 'You know I've never been much in the petticoat line.' He lowered his fists as it occurred to him that, actually, Chepstow might be the very chap to help him, after all.

'You have been though, Chepstow. You've had some really high-flyers in keeping, haven't you? And still managed to stay popular with ladies of the *ton*. How d'ye do it, man? How d'ye get them all eating out of your hands, that's what I need to know.'

'By opening my purse strings to the high-flyers,' said Chepstow candidly, 'and minding my manners with the Quality. It's perfectly simple….'

'Yes, if all you are looking for is something of a temporary nature. But if you had to get married, what kind of woman would you ask? I mean, what sort of woman do you think would make a good wife? And how would you go about finding her, if you only had a fortnight's grace to get the knot tied?'

Chepstow froze, like a stag at bay. 'Me? Married?' He slowly shook his head. 'I wouldn't. The trick is avoiding the snares they lay for a fellow, not deliberately walking straight into one.'

'You don't understand,' Havelock began to say. But Chepstow wasn't listening. He was looking wildly round the room, like a hunted animal seeking cover. And then, with obvious relief, he found it in the form of a pair of young men just barely visible above an enormous mound of books on one of the reading desks, engaged in earnest conversation.

'Let's ask Ashe,' he said, grabbing Havelock by one arm and towing him across the floor with an air of desperation. 'Kind of chap who reads books when he don't need to is bound to know something worth knowing about matrimony.'

Which was rot, of course. But Chepstow was clearly panicking. Anybody who thought they could get away with manhandling him across a room, whilst babbling about books, had obviously lost his wits.

But then the topic of matrimony was apt to do that to a fellow. He wouldn't willingly put his head in the noose if there was any alternative. But, having racked his brains for hours, Havelock simply couldn't find one.

So he'd decided that the only thing to be done was to see if he couldn't somehow sugar-coat the pill he was about to swallow. Find some way, unlikely though it seemed, to find a woman who wouldn't oblige him to alter his entire way of life.

Who wouldn't try to alter *him*.

'Ashe, and, um…' Chepstow floundered as he shot a blank look at the second man at the table with Ashe.

'Morgan,' said the Earl of Ashenden, waving a languid hand at his companion. Havelock had seen Morgan about, at the races, Jackson's, this club and various social events, though had never had cause to speak to him before. Son of some sort of nabob, if memory served him. Nothing wrong with him, so far as he knew. Just not out of the top drawer.

Not that he cared a rap for any of that. Not at a time like this.

Introductions dealt with, Chepstow thrust Havelock into a chair, then perched on the edge of his own as though ready to take flight at a moment's notice.

'Havelock has decided he wants to get married,' he announced, rather in the manner of a man who has just tossed a hot potato out of his burnt fingers. Then he practically pounced on the waiter, who'd ventured into the library to see if any of the young gentlemen needed refreshment.

'We need a bottle of wine,' declared Chepstow with feeling.

'Not *want* to,' Havelock explained once the waiter was out of earshot. 'Have to. Need to. And before you start questioning my *ton*, no, it isn't because I've suddenly started seducing innocents,' he growled, shooting Chepstow a resentful look. 'That's not it at all.'

'Steady on,' said Chepstow, pushing enough books aside that the waiter would have room to put a bottle and some glasses down when he returned. 'Sort of mistake anyone could make. With you looking so…out of sorts. And then broaching the topic the way you did.'

'Gentlemen,' said Ashe in that quiet way he had that somehow made everyone listen. 'Perhaps the best thing to do would be to let Havelock explain, in his own words, just what his problem is and how he thinks we may be of assistance? Before he feels compelled to call on his seconds.'

At Morgan's look of alarm, Ashe chuckled quietly.

'It is a foolish man who casts a slur on Havelock's honour these days.'

'I don't, and never have, challenged my friends to duels.'

'You shot off half of Wraxton's ear,' put in Chepstow.

'He wasn't my friend.' Havelock folded his arms over his chest and glared across the table at Ashe. 'And it wasn't me he insulted. But…a lady.'

'Oho! And I thought you said you weren't in the petticoat line.'

'I'm not. Never have been. It wasn't like that—'

'From what I heard,' put in Ashe mildly, 'if it hadn't been you, it would have been her husband who challenged him.'

'He should have done,' snapped Havelock. 'Only…' He sighed, and pushed his fringe out of his eyebrows irritably. '*I* lost my temper with him first.'

'Never mind,' said Ashe soothingly. 'At least *someone* shot him. That is the main thing.'

'I shouldn't have done it,' admitted Havelock, as the waiter returned with a tray of wine and clean glasses. Meeting Wraxton had been nothing like the first duel he'd fought. Wraxton would have killed him stone dead if his pistol hadn't misfired. And therefore he'd wanted to kill him right back. If it hadn't been for a freakish bout of hiccups throwing his aim off, causing him to nick the man's ear rather than put a hole through what passed for his heart, he would have done. And would then have had to flee the country or face charges for murder.

Seeing how close he'd come to bringing dishonour on his family through sheer anger had pulled him up short. Since then, he'd made much more effort to keep a rein on his temper.

Although few people were foolish enough to think they could get away with goading him, after the affair with Wraxton. The tale had got about that he'd deliberately marked the man. That he was a crack shot.

Which just went to show what idiots most people were.

'I only wish,' he said, pouring himself a generous measure of wine, 'my problems now could be solved by issuing a challenge, picking my seconds, then putting a bullet into…someone. But the fact is I need to get married,' he said glumly. 'And soon. But I don't want to end up shackled to some harpy who will make my life a misery by constantly nagging at me to reform. And the thing with women,' he said, lifting the glass to his mouth, 'is that you never can tell what they're really like until *after* they've got you all legally tied up.' He took a gulp as he recalled just how many times he'd seen it happen. One minute they'd been blushing brides, tripping down the aisle all sweetness and light, and the next they'd become regular harpies, henpecking the poor devil who'd married them into an early grave.

'Well, the answer, then, is to make sure of the woman's character before you wed her,' said Ashe with infuriating logic.

'And just how am I supposed to do that in the limited time I have available?'

'Marry someone you know well,' said Morgan as though it was obvious.

'God, no!' Havelock seized his glass and threw the rest of its contents back in one go. 'I can't face the thought of actually *living*, in the *same house*, with *any* of the girls I know really well. And anyway, they wouldn't oblige me by marrying quickly. They'd want a big society affair.' He shuddered. 'Not to mention a massive trousseau, and so forth.'

'So, to be blunt, you want a girl who will take you exactly as you are, and won't demand a big society wedding.'

'Exactly.'

'You are looking for a mouse,' put in Morgan. 'A mouse so desperate for matrimony she'll take what little you're prepared to offer.'

'That's it,' he cried, startling the sneer from Morgan's face. 'That would work. Morgan, you are a genius.'

'You'd better be prepared to accept someone plain, then,' returned Morgan, somewhat taken aback by his enthusiasm for a suggestion he'd made with such sarcasm. 'And probably poor, as well.'

Havelock leaned back for a moment, considering. 'Don't think a plain face would put me off, so long as she's not a complete antidote.'

'Just a moment,' put in Ashe. 'Though, for whatever reason, you have decided to marry *now*, and in such haste, you must not forget the matter of succession. All of us, except perhaps you, Morgan,' he said, giving the nabob's son a dry smile, 'have a duty to marry and produce sons to take over our responsibilities in their turn.'

'Point taken,' said Havelock before Ashe could state the obvious. It went without saying that he'd have to find someone it wouldn't be too much of a hardship to bed.

'I notice you haven't denied needing a girl with a sizeable dowry,' said Morgan, looking at him through narrowed eyes. 'Is that why you need to marry in such a hurry? In need of an heiress, are you?'

At that point Chepstow, who'd got through two drinks to Havelock's one, let out a bark of laughter.

'Just because I'm not one of the dandy set,' said Havelock, self-consciously putting his hand to his neckcloth, which he'd knotted in a haphazard fashion much, much earlier that day, and no doubt looked even further from the apparently effortless elegance attained by the other men about the table, 'that don't mean I haven't a tidy income.'

Morgan eyed the pocket of Havelock's jacket, which had somehow got ripped half off during the course of the day, and then lowered his gaze to his muddied boots, which he hadn't stopped to change after the devastating interview with his lawyers. He'd walked and walked whilst trying to come up with a solution, before he'd noticed he was passing his club, and decided to come in and see if anyone else could come up with any better ideas.

'I don't need a woman to bring anything but herself to the union,' he finished belligerently.

Once again it was Ashe who defused the tension, by summoning the waiter who'd been hovering at a discreet distance, and asking him to fetch ink and paper.

'What we need to do, I think, is to make a comprehensive list of exactly what you do need, before we set our minds to the problem of how you may acquire it.'

'There,' cried Chepstow triumphantly. 'Didn't I say that Ashe was the very fellow to help? I'll just…' He half rose from his chair.

Havelock only had to glare at him for a second or two to take the wind out of his sails. A gentleman didn't bail out on his friends when they'd gone to him for help. Havelock had stood by Chepstow every time he'd needed help getting out of a scrape. Now the boot was on the other foot, he expected a similar show of loyalty.

Chepstow subsided into his seat with an air of resignation and, in a hollow voice, asked the waiter, who just then arrived with the writing materials, to bring them another bottle of wine.

'So,' said Ashe, dipping the pen into the ink, 'you do not require beauty, or wealth, in your prospective bride. But you do require a compliant nature—'

'A mouse,' repeated Morgan derisively.

Ashe shot him a reproving look over the top of his spectacles.

'Undemanding. And not one of the circle in which you habitually move.'

At Havelock's shudder, Ashe wrote, *not of the upper ten thousand* on his list.

'Any other requirements?' He paused, his hand hovering over the paper.

Havelock frowned as he considered.

'Quite a few, actually. That's what makes it all so damned difficult.' He ran his fingers through his hair, for what felt like the thousandth time that day. Not that it made any difference to the style, or rather lack of it. It was fortunate he wasn't obsessed with his appearance, for his thick, curly hair did whatever it wanted. Impervious to comb, or pomade, the only thing was to keep it short and hope for the best.

'I don't want a woman with *any* family to speak of,' he said with feeling.

'You mean…no titled family?' The nabob's son shot him a glance loaded with sympathy. 'Wouldn't want them looking down on you.'

Before Havelock had a chance to get up, seize the fellow by the throat and give him a shaking, Ashe put in mildly, 'Morgan is not aware of how very well connected you are, Havelock. I am sure he meant no insult.'

No, Havelock sighed. He probably didn't. And anyway, he'd already decided to forgo the pleasure of indulging in a decent set-to with anyone within the walls of this club.

'Look, I'm related to half the bloody *ton* as it is,' he explained to the bemused Morgan. 'What with stepbrothers, and stepsisters, and all the attendant stepcousins and aunts and uncles and such like all thinking they have a right to poke their nose into my affairs, I don't want someone bringing yet another set of relatives into my life and making it any more complicated, thank you very much.'

He saw Ashe write the word *orphan* on the list.

Morgan nodded. 'Makes sense. And an orphan, a girl with no family to support her, is all the more likely to agree to the kind of bargain you seem determined to strike.'

'What do you mean by that?'

Chepstow poured a large measure of wine into Havelock's empty glass and nudged it towards him.

'I am sure Morgan meant nothing you need take offence at, Havelock,' reproved Ashe in the reasonable tone that so many men found damned supercilious.

He was beginning to understand why.

Havelock folded his arms and glared across the table.

To his credit, Morgan met his look without blinking.

Ashe removed his spectacles and set to polishing them with a silk handkerchief he produced from an inner pocket of his tailcoat. 'May I make a suggestion?'

'I wish you would. It's why I came in here, after all. See if anyone could help me find a way through this… morass,' said Havelock.

'Well, for myself,' said Ashe diffidently, 'I could not

stand to be married to a woman who did not possess a keen intellect.'

'Lord,' said Havelock, aghast. 'I wouldn't know what to do with a bluestocking!'

'Oh, come,' said Lord Chepstow, his devilish grin returning for the first time since they'd sat down. He then proceeded to offer a variety of suggestions about what exactly a man could do with a bluestocking, her garters, and various other items of apparel before descending into a spate of vulgarity that, though a little off the topic at hand, did at least serve to lighten the atmosphere.

When they'd stopped laughing, had wiped their eyes, topped up all their glasses and called for another bottle of wine, Ashe brought them all back to the point.

'You mustn't forget that this woman, whoever she may be, will be the mother of your children, Havelock. So, as well as considering what kind of woman you could tolerate living under your roof, you should also ask yourself what kind of children do you want to sire? For myself, I would hope my own offspring would have the capacity to make me proud. I would hate to think,' he said, giving Havelock a particularly penetrating look, 'that I had curtailed my own freedom only to produce a brood of idiots.'

Havelock ran his fingers through his hair yet again. 'You are in the right of it.' He sighed. 'Must think of the succession. Very well, put that on your list, Ashe. Not completely hen-witted.'

Since Ashe was taking a sip of wine it was Morgan who picked up the pen and wrote that down.

'I want her to be kind, too,' declared Havelock with some force. 'Good with youngsters. Not one of these women who think only of themselves.'

'Good, good, now we are really getting somewhere,' said Ashe, as Morgan added these further points to the steadily growing list.

'It's all very well making a list,' put in Morgan, tossing the pen aside. 'But how do you propose finding a woman who meets all your requirements? Put an advertisement in the papers?'

'God, no! Don't want the whole world to know how desperate I am to find a wife. I'd have every matchmaking mama within fifty miles of town descending on me with their simpering daughters in tow. Besides…' he shook his head '…it would take too long. Much too long. Only think of having the advertisement put in, then waiting for women to reply, then sifting through the mountain of responses, then having to interview them all…'

Morgan let out a bark of laughter. 'You are so sure you will have hundreds of replies, are you?'

'Oh, yes,' said Havelock testily. 'I've had women flinging themselves at me every Season for the past half-dozen years.'

'And during summer house parties,' put in Chepstow.

'There was that Christmas house party, wasn't there,' Ashe added, 'where—'

'Never mind that!' Havelock interrupted swiftly. 'I thought we'd agreed never to speak of *that* episode again.'

'Then there was that filly at the races,' said Chepstow.

Morgan laughed again. 'Very well. You have all convinced me. Havelock is indeed one of those men that society misses regard as a matrimonial prize.' Though the way he looked at Havelock conveyed his opinion that there was just no understanding the workings of the female mind.

'And you wouldn't believe some of the tricks they've employed in their attempts to bag me,' he said bitterly.

'Couldn't you simply settle with one of these women who've shown themselves so keen to, um, bag you? That would save you time, wouldn't it?'

Havelock gave Morgan a cold stare, before saying, 'No. Absolutely not. Can't stand women who flutter their eyelashes and pretend to swoon, and flaunt their bosoms in your face at every opportunity.'

Modest, he noted Ashe write on the bottom of the list, out of the corner of his eye.

'And anyway, the girls I already know, the ones who have made it plain they want me, have also made it plain they want a damn sight more from me than I'm willing to give. I'd make them miserable. So then they'd make damn sure they made me miserable.'

Ashe dipped his pen in the inkwell one more time, and wrote, *not looking for affection from matrimony.*

Morgan frowned down at the list, sipping at his drink. 'What this list describes,' he said thoughtfully, 'is a woman who is willing to consider a businesslike arrangement. Someone from a respectable family that has fallen on hard times, perhaps. Someone who would like to have children, but has no hopes of gaining a suitor through the normal way.'

'Normal way?'

'Feminine wiles,' supplied Morgan helpfully.

'Oh, them,' huffed Havelock. 'No. I definitely don't want a wife who's got too many feminine wiles. I'd rather she was straightforward.'

Honest, wrote Ashe.

'Good grief,' said Chepstow, peering rather blear-
ily at the list. 'You will never, ever, find a woman who
has all those attributes, no matter how long you look.'

'Oh, I don't know,' said Morgan. 'There are any number of genteel poor eking out an existence in London
right at this moment. With daughters aplenty who'd give
their eye teeth to receive a proposal from a man of Havelock's standing, from what you tell me. I'm tolerably
sure that he could find one or two amongst them who
would have at least a couple of the character traits he
finds important. Particularly if he's not going to be put
off by a plain face.'

Havelock leaned forward in his seat. 'You really think
so?'

'Oh, yes.'

'And do you know where I might find them?'

Morgan leaned back, crossing one long leg over the
other, and stared hard at the wall behind Havelock's
head. The other men at the table waited with bated breath
for his answer.

'Do you know, I rather think I do. I could probably
introduce you to a couple of likely prospects tomorrow
night, if you don't mind—' He broke off, eyeing Havelock's less-than-pristine garb, and laughed. 'No, you
don't look like a chap who stands on ceremony. And I
have an invitation to a ball, given by people who will
never be accepted into the very top echelons of society,
for all their wealth. Yet, amongst their guests, there are
always a number of people in the exact circumstances
to be of use to you. Good families, fallen on hard times,
who have to put up with what society they can get. I dare
say every single female there of marriageable age will
look upon you as a godsend.'

'And you wouldn't mind taking me to such a ball?'

'Not in the least,' said Morgan affably. 'Is that not what friends are for? To help a fellow out?'

It was. He'd been on the verge of being disappointed in Chepstow. But really, the fellow had done what he could. He'd brought him to Ashe, who'd helped him to get his thoughts set down in a logical fashion, and introduced him to Morgan, who was going to give him practical assistance.

'To friendship,' he said, raising his glass to the three men sitting round the table with him.

'And marriage,' said Ashe, lifting his glass in response.

'Let's not get carried away,' said Lord Chepstow, his glass stopping a mere inch from his lips. 'To Havelock's marriage, perhaps. Not the institution as such.'

'Havelock's marriage, then,' said Ashe.

'Havelock's bride,' said Morgan, downing his own drink in one go and reaching for the bottle.

'Yes, don't mind drinking to her,' said Chepstow. 'Your bride, my friend.'

And let's hope, thought Havelock as he carefully folded the list and put it in his pocket, *that the woman who possesses at least the most important of these attributes will be at the ball tomorrow night.*

Chapter Two

'Can you really do nothing better with your hair?'

Mary lowered her gaze to the floor and shook her head as Aunt Pargetter sighed.

'Couldn't you at least have borrowed Lotty's tongs? I am sure she wouldn't begrudge them to you. If you could only get just a *leetle* curl into it, I am sure it would look far more fetching than just letting it hang round your face like a curtain.'

Mary put her hand to her head to check that the neat bun, in which she'd fastened her hair earlier, hadn't already come undone.

'No, no,' said Aunt Pargetter with exasperation. 'It hasn't come down yet. I am talking in generalities.'

Oh, those. She'd heard a lot of those over the past few months. Generalities uttered by lawyers about indigent females, by relations about the cost of doing their duty and by coach drivers about passengers who didn't give tips. She'd also heard a lot of specifics. Which informed her exactly how she'd become indigent and why each set of people she'd been sent to in turn couldn't, at present, offer her a home.

'Now, I know you feel a little awkward about attending a ball when you are still in mourning,' Aunt Pargetter went on remorselessly. 'But I just cannot leave you here on your own this evening to mope. And besides, there will be any number of eligible men there tonight. Who is to say you won't catch someone's eye and then all your problems will be solved?'

Mary's head flew up at that, her eyes wide. Aunt Pargetter was talking of marriage. Marriage! As if that was the answer to *any* woman's problems.

She shivered and lowered her gaze again, pressing her lips tightly together. It would solve Aunt Pargetter's problems, right enough. She hadn't said so, but Mary could see that keeping her fed and housed for any length of time would strain the family's already limited resources. But, rather than throwing up her hands, and passing her on to yet another member of the family upon whom Mary might have a tenuous claim, Aunt Pargetter had just taken her in, patted her hand and told her she needn't worry any longer. That she'd look after her.

Mary just hadn't realised that Aunt Pargetter's plan for looking after her involved marrying her off.

'You need to lift your head a little more and look about you,' advised Aunt Pargetter, approaching her with her hand outstretched. She lifted Mary's chin and said, 'You have fine eyes, you know. What my girls wouldn't give for lashes like yours.' She sighed, shaking her head. And then, before Mary had any idea she might be under attack and could take evasive action, the woman pinched both her cheeks. 'There. That's put a little colour in your face. Now all you need to do is put on a smile, as though you are enjoying yourself, and you won't look quite so…'

Repulsive. Plain. Dowdy.

'Unappealing,' Aunt Pargetter finished. 'You could be fairly pretty, you know, if only you would…' She waved her hands in exasperation, but was saved from having to come up with a word that would miraculously make Mary not sound as though she was completely miserable when her own daughters bounced into the room in a froth of curls and flounces.

Aunt Pargetter had no time left to spare on Mary when her beloved girls needed a final inspection, and just a little extra primping, before she bundled them all into the hired hack they couldn't afford to keep waiting.

'We have an invitation from a family by the name of Crimmer tonight,' Aunt Pargetter explained to Mary as the hack jolted over the cobbles. 'They are not the sort who would object to me bringing along another guest, so don't you go worrying your head about not receiving a formal invitation.'

Mary's eyes nevertheless widened in alarm. She hadn't any idea her aunt would have taken her to this event without forewarning her hosts.

Aunt Pargetter reached across the coach and patted her hand. 'I shall just explain you have only recently arrived for a visit, which is perfectly true. Besides, the Crimmers will love being able to boast that their annual ball has become so popular *everyone* wants to attend. But what is even more fortunate for you, my dear, is that they have two sons to find brides for, not that the younger is quite old enough yet, and I've heard rumours that the older one is more or less spoken for.'

As Mary frowned in bewilderment at the contradictory nature of that somewhat rambling statement, her aunt explained, 'The point is, they have a lot of wealthy friends with sons who must be on the lookout for a wife, as well. Especially one as well connected as you.'

'What do you mean, Mama?' Charlotte shot a puzzled glance at Mary. It had clearly come as a shock to her to hear there might be anything that could possibly make Mary a likely prospect on the marriage mart, when all week they'd been thinking of her as the poor relation.

'Well, although her poor dear mama was my cousin, by marriage, her papa was a younger son of the youngest daughter of the Earl of Finchingfield.'

Mary's heart sank. Her well-meaning aunt clearly meant to spread news of her bloodlines about tonight as though she were some...brood mare.

'But if she's related to the Earl of Finchingfield, why hasn't she gone to him?' Dorothy, Charlotte's younger, and prettier, sister, piped up.

That was a good question. And Mary turned to Aunt Pargetter with real interest, to see how she would explain the tangle that had been her mother's married life.

'Oh, the usual thing,' said her aunt with an airy wave of her hand. 'Somebody didn't approve of the marriage, someone threatened to cut someone off, people stopped speaking to one another and, before you knew it, a huge rift had opened up. But Mary's mother's people still know how to do their duty, I hope, when a child is involved. Not that you are a child any longer, Mary, but you know what I mean. It isn't fair for you to have to suffer the consequences of the mistakes your parents made.'

Charlotte and Dorothy were both now looking at her with wide eyes. Mary's heart sank still further. In the few days she'd been living in their little house in Bloomsbury, she'd discovered that the pair of them had a passion for the kind of novels where dispossessed heiresses went through a series of adventures before winding up married to an Italian prince. She was very much afraid they'd suddenly started seeing her as one of those.

Still, since the Crimmers, who were in trade, weren't likely to have invited an Italian prince to their ball, she needn't worry they would attempt to push them into each other's arms. Actually, she needn't worry that either Lotty or Dotty would push her into anyone's arms. They were both far too keen on eligible bachelors themselves to let a single one of them, foreign or not, slip through their own eager fingers.

She pulled her shoulders down and took a deep breath. No need to worry. Aunt Pargetter might talk about her suitability for marriage as much as she liked, but that didn't mean she was at risk of having some marriage-minded man sweeping her off her feet tonight. Or any night. She wasn't the type of girl men did want to sweep off her feet.

Men didn't tend to notice her. Well, she'd made sure they wouldn't by developing the habit of shrinking into the background. And by dint of following just a few steps behind her more exuberant cousins, she very soon managed to fade into the background tonight, as well. It was never very hard. Most girls of her age actually *wanted* people to look at them. Especially men. So there was always someone to hide behind.

Mary found a chair slightly to the rear of her aunt and cousins when they all sat down. By shifting it, only a very little, she managed to make use of a particularly leafy potted plant, as well.

Though she was now shielded from a large percentage of the ballroom, she had a good view of the main door through which other guests were still pouring in, greeting one another with loud voices as they flaunted their evening finery. If she hadn't already decided to keep out of sight, the wealth on display in this room would have totally overawed her. Dotty and Lotty scanned the crowd with equal avidity, whispering to each other behind their fans about the gowns and jewels of the females, the figures and incomes of the males.

'Oh, look, it's Mr Morgan,' eventually exclaimed Lotty, as a pair of young men entered the ballroom. 'I really didn't think he'd be here tonight.'

From that comment, and the fact that she and Dotty immediately sat up straighter, their fans fluttering at a greatly increased tempo, she guessed the man in question was what they termed 'a catch.' She could, for once, actually see why. The shorter of the two men was extremely good-looking, in a rugged sort of way, besides being turned out in a kind of casual elegance that made him look far more approachable than others of his age, with their starched shirt points and nipped-in waists.

'Who is that with him?'

Following slightly behind the handsome newcomer was a taller, rather rangy man with ferocious eyebrows.

'He must be a friend of his from school, or somewhere,' whispered Lotty. 'See the way Mrs Crimmer is smiling at him, giving him her hand and sort of... fluttering?'

Mary joined her cousins in watching the progress round the room of what must be decidedly eligible bachelors, given the way the ladies in every group they approached preened and fluttered for all they were worth.

By the time they reached their corner of the ballroom, Dotty and Lotty were almost beside themselves.

'Good evening, Mrs Pargetter, Miss Pargetter, Miss

Dorothy,' said the tall, slender man, somewhat to Mary's confusion. *This* was the man who'd set her cousins all aflutter?

He must be very wealthy then, because he certainly didn't have looks on his side. Not like his companion.

'Allow me to present my friend,' Mr Morgan added. 'The Viscount Havelock.'

Dotty's and Lotty's heads both swivelled in unison as they tore their eyes from the man they considered the prize catch of the night, to the man they'd just discovered to be a genuine peer of the realm. They both pushed their bosoms out a little further, fluttering their fans and eyelashes at top speed.

The viscount, apparently unimpressed by their ability to do all three things at once, accorded them no more than a curt nod.

Then his gaze slid past them, caught her in the act of biting back a smile and stilled.

'And who is this?'

'Oh, well, this is my…well, almost a niece, by marriage,' said her aunt. 'Miss Carpenter.'

Mary's cheeks heated. She really shouldn't have been mocking the ridiculous way her cousins had been preening just because a titled man was standing within three feet of them. But he didn't look as though he minded. On the contrary, that bored, slightly irritated look he'd bestowed on them had vanished without trace. If anything, she would swear he looked as though he shared her view that they were being a little silly.

And then he smiled at her with what looked like… Well, if she didn't know better, as if he'd just found something he'd been looking for.

'Do you care to dance, Miss Carpenter?'

'Me?' Her jaw dropped. She closed her mouth hastily, then shook her head and lowered it.

'N-no. I couldn't…' Lotty and Dotty would be furious with her. And insulted. And rightly so. It was almost a snub, to ask her, in preference to them, after they'd made their interest so blatant.

Could that be the reason he'd asked?

You never could tell, with men. What looked like an act of charity could be performed deliberately to spite someone else, or in order to put someone in their place. She stared doggedly at her shoes, her spirits sinking to just about their level. You couldn't judge a man by the handsome cast of his features. And she'd been foolish to have been even momentarily deceived by them and that rather…heartening smile.

It was a man's actions that revealed his true nature.

'My niece is in mourning, as you can see,' her aunt was explaining, waving her hand towards Mary's plain, sober gown.

'Really?'

She couldn't help looking up at the tone of the viscount's voice. It was almost as if he… But, no, he couldn't be pleased to hear she was in mourning, could he? That was absurd.

And there was nothing in his face, now she was looking at it, to indicate anything but sympathy.

'Perhaps,' he said, in a rather kinder tone of voice, 'you would be my partner for supper, later?'

'Oh, well, I…' The look in his eyes made her tongue cleave to the roof of her mouth. It was so…intent. As though he wanted to discover every last one of her secrets. As though he would turn her inside out and upside down, until he'd shaken them all from her. As though nothing would stop him.

It made her most uncomfortable. But at the exact same moment Mary decided she would have to somehow refuse his invitation, her aunt accepted it on her behalf. 'Mary would be honoured. Wouldn't you, dear?' She poked her with the end of her furled fan, as if determined to prod the approved response from her.

When she still couldn't give it, the viscount smiled again, then turned his attention to her cousins.

'And in the meantime,' he said, with surprising enthusiasm, 'would either of you two lovely young ladies show pity on a stranger, by dancing with me?'

Fortunately, before they could elbow one another out of the way in their eagerness to get their hands on him, the tall thin one held out his hand to Charlotte.

Mary sighed with relief as the foursome made their way out on to the dance floor. But her relief was short-lived.

'I believe you have made a conquest,' breathed her aunt in rapturous tones as she sidled closer, pushing a palm frond out of the way. 'Lord Havelock seemed most interested in you.'

'I cannot think why,' said Mary. She'd practically hidden herself behind a potted palm, she was wearing a plain gown that did nothing for her pale complexion and she'd turned down his offer of a dance. 'Perhaps he needs spectacles,' she wondered aloud. 'That might account for it.'

'Nonsense! He can clearly see that you have good breeding. My girls may be prettier than you,' she said with blunt honesty, 'but neither of them would know how to go on in his world.' She nodded towards the viscount, who was leading a glowing Dotty into the bottom set.

'Well, I don't suppose I would, either,' retorted Mary. 'It's not as if I've ever been a part of it.'

'No, but your mother was far more genteel than I've ever been. And your father, too—I dare say he taught you how a real lady should behave.'

Mary did her best not to react to that statement, though something inside her shrivelled up into a defensive ball at the mere mention of her father.

'Papa was…very strict with me, yes,' she admitted. Not that she would ever mention the form his strictness took, not to a living soul. Particularly not as he directed most of it firmly, and squarely, at her mother, rather than her.

'And he certainly did have strong opinions about how a lady should behave,' she also admitted, when her aunt kept looking at her as though she expected her to say something more. And he enforced those opinions. With loud demands, interspersed with terrifyingly foreboding silences, when he was sober, fists and boots when he was not.

'I really do not want,' she said tremulously, 'an eligible *parti* to prefer me to either of my cousins. Especially not when they seem so taken with him.'

'Well, that's all very well and good, but he's plainly only got eyes for you. Besides, both my girls would be far more comfortable with Mr Morgan. Not out of their reach, socially, you see, for all his wealth.'

Mary took a second look at her cousins as they skipped up and down the set. Though Dotty looked as though she was enjoying herself, Lotty was positively glowing. And had Dotty just shot Mr Morgan a coy glance over her shoulder while the viscount's back was towards her?

She frowned. How could either of them prefer that great long beanpole of a man to the dashing viscount? Not only was he much better looking but he had a more amiable expression. She'd even thought she might have detected a sense of humour lurking in the depths of those honeyed hazel eyes. When he'd caught her smiling at the way Dotty and Lotty had reacted on learning he had a title, it had been like sharing a private joke.

Only, she reminded herself tartly, to suspect him of snubbing them rather unkindly a moment later.

She was in no position to judge him. Or think her own observations could have any sway over Dotty's or Lotty's decisions. Lords were notorious for being as poor as church mice. If his pockets were to let, then he'd be looking to marry an heiress. Which ruled them both out.

Besides, they knew Mr Morgan was wealthy. Which must make him terribly tempting.

Anyway, she was not going to harbour a single uncharitable thought towards them. Not when they'd been the only ones of her extended family to make room for her in their lives. The girls could have protested when their mother told them Mary was to share their room. But they hadn't. They'd just said how beastly it must be for her to have nowhere else to go and emptied one of the drawers for her things.

Mary had tried to repay them all by making herself useful about the house. And until tonight, she'd thought she was beginning to make a permanent place for herself.

But it was not to be. Aunt Pargetter, who wasn't even really an aunt at all, but only a distant connection by marriage, might be kinder than most of the relatives she'd met so far, but it was absurd to think she would house her indefinitely.

Even so, she was not going to tamely submit to her misguided plans to marry her off. No matter how kindly meant the intention was, such a scheme wouldn't do for her.

In the morning, she would find out where the nearest employment agency was located and go and register for some kind of work. Not that she had any idea what she might do. She darted a look at Aunt Pargetter, wishing she could ask her advice. But it would be a waste of time. Aunt Pargetter, though kindness itself, was also one of those females who thought marriage was the height of any woman's ambitions and wouldn't understand her preference for work.

Well, then, she would just have to, somehow, discover where the agency was on her own. Although what excuse she could give for wishing to leave the house, she could not think. Everyone knew she had no money with which to go shopping. Besides, since she was a stranger to London, either Dotty or Lotty, or probably both, would be sent with her to make sure she didn't get lost.

She became so wrapped up in formulating one plan after another, only to discard it as unworkable, that she scarcely noticed when the dancing came to a halt and people began to make their way to the supper room. Until Viscount Havelock brushed the fronds of the potted palm to one side, smiling down at her as he offered her his hand.

'Are you ready for a bite to eat? I must confess, all this dancing has given me quite an appetite.'

'Oh. Um…' He wasn't out of breath, though. Her

cousins were fanning their flushed faces, Mr Morgan was mopping his brow with a handkerchief, but Lord Havelock wasn't displaying the slightest sign of fatigue. He was obviously very fit.

Not that she ought to notice such things about a man.

Flustered by the turn of her thoughts, she took the viscount's hand and allowed him to place her hand on his sleeve.

It must just be that something about him reminded her of her brother's friends. Several of them had been of his class and had about them the same air of...vitality. Of vigour. And the same self-assurance that came with knowing they were born to command.

She regarded her hand, where it lay on his sleeve. The arm encased in the soft material of his evening coat felt like a plank of oak. Just like her brother's had. And those of his friends he'd sometimes brought home, who'd escorted her round the town. Not that this viscount actually worked for his living, like those lads who'd served in the navy. From what she knew of aristocrats, he probably maintained his fitness by boxing and fencing, and riding.

He was probably what her brother would have called a Corinthian. She darted a swift glance at his profile, taking in the firm set of his jaw and the healthy complexion. Yes, definitely a Corinthian. At least, he certainly didn't look as though he spent his days sleeping off the effects of the night before.

And, if he was one of the sporting set, that would explain why he wore clothing that looked comfortable, rather than fitted tightly to show off his physique. He might not be on the catch for an heiress at all.

Her cheeks flushed. She couldn't believe she was speculating about his reasons for being here. Or the body underneath his clothing. Not that she'd ever spent so much time thinking about a man's choice of clothing, either. Just because he seemed better turned out than any other man present, in some indefinable way, she had no business making so much of it.

'I hope the crowd of people we are following *are* heading to the supper room,' he said, breaking into her thoughts.

'I…I suppose they must be,' she replied, but only after casting about desperately for an interesting reply and coming up empty.

'You are not a regular visitor to this house?'

She shook her head. 'I have only been in London a few days,' she admitted. 'I don't know anyone.'

'Apart from the lady you are with. Your…aunt?'

Mary shook her head again. 'I had never even met her before I turned up on her doorstep with a letter of introduction from my lawyer. And to be perfectly frank, I'm not at all sure the connection is…'

Suddenly Mary wondered why on earth she was telling this total stranger such personal information. It couldn't be simply because there was something about him that put her in mind of her brother and his fellow officers, could it? Or because he'd given her that look, earlier, that had made her feel as though he was genuinely interested?

How pathetic did that make her? One kind word, one keen look, a smile and a touch of his hand and she'd been on the verge of unburdening herself.

Good grief—she was as susceptible to a good-looking man as the cousins she'd decried as ninnies not an hour earlier. She, who'd sworn never to let a handsome face sway her judgement, had just spent a full five minutes wondering how he managed to keep so fit and speculating about the cut of his clothes, *and* what lay beneath them.

'You don't really have any family left to speak of, is that what you were about to say?'

She couldn't recall what she'd been about to say. Nor even what the question had been. Her mind kept veering off into realms it had never strayed into before and consequently got lost there.

'Your…aunt, or whatever she is,' he persisted, while her cheeks flooded with guilty heat, 'said you are in mourning. Was it…for someone very close?'

Well, that dealt with the strange effects his proximity had been wreaking in her mind and body. He might as well have doused her with a bucket of cold water.

'My mother,' she said. 'She was all I had left.'

She might be in a crowded ballroom tonight, on the arm of the most handsome and eligible man in the room, but the truth was that she was utterly alone in the world, and destitute.

'That's c…' He pulled himself up short and patted her hand. 'I mean to say, dreadful. For you.'

They'd reached the doorway now and beyond she could see tables laid out with a bewildering array of dishes that looked extremely decorative, but not at all like anything she might ever have eaten before.

Since they'd both come without an invitation, space was found for them at a table squeezed into the bay of a window.

'Don't worry,' he said when he noted her gaze darting about anxiously. 'I shall make sure we find your aunt once we have eaten and return you to her side in complete safety.'

She was amazed he'd noticed how awkward she felt. And that he'd correctly deduced it was being separated from her aunt that had caused it. Most men couldn't see further than the end of their noses.

He must have noticed the way she'd eyed the food with trepidation, too, because he took great care, when offering her dishes, to ask if she liked the principal ingredient of each. Which deftly concealed her ignorance. For he could have explained what everything was, making her feel even more awkward, whilst puffing off his own *savoir faire*. As it was, since the other men at their table were passing dishes round, and helping the ladies to slices of this, or spoonfuls of that, nobody noticed anything untoward.

Eventually, her plate, like that of everyone else at the table, was piled high and conversation began to flow.

Except between Lord Havelock and her.

She supposed he'd gone to the length of his chivalry. She supposed he was waiting for her to make some kind of remark that would open up the kind of light, inconsequential conversations that were springing up all around them.

But for the life of her she couldn't dredge up a single topic she could imagine might be of interest to a man like him. Or the kind of man she suspected he was. She didn't really know a thing about him.

And though she was grateful to him for the way he'd behaved so far, she began to wish she was with her aunt and cousins. *They* would know how to entertain him, she was sure. They wouldn't let this awkward silence go on, and on, and on…

He cleared his throat, half turned towards her and said, 'Do you…?' He cleared his throat again, took a sip of wine and started over. 'That is, I wonder, do you enjoy living in town, or do you prefer the country? I suppose,' he said with a swift frown before she could answer, 'I should have enquired where you lived before you had to come to London, shouldn't I? I don't know why I assumed you had lived in the country before.'

'I lived in Portsmouth, actually,' she said, relieved to be able to have a question she could answer without having to rack her brains. 'And I haven't been here long enough to know whether I prefer it, or not.'

'But do you have any objection to living in the countryside?'

It was her turn to frown. 'I cannot tell. I have never lived anywhere but in a town.'

Oh, what a stupid, stupid thing to say. She should have made some remark about how…bustling London was in comparison to Portsmouth, or…or how she missed the sound of the sea. Or even better, asked him about *his* preferences. That was what men liked, really, wasn't it? To talk about themselves? Instead, she'd killed the potential conversation stone dead.

They resumed eating in silence for a few more minutes before he made a second, valiant attempt to breach it. 'Well, do you like children?'

'Yes, I suppose in a general way,' though she couldn't imagine why he might ask that. But at least she'd learned her lesson from last time. She would offer him the chance to talk about himself. 'Why do you ask?'

'Oh, no reason,' he said airily, though the faint blush that tinged his cheeks told her he was growing a bit uncomfortable. 'Just making conversation.' He reached for his wine glass and curled his fingers round the stem as though in need of something to hang on to. And then blurted, 'What do people talk about at events like this?'

For the first time in her life, she actually felt sorry for a man. He'd come here expecting to enjoy himself and ended up saddled with the dullest, most boring female in the room. And far from betraying his exasperation with her ignorance, and her timidity, he'd done his best to put her at ease. He'd even been making an attempt to *draw her out*. And wasn't finding it easy.

'I expect it is easier for them,' she said, indicating the other occupants of the table. 'That is…I mean…they all know each other already, I think.'

He looked round the table and she couldn't help contrasting the animated chatter of all the other females, who were universally fluttering their eyelashes at their male companions in the attempt to charm them. Then he looked back at her and smiled.

'Well, we'll just have to get to know each other then, won't we?'

Oh, dear. Did he mean to ask her a lot of highly personal questions? Or expect her to come up with some witty banter, or start flirting like the other women? That's what came of throwing a man even the tiniest conversational sop. She'd made him think she was interested in *getting to know* him.

'What,' he said abruptly, 'do you think about climbing boys?'

'I beg your pardon? Climbing boys?'

'Yes. The little chaps they send up chimneys.'

All of a sudden, the odd things he said, and the abrupt way he said them reminded her very forcibly of her own brother's behaviour, when confronted by a female to whom he was not related. He was trying his best, but this was clearly a man who was more at ease in the company of other men. Lord Havelock had no more idea how to talk to a single lady than she had as to how to amuse an eligible male.

He was staring at his plate now, a dull flush mounting his cheeks, as though he knew he'd just raised a topic that was not at all suitable for a dinner table, let alone what was supposed to be the delicate sensibilities of a female.

And once again, she felt...not sorry for him. No, not that. But willing to meet his attempts to entertain her halfway. For he was exerting himself to a considerable extent. A thing no other male she'd ever encountered had ever even *considered* doing. And though men did not usually want to hear what a woman thought, he had asked, and so she girded up her loins to express her opinion. It wasn't as if she was ever likely to see him again, so what did it matter if he *was* offended by it?

'It is a cruel practice,' she said. 'I know chimneys have to be cleaned, but surely there must be a more humane way? I hear there are devices that can produce results that are almost as good.'

'Devices,' he said, turning to her with a curious expression.

'For cleaning chimneys.'

'Really? I had no idea.'

'Oh? But then why did you ask me about them?'

His brows drew down irritably.

'I beg your pardon,' she said hastily, hanging her head meekly. Whatever had possessed her to question him? How could she have forgotten the way her father had reacted should her mother have ever dared to question his motive for saying *anything*, no matter how absurd?

There was a moment's awkward pause. She darted

him a wary glance to find he'd folded his arms across his chest and was glaring at his plate as though he was contemplating sweeping it, and its contents, from the table before storming off.

A kind of dim terror crept over her. A mist rising up from her past. Her own appetite fled. She pleated her napkin between nervous fingers, fighting to stay calm. He couldn't very well backhand her out of the chair, she reminded herself. Not even her father had taken such drastic action, when she'd angered him, not in public, at any rate.

No—Lord Havelock was more likely to return her to her chaperon in frosty silence and vow never to have anything to do with her again.

She felt him shift in his seat, next to her. 'Entirely my fault,' he growled between clenched teeth. 'No business bringing such a topic up at a dinner table. Cannot think what came over me.'

The mist shredded, blasted apart by the shock wave of his apology. She turned and stared at him.

'I dare say you can tell that I'm just not used to conversing with…ladies.'

Good grief. Not only had he apologised, but he, a *man*, had admitted to having a fault.

'I…I'm not very good at it myself. Not conversing with ladies, obviously, I can do that. I meant, conversing with members of the opposite…' She floundered on the precipice of uttering a word that would be an even worse *faux pas* than mentioning the grim reality of chimney sweeps.

And then he smiled.

A rather devilish smile that told her he knew exactly which word she'd almost said.

With an unholy light in his eyes that sent awareness of her own sex flooding from the pit of her stomach to the tips of her toes.

Chapter Three

'So you found your mouse,' remarked Morgan, as they strode out into the night.

'I've found a young lady who appears to meet many of my requirements,' Havelock testily corrected him. He hadn't been able to believe his luck when the bashful creature he'd had to coax out from behind her potted plant had admitted to being an orphan.

'The only problem is,' he said with a scowl, 'the very things I like most about her make it devilish difficult to find out what her character is really like.'

'How so?'

'Well, it was damn near impossible to pry more than a couple of words out of her at a time.' To think he'd congratulated himself on so deftly separating her from her more exuberant cousins, only to come unstuck at the dinner table.

'I made a complete cake of myself.' He sighed. She wasn't like the girls he was used to sitting with at such events. Girls who either flirted, or threw out conversational gambits intended to impress and charm. She'd left all the work to him. And he discovered he was a very poor hand at it. In his determination to delve to the heart of her, he'd asked the kind of questions that had both puzzled and alarmed her.

Climbing boys, for God's sake! Who in their right minds asked a gently reared girl about such a deplorable topic? Over a supper table?

Though in fairness to Miss Carpenter, she'd swiftly rallied and given an answer of which he could heartily approve. And shown her head wasn't stuffed with goose down. Devices for sweeping chimneys, eh? Where could she have heard about them? If they even existed.

'You know,' said Morgan as they turned in the direction of their club, 'either of her cousins would be only too glad to get an offer from you. Wouldn't be so much work, either. That's why I made them known to you. Family not that well off, eager to climb the social ladder. Have known them some time, so I can vouch for them both being good girls, at heart.'

'No, thank you,' said Havelock firmly, recalling the way they'd fluttered and preened the moment they heard he had a title. 'Miss Carpenter is the one for me.'

'Very well,' said Morgan with a shrug. 'Perhaps you will get a chance to discover more about her when we go and visit her tomorrow.'

'Perhaps,' he said gloomily. He wished now that he *had* been more in the petticoat line. Had more experience with plumbing the depths of women's natures. He'd plumbed other depths, naturally, to the satisfaction of both parties involved, but had always avoided anything that smacked of emotion. The moment a woman started to seem as though she wanted to get 'close', he'd dropped her like a hot potato.

He'd thought it was safer.

And it had been. Not one of them had ever managed to get under his skin. The trouble was, keeping himself heart whole had left him woefully unprepared for the most important task of his life.

'Good morning, my lord,' gushed Mrs Pargetter.

Havelock favoured her with his most courtly bow. If he was going to be frequenting these premises, he needed to be on good terms with the hostess.

Miss Carpenter's cousins, whose names escaped him for the moment, fluttered at him from their strategic locations on two separate sofas, indicating their willingness to have him join them. Or Morgan. The hussies didn't appear to mind which.

Miss Carpenter, on the other hand, was sitting on a straight-backed chair by the window, looking very much as though she would like to disappear behind the curtains.

Morgan made straight for the younger chit, so he went and sat beside the elder. He'd paid this kind of duty visit to dance partners, the day after a ball, before. But he'd never realised how frustrating they could be if a fellow was serious about pursuing a female. You couldn't engage in meaningful conversation with teacups and macaroons being thrust under your nose every five minutes. Not that he'd had much success in the field of conversation when he *had* got her to himself.

'We hope you will permit us to take your lovely daughters out tomorrow,' Morgan was saying. Havelock scowled. He didn't want to take either of *them* anywhere.

The girls looked at each other. Then their heads swivelled towards the window where Mary was sitting.

'And you, too, Miss Carpenter, of course,' said Havelock, taking his cue from them. Morgan had been right. Man-hungry they might be, but they weren't totally ruthless in their pursuit of prey. They were willing to offer Miss Carpenter a share in their spoils.

'Oh, no,' said Miss Carpenter, blushing. 'Really, I don't think…'

'Nonsense, Mary,' said her aunt briskly. 'It will do you the world of good to get out in the fresh air.'

Her brows rose in disbelief. Since rain was lashing at the windowpane, he could hardly blame her.

'It isn't really the season for driving in the park, now, is it,' said Morgan with just a hint of a smile. 'I was thinking more in the lines of visiting somewhere like Westminster Abbey.'

Westminster Abbey? Was the fellow mad? Walking about looking at a bunch of grisly tombs? How was he going to find out anything, except whether the girl knew her kings and queens, by taking her to Westminster Abbey?

'It is so kind of you,' said the girl he was sitting next to, with a flutter of eyelashes up at Morgan, 'to think of taking us all out to see the sights. And Mary would love that, wouldn't you, Mary? She hasn't seen anything of London at all.'

Before Miss Carpenter had the chance to voice her horror at the prospect of being dragged out on an expedition to examine a lot of mouldering tombs, the door flew open and a boy, who looked as if he was about eight or nine years old, and was covered in flour, burst in.

'Mother, Mother, you have to come see…'

'Will, how many times have I told you,' shrieked Mrs Pargetter, 'not to come barging in here when we have callers?'

At the same moment, Miss Carpenter leapt from her chair and cut off his headlong dash into the room by dint of grabbing him about the waist.

She alone of the four women in the room was smiling at him.

'You're all over flour, Will,' she pointed out as he looked up at her in bewilderment. 'You don't want to spoil your sisters' pretty clothes, do you?'

She didn't seem to care about her own clothes, though. There was a little boy-shaped smudge on her skirts and a white handprint on her sleeve.

'No, 'spose not,' he said grudgingly, rubbing his twitching nose with the back of one hand, making him twice as likely to sneeze. 'But you've just got to see...'

'Come on,' said Mary, taking his dough-encrusted hand in hers. 'You can show *me* whatever it is that's got you so fired up. And later, when these visitors have gone, I'm sure your mama will want to see, as well.'

The boy glared at him, then at Morgan, then turned his floury little nose up at his sisters, as though roundly condemning them for considering the state of their clothes more important than whatever exciting development had occurred in the kitchens.

'Oh, thank you, Mary,' said her aunt.

'Not at all,' she replied, with what looked suspiciously like heartfelt relief.

'Did you see that?' he asked Morgan later, as they were going down the front steps. 'Her reaction to the floury boy?'

'Indeed I did,' he replied. 'Another item on your list ticked off. Or two, perhaps. She's not totally selfish and appears to be kind to children. Unless…well, I suppose she could have been using the child to make her escape.'

'Blast.' He peered out from under the front porch into the teeming rain. 'She might not have been thinking of the child at all. She might have just wanted an excuse to bolt. And she might well have given him a good scolding for spoiling her gown, once she was safely out of our sight. You see, that's the trouble with women. They put on a mask in public that makes you think they have the nature of an angel, but it comes straight off when they think nobody's watching. If only there was some way I could be sure of getting a genuine reaction from her.'

'Our trip to the Abbey tomorrow would be a perfect opportunity,' said Morgan as they dashed across the pavement into his waiting carriage, 'to set up some kind of scene,' he said, wrenching open the door, 'where she will be obliged to react without thinking too much about it.'

In the time it took Lord Havelock to get into the carriage as well and slam the door on the filthy weather, he'd gone from wanting to tell Morgan he hadn't been serious—for what kind of man deliberately set a trap to expose a lady's faults?—to realising that too much was riding on his making a successful match, in the shortest possible time, for him to take the conventional route.

So when Morgan said, 'Best if you leave the details to me', he raised no objection.

'I'll stage something that will take you as much by surprise as her,' said Morgan. 'So that if she's clever enough to work out what's afoot, the blame will fall upon me, not you.'

'That's…very decent of you,' he said. And then wondered why Morgan was being so helpful. They'd only met, properly, a couple of nights ago. And Morgan had sneered, and mocked, and generally behaved as though he'd taken him in immediate dislike.

'What's your lay, Morgan?'

'I beg your pardon?'

'I mean, why are you so keen to get involved in my affairs?'

'Just what are you accusing me of?'

'Don't know. That's the thing. But it seems dashed smoky to me. When you consider that Chepstow, a man I've known all my life, skipped town rather than risk getting tangled with females intent on marriage.'

'You can't know that. He could have left town for any number of reasons.'

'He's running scared,' Havelock insisted. 'He would have bolted from the club after foisting me on to Ashe, if he'd thought he could get away with it.'

Morgan looked out of the window. Sighed. Looked back at Havelock. Lifted his chin so that when he spoke, he did so down his nose.

'I have a sister,' he said defiantly. 'Who is of an age to get married. And I would walk over hot coals rather than see her married to a man like you.'

'A man like me?' His voice came out rapier sharp. 'What, precisely, do you mean by that?' He was from one of the oldest families in the land. Everyone knew him. He was welcome everywhere. Not a scandalous word had ever been whispered about him.

Except, perhaps, about the duels he'd fought.

Though he'd fought them over matters of honour, not *dis*honour.

'A man,' said Morgan in an equally chilling tone,

'who won't love his wife. The last thing I want is for my sister to get drawn into a loveless marriage.'

'Oh.' He shrugged. 'That puts a different complexion on the matter. I have a sister myself. Well, half-sister, to be precise. But even so, I would walk over hot coals for her.' In fact, that was very nearly what he was doing.

'So you see why I'm keen to get you off the marriage mart, before she comes to town?'

'Oh, absolutely. Would do the same myself, if I thought Julia was in danger of getting tangled up with an unsuitable man. Like a shot.'

They nodded at each other with grudging respect.

'Westminster Abbey, though? Really, Morgan, could you not have thought of somewhere a little more conducive to courtship?'

Morgan's craggy face relaxed into something resembling a smile. 'You are the only one thinking in terms of courtship. I have no intention of taking a risk with either of those Pargetter girls. But it will be out of the wind and rain, at all events. And large enough that our two parties may drift apart...'

'So that I can get Miss Carpenter to myself while you play the elder off against the younger,' he said. 'Morgan, you're as cunning as a fox.'

'Not really,' he said diffidently. 'Just well versed in the ways of women. I have,' he added with a wry twist to his mouth, '*two* half-sisters, and a stepsister under my guardianship. There's not much you can tell me about tears and tantrums, scenes staged to persuade me to do something against my better judgement, campaigns designed to wear a man down...'

'I get the picture,' he said with an appreciative shudder. 'You clearly know exactly how the female mind works.' And thank God for it. And for Morgan's willingness to see him safely married before his own sister came to town for her Season.

'Come *on*, Mary,' Dotty urged. 'That's Mr Morgan and Lord Havelock knocking on the front door now and you haven't even chosen which bonnet you're going to wear.'

The girls, determined they should all look their best for this outing with the most eligible men it had ever been their good fortune to come across, had spent the previous evening, and the best part of this morning, ransacking their wardrobe for items to lend Mary.

'The brown velvet,' said Lotty firmly, ramming the bonnet on to Mary's head. 'Sober colour, to suit your sense of what you should be wearing for mourning, yet the bronze satin rose just takes the plainness off. And if you say you don't care what you look like one more time,' she said, tying the ribbons deftly under her chin, 'I shall go off into strong hysterics.'

There was no arguing with the sisters. And if she persisted, she was afraid she was going to take the shine off their own pleasure in the outing.

Resigned to her fate, Mary trailed the girls down the stairs, hanging back while they launched themselves with great gusto, this time, at *both* of the gentlemen who'd come to take them out.

For Mr Pargetter, upon hearing Lord Havelock's name, had divulged that though he was only a viscount, and never likely to be an earl, he was very well-to-do.

While that information had sent his daughters into raptures, it had just made Mary wonder, again, what on earth he'd been doing at such an unfashionable event as the Crimmers' annual Advent ball. If he was as wealthy as Mr Pargetter thought, he couldn't have been searching for an heiress. She peered up at him, perplexed, as he handed her into the carriage. Could he possibly be thinking of going into politics? Perhaps he'd decided to mingle with the kind of men whose votes he would have to canvass and find out what they thought about various issues. Climbing boys, for instance.

Only, that didn't explain why he'd wasted so much time with her, when he could have been mingling with the men, who were the ones who had the votes.

It was only when he smiled at her that she realised she'd been staring at him with a puzzled frown all the while he'd been taking his own seat opposite her.

Swiftly, she averted her gaze and peered intently out of the window. She had to stop making conjectures about what drove Lord Havelock and make the most of her first foray out of the immediate vicinity of Bloomsbury to see if she could spot an employment agency. But no matter how she strained her eyes, she simply couldn't make out what might be engraved on any of the brass door plates of the buildings they passed. And it wasn't the kind of thing she could ask.

Lotty and Dotty wouldn't understand her desire for independence. The yearning to be able to stand on her own two feet and not have to rely on a man for anything.

Though at least they weren't making any attempt to include her in the flirtatious sallies they were directing at Mr Morgan and Lord Havelock. They'd drawn the line at getting her dressed up smartly and practically bundling her into the carriage.

And so intent were they on dazzling the two gentlemen that they didn't appear to notice when she started lagging behind them the minute they got inside the Abbey.

She'd started hanging back more out of habit than anything, but before long she was craning her neck in genuine awe at the roof, wondering how the builders had managed to get stone looking like acres of starched lace. She barely noticed their chatter gradually fading into the distance.

'Miss Carpenter?'

Lord Havelock was standing watching her, a concerned expression on his face. And she realised she ought to have made an effort, for once, to stay part of the group. Loitering here, obliging him to wait for her, might have made it look as if she wanted to be alone with him. And she didn't want him thinking that!

'It has just occurred to me,' he said, preventing her from stammering any of the excuses that leapt to mind, 'that it wasn't particularly tactful of us, was it, to arrange an outing to a place like this. With you so recently bereaved?'

Goodness. It wasn't like a man to consider a woman's feelings.

'I can clearly recall how it felt to lose my own mother,' he said, when she carried on gaping at him in complete shock. 'I was only about…well, a similar age to the floury boy of yesterday…'

'You mean Will?' The mention of her favourite cousin brought a smile to her lips without her having to make any effort whatever.

Lord Havelock smiled in response, looking very relieved. It was a warning that she really ought to make more effort to conceal her thoughts, if even a stranger could tell she was blue-devilled.

'You like the boy?'

'He's a little scamp,' she said fondly. 'The hope of the family, being the only surviving male, you see, and hopelessly indulged.'

'Hmm.' He crooked his arm and she laid her hand on his sleeve for the second time. The strength of his arm wasn't as alarming this time. Perhaps because he'd shown her several kindnesses. Besides, if they walked swiftly, they could soon catch up with her cousins and Mr Morgan.

Only, how could she get him to walk faster, when he seemed set on strolling along at a snail's pace?

'But to return to your own loss,' he said. 'The one thing I would not have wanted to do, in the weeks immediately following my own mother's funeral, was spend an afternoon wandering through a lot of tombs.'

'Oh? But this is different,' she said. 'These tombs are all of very grand people. Not in the least like the simple grassy plot in the churchyard where my mother was laid to rest. No…this is…is history. I confess, I didn't really want to come here. But now we are here…'

His face brightened. 'Would you care to have a look at Shakespeare's monument, then? I believe it is this way,' he said, indicating an aisle that branched away from the direction the rest of the party were headed.

'Oh, um…' She couldn't very well object, not when she'd just claimed to have an interest in old tombs, could she?

And what could possibly happen to her in a church, anyway?

'Just a quick look, before we join the others,' she said. 'I don't expect I shall have leisure to do much sightseeing, before much longer, and I would—'

She broke off, flushed and curled into herself again. She'd almost let slip that she was only going to stay with the Pargetters until she could find a paid position. What was it about this man that kept on tempting her to share confidences? It was time she deflected attention away from herself. It shouldn't be too hard. All she'd have to do would be to ask him about himself. Once a man started talking about himself, nothing short of a riot would stop him.

'You said you lost your own mother at a very young age. That must have been very hard for you.'

'Oh, my father pretty soon made sure I had another one,' he said with evident bitterness.

She wished she hadn't said anything now. It was clearly a painful topic for him. And though she racked her brains, she couldn't think of anything to say to undo the awkwardness she'd caused. An awkwardness that resulted in them walking the entire length of the south transept in silence.

'What did you mean, Miss Carpenter,' he eventually said, once they'd reached their destination, 'about not having leisure to do much sightseeing?'

Oh, drat the man. Why did he have to keep asking such personal questions? He couldn't really be interested. Besides, she had no intention of admitting that she wasn't totally happy to reside with the Pargetters. Especially not now, when she could see Dotty and Lotty sauntering towards them. They'd been so kind to her. She couldn't possibly hurt them by broadcasting the fact she wanted to leave.

'Oh, look,' she exclaimed, to create a diversion. 'Sheridan!'

'What?'

She pointed to the nearest monument. 'Only fancy him being buried here. And Chaucer. My goodness!'

He dutifully examined the plaques to which she was pointing, though from the set of his lips, he wasn't really interested.

'Hi! You, boy! Stop!'

Mary whirled in the direction of the cry, shocked to hear anyone daring to raise their voice in the reverent atmosphere of the ancient building, and saw Mr Morgan shaking his fist at a raggedy urchin, who was running in their direction.

Lord Havelock let go of her arm and grabbed the boy by the collar when he would have darted past.

The urchin squirmed in his grip. Lashed out with a foot. Lord Havelock twisted his fingers into the material of the boy's collar and held him at arm's length, with apparent ease, so that the boy's feet, and swinging fists, couldn't land any blows on anyone.

The boy promptly let loose with a volley of words that had Lord Havelock giving him a shake.

'That's enough of that,' he said severely. 'Those aren't the kind of words you should ever utter when ladies are present, leave alone when you're in church. I beg his pardon, Miss Carpenter,' he said, darting her an apologetic look.

She was on the verge of admitting she'd heard far worse coming from her own father's lips, but Morgan was almost upon them, his beetling brows drawn down in anger. And her brief urge to confide in anyone turned tail and fled.

'What's to do, Morgan?'

'The little b—boy has lifted my purse,' Mr Morgan snarled. Reaching down, he ran his hands over the squirming boy's jacket, evading all the lad's swings from his grubby little fists.

A verger came bustling over just as Mr Morgan recovered his property. 'My apologies, my lords, ladies,' he said, dipping into something between a bow and a curtsy. 'I cannot think how a person like this managed to get in here.'

Dotty and Lotty came upon the scene, arm in arm as though needing each other for support.

'If you will permit me,' said the verger, reaching out a hand towards the boy, who had ceased struggling as though realising it was pointless when he was so vastly outnumbered. 'I will see that he is handed over to the proper authorities.'

'Yes, see that you do,' snarled Morgan as the verger clamped his pudgy hand round the boy's wrist. 'It comes to something when a man cannot even safely walk through a church without getting his pockets picked.'

'He will be suitably punished for his audacity, attacking and robbing innocent persons upon hallowed ground, never you fear, sir,' declared the verger.

Mary's heart was pounding. Could Mr Morgan really be so cruel as to have him dragged off to prison?

Lord Havelock, she suddenly noticed, hadn't relinquished his hold on the boy's collar.

'Hold on,' he said. 'Morgan, this isn't… I mean, I think this has gone far enough.'

The two men glared at each other, locked in a silent battle of wills.

The boy, sensing his fate hung in the balance, knuckled at his eyes, and wailed, 'Oh, please don't send me to gaol, sirs. For lifting a purse as fat as yours, I'd like as not get me neck stretched. And I wouldn't have lifted it if I weren't so hungry.'

'A likely tale,' said the verger, giving the boy's arm a little tug. But Lord Havelock kept his fingers stubbornly twisted into the boy's clothing.

Mary saw that Dotty and Lotty were clinging to each other, clearly appalled by the situation, but too scared of offending Mr Morgan to say what they really thought.

Well, *she* didn't care what he thought of her. She couldn't stand by and let a child suffer such a horrid fate.

'For shame,' she cried, rounding on Mr Morgan. 'How can you want to send a child to prison, when his only crime is to be hungry?'

'He lifted my purse....'

'Which he can see you can spare! You are so rich, I don't suppose you have ever known what it is to be hungry, to be desperate, to have nowhere to go.'

'Now, now, miss,' said the verger. 'We don't want raised voices in here. Please moderate your tone....'

'Moderate my tone!' She whirled on the plump, cassocked man. 'Your creed demands you *feed* the hungry, not toss them in prison. You should be offering him food and shelter, and help, not punishing him for being in want!'

Lotty and Dotty stared at her as though she had gone quite mad. Actually, everyone was staring at her. She pressed her hands to her cheeks, shocked at herself for speaking with such fervour, and disrespect, to a man of the cloth. For raising her voice at all. Whatever had come over her?

But then, the shocked silence that echoed round them was broken by Lord Havelock's crisp, biting voice.

'Quite,' he said with a decisive nod. And then turned

to the verger. 'And I really don't care for the way you just spoke to Miss Carpenter. Look, Morgan, you have your property back, can you not…let him go?'

Mary took a step that placed her next to him. Side by side they faced the rest of the group.

He really was rather a…rather a wonderful person. She'd been able to tell he hadn't liked the notion of throwing the pickpocket in gaol, from the way he'd refused to relinquish him into the verger's custody. But she'd never expected him to spring to *her* defence, as well. It was just about the most…amazing, surprising thing that had ever happened to her.

'Thank you, my lord,' she breathed, darting him a shy glance. And noting that the way the sunlight glanced off his bright bronze curls made him look like… Well, with his strong hand clamped firmly behind the little boy's scrawny neck, he could have been a model for a guardian angel. The rather fearsome kind who protected the weak and downtrodden against oppression.

'Not at all, Miss Carpenter,' he replied grimly. 'I believe you have the right of it. This boy's nothing but a bag of bones. When,' he said, turning his attention to the dirty scrap of humanity he held in one fist, 'did you last have anything to eat?'

The boy squinted up at him. 'Can't remember. Not yesterday, that's for sure. Day before, mebbe…'

At that, even Morgan looked taken aback. 'Look,' he began, 'I had no idea…'

The boy's face twisted into an expression of contempt. 'Your sort never do. She's right…' he jerked his head in Mary's direction '…got no idea what it feels like to have nuffink. Or what you'll do just to earn a penny or two.…'

'If you had the means to earn an honest living, would you, though?' Havelock shook him by the coat collar. 'Or would you just keep right on thieving?'

The boy snorted in derision. 'Who'd give me a job? I ain't got no trade. No learnin' neither.'

'If you can learn to pick pockets, you can learn an honest trade,' said Lord Havelock witheringly. Then he frowned. 'Don't suppose anyone would want to take the risk, though.' He closed his eyes, drew a deep breath and sighed it out.

'My town house could probably use a boot boy,' he said. 'You'd get a bed to sleep in, meals provided and a wage, if you kept your nose clean.'

The boy promptly straightened up and wiped his nose with the back of his hand.

'I got no wiper, but I'd try and keep it clean if I got all what you said.'

'Morgan? Will you let the matter drop if I take charge of the boy?'

'I… Well, if you are prepared to attempt to rehabilitate him, I suppose I can do no less.'

Dotty and Lotty heaved a sigh, showing they were as relieved as Mary to see the boy escape the full force of the law.

'Then if you will excuse me, ladies,' he said, bowing first to her cousins, and then to her, 'I had better take him there myself. Straight away. And hope that his arrival won't induce my butler to leave,' he grumbled.

He was scowling as he led the boy down the aisle. He didn't slacken his hold on his collar, either. Which was probably wise. Who knew but if he let the lad go, he wouldn't run straight back to whatever gutter he'd sprung from, and the associates who'd probably led him into his life of crime in the first place?

Damn Morgan for foisting this guttersnipe on him. Obliging him to leave, just when he was beginning to coax Miss Carpenter out of her shell.

Still, he supposed this little test had proved that she was capable of coming out of it when sufficiently roused. She'd been shaking like a leaf, but she'd managed to speak out against what was clearly a gross injustice.

For the sake of a child.

He pulled up short, turned and glanced back at her.

To find her gazing back at him, with a rapt expression on her face.

She hid it at once, by bowing her head and turning away, but he'd caught something in her look that had been encouraging. It was approval. And warmth. And, not to put too fine a point on it, something that verged on downright hero worship.

There would be no trouble getting to speak to her next time he paid a call. He could use the pretext of telling her how the boy had settled in to his new life. And take it from there.

'I want me penny,' said the boy, the moment they emerged from the great church door into the drizzle that they'd gone inside to escape.

'Your what?'

'My penny,' said the boy. 'That other cove said as how you'd give me a penny if I lifted his purse, then ran straight into you and let you catch me.'

'I,' said Havelock firmly, 'am not going to give you a penny.'

'I might have known. You swindler...'

'I'm going to give you something better,' he interrupted.

'Oh, yeah?' The boy's face brightened.

'Yes. I'm going to give you that job I promised. A man has to keep his word, you see? Especially when he gives it to a lady.'

Chapter Four

Overnight the drizzle drifted away, leaving the sky cloudless. When the girls awoke, there was a layer of frosted ice on the inside of their bedroom window.

They shivered, red-nosed, into their clothes and rushed downstairs to the warmth of the parlour.

The moment she got downstairs though, Mary wished it wasn't quite so cold in their room, or she could have found some excuse to stay there. For her aunt was still upset with her over what the girls had told her of their outing to Westminster Abbey.

'I cannot think what came over you,' said Aunt Pargetter as she poured Mary's tea. 'To have raised your voice to Mr Morgan…'

'I am sorry, truly sorry, if my behaviour has offended you.'

'It didn't offend me,' said Lotty, wrapping her fingers round the cup that contained her own, freshly poured, steaming hot tea.

'Nor me,' added Dotty. 'I only wish I'd had the courage to speak up for the boy when that nasty verger threatened him with gaol. He couldn't have been any older than Will.'

'It wasn't a matter of *courage*,' Mary protested. She wasn't a courageous person. Not at all. 'I just...' She shook her head. To be truthful, she had no idea why she'd picked that particular moment to finally speak her mind. She just... She'd had to endure so much, in silence, for so long. She knew what it felt like to have nothing. To be at the mercy of strangers. And yesterday, it was as though a lifetime of resenting injustice, of knowing that the strong naturally oppressed the weak and trampled down the poor for being of no account, all came to a head and erupted without, for once, her giving a fig for the consequences.

'I just couldn't help myself.'

'I'm not denying you were right to *feel* as you did,' said Aunt Pargetter. 'But to risk driving away such an *eligible* suitor, by openly *challenging* him like that...'

'Mary did just as she ought,' said Mr Pargetter, folding up his newspaper and getting to his feet. 'The consequences must take care of themselves.'

A tense silence hovered over the breakfast table after he'd left the room. Until Dotty cleared her throat.

'You know,' she said, 'it didn't do Mary any harm in Lord Havelock's eyes.'

'No,' added Lotty. 'He looked at her as though he thoroughly approved of her standing up for the boy.'

'Hmmph,' said her aunt. 'Well, I suppose that is something.'

And though her aunt let the subject drop, the atmosphere remained tense throughout the rest of the morning, as they all waited to see if either of the gentlemen would call upon the house again.

Either Dotty or Lotty kept a vigil by the window,

while Mary kept close to the fire, steadily working her way through a basket of mending.

Until at length, Lotty let out a squeal of excitement.

'It's him! Them! Both of them! They've just got out of their carriage!'

Her cousins rushed to the mirror to check their appearance, before dashing to the sofa and striking relaxed poses. Which were only slightly marred by the way their chests rose and fell so rapidly.

It puzzled Mary to see the girls greet Mr Morgan with such enthusiasm, when his callous behaviour the day before had shocked them all so much.

She could have understood it if they'd flown to Lord Havelock's side, and showered *him* with praise, and pulled *him* down on to the sofa between them.

Instead, he was left standing just inside the door, watching them with a kind of amused disbelief.

Couldn't they see how…superior he was to Mr Morgan, in every way? When she thought of the way he'd lifted that boy out of the verger's reach…

Just as she was reflecting that she'd never seen a man use his physical strength to protect the defenceless before, he turned, caught her watching him and smiled at her.

Her stomach gave a funny little lurch. Her heart sped up.

She hastily lowered her head to stare at the sewing that lay in her lap.

She *wasn't* interested in him, not in the way Lotty and Dotty were interested in Mr Morgan. She just…she just couldn't deny it was flattering to have such a handsome, personable young man smile at her like that.

She hadn't been able to forget the look he'd shot her as he'd left the Abbey with the pickpocket still held firmly by his collar, either. Or the feeling that had come over her when he'd defended her from the verger's censure. It had washed over her again, several times the night before, while she'd been trying to get to sleep.

And it positively surged through her when he took a chair, carried it to her side and sat down.

'I bring good news,' declared Mr Morgan once the flurry of greetings had died down. 'The Serpentine has frozen over. Hard enough for us to go skating, if you ladies would enjoy it?'

Dotty and Lotty beamed and clapped their hands, saying what a wonderful idea it was. Just as though the incident the day before had never happened.

'You will be coming with us, won't you, Miss Carpenter?' said Lord Havelock, with a hopeful smile.

She shook her head.

'I cannot skate,' she said with what felt suspiciously like regret.

Regret? No! She didn't want to spend any more time than she had to with these two men. They both made her uncomfortable—Mr Morgan because of his harsh manner and Lord Havelock because of the tendency she had to say far more than she should when she was with him. And for feeling that she could say it to him. And most of all—she had to be honest with herself—because she found him so…attractive. Which made him downright dangerous.

'I will teach you,' said Lord Havelock, somehow turning up the warmth in his smile in such a way that she wished it wouldn't be such a terrible idea to draw closer to him and warm herself at it.

'Oh, Mary, please! You have to go,' begged Dotty.

'Yes. For we cannot go out and leave you here on your own,' pointed out Lotty.

And they both really, really wanted to go.

There was nothing for it but to surrender with good grace.

With cries of glee, the girls took her upstairs to ransack their wardrobe again, going back down only when all three of them were swathed in gloves, scarves, boots and several extra layers of petticoats.

Her cousins sat one on either side of Mr Morgan in the carriage, which meant that she and Lord Havelock were sat next to each other, with their backs to the horses.

Once they'd tucked luxurious fur rugs round their legs, they set off. Even though the carriage was very well sprung, and they had far more room than the three squeezed together on the opposite seat, every so often the jolting of the carriage meant that their legs bumped. Whenever she felt the warmth of Lord Havelock's thigh pressing against hers beneath the concealment of the fur, everything else faded into the background. The chatter of her cousins, the buildings at which she was pretending to look through the window—none of it reached her senses. Once or twice, he made an attempt to speak to her, but she wasn't able to give a coherent reply. It was a relief when they arrived, and the gentlemen got out so they could help the ladies down.

Lotty and Dotty stuck close to Mr Morgan, which meant Lord Havelock was left to escort Mary.

She laid her gloved hand on his outstretched arm and let him lead her to the frozen expanse of water, besides which several enterprising people had set up various stalls to earn what money they could from this unexpected cold spell.

The men hired skates from a booth where a ruddy-cheeked woman helped to fit them over their boots.

Dotty and Lotty rushed on to the ice, shrieking with laughter and clutching at each other for support as they almost fell over. Mr Morgan went to their rescue, offering them one arm each. Clinging to him, the trio set out, wobbling and giggling, across the frozen lake.

Which left her alone with Lord Havelock.

'Come, you need not be afraid,' he said with a sincerity that made her wish she could trust him. Made her wish she could let go of her habitual distrust of the entire male sex, just once.

'I won't let you fall.'

It wasn't falling she was worried about. It was the increasing frequency with which she was having foolish, feminine thoughts about him. Foolish, feminine reactions, too.

She gave Lotty and Dotty a wistful look. They weren't tying themselves up in knots about the wisdom of plastering themselves to a man and relying on his strength and balance to keep them from falling over. They were just enjoying themselves.

There were skaters of all ages, shapes and sizes twirling about on the ice. All looking as though they were having a splendid time. Life didn't offer many opportunities like this, to try something new and exciting. And the ice probably wouldn't last all that long. She might never get another chance to have a go at skating.

When had she last let herself go, the way they were doing? Living in the moment?

Having fun?

When had she got into the habit of being too afraid to reach out and attempt to take hold of the slightest chance at happiness?

She reached out and took the hand Lord Havelock was patiently holding out to her, vowing that today, at least, she would leave fear on the bank, launch out on to the ice and see what happened.

What happened was that the moment she set her feet on to the slippery surface, she very nearly fell over.

With a shriek that sounded remarkably similar to the ones erupting from her cousins' lips, she grabbed at Lord Havelock, who was maintaining his own stance with what looked like total ease.

'I hadn't thought it would be so hard to just stand upright,' she said. 'How do you manage to make it look so effortless?'

He shrugged. 'I've skated a few times before. But I had my share of falls the first time I tried it, I can tell you. If you have any sense of balance, you'll get the hang of it in no time.'

Mary made a tentative effort to let go of his arm. Each of her legs promptly attempted to go in opposite directions. How vexing. It was only by clinging to Lord Havelock that she could even manage to stay upright.

'Perhaps you will fare better once we get going,' he suggested. And then, without waiting for her agreement, made a move that somehow set them both gliding away from the shore.

'See? That's better, is it not?'

'Not,' she gasped, clinging to his arm for dear life. She had no control over the situation at all. Whenever she attempted to wrest it back, her feet went skittering off all over the place, resulting in her having to clutch at him with increasing desperation.

Though neither Lotty nor Dotty looked any more accomplished. They were both clinging to Mr Morgan with what looked like the same desperation she felt, though being far more vocal about their slips, shrieking and laughing with an abandon that she almost envied.

'Oh! Oh, dear,' she gasped as, once again, her outside leg shot off on a course she hadn't expected.

'This will never do,' said Lord Havelock. 'You'll fare a lot better if you let me put my arm round your waist, see, like this.'

He did so, tucking her into his side, and then pushing off with the leg that was nearest her own. She felt the power of it propelling them forward as he reached across her front and took hold of her other hand.

'My lord, I'm not at all sure this is quite proper,' she squeaked in something very close to panic.

'It's only like a sort of dance hold.'

That was true. But in a dance they'd only be as close as this for a moment or two, whilst turning into a new figure. Not plastered to each other from hip to shoulder for as long as he chose to keep them like that.

'Please,' she begged him. 'This is making me feel...' warm. Yearning. Excited '...most uncomfortable.'

He glanced down at her. She was sure her cheeks must be bright red.

'I beg your pardon,' he said, with a sigh of what sounded like regret. 'I did not mean... That is, I do not want you to feel I'm taking advantage. Let me just steer us both across to the side, there, and you can catch hold of that tree and see if you can manage to stand up on your own, now you've had a bit of a go.'

'Thank you,' she managed to say, since it was the polite response to the gentlemanly way he'd reacted to her protest. But it wasn't easy to thank him for finding it so easy to let go of her. It meant he wasn't all that keen on having her hang on to his arm. Though why she should find that so disappointing she couldn't think. What on earth was the matter with her?

'Thank you,' she gasped, again, when he'd delivered her to the promised tree, untangled their arms and helped her to get a good hold on a low branch. 'Oh, dear, this is most awkward.' Her legs were shaking so much, she felt sure he must be able to see it. She glanced his way, expecting to encounter a look of masculine scorn, only to find that he'd taken up the kind of stance she'd seen fielders take on a cricket pitch. As though he was braced to catch...her. Should she fall.

He had very strong, very capable hands. She'd thought so the day before, when he'd had hold of the little boy.

'How did he go on? The little boy you took home with you yesterday?'

He blinked.

'It was very good of you to offer him work, instead of letting Mr—' She broke off as the branch she'd been holding showed signs of giving way. With a wobble, and a lunge, she got hold of another one.

'I couldn't bear to think of him being thrown in prison. It's been on my mind all night. I'm glad,' she said, lifting her chin, 'that we are a little apart from the others so I can ask you about it.'

He didn't reply straight away. In fact, he looked a touch...uncomfortable.

'You don't mind me asking you about him, do you?' Oh, dear. Perhaps she shouldn't have said anything. But it felt so very strange being alone with him like this, under the shelter of the tree. Not that they were alone, exactly. There were dozens of other people whizzing about on the ice. Yet there was a certain intimacy about the way there was nobody else within hearing distance. An intimacy that she'd instinctively tried to dispel.

'First of all,' he said, squaring his shoulders, 'I have to confess that I didn't exactly take him home. I live in a cosy little set of rooms, y'see, which are too small to take in stray boys. Besides, I wouldn't know what to do with a lad like that. And nor would my valet.'

'Oh, never say you abandoned him?'

'Absolutely not!'

He looked so affronted she immediately wanted to beg his pardon. But before she could do so, he went on, 'I have another property in town. Durant House. Huge great barn of a place. I took him there.'

'Then why…?'

'If you must know, I feel a bit of a fraud accepting any praise for my actions when the task of reforming the wretch will fall to the staff of Durant House. I really did very little.'

'Oh.'

'Please don't be too disappointed in me.'

Her gaze flew to his face. The words were apologetic, but his tone was confrontational.

'I could have made up some tale that would have made you look at me the way you did yesterday,' he pointed out a touch belligerently. 'As though I were some kind of hero. Instead I've chosen to tell you the truth. Because I never want there to be any misunderstanding between us.'

Well, how was she supposed to respond to that? Given

the choice, she would have mumbled something vapid and moved away. But she couldn't go anywhere. All she could do was cling to the tree, study his boots and tell herself he couldn't possibly be implying he was planning to prolong their acquaintance.

And yet, the way he kept looking at her...

'And while we're about it, I have something else to confess, too. I deliberately got you alone, so that I could talk to you freely. For I have something I particularly wanted to ask you.'

'Oh?' She winced. How many times had she said that this afternoon? He must be starting to think she was a complete ninny.

'Yes. You said something about not being in London long and having plans. I know you do not want your cousins to know about these plans. But perhaps you might feel you could confide in me?'

'Why would I want to do that?'

'I may be able to help you.'

'I doubt that very much.'

'You won't know unless you tell me.'

'Why would you even want to help me? I am a complete stranger to you.'

'And yet something about you calls to me,' he said, giving her a look that was unlike anything she'd ever seen in a man's eyes before.

'You do not appear to have anyone to help you. You need...a friend.'

Suddenly everything fell into place with sickening disappointment. She couldn't bear to think Lord Havelock was the kind of man who preyed on defenceless females. When he'd taken that robber boy under his wing, she even started to think that...to think that...

Oh, how could she have been so naïve?

'I do not want the kind of friendship you are offering me,' she snapped. 'Poor I may be, but I would never, ever…'

His brows snapped down. 'Nor would I, ever, make a gently bred girl the kind of offer you seem to think I'm about to make. What kind of man do you think I am?'

She flushed. Felt her insides skid about as much as when she'd tried to walk a straight path on the ice. 'I…I don't know what kind of man you are, that's just the point. I just cannot see why you should concern yourself over someone like me. I'm nobody. And it's not as if I'm even pretty. And you're so handsome and dashing you could have any girl you want at the snap of your fingers.'

In mortification, her hand flew to her mouth, though it was too late to stop the words that had tumbled out.

And letting go of the branch proved to be as reckless as speaking her mind. For her left leg promptly shot off to the right while her right leg went straight forward. She had no choice but to grab hold of the front of Lord Havelock's coat, which had the effect of spinning them both right round, then landing her flush up against the tree trunk, with her wedged between it and the solid bulk of his body.

'So. You think I'm so handsome I could have any girl I wanted, do you?'

'I didn't mean it!' She uncurled her fingers and gave his coat a firm shove. It only had the effect of propelling her harder against the tree. 'At least,' her honesty compelled her to admit, 'I didn't mean to say it out loud.'

'But you did say it,' he replied with a grin, closing the small gap she'd opened up between them. 'Which gives me hope. I was beginning to think I'd never break through your defences.'

'B-break through my defences? Why would you want to do that? And as for saying never…why, we only met a handful of days ago.'

'And yet the attraction was instant. And powerful. You feel it, too. Though you are trying to resist it.'

She hadn't thought it possible to feel more embarrassed, but hearing him lay her innermost soul bare in that way, when she hadn't even worked it all out for herself, was utterly mortifying.

'You don't need to resist it, Miss Carpenter. For I want you, too. Very much. And just so there is no misunderstanding about it, I mean, as my wife.'

It was just as well she was wedged between the tree, and his body, because the shock of hearing him propose took all the strength from her legs.

'Your wife? But you cannot!'

'Why not?'

'Because we know nothing about each other.'

'We know enough,' he said, giving her another one of those melting looks. She was suddenly very aware of how close they were. And how their breath, rising on the air in two plumes of white vapour, mingled and merged not very far up into one cloud.

'Let me prove it to you.'

He began to lower his head. Her breath hitched in her throat. He was going to attempt to kiss her. And there was no way to escape. If he let go of her, she would fall over.

That was the moment she realised he wasn't actually holding her. No, she was the one who was clinging to him, or at least, to his coat. But it was only so that she wouldn't fall over. Not because…

Not because…

And anyway, if she really, really didn't want him to kiss her, all she would have to do was turn her head away and his lips would land relatively harmlessly on her cheek.

But she couldn't move her head. She stayed frozen in place while his mouth came closer and closer to hers. Until his lips touched hers. Pressed, and caressed, and coaxed her own apart. And then their breath was mingling not five feet up in the air, but in her very mouth. And the swirling sensation went right down through her stomach, getting hotter, and hotter, until she wondered that the ice beneath their feet did not melt and suck them down into a vortex that would drown them both.

She'd never felt anything like it in her life. So powerfully all-consuming. So compelling that she didn't care if carrying on experiencing it did melt the ice and she drowned.

With a whimper, she pressed up against him and slid her arms round his waist. His own went round hers, so that she was no longer the one clinging to him, but they were clinging to each other.

'So,' he breathed, ending the most wonderful encounter she'd ever had in her life, 'you will marry me, then?'

'What?' Hearing him persist in talking of marriage felt like plunging right through the ice into the black void beneath. 'No!'

She tried to pull out of his arms, skidded and had no choice but to grab hold of him again.

'What do you mean no?' He frowned down at her. 'You enjoyed that kiss as much as I did.'

'That is not the point.'

'Then what is the point? What can you possibly want from life, if you can turn up your nose at a proposal from a *dashing*, *handsome*, and I'll have you know, solvent peer of the realm? Who could have any other woman for the snapping of my fingers?'

She sucked in a short, shocked breath. How cruel of him to fling her very own words back in her face.

And his face was hard now, harder than she'd ever seen it. Gone was the mask of affability he'd worn when he'd been trying to win her round. Gone the charming smile and the warmth in his eyes. It had been replaced by something with which she was far more familiar.

Cold, hard anger.

Oh, but it was just as well she'd seen this side of him, before it was too late. Before she'd forgotten just how miserable her father had made her mother, within the cage that their marriage had become. She would never, ever, let a man bully her and break her down. Nor coerce her with…with deceitfully delightful kisses!

This time when she tried to break from his hold, he let her go. As though he'd recognised the determination in her eyes and realised it was over.

'The only sort of man I would even consider marrying,' she retorted, 'not that I have any intention of doing anything so stupid, would be…would be…a sailor!'

'A what?'

'You heard me. A sailor.'

'Why the deuce would you prefer a sailor to me?'

'Because a sailor,' she snapped, almost beside herself with fury at the way she was having to hang on to a tree merely to maintain her upright position, while he was standing there, hands on his hips, looking down his nose at her with the kind of disdain only an aristocrat could ever muster, 'would hand over his money, and go off to sea for months, perhaps even years, and leave me in peace to live exactly as I wished!'

There. That had done it. He'd stalk away now—or rather skate away—without a backward glance. And never deign to so much as recognise her if he saw her in the street.

But to her astonishment, he did no such thing. On the contrary, the anger that had seemed to consume him vanished as he flung back his head and burst out laughing.

'You are perfect,' he cried, taking hold of her by the elbows and restoring her to a more upright stance. 'Absolutely perfect. You no more want to get married than I do!'

'But...if you don't want to get married, then why...?'

'Look, there are reasons why I need to have a wife. Which I won't go into just yet. But I am definitely willing to hand over a deal of my money, and leave you alone, if that's what you want. We can live virtually separate lives, if, after an initial period, you find you really can't stand the sight of me. I shan't cut up rough. You'll still have a generous allowance.'

'An allowance?' She couldn't quite get her breath. She shook her head. 'I don't understand....'

'Come, Miss Carpenter, I can see you are tempted, if not by my kisses, then at least by my money.'

'That sounds... You're making me sound horrible. Mercenary....'

'Then what can I offer you, that would make you agree to take my hand? Name it. Whatever it is you've always craved, and feared you could never have, I will give it to you.'

'You can't want to marry me that much….'

'So there is something? I knew it. Tell me and it shall be yours.'

'It isn't anything…really.'

'It's something.'

'Well, it's just that of late…' She stopped and shook her head.

'Yes? Come on, tell me. If it is in my power to give it, I will.'

'It will probably sound silly to you. But…oh, I so wish I could have a room of my own. A room I can do whatever I want in. Where people have to knock before they come in. A room that nobody can ever turn me out of…' She faltered to a halt as tears stung her eyes. She hadn't realised how precious privacy was, until she'd been forced out of her childhood home, and had to rely on the grudging charity of others. Even here, in London, she had to share not only a room, but a bed, with two other girls. They'd made space for her, but it was just a corner. And she was sick of having to make do with just claiming a corner of other people's rooms.

'You want security,' he said, once more hitting the nail on the head. 'I can give you that. And as for privacy, well, I have several properties. And you may have your very own room in each one of them.'

'Really?' It sounded too good to be true. 'But I still don't understand why…'

'Never you mind about why,' he grated. 'Just think about this.' And without further ado, he pulled her into his arms, and kissed her again. And this time, there was nothing gentle, or tentative, about it. This kiss was one that claimed her, body and soul. She had no more chance of escaping him than a snowball did of surviving in the kitchen fire.

She melted into him, swept away by his ardour, her own body's clamouring and the joyous thought that if she agreed to his proposal, she would have a place of her own. Money to spend as she wanted.

And kisses like this.

She came out of her blissful haze to the sound of Dotty and Lotty, shrieking.

And opened her eyes to see them speeding across the ice towards her.

Lord Havelock spun round to face them, his arm snaking round her waist as they offered their congratulations on a betrothal she hadn't actually voiced her agreement to.

But she couldn't very well say so. Why else would she have been kissing a man, in broad daylight, unless it was because they'd just become engaged?

Then something struck her. 'You can both skate. You don't need Mr Morgan to stop you falling over at all!'

Dotty and Lotty, completely unabashed, giggled, took her by an arm each and towed her away from her...well, she supposed she had to call him her fiancé.

'If he'd known we could skate, do you think he would have let us hang on to him like that? He's the most hardened case in town. Girls have been trying to get him to the altar since...oh, for ever, and nobody has yet got as far as either of us did today.'

She blinked at them in shock. They'd been pretending they couldn't skate, just so they could get close to him?

She'd never heard of anything so...unscrupulous!

Unless it was letting everyone think she'd just accepted a proposal, when she had no intention of doing any such thing.

Chapter Five

He held her hand, in the carriage, all the way home.

She could have tugged it free, she supposed, but then she would have to explain herself.

And she had no excuse. None. She couldn't very well claim Lord Havelock had forced those kisses on her. She'd put her arms round him and kissed him back. With some enthusiasm.

And Dotty and Lotty looked so pleased for her. Even Mr Morgan had a twinkle in his eye, and a smile that softened that stern mouth whenever he glanced at their clasped hands.

Her stomach clenched into a cold, hard knot. If she made any attempt, now, to tell them they'd all made a terrible mistake, then…well, she wasn't sure quite what would happen, but there was bound to be a dreadful scene. She'd upset everyone badly enough by shouting at a man in public. What would they make of her *kissing* one?

It would be better to wait till they got home. She'd beg a few moments alone with her aunt, and try to explain what had happened. And then…

And then the carriage stopped, and Lotty and Dotty leapt out and went bounding up the front steps, shrieking out the news of her betrothal.

And when Aunt Pargetter came to the front door, it was to Lord Havelock she held out her hands. Even when Mary made frantic signals, behind his back, to try to convey her need to speak with her, she paid no heed.

'In a moment, Mary,' she said. 'His lordship wants to have a private word with me first. Since Mr Pargetter is not at home just now. Though I can guess what you want to say,' she finished, shooting him an arch look.

'No, no, I don't think you could possibly...' she said, though her voice was drowned out by Lord Havelock saying, 'My behaviour has been a little unconventional. I should have approached you, that is to say, Mr Pargetter, first, and asked your permission to pay my addresses.'

'Not at all,' said Aunt Pargetter, ushering him into her husband's study. 'We aren't legally Mary's guardians, you know. She is free to make her own choices.'

'Nevertheless...'

And then the study door closed on whatever he'd been about to say, leaving Mary on the wrong side of it.

Free to make her own choices! If only that were true.

And then Dotty and Lotty were shooing her into the front parlour and divesting her of her coat.

'She's in a complete daze,' said Dotty, untying the ribbons of her bonnet.

'No wonder,' said Lotty, pushing her into a chair. 'His lordship swept her completely off her feet.'

'No, he didn't, it was the opposite. He stopped her slipping over,' quipped Dotty with a giggle. 'Got his arm round her waist and held her so tight she couldn't possibly have lost her footing.'

'Oh, I've never seen anything so romantic.'

'Romantic? No! I…'

'Oh, but it was,' sighed Dotty, pressing her hands to her heart and flinging herself backwards on to the sofa as though in a swoon.

'Aren't you cross with me? Why aren't you cross with me? When the whole purpose of going skating at all was to try and…and… Well, you were both trying so hard to attract Mr Morgan.…'

Who was nowhere in sight, she suddenly realised. The moment they'd gone into the house, he'd slipped away, unnoticed in all the excitement.

'Oh, that's so sweet,' said Lotty. 'And so like you, to think of us, rather than yourself.'

Dotty bounced off the sofa, and flung her arms round her neck. 'You mustn't feel bad because you got a proposal, today, and not us. And as for Mr Morgan…' She made an airy gesture with one hand. 'When a man as wealthy as that, and single, comes your way you simply have to make a push to get him interested. But it's not as if either of us developed a *tendre* for him, did we, Lotty?'

Lotty shook her head so hard her ringlets bounced.

'Yes, but…' As she floundered to a halt against the impenetrable barrier of her own behaviour, Lotty and Dotty both collapsed in giggles again.

And then they heard the front door slam, and Aunt Pargetter came in, beaming all over her face.

'Mary, I'm so proud of you,' she said, enveloping her in a lavender-scented hug.

'No…you shouldn't be. I didn't mean to…'

'Well, I dare say that is what won him round. You are so very…modest. And…and, oh, everything a lady ought to be, I'm sure. A viscountess,' she exclaimed, sinking on to the sofa next to Dotty, gazing at her with starry eyes. 'You will be presented at court...'

The girls both squealed with an excitement that passed Mary by completely.

'And you will go to all the most *tonnish* events.'

'But...' Mary attempted to protest.

'And then,' she carried on, regardless, 'once you are established, you will be able to invite all those *tonnish* people to parties you throw.'

Mary blinked, completely unable to envision herself ever throwing any kind of party.

'And I just know you are too kind-hearted to forget my girls. This will be a foot in the door to a world they'd had no hope of entering otherwise. And with both of them being so pretty—no offence to you, my dear, but if you managed to land yourself a viscount, without even trying, only think what my girls could accomplish. I shouldn't wonder at it if this means an earl, or perhaps even a marquis....'

No wonder they'd let Mr Morgan escape without a twinge of regret. The girls now had visions of getting themselves a title apiece.

'Aunt Pargetter, please! You don't understand. I never actually wanted to get married. I thought I would...find work as a housekeeper, or a governess, or something....'

'Well, that is because you lived in such an out-of-the-way spot, and didn't have any prospects,' said her aunt complacently.

'And she feels a touch guilty,' explained Dotty. 'For stealing a march on us.'

'Oh, we don't begrudge you your good fortune,' said her aunt kindly.

'No, but...'

'Well, I can see this sudden reversal in your prospects has overwhelmed you,' she said, tilting her head to one side. 'And no wonder, if all you ever hoped for was to obtain some menial position. A good strong cup of tea is what you need.' She flicked her hand to Lotty, who went to the fireplace and pulled the bell to summon the maid.

'And you are so shy,' she added with a knowing nod, 'that having such a very…masculine man as Lord Havelock positively…bowl you over…'

'Yes, he did, Mama. He kissed her quite passionately.'

'Twice!'

Oh, if only the chair cushions would open up and swallow her whole.

'Oh,' said her aunt with a sympathetic look as Mary's face heated to what felt like boiling point. 'I see what this is. But, my dear,' she said, reaching across to pat her hand, 'Lord Havelock must be very taken with you, to propose so quickly. You know, I saw there was something, that very first night at the Crimmers'. Why, he started at the sight of you as though…as though his ship had come in, as you would probably say. It is clearly a case of love at first sight.'

As though that made it all right.

Except that it was most definitely *not* love at first sight. The things he'd said made that crystal clear. Like, going their separate ways, for instance. And being glad she was no more keen to marry than he was. Immediately after he'd proposed.

She shook her head in complete frustration. There was no way she was going to be able to get Aunt Pargetter to understand her reluctance to marry. Or the girls, not now their heads were full of eligible titled men.

There was only one thing for it. She would have to tell

Lord Havelock, to his face, that she couldn't go through with it.

And then—she glanced at the happy, glowing faces of her aunt and cousins—she'd have to endure their disappointment.

Lord Havelock was coming to call on Mary the very next day, Aunt Pargetter informed her husband over dinner that night. To talk about arrangements.

So Mary had all night to marshal her arguments. And the longer she thought, the more convinced she became that he wouldn't be all that bothered to have it all come to nothing. Hadn't he said he was no keener to get married than she was? He'd probably just thought he *had* to propose, after kissing her in such a public place. Especially as she'd made it crystal clear she wouldn't be his mistress.

It was the only reason that could possibly account for it.

Satisfied she'd reached the nub of the matter, and that Lord Havelock would be positively grateful when she let him off the hook, Mary finally drifted off to sleep. And if a few tears leaked from under her tightly closed eyelids, they were only a symptom of the extreme stress she'd been under all day. She was relieved, truly she was. And quite calm, now that the terrifying prospect of being shoehorned into a marriage she really, really didn't want was over.

It was strange, therefore, that the next morning she felt as though her limbs were weighted with lead.

It was worry, that was what was making it so hard to dress, or eat breakfast. Worry that she might not be able to persuade her aunt to let her have a few moments alone with Lord Havelock. The fear she might have to continue with the charade one moment longer.

So why did her heart sink still further when Lord Havelock was the one to ask if he could have some private speech with her? He was giving her the very opportunity she sought, to speak freely.

'Won't you sit down?' It was the only thing Mary could think of to say. She'd never been on her own in a room with a man and this one seemed to fill it with his presence. It wasn't as if he was particularly tall, but he was so full of energy. She could still feel the strength of him as he'd guided her round the ice the day before, his arm effortlessly pinning her to his side. How immovable he'd been when she'd tried to push him away after the kiss.

The kiss. She shouldn't have thought about the kiss. It made every single inch of her feel far too…feminine.

He took a seat as close to hers as he could find, which didn't help. Now he could reach out and take her hand, if he wanted. Or she could reach out and take his.

Not that she wanted to. Absolutely not!

'Thank you for agreeing to speak with me alone,' he said. 'I know it is a little unconventional, but there are things we do need to talk about.'

'Yes, there are,' she agreed. 'I understand that you felt obliged to make me an offer of marriage, yesterday, after kissing me.' She couldn't look at his face. Not with his mouth right there, close enough that if she leaned forward, and he leaned forward, just the tiniest bit, they could be kissing again. She looked hard at her hands instead, which she was clasping tightly on her lap. 'And

I'm also aware that you do not truly wish to marry me. And so I release you—'

'You jolly well don't!' He leapt to his feet again. 'No wriggling out of this. You gave me your word....'

'Actually, I didn't. You said a lot of things, and everyone congratulated us, but I never, not once, said I would marry you.'

'Well, you are going to marry me and that's that.'

'No.' She got to her feet, as well. She wasn't going to risk backing down simply because she felt intimidated with him looming over her like that. 'It is better to end this engagement now than to take a step we will both regret for the rest of our lives.'

She'd seen, at close quarters, just how miserable two people could become when bound together by chains of matrimony that neither of them wished for any longer.

'Our engagement will only end one way,' he growled, jabbing his forefinger at her. 'In marriage.'

She flinched at the first physical expression of his anger, but held her ground.

'I've already purchased the licence,' he rapped out. 'And spoken to your uncle, and taken a light-fingered guttersnipe into my employ all on your account. We. Are. Getting. Married.'

As the volume of his voice increased, the memories of raised voices that led to clenched fists, and thence to bruised ribs, made her recall how dangerous it was to be some man's wife, some man's property to deal with as he saw fit. And she began to tremble.

'If this is an indication of the way you mean to go on, whenever your will is crossed, then...'

His eyes widened. He shook his head and ran his fingers through his hair.

'I didn't mean to scare you. Please...' he waved a hand at the chair '...sit down again and I will try to talk this over calmly.'

'Only if you sit down, too.'

He frowned, then nodded.

Gingerly, she sat in the chair he'd indicated and he sat down, too.

'Look, Miss Carpenter. I have a terrible, hasty temper. Bane of my life, actually, but I do try not to let it govern my actions, the way it once did. I am sorry I let it get the better of me this morning. Ungentlemanly of me.' He lowered his head for an instant, the picture of contrition, before lifting it, looking directly into her eyes, and saying, 'Do you think you could find it in your heart to forgive my...outburst and start this interview again?'

She could hardly believe it. He didn't appear to believe, the way her father had, that it was his God-given right to harangue a female, when he had her behind closed doors. On the contrary, he'd said it was 'ungentlemanly' behaviour. And had asked her to forgive him.

How could she do anything *but* forgive him? When she nodded, mutely, he heaved a sigh of relief.

'Thank you. It is just that...this means so much to me. And I was so certain you felt the same way I did. That the fact you were a touch reluctant to get married would make us...allies. Then the cool way you talked about pulling the rug from under my feet just made me—' He broke off, shaking his head as though he didn't have the words to describe what he felt.

She felt every bit as confused as he looked.

'But if you don't truly want to get married, then...'

He heaved another sigh and ran his fingers through his unruly curls again.

'I don't truly *want* to get married, no,' he admitted. 'But I cannot see any other way out. But it's not because I'm in debt, or anything of that nature. My trustees have done a sterling job of managing my capital, up till now. Of course the trust will wind up when I get married,' he said gloomily. 'So I'm going to have to learn all that side of things myself now.'

'And you don't want to.'

He shrugged. 'In some ways it will be good to take up the reins myself instead of letting others drive the team. But I'm going to be far busier with that sort of thing than I'd like.' He slouched back into his seat, his expression mulish.

'Well, then, why? If it isn't money? And you aren't really ready to…take up the reins…' And it certainly wasn't because he'd fallen in love with her. There was nothing lover-like in the way he'd reacted to her rejection. Besides, men only fell for beautiful girls.

'I suppose I should blame Ashe for suggesting I court a girl with brains,' he said cryptically. 'You aren't going to be fobbed off with the usual nonsense, are you?'

'Nonsense?'

He tilted his head to one side and made a wry attempt at a smile.

'Nothing of nonsense about you at all, is there? Very well,' he said, leaning forward and clasping his hands between his knees. 'I will take you into my confidence. I hadn't meant to until after we were married, but I can see you're unlikely to marry me at all unless I give you a very good reason for me acting in a way that must make you think I've taken leave of my senses. I have a sister, you see.'

She didn't see, but before she could say so he leapt

to his feet and, clearly in some agitation, paced away from her. 'Or, to be more precise, a half-sister.' He had to stop when he got to the window, but instead of turning round, he stayed just where he was, his shoulders hunched, and started fiddling with the curtain tie-backs.

'My mother died when I was eight, as I told you before, and then my father remarried pretty swiftly. Before another year was out, she presented him with a daughter. The marriage lasted a few more years before he died. And then my stepmother—' He started in surprise as an ornamental tassel came off in his hand. He laid it down on the windowsill and, taking a step back from further temptation, turned towards Mary and kept his eyes fixed firmly on her as he took up his tale again.

'My stepmother remarried. She…she was only the daughter of our village grocer. But she was beautiful. Her parents, I found out some years later, were so thrilled to have her elevated to the ranks of the peerage, that they pushed her into accepting my father's proposal. She tried to make the best of it, but she was never very happy with him. Anyway, the minute Father died, she took up with the man she'd loved all along. A pretty decent fellow, actually. At least, he was good to me. Paid me more attention than my own father ever had, to tell you the truth, but that's beside the point. He was a nobody, that's what my own father's family said. And they were correct. He hadn't a title. Little money. No land, nothing of that sort, but…'

He turned and paced up and down, raking his fingers through his curls yet again.

'It's all such a tangle it's hard to know how to explain it. You see, my legal guardians didn't actually want me to live with them, but they didn't want me contaminated by the man they called a commoner, either. So they sent me away to school. But you know what? My stepmother, my half-sister and her new stepfather were the only ones to show a real interest in me. Their letters kept me from… Well, school can be a pretty harsh sort of place. I got through because I knew how to defend myself. Thanks to the very man my guardians said I shouldn't go near. He taught me to box.' He glanced down at his fists, which he'd clenched the moment he'd mentioned his school.

'It was to his home I went during school vacations. With him, and my stepmother and Julia I felt I had the nearest thing to a home. I was…very cut up when he died. And for his sake, I kept in contact with his sons. The sons my half-sister's mother bore him.'

She blinked. He caught the bewildered expression in her eyes, at the end of one of his circuits of the room, and pulled a wry face.

'I warned you my family ties are complicated. But that is only the start. You see, after he died, she—that is my stepmother—was left in slightly tricky circum-stances. There was talk of taking Julia away from her and having her brought up by her father's—*my* father's family. Only she hadn't been all that impressed by the way they'd treated me up to then. So when she got an offer of marriage from yet another titled man, she agreed, in an attempt to keep them all, Julia and her two sons, together as a family. Following it so far?'

'Yes, I think so.'

'Well, although financially she did well, she was even more miserable with her third husband than she was with my father. Died giving him his heir. And then… well, for the next few years it felt as though every long vacation I went back to a different marital home as either the husband or the wife died and remarried. It was like living through some bizarre form of farce, with a different infant squalling in a crib, being introduced to me as my new brother or sister, by an adult I was supposed to call Mother or Father.'

'Hold on,' said Mary. 'Why were you calling all these strangers Mother? I don't quite understand.'

'Well, nobody really wanted to take on Julia's brothers, because of who their father was.'

'The decent, but common man.'

'That's him. But they all wanted to keep Julia under their wing, because she has a great deal of money settled on her, and whoever has wardship gets to control it. And wherever she went, I went, too. Because—well, I didn't have anywhere else to call home. And by that time I'd gained a bit of a reputation for being a hellion. Not the trustees or any of my father's extended family thought it worth the bother of attempting to discipline me, or cross my will. If I wanted to take myself off to the wilds of Wiltshire, or Yorkshire or Devon so I could be with my half-sister, they were only too glad to see the back of me.'

Mary's heart went out to him, or rather, the abandoned, unloved little boy he'd been. No wonder he went a bit wild. No wonder he made a point of going where he truly was wanted. Where he would be loved.

'I…I see….'

'No, you don't.' He shook his head and grinned at her. 'My family connections are so incredibly complicated that even I cannot keep track of all the people who claim kinship with me these days. Suffice it to say that Julia is the only one of them I give a rat's a— I mean, care very much about.'

She ought to have been offended by the way he'd almost slipped into vulgarity. But she was beginning to find his very clumsiness of speech rather endearing. In a way, he was treating her with a unique form of respect by saying whatever came into his head, rather than trying to bamboozle her with glib speeches. As was the way he pulled himself up, without her having to so much as lift a brow in reproof, either.

'Very well,' she said. 'Go on.'

'Thank you.' He sat down in the chair he'd used before, leaned his elbows on his knees and clasped his hands.

'Now, the thing is, the woman who is currently standing in the place of Julia's stepmother is about to get married again. And the man she's marrying is…' He scowled. 'Well, put it this way. I wouldn't want *any* innocent girl to have to live under the same roof as him. Julia's fifteen now and pretty as a picture. And Lord… Perhaps I shouldn't tell you his name.' He frowned, rubbing his thumb across his nose. 'Although, if people didn't gossip about him, I never would have found out that he's assuming nobody cares what becomes of Julia, given the way she's been passed round like a parcel up till now.'

'Oh, I see.' Mary leaned forward, clasping her own hands. 'By marrying, you are launching a rescue. You plan to provide a stable, safe environment for her to live in. That's…' she smiled at him a little mistily '…that is truly noble of you.'

He sat up straight again. 'Is it? I hadn't thought of it like that.' He shook his head. 'I just couldn't think what else to do. I spent hours discussing Julia's future with my lawyers, and hers. My first thought was to make an attempt to be declared her legal guardian. I'm pretty nearly old enough now, you see. But found out that would take too much time. Couldn't very well drag her out of the house and take her back to live in my bachelor lodgings either, while the lawyers worked through all the red tape. It would look damned peculiar. Probably cause the very kind of talk I don't want her exposed to. But if I got married, they said, and moved back to Mayfield, it would seem perfectly natural to invite her to live with us. Reunite the Durant family in the ancestral home, sort of thing.'

And if she didn't marry him now, he'd have to abandon that plan. Start all over again trying to find someone else to become his convenient wife. For that was what he wanted, she finally saw. Just a woman to make his rescue of his sister appear respectable and above board.

Could she really let him down, this way, after he'd confided the delicacy of his sister's plight to her? Could she let the girl, Julia, down, for that matter? She knew what it felt like to be all alone in the world, a burden to everyone, yet nobody's responsibility. Though she'd never been in the kind of peril that faced Julia. She simply wasn't pretty enough.

And then there were the Pargetters, who'd been so kind to her when she was just about at the end of her tether. They were banking on her to launch Dotty and Lotty into society. Give them the chance their beauty and vivacity deserved.

Could she trust him though, to keep his word? To grant her an allowance and treat her with respect?

From the way this interview had gone so far she thought, yes, perhaps she could.

And as for his temper, which seemed to flare out of

nowhere—well, at least he regarded it as the bane of his life and tried to keep it in check.

And apologised when he couldn't.

'Very well,' she said. 'I will help you. Of course I will, now I understand what is at stake.'

'Thank you.' He heaved a sigh of relief. Reached across the small gap that divided them, took both her hands in his and gave them a little squeeze.

'I have been at my wit's end. I couldn't tell anyone of my fears for her, in case it started the very kind of gossip that would be almost as bad as the fate I was afraid would await her if she ever got into Lord Wakefield's clutches. Now we can nip any schemes he might have been hatching in the bud. But…you must understand, time is of the essence. I want a place made ready for her to come to, a place she can feel safe, before her current stepmother marries him.'

'Which is why our wedding must take place so soon.'

'That's it. In fact, I was hoping we could get the knot tied tomorrow, then travel straight down to Mayfield and look the place over.'

'Mayfield? Why, is there something wrong with it?'

'I shouldn't think so. But I do want to just make sure before I tell Julia she can move in. You see, when my father died, I was too young to live there alone, so, as I mentioned, my guardians packed me off to school and let the place out to tenants. Better than letting it stand empty, they reckoned, and renting it out paid for its upkeep.'

'Oh, dear. Are you going to have to evict the current tenants? It's so near to Christmas….'

'And it may very well snow, too.' He chuckled. 'No, I'm not going to play the part of an evil landlord, don't worry about that,' he said, chucking her chin. 'Fortunately, a couple of years ago, when it fell vacant, I told the letting agent I didn't want them to find another tenant. Don't need the money and have never liked the thought of strangers living there. Good country round about, too. Had some thoughts of doing a bit of entertaining, having some fellows down for the hunting, that sort of thing, though I never got round to it. And just as I told you before, the trustees never bother arguing when they can see I've made up my mind. For some reason, they stopped letting out Durant House, too.

'Oh, hang it! I suppose I shall have to reside there once I'm married and have Julia in tow.'

'You don't like the place?'

'It's like a cross between a barn and a mausoleum,' he said gloomily.

'Can you not make it more comfortable?'

'I don't see how.'

'W-well, I've never lived anywhere that cannot be made more…cheerful, by the strategic placement of furniture and a lick of paint.'

'If you can make Durant House anything like approaching cheerful,' he said fervently, 'I will consider myself for ever in your debt.'

'R-really?'

He pounced on the hopeful note she couldn't help trembling through her voice.

'I'll give you a completely free hand. In fact, I would prefer it if you didn't bother me with any of the details of the refurbishment at all.'

'You are willing to give me a totally free hand in the redecoration of your town house?'

'Mayfield, too, if you think you'd enjoy it. The only

stipulation I will make is that I want it to feel like somewhere Julia can really feel at home.'

'A…a home.' She pressed her hands to her cheeks. 'You want me to turn your ancestral seat into a home?'

'Actually,' he said, as though it had just occurred to him, 'it's *traditional* for the new bride to make some changes.'

'Oh,' she breathed, her hands clasped at her bosom now. She'd asked him for one room to call her own and he was presenting her with two whole houses.

'You'd *really* enjoy doing that?'

'Yes. Very much.'

'Good. Told you I wanted you to be happy! And if buying new carpets and wallpaper will do it, then so much the better. Though…' He rubbed his nose with his thumb as though a thought had just struck him. 'If your taste really runs counter to mine, I might just have to reserve a room or two for myself.'

'I wouldn't dream of making you uncomfortable anywhere in your own homes,' she protested.

'You won't,' he said firmly. 'This will be a very… That is, I've already told you I don't want us to be in each other's pockets all the time. You can go your way and I'll go mine. Within limits.' He frowned. Then shook his head. 'No, no, never mind. I trust you to set a good example for Julia to follow. You won't go creating any sort of scandal, will you?'

'I…I don't think I'd know how to,' she said, a little stung by his warning, even though he had retracted it almost at once.

He smiled at her again. A smile so warm and full of approval that she quite forgave his blunt speaking yet again. It was just the way he was and she was going to have to get used to it.

'So, you have no objection to marrying tomorrow and heading straight down there, then?'

'What?' She wasn't sure how they'd moved from living separate, but parallel lives, the way she'd heard many *tonnish* people did, to rushing into the wedding itself.

'Your aunt tried to make some objection about not having time to get a trousseau together, but do you really need one?'

'N-no, of course not.' She hadn't even thought about it. All that had exercised her mind since the day before had been how to avoid marriage altogether.

He frowned. 'You do mind. I can tell. Your aunt is right. It is downright selfish of me to deny you all the folderol most brides have. You'll want a new gown at the least, and shoes.'

'I...I think I could contrive to get something you won't be ashamed to see me in, by tomorrow,' she said.

His face lit up. 'I'll pay for it, of course. Send whatever bills you run up to me. Well, I think that's all settled, then.'

He reached into his pocket and pulled out a sheet of paper. Having scanned it swiftly, he thrust it back, his face flushing. 'You wouldn't believe how many things a chap has to remember,' he said, fishing around in another pocket, from which he produced a second list.

'No wonder most women insist on having several weeks to organise a wedding. Ah. Yes, thought so,' he said, thrusting the list back into his pocket. 'There is just one more thing I do need to discuss with you, before we tie the knot.'

He cleared his throat.

'This may be a businesslike arrangement, but it won't be a paper marriage.'

'I don't follow.'

'To be blunt, I need an heir. I've thought about this a lot, since…well, since I decided on marriage. And I've come to the conclusion we should get that side of things started straight away. I can tell you're quite a bashful sort of girl and that you might think I ought to give you time to become accustomed to the idea of being married, before I make any demands of that nature. But it's like this…'

He leaned forward and took hold of both her hands in his. 'At the moment, we both like each other. Don't we?'

When she nodded, shyly, he smiled. 'Now, the sad fact is marriages can turn sour remarkably quickly. I've seen it time and time again. If we get to the point where we cannot stand even being in the same room as one another…well, let's just say attempting to get an heir in those conditions won't be pleasant. Not for either of us. But at the moment, when we kiss…'

He looked at her mouth. Her lips tingled in remembrance of the kisses they'd shared the day before. And then every other part of her began to tingle, as well.

He was probably right. She'd grown up in a house where husband and wife could barely stand to be in the same room as each other. Whereas now…

Well, it really sounded as though he wouldn't try to suffocate her. He had at least two houses that she knew of. So they needn't ever be cooped up in a cramped little cottage, resenting the very air that each breathed. And they weren't marrying for love, so they couldn't fall out of it and grow bitter and resentful.

But, oh, she did like kissing him. And now that he'd

mentioned it, and was looking at her mouth that way, she wanted him to take her in his arms again, the way he'd done yesterday. And…she blushed, and the rest.

As if he knew the direction of her thoughts, he dropped to his knees in front of her, never letting go of her hands, leaned forward and touched his lips to hers. Just lightly.

Her eyes fluttered shut. She gripped his hands tightly. And she leaned forward, too, this time pressing her lips to his.

In a heartbeat, he'd got his arms round her, she'd put her arms round him and each was kissing the other for all they were worth.

'Mmnhh…stop,' he mumbled, pulling away. 'We have to stop,' he said, staggering to his feet and backing across the room. 'Or I won't be able to. You…' He drew in a great, ragged breath.

'My God,' he said unsteadily. 'I would never have believed it, but do you know, I'm actually looking forward to my wedding day.'

'Me, too,' she admitted, stunned. 'And I wouldn't have believed it, either.'

'See?' He grinned. 'We're perfect for each other.'

To her amusement he then sidled round the edge of the room to the door, as though avoiding a dangerous precipice.

As though she was utterly irresistible.

Just for a moment, she almost believed it herself.

Chapter Six

Wedding fever swept through the household. Aunt Pargetter took Mary to a street where there was a whole parade of shops where you could buy clothing ready-made. And not all of it used. And by dint of sitting up well into the night, with as many lamps as they could gather, the four women, working together, had both her gown, and the coat they'd bought to wear over it, altered to fit as though it had been made for her, then trimmings added so that the whole ensemble looked as though it had been designed from the outset instead of bought piecemeal and cobbled together.

She slept surprisingly well considering she was about to take a step she'd once vowed she would never take at all. Even though she'd only met Lord Havelock a matter of days before, the prospect of marrying him didn't fill her with dread. Every time either Dotty or Lotty rolled over, kicking her in the shins in their sleep, it reminded her of their willingness to make room for her when they had so little of it themselves. And she got a warm glow of satisfaction, knowing that she would soon be in a position to help this family, the only ones who'd shown her any compassion when she'd been at her most desperate.

And help Lord Havelock's sister, too.

How many men, she sighed, would make the supreme sacrifice of surrendering their bachelor freedom for the sake of a sister? Not her own brother, that was certain. He'd escaped their unhappy household as soon as he could and never looked back. Oh, he'd visited when on shore leave, but during those brief visits their father had been on his best behaviour and Kit had never once looked beneath the surface....

Not that she had begrudged him his career. Not in the light of how it ended....

She turned on to her side, resting her cheek on the palm of her hand. No point dwelling on the failings of a brother who was no more. Besides, she'd much rather dream about her husband-to-be. She smiled into the darkness as she recalled his insistence they get the business of providing an heir to his estates settled quickly, *before they went off each other*. Some women might have taken his attitude as an insult. She preferred to regard it as eminently practical. And a touch flattering that though he assumed his ardour would cool, he really felt some now. Quite a lot, if that last kiss in the parlour was anything to go by. And the difficulty he had in breaking it off.

Which meant that very soon she would have a baby to hold. Possibly even a couple before he went back to his... Well, a man as energetic and healthy as he was bound to have some arrangement to satisfy *that* form of appetite. Though even when it got to that stage in their marriage, she was not afraid he would become a cruel, or even an indifferent, parent. The lengths to which he was prepared to go for his sister assured her of that.

The next morning, when she stood before the mirror, she couldn't help exclaim in thanks for the Pargetters' hard work and inventiveness. She'd never looked better dressed.

Oh, if only her mother could see her now. Or her brother…though it wasn't likely he would have been on leave to walk her down the aisle even if his ship hadn't gone down with all hands.

For a moment, stark loneliness had tears welling in her eyes. Resolutely she dashed them away. She didn't want to appear in church with red eyes, as though she was going to the altar like some…sacrificial lamb. Besides, she was gaining a new family today, a husband who didn't seem as though he had the slightest inclination to browbeat and control her, a sister who would need her and eventually children of her very own to love her.

It was with a pale, but determined face that she left the room she'd shared with her cousins and made her way downstairs and to the carriage waiting to carry her, her aunt, uncle and cousins to church.

Her uncle Pargetter had taken leave from his place of work so that he could walk her down the aisle. The gesture should have made her feel less alone, but somehow the fact that she knew him as little as the man who was waiting for her at the altar merely lent the proceedings an air of unreality.

It had all happened so fast. And before she knew it, the vicar declared they were man and wife, and Lord Havelock was bundling her into a carriage, which

whisked them off to the Clarendon, where Lord Havelock treated them all to a splendid breakfast.

'You've landed on your feet and no mistake,' her uncle
commented as he shook her hand before leaving. 'Very
open-handed, this new husband of yours.'

'Yes, and so handsome,' added Aunt Pargetter, giving
her a kiss on the cheek. She added a hug to the parting
kiss, so that she could whisper into her ear.

'But please, don't think of this as a permanent parting. You must feel free to come and talk to me, or write,
if you have any little problems. Getting used to the married state can be a touch tricky and I know you have no
other female relative in whom you can confide.'

She didn't know how her aunt had guessed, but she
did feel rather as though she was sailing into uncharted
waters without a compass. And also now she'd boarded
this ship called matrimony, it wouldn't be possible to
return to the shore from which she'd embarked. Her
aunt's willingness to give her the benefit of her advice,
should she reach troubled waters, made her feel not quite
so alone.

She hugged her aunt back, fiercely.

'Thank you' was all Mary managed to say, with a
voice thickened with emotion. She was going to miss
them, all the Pargetters. They were good people. They
didn't have much, yet they'd been far more generous
than closer relations who were far better off.

'Our rooms are this way,' said Lord Havelock, the
moment the last of the Pargetters had exited the hotel
and she'd dabbed her eyes dry with a darned handkerchief. He offered her his arm, and she laid her hand on
his sleeve.

They mounted the stairs in silence, in the wake of a

smartly liveried hotel porter. The man opened a door with a flourish and bowed them into what looked like some wealthy person's best parlour.

'I took a suite of rooms,' said Lord Havelock once he'd dismissed the porter. 'I hope they meet with your approval.'

'In all honesty,' she said, hands clasped to her bosom, 'I have never seen such a magnificent room in all my life.' The thickness of the carpet alone made her yearn to take off her shoes and stockings so she could sink her toes into it. A fire blazed heartily from an ornate marble fireplace and all the furniture looked as though it had been specially selected to match not only every other piece in the room, but also the wallpaper and curtains.

He had casually mentioned having both a country estate and a town house, as well as his more comfortable bachelor rooms, but it hadn't really struck her, until this moment, what it meant. A man who could afford to buy a marriage licence and get a ceremony organised within a couple of days, splash out for a wedding break-fast in a hotel notorious for the expense of its meals and hire a whole suite of rooms like this, must be very, very wealthy indeed.

In a daze, she let him lead her across the room.

'This is your bedchamber,' he said, throwing open the door to the right of the fireplace. 'I did promise that you would always have your own room, a room that nobody could enter without your permission.'

'You did,' she said, hovering tensely on the thresh-old, looking in. The room was as tastefully opulent as the sitting room. But what caught her eye, and held her rooted to the spot, was the enormous four-poster bed it contained.

He came to stand very close behind her.

'I shall be knocking on this door later on,' he said, his breath rushing over the back of her neck and giving her goosebumps in the most remarkable places. 'I hope very much you will let me in, but if you really don't want me...bothering you in that way, tonight, then of course you only have to say so.'

Well, that was very considerate of him. And perhaps she ought to feel reluctant to welcome him into that bed when she scarcely knew him. Except that the heat of his kisses would keep searing into her mind at the most unlikely moments, making her squirm and melt inside. And she wasn't ever likely to get any less shy of him than she felt now. And they were married. Making a baby was one of the reasons he'd given for marrying her. And it was his right...

'I won't *demand* my husbandly rights, if that is what is making you blush,' he murmured into her ear. 'Not until you are ready. Though I do want you. Badly.' He leaned down and brushed a tantalisingly barely there kiss on her neck, just below her ear. 'And I really do think,' he growled, 'it would be better to jump this hurdle before too long.'

Was she blushing? She pressed her hands to her cheeks, which did indeed feel as if they were on fire. Because she was ready right now. And rather ashamed that what he was taking for maidenly modesty was a complete inability to know what to do with her reaction to the nearness of his body. The seductive pull of his mouth on her skin...

'Beg pardon,' he said, stepping away just as she was on the point of turning and flinging her arms round his neck. 'I'm being a bit too blunt for you. But, look, you may as well know that I'm not a man given to fancy speeches and wrapping things up in metaphors. I hope you will soon get used to me and learn not to take offence, because I won't change.'

There was a touch of belligerence to his voice that made her turn to look warily up into his face. Was he angry with her? He probably thought he had a right to be, having spent so much money, only to have her appear to...shy at the first fence.

He was frowning, but before she could stammer out the confession that he'd got it all wrong, that not only did she agree that it was better to get on with the physical side of their marriage, but was actually rather looking forward to it, he'd turned away, and was striding across the room to a door on the other side of the fireplace.

'This is my chamber,' he said gruffly, 'where all my things are stowed.' He whirled round, his frown deepening.

'Was that luggage I saw, next to your bed, all you have with you?'

She nodded. 'It's all I have.'

'All you have?' The frown altered in tone. He came to her and took her hands. 'We really ought to be spending a few days in town putting that right, but... Look, I'm sorry, I've already made arrangements to travel down to Mayfield and get the place ready for Julia to come. Still, there's bound to be a dressmaker in Corleywood—that's the nearest sizeable town—who can fit you out with some new gear.'

'I don't mind about clothes,' she said. 'I know it is more important to ensure Julia's safety.'

His handsome face broke into a grin. 'I don't know another woman who'd look at it like that.' He lifted her hands to his mouth and kissed them. 'But you must have some decent things to wear, before the local gentry all turn out to have a look at you. Once word gets out in the neighbourhood that I've married and brought my bride to Mayfield, they'll all be coming to call. And you will want to be able to look 'em in the eye.'

Meaning, she wasn't able to now? In the outfit she'd been so proud of that very morning?

'Well, that's another thing to add to my list.' He gave her a rueful smile. 'Every time I think I've got everything organised, something else crops up that I've entirely overlooked.'

'I'm quite capable of buying my own clothes,' she began indignantly, only to founder on the rock of her completely penniless state.

'You just get whatever you want and have the dressmakers send the bills to me,' he said. 'You'll have an allowance, too. That's one of the things... Damn!' He let go of her hands and thrust his fingers through his hair. 'I've an appointment with my lawyers in...' he glanced at the clock on the mantelshelf '...about half an hour's time. I've a deal of stuff to discuss with them, documents to sign and so forth, which couldn't be done until I'd got the marriage lines. I know it's not the thing to leave a bride alone, so soon after the ceremony, but...'

'I understand.' He'd married her for necessity, not inclination. And if she took offence every time he reminded her of that fact, she was going to end up being badly hurt a dozen times a day. 'Go. Do what you have to do. I shall be quite content here, in this beautiful room.'

In a way it would be good practice for her. She was going to have to get used to spending large amounts of time on her own while he went off doing whatever it was he spent his days doing.

'Thank you,' he said, his look of relief being the only indication that, up till that point, he had been concerned about her reaction.

'I will return as soon as possible, I promise you.' With a heartbreakingly compelling smile, he leaned forward and gave her a peck on the cheek. Then he turned and left her, and she pressed one palm to her face as though to cling on to it, on to him, as long as she could.

For a few moments after the door closed behind him, Mary just stood there, in the stately isolation of the sitting room, marooned on her desert island of Axminster.

But there was no point in moping. Better to keep herself busy. She might as well use the spare time to unpack. Only...they would be setting off for his country estate the next morning, so it hardly seemed worthwhile. She'd only have to pack all over again.

She wandered over to the window, from where she had a good view over Blackheath, if she'd *wanted* to look at it. She shook her head reproachfully over her spurt of pique. Lord Havelock had warned her that he didn't want them to live in each other's pockets and she'd agreed it sounded much better than having a jealous, vengeful sort of husband who'd be breathing down her neck the whole time. She was going to have to cultivate the habit of finding things to do, when she was on her own. And not dwell on what it had made her feel like when he *had* been breathing on her neck, brushing that kiss on it…

She shook herself. What did married ladies do when their husbands were out on business, that was what she should be thinking about. Drank tea, probably. There.

That was something she could do. She would definitely feel better for a cup.

She rang for a servant, and before much longer she had not only tea, but also a selection of cakes and sandwiches brought up. As the waiter set them out on one of the many small tables scattered about the sitting room, she had to suppress a wild urge to giggle. It was like being a little girl, play-acting at being a princess, clapping her hands only to have invisible servants magic up food and drink out of thin air.

She couldn't look at him as he bowed himself out of the room, lest she really did burst out laughing. And so, when the door slammed, she was looking in exactly the right direction to see a sheet of paper, lodged under her husband's bedroom door, flutter in the draught.

Even from where she was sitting she could see it was some kind of list. And the moment she registered what it was, she recalled him saying how many things he had to remember, how he'd frowningly pulled not just one, but two lists out of his coat pocket the day he'd called to discuss arrangements.

Oh, dear, she hoped this one wasn't important. But if it was, perhaps she could summon up one of the hotel genies to whisk it to the meeting he was having. That would prove what a good and useful wife he'd married.

She bent down and pulled it out from under the door, her eyes snagging on the first item.

Compliant, it said, in an elegant copperplate script. And then next to it, in heavier, darker letters, another hand had added, *A Mouse*.

What kind of list was this?

Needn't have any dowry.

Oh. Oh! She clapped one hand to her mouth as she read the next item: *Won't demand a society wedding.*

This wasn't a list of things he needed to remember at all, but a list of what he was looking for in a wife.

A Mouse, the heavier hand had scrawled next to the bit about the ceremony, and underlined it.

Not of the upper ten thousand, her shocked eyes discovered next.

Orphan.

Her stomach roiled as she recalled the look on Lord Havelock's face when she'd told him, that fateful night at the Crimmers', that she'd just lost her mother. She'd thought he couldn't possibly have looked pleased to hear she was all alone in the world, that surely she must have been mistaken.

But she hadn't been.

She tottered back to the tea table and sank on to the chair the waiter had so helpfully drawn up to it. And carried on reading.

Not completely hen-witted, the sloppier of the two writers had added. And she suddenly understood that cryptic comment he'd made about finding a wife with brains. Suggested by someone called…Ashe, that was it. How she could remember a name tossed out just the once, in such an offhand way, she could not think.

Unless it was because she felt as though the beautiful little dainties set out on their fine china plates might as well have been so many piles of ash, for all the desire she had now to put one in her mouth.

Good with children, *Not selfish*, the darker hand had scrawled. Then it was back to the neater hand again. It had written, *Modest*, *Honest* and *Not looking for affection from matrimony.* And then the untidier, what she'd come to think of as the more sarcastic, compiler of wifely qualities had written the word *Mouse* again, and this time underlined it twice.

But what made a small whimper of distress finally escape her lips was the last item on the list.

Need not be pretty.

Need not be pretty. Well, that was her, all right! Plain, dowdy, mouse that she was. No wonder he'd looked at her as though—what was it Aunt Pargetter had said— as though his ship had come in?

But which of the men who'd compiled that list had harped on about the need to find a mouse, that was the question that now burned in her brain like a fever. Had Havelock's been the hand to scrawl that word, not once, but three times?

Getting to her feet, she strode to his bedroom door and flung it open. Somehow she had to find a sample of his handwriting to see if he'd been the one to...to mock her this way, before he'd even met her. And then she would... She came to an abrupt halt by his desk, across the surface of which was scattered a veritable raft of papers. What would she do? She'd already married him.

With shaking hands she began to sift through what looked like a heap of bills, some of them on the hotel's headed notepaper. Until she came to what was unmistakably a letter. *Dear Lady Peverell*, it began. There was another underneath, in the same bold scrawl, which started, *Dear Chepstow.* She flipped to the bottom of the page. The one to Lady Peverell was signed *Havelock.* And she couldn't help noticing, on her way to the end of the sheet, that he was informing her of his marriage. He hadn't got very far with the other letter, so there was no signature, but it began in the same vein. Except...

Oh! He'd informed his friend that *She meets all the requirements we fixed on, bar one.*

The room seemed to swim as several facts all jostled rudely into her mind at once. This Chepstow person had taken part in compiling the wife list. Ashe was another. Were theirs the two sets of handwriting? And then there was Morgan. She'd wondered why Lord Havelock had come to such an unfashionable place as the Crimmers', but now she understood perfectly. He had been looking for a wife who didn't come from the upper ten thousand and Mr Morgan had made it possible to meet one, by taking him there.

So, Mr Morgan, too, must know about the infamous list.

And how many others?

She had a sickening vision of half a dozen drunken bucks sitting round a table in some crowded tavern, suggesting what Lord Havelock should look for in a wife who would be so grateful to receive a proposal at all, that she'd never dare lift her voice in complaint about any treatment he might decide to mete out.

With an expression of disgust, she dropped the list on to the rest of his papers and hurried from his room.

Which didn't look like a palace out of a fairy tale any longer, but a gilded cage.

A cage she'd walked into with her eyes wide open.

Or so she'd thought. But that was before she'd discovered he'd made out a list of what he wanted from a wife. Just as though he was going shopping for groceries!

She stood quite still, eyes closed, head bowed against the tide of humiliation that washed over her.

She was such a fool.

He'd been honest with her from the start. He'd told

her he was looking for a convenient wife. That he'd been in a hurry to get one, so that he could get on with the far more important business of rescuing Julia.

At what point had she forgotten that? When had she started hoping there might be a glimmer of truth in what Aunt Pargetter said about him falling for her? Men didn't need to even *like* a woman to want to get her naked and in a bed. She knew that. She'd been brought up in a coastal town swarming with lusty sailors, for heaven's sake!

She clasped her hands to her waist as her middle lurched almost painfully. How on earth could she possibly have thought that such a handsome, wealthy, titled man would suddenly become enamoured of a penniless, plain little...*mouse* of a creature like her? She'd mistaken his relief at finding a compliant, orphaned, modest woman to be his convenient wife so quickly for delight in *her*.

She shook her head. It had been useless flinging the list back amongst his other papers. The words of it were scored into her brain as though carved with a knife.

The sound of footsteps striding along the corridor had her opening her eyes and gazing in horror at the door. She couldn't face him, in all his good humour, not now, not while she felt so...wounded!

To her relief, the feet kept on walking. It must just have been another guest returning to his room, or one of the hotel staff bustling about their business.

Still, it had been a warning. With fingers that shook, she poured some tea into her cup, selected a pastry at random and put it on to a plate. If he walked in now, he would simply see a woman taking tea. She would make her face show nothing of what she felt.

And she would *not* weep.

* * *

When Lord Havelock eventually returned, she was still doggedly dry-eyed. Sitting stock-still at the table with her cup of tea, untouched, in front of her.

'Sitting in the dark?' He frowned at her as she started, then stared at him as though she wasn't quite sure who he was.

'You should have rung for candles.' He strode across and tugged on the bell pull. 'And the fire has almost gone out, too.'

She turned, slowly, to look at it.

'At least you've had something to eat…' He frowned as he noted that nothing appeared to have been touched. Even her teacup was full.

Though her eyes were empty.

'I've been a perfect beast, haven't I,' he said, pulling up the other chair to the table and grasping her hands. 'To leave you alone for such a long time.' He raised each hand in turn, kissing it penitently.

She looked at him in confusion. No wonder she'd started to think he was developing some real affection for her. But this was just…gallantry. If she'd had any experience of suitors, in the past, she would have known that this was how men behaved with women. That it meant nothing.

He should have picked either Dotty or Lotty. Either of them would have coped with him far, far better than she was doing.

'Well,' he said, starting to chafe her hands between his own. 'I've achieved everything I needed to get done today, so now I'm all yours.' He gave an uneasy laugh. 'Though from the look you're giving me that information doesn't exactly please you. Dash it, where's that waiter? Your hands are like ice. Your feet, too, I dare say.'

She thought she'd kept her face impassive, but something must have shown, for he shook his head and said ruefully, 'Ah, Mary. You don't have anything to worry about. On my word of honour, I'll do better from now on. To start with, we'll have a slap-up meal, and…and talk to each other. Yes? Not downstairs in one of the public rooms, but up here, since you are looking a little…'

Plain? Mousy? Not smartly dressed enough to be able to look the well-heeled clientele in the eye?

'Uncomfortable,' he finished.

'I…I don't feel very hungry,' she said. 'Today has been…just a bit…rather…'

'Hasn't it, though? Not two weeks ago I thought I'd *never* get married. Now here I am in a hotel room with my bride, on my wedding night. Takes your breath away, don't it?'

She nodded.

'Do you know what I think?'

She shook her head. That was the trouble. She kept imagining he was thinking things he'd told her pointblank he wasn't going to think.

'I think by leaving you hanging all afternoon, you've ended up feeling like a game bird ready for plucking. And that I ought to set about making you feel like a bride, instead.'

'What do you mean?'

'I think you know very well what I mean,' he growled, pulling her to her feet.

She uttered a squeak of surprise when he hefted her into his arms.

A woman with more pride, she expected, would have put up some form of protest.

Mary put her arms round his neck, buried her face in his shoulder and clung to his solid warmth as he strode with her over to his bedroom.

Chapter Seven

He tumbled them both on to the bed and kissed her with an ardour that left her breathless. And strangely comforted.

Even though he'd only chosen her with his head, not his heart, he had chosen *her*. There must be dozens of poor, plain, penniless orphans in London, yet he hadn't looked any further once he'd met her.

And, yes, maybe that was only because he was in such a hurry to get married, but...

With a moan that was half distress, half desperation, she curled her fingers into the luxuriant softness of his hair and kissed him back for all she was worth.

They were married now. Did it really matter how it had come about? No. It was what they made of their future that mattered.

Her response brought a feral growl of appreciation from his throat. And then, for a few moments, it was as though he had been let off some invisible leash. His hands were all over her while his body strained against hers in a way that thrilled her to the soles of her boots.

His excitement called to something buried deep in

the heart of her. Something wild and wanton that came roaring to life and swept aside her every inhibition. Her hands were every bit as greedy as his, seeking and stroking and learning. She couldn't get close enough to him. She wanted to wrap herself round him. Press every single inch of her against every marvellously thrilling inch of him.

Until, quite without warning, he reared back.

'This is going too fast,' he panted, frowning.

'What do you mean?' It all felt perfectly wonderful to her.

'This is your first time,' he gritted out between clenched teeth. 'I should be taking it far more slowly. Making it good for you.'

Well, she couldn't argue with that. After all the horrible things she'd read on that list, the dreadful afternoon she'd spent sitting alone, cold and brutally wounded, the least he could do was make *this* part of their marriage good.

He'd closed his eyes on a grimace. When he opened them again, only a few seconds later, he'd calmed down considerably.

'I didn't even pause to get our shoes off.' He sighed, with a shake of his head.

He sat up, scooted down the bed and rapidly unlaced her rather worn leather half-boots. Aunt Pargetter had wanted to get her some dainty footwear to go with her wedding finery, but there hadn't been time. And she'd thought her own comfortable boots would stand her in better stead, considering the coldness of the season. Only now did she wish she'd taken them off herself, during the hours he'd been away seeing his lawyers.

He didn't say anything about the patched soles, or

the worn-down heels, but his frown did deepen once his fingers encountered her stockinged feet.

'Your feet are like ice! Well, that won't do.' Taking her left foot between both hands, he first chafed it, then raised it to his mouth to plant a hot kiss on the sole. The action sent her skirts slithering up her legs.

His hot eyes followed their movement. Swiftly followed by his hands.

'I need to get these stockings off,' he said, as though warning her of his intent.

She shivered with pleasure when he deftly undid her garter, then slid one stocking down.

'Cold?'

She shook her head. Far from it. It felt as though a bolt of lightning streaked from the heat of his hands against her bared skin, right to her very core. She subsided into the pillows again, luxuriating in the sensations he evoked whilst removing her other stocking—with slow deliberation.

Her eyes half-closed, she watched with growing interest as he got up, shrugged off his jacket, undid his shirt and yanked it impatiently off over his head.

He had, without doubt, the most impressive masculine torso she'd ever seen. And she had seen many. Sailors often worked in just their ragged breeches, when loading and unloading ships during the hottest months of the year.

But she'd always averted her gaze and hurried past. She'd never been even remotely tempted to pause and drink her fill of any single one of them. She hadn't struggled to keep her hands neatly placed at her sides, rather than reaching out and running her fingers over each clearly delineated muscle. Or thought about letting her tongue follow in the wake of her fingers. Or got a mad urge to lick her way up that strong column of a masculine throat to the stubbled texture of his chin.

Not that she was bold enough to do any such thing. Besides, he'd just said he was going to make it good for her. And part of her, the part that was still smarting over the things she'd read on the list, wanted him to exert himself to make it up to her. Not that he would be aware he was doing any such thing, but still, she would know.

Anyway, he inadvertently helped her to resist the temptation by sitting down on the edge of the bed to remove his boots, which gave her eyes an entirely new view to appreciate. His back. The broad shoulders, the ridges of muscle down either side of his spine, which disappeared into the narrow waistband of his breeches.

She was a little disappointed when he drew the line at removing them. Although perhaps it was only fair. After all, she was still in her gown. Not that it took him long to take it off her once he set to it. My, but he certainly knew his way round lacings, and corsets.

Her heart was beating nineteen to the dozen by the time he lay down beside her and put his arm about her shoulders. The dexterity he'd just displayed with her clothing convinced her that he truly could make this experience good for her.

Even though he wasn't all that proficient at flirting and charming his way into a woman's bed, it didn't mean he hadn't had encounters of an…earthy nature, with willing women.

Willing? Oh, what an inadequate word. If any of them had guessed what kind of body he concealed beneath his casually comfortable clothing, plenty of them would have ripped them off just to get their greedy hands on it.

Just as she wanted to get her own hands on it.

She was so glad he didn't wear the kind of clothing that showed his stunning physique to better advantage. If he'd needed a couple of valets to peel a tightly fitted coat from those bulging biceps, she would have missed the enthralling spectacle of him gradually revealing more and more of his masculinity for her eyes alone.

He wouldn't have been able to just take her to bed because he felt it was time, either. She liked that they could be spontaneous about this, rather than having to involve servants.

She reached for him as he ran his fingers through her hair—hair that had come out of its fastenings during their first bout of kissing on this bed.

As she ran her hands down his back, glorying in the fact that there were no longer any clothes to impede her exploration, it occurred to her that a 'modest' woman wouldn't be doing this. Wouldn't have clawed her way under his waistcoat and writhed up against him like some kind of snake when he'd tumbled her on to the bed earlier, either. Nor would a 'modest' woman let her husband strip her naked at four in the afternoon—even if daylight was fading—and be glad of the way firelight bathed the room in a warm glow, so she could feast her eyes on her new husband's magnificent masculine nakedness.

But then, nor would a man who truly wanted a modest wife be looking at her like that—as if he wanted to devour her.

Which was pretty much what he did next, tasting and nibbling her all over as though she was some rare delicacy. He didn't leave an inch of her unexplored. And everywhere he put his mouth, he left behind such glorious feelings she didn't know how to describe them.

She bit down on her lower lip when he finally stroked her legs apart and began trailing kisses up the inside of her thighs.

Her aunt Pargetter had warned her, during a private little talk the night before, that the things her husband might wish to do to her, once in the marriage bed, might seem strange and perhaps a little frightening at first. She had advised her against resisting, or protesting, because nine times out of ten he would have more of an idea what would end up making it lovely.

It was all she could do not to laugh out loud. Resist him? Protest about this? Oh, no. The slow slide of his tongue, the little nips of his teeth, combined with the firm caresses of those strong hands, those knowing fingers, were exactly what she wanted.

Oh, very well, so her aunt had got part of it right. He did know more than her about this.

And he was taking the time to make it lovely for her, too. Which was somewhat surprising, considering he'd so far given the impression of always being in a hurry to get things done.

There was just one awkward little interlude, after he'd shucked off his breeches, where what he did hurt quite a bit, but then he brought the lovely feelings back, with skill, with patience, until…until…oh, utter rapture. It was as if she had completely left her body behind. She was floating somewhere—somewhere he'd taken her. And he was there, too. She could tell. His whole body was quivering with it. Pulsing with it.

'Mary.' He sighed, as she began to drift back to reality. A reality that had somehow been transformed, though she couldn't have explained how. And anyway, she felt too peaceful to rack her brains over what had changed between them, or within her, or…

He shifted his weight to one side and dropped a kiss on her forehead. Though how he found the energy to move so much as one eyelid, she couldn't imagine. She felt as though all her bones had melted. And as for muscles— there was not one left, in her entire body, that wasn't completely and utterly drained.

'Thank you for being so generous,' she heard him murmur, as he tucked her into his side.

Just before she drifted into sated oblivion.

There was no need to panic. He'd managed to bite back his urge to tell her that the way they'd reached the pinnacle of rapture together had been just about the most blissful experience of his life. He'd turned it into a far more temperate expression of gratitude, thank God.

And he was grateful. Grateful that they were so compatible, sexually. He'd specifically sought a woman he could enjoy taking to bed, hadn't he? So that getting an heir wouldn't be a hardship. She'd just ticked off another item on the list, that was all. His heart wasn't going to be at risk, just because he'd had a momentary, overwhelming feeling of rightness. Of belonging.

No. It just meant he'd made a very sensible choice of bride.

The next time Mary opened her eyes, it was because someone was insistently shaking her shoulder, pulling her up from a dream that featured her new husband, shirtless, skilfully skating away from her and disappearing into a thick swirling fog while her own useless legs melted away from under her.

'I am a little sorry to have to wake you,' said Lord Havelock gruffly.

She blinked up at him sleepily. Last thing she knew he'd been wrapped round her like a living blanket. Now there was a real blanket tucked up to her chin, and he was... She frowned. He was dressed and standing over her looking a touch reproachful.

'Lying there like that you look...'

He paused, searching no doubt for a polite way to tell her she looked a mess, with not a single pin remaining in her hair, which was more than half over her face. Still, at least that would be concealing the sleep creases she'd no doubt have from the embroidered pillow slip.

'Absolutely edible,' he finished with a wicked grin. 'And speaking of edible, while you slept I ordered that supper I promised you earlier. And it's arrived. I'm having them set it out in the sitting room, if you'd care to join me?'

He indicated the foot of the bed, where, to her astonishment, she saw the nightgown and wrap her cousins had given her, because, they'd said, her much darned and patched nightgown and a woollen shawl would simply not do for her wedding night.

The nightgown was of the sheerest lawn she'd ever seen. Even when she'd folded it into her portmanteau she'd been able to see the outline of her hand through it. And the wrap was of scarlet silk, patterned all over with lush oriental flowers of some sort.

But he was indicating he wanted her to wear them and join him for supper in the sitting room.

'I thought you'd prefer a private supper, up here,

rather than go through all the bother of getting fully dressed and dining in one of the public rooms.'

Well, there was that.

And also, she'd like to see how he reacted when she walked around wearing a nightgown that revealed as much as it covered. With her hair loose, she suddenly decided, and flowing unbound all the way down her back to her waist. She'd wager he wouldn't reprove her for not being modest. Given the way he was watching the blankets now, which were only just covering her breasts, he was more likely to enjoy the show.

But all she said was 'That was very thoughtful of you.' Because, to be fair, it did sound as if he'd actually thought about how she might feel. This once.

'I will join you in a moment.'

After catching a glimpse of herself in the mirror, she had to steel herself to walk into the next room. It wasn't as easy to walk about wearing attire that was outrageously seductive as it had been to roll about on the bed stark naked.

But she wasn't, most definitely wasn't, going to let him get away with claiming he wanted a modest bride, when his behaviour earlier had shown it was the exact opposite.

She made it to the threshold, and paused, certain that her face had gone the same shade of scarlet as the silken wrap. For it wasn't only her husband who could see her in her scanty nightclothes. But also the two waiters who were setting out their supper.

'Ah, here she is now,' he said, drawing the eyes of the two male staff in her direction. Her face went a shade hotter as they looked her up and down before swiftly bending their heads to concentrate on their tasks.

As if that wasn't bad enough, she now noticed that he wasn't fully dressed at all, but only wearing his breeches and the shirt he'd earlier tossed on to the floor.

'You can be off,' he said to the waiters, without the slightest hint of self-consciousness. 'I will serve my wife.'

She supposed people who worked in hotels must be used to having guests who wandered around half-dressed, at all hours of the day. Who'd very clearly spent most of the afternoon in bed. But she couldn't bring herself to look their way as they melted out of the room, dreading what she might see written in their faces.

'You certainly look like a bride now,' said Lord Havelock, in a tone that had her lifting her head again. Just as she'd hoped, his eyes were gleaming with appreciation as they roamed her diaphanous gown.

'How do you feel?'

Embarrassed. Rather foolish. Out of her depth, for trying to play the wanton, only to run aground on the shoals of slippery-eyed waiters.

He crossed the room to her, tilted her chin up with one finger and planted a brief kiss on her flaming cheek. And she no longer felt anything but aware of him, standing so close. His warm breath on her face. And the way he'd made her feel in the bed that was only a few faltering footsteps away.

But before she could summon up the words to express even a tithe of what she was feeling, her stomach rumbled. Rather loudly.

He grinned. 'Hungry! Good. So am I. I hope you like what I've ordered,' he said, taking her hand and leading her across to the table the waiters had been so busy over just moments before.

'It...it certainly all looks lovely,' she managed to stammer. The table had been set for two, with fine linen and sparkling crystal, delicate china and fresh flowers. The fire, she also noted, had been stoked up again so that the room was warm enough for them to sit about in a state of undress.

She was excruciatingly aware of his body now. Of exactly where it was and how it all felt. Whenever his legs so much as brushed against the hem of her night-gown, under the table, it brought back how they'd felt, pushing her own sleeker, softer legs apart. The muscles bunching and flexing as he'd...

He'd apparently lost the ability to talk, as well. In fact, the atmosphere reminded her very much of the time they'd striven in vain to make some sort of conversation over the supper table at the Crimmers'. Except that now it was charged with sexual awareness.

His as well as hers, she would stake her life on it.

He might be frowning as he spooned a helping of fric-assee on to her plate, but it wasn't the frown of an angry man. She'd spent years studying her father, learning his moods in the faint hope she could avoid the worst of them. And that frown wasn't one of displeasure.

If anything, she would say he felt awkward. Though that was absurd! He'd wandered around earlier, ordering the waiters about as though it meant nothing....

But now they were alone.

And he'd readily admitted, that night at the Crim-mers', that he didn't know how to converse freely with ladies.

Particularly not to ones he'd just married, apparently.

Perhaps it wasn't so surprising he'd got friends to

help him compile a list when he'd decided he had to get married.

Perhaps she'd overreacted when she'd found and read it. He hadn't intended her to know he'd resorted to such lengths, after all.

And hadn't she already decided that she ought not to dwell on how this marriage had come about? But to just make the most of what they had?

And when it came right down to it, wouldn't she rather be married to him, with all his faults, than a glib-tongued man whose charm marked him down as a seasoned womaniser?

So she met his eye and gave him a tentative smile.

He smiled back, his shoulders dropping a good inch as some of his tension melted away.

I did that. I put him at ease.

Her aunt Pargetter had hinted that if their marriage was to be a happy one, it would be up to her. She hadn't seen how that could possibly be true, but already, today, she'd made a start. She could have flung the list at him when he returned from the lawyers and demanded an explanation, and an apology. She wouldn't have received one. Instead of making such wondrous love together, they would have had a fight. They wouldn't be sitting here, remembering how good it had been, and wondering when they could do it again, either. They would be at daggers drawn.

Not that she would ever let him treat her with such disrespect in future. She was *not* a mouse. And she had no intention of letting him turn her into one. The thought she might ever end up like her mother, too scared to draw a breath without the permission of her tyrannical husband, had almost made her cry off altogether.

Except that she'd seen Lord Havelock was nothing like her father. And they weren't eloping, in the face of opposition from both their families. They'd come together for very practical reasons.

Not that she felt very practical about him at this moment. Her mind was a whirling jumble of emotions and desire and, above all, hope.

All of a sudden, Lord Havelock broke into her musings by uttering an oath and throwing the serving spoon back into the dish with a clatter.

'I should have taken you out to the theatre, or something, shouldn't I? Not kept you cooped up indoors all evening, with only me for company.'

And that was the nub of the matter. He wasn't an unkind man. Only a touch thoughtless.

And apparently willing to learn to do better.

'It was just,' he said, seizing her hand across the table, his face screwed up with contrition, 'that I'd planned on getting an early night.'

When she flushed, and dropped her head to gaze at her plate, she heard him chuckle.

'Not because of *that*. Well, not only that. You see...' he gave her hand a slight squeeze '...we need to get on the road as early as we can, with the days being so short. I don't want you to have to put up at any of the inns on our way. And if we make an early enough start, providing we don't encounter any problems, we should be able to make it in one stage.'

'Yes, I see. Well...um...' Her heart was pounding so hard she was amazed he couldn't hear it.

'I...I don't mind having an early night,' she finally managed to confess, shooting him a coy look from under her eyelashes.

'Well, yes, but that was before my patience ran out and I swept you off to bed the minute I got back from the lawyers. And...' He cleared his throat. 'It probably isn't such a good idea to attempt... I mean...' He coughed. 'You are probably a bit... That is, I've heard...' he flushed '...that the first time can leave a lady feeling a bit, um, sore.'

'I don't feel sore.' What she did feel, had started to feel from the moment he'd hinted he wanted to take her again, was an ache. An ache that she knew only he could assuage. 'You were so careful with me that I...'

'I will be careful again,' he vowed, cutting her hesitant response off so swiftly, and with such fervour, that she could tell he wanted her as much as she wanted him.

It was the greatest compliment he could have paid her.

Holding both her hands in his, he looked straight into her eyes.

'That is, if you want to... I mean, I don't expect you to...only hope that you...'

He pulled himself up straight, giving his head a little shake, then laughing ruefully.

'Here's the thing. Lady Havelock, I would like to invite you to come to my room now, for an evening of... exploration, let's call it that. I'd like to find out what gives you pleasure. So if, at any time, anything I do causes you discomfort, you have only to tell me, and I will stop. And move on until we find something that you do enjoy. Will you...will you come with me?'

He wanted to spend the evening discovering what gave her pleasure?

How could she possibly refuse?

For one thing, he was only inviting her to do exactly

what she'd wanted from the moment she'd woken up, naked, to find him standing over her.

For another, he'd warned her that this stage of their married life might not last long. One of them might take the other in dislike and then all this ardour would cool.

But most of all, only an idiot wouldn't make the most of having a man like Lord Havelock take her to bed.

And she most certainly wasn't an idiot.

It was still dark when the porter came next morning with hot water for her husband to wash. She slid as far beneath the blankets as she could, until he'd gone, then flung back the covers with grim determination and sa-shayed across the room to pick up her robe, which was lying in a scarlet puddle by the door.

'I will go to my own room to wash and dress,' she said as she plunged her arms into the sleeves and fum-bled for the sash. It was all very well, she'd discovered, attempting to flout his hope she would behave modestly, but she really didn't have the stomach for it.

From his bank of pillows, her husband stretched and gave her a lazy smile.

'I will meet you back in the sitting room. They'll be setting out breakfast in there, so you might want to, um…' He indicated the neckline of the robe, which was revealing rather more of her than she'd like.

She gripped the edges close over her throat, leaving the room to the sound of her husband's throaty chuckle.

It didn't take her long to wash and dress.

'You'd better make the most of this,' he said, indi-cating the array of dishes set out on the table when she joined him. 'I won't be making long stops on the way, if I can avoid it. Besides, none of the inns I've ever tried on the way to Mayfield can offer anything half so good.'

Mary dipped her head as she sat down. How could he be talking in such a matter-of-fact way when she was feeling so…so awkward? So vulnerable? Didn't he care?

Or hadn't he noticed how hard this was for her?

Though perhaps that was for the best. After all, she'd vowed he would never have cause to think of her as a mouse.

And anyway, he was at least explaining his reasons for making the travelling arrangements the way he had. Which sounded as though he was looking out for her, in his own way.

She sat up a little straighter and began to nibble at a slice of toast while he demolished a vast quantity of steak and eggs, and ale and coffee. Lord, but he had a healthy appetite.

In more ways than one. She flushed as her mind flew back to the boundless energy he'd displayed the night before. The inventiveness, and the patience, and the amazing stamina…

He looked up and caught her looking at him in a sort of sexual haze. His fork faltered halfway to his mouth.

'Eat up,' he said gruffly. 'You need to keep your strength up. It will be a long and arduous day, and after such a long and…energetic night…'

She lowered her head and slid a mound of fluffy scrambled egg on to her fork. It wasn't easy to sit at table with a man who'd had his hands and mouth all over her. She knew this was what married people did—and quite a few people who weren't married, too—but how did they hold conversations, as though they hadn't done the most shocking things to each other under cover of darkness?

She raised the fork to her mouth. As she parted her lips, her husband gave a strange, choking sort of sigh. When she raised her eyes to his in enquiry, she saw him looking at her lips. His fingers were clenched tightly round his own fork, which hadn't travelled any nearer to his own mouth.

So he wasn't as unaffected by their night of intimacy as she'd at first thought. With a little inward smile, she reached for her cup and took a delicate sip of tea, shooting him what she hoped was a saucy look over the rim as she drank. The look he sent her back was heated enough to make her toes curl.

It kept her warm for the rest of the morning. As did his constant care for her comfort. Though he'd warned her that the journey was likely to be arduous, she found it the least unpleasant she'd ever undertaken. For one thing, she was sitting in a comfortable post-chaise, swathed in travelling furs with a hot brick at her feet, next to a man she…really liked. A man who kept her entertained with a fund of anecdotes about adventures he'd had whilst travelling this route before. It was a far cry from being cooped up inside the common stage with a bunch of malodorous strangers. Then again, wherever they stopped, the landlords gave him swift and respectful service. No waiting around in draughty public rooms, suffering rude stares and coarse remarks. They made good speed and dusk was only just descending into true night by the time their carriage swept through the gates of what he told her was to be her new home.

'I am sorry you cannot see very much of it,' he said as they bounced up a lengthy drive. 'I will show you around tomorrow. The horses should have settled in by then. I had them sent on ahead, by easy stages, the minute I knew we'd be coming down.'

She turned, slowly, and looked at him. He'd sent his horses by easy stages, but pushed her to make the journey in one day?

Just when she'd made allowances for him writing that dreadful list, he…he…

She drew in a deep breath, grappling with the wave of hurt that had almost made her lash out at him. She would *not* take his casual remark about his horses as a sign he didn't care about her. Hadn't he proved that, in his own way, he did? As he'd related all those tales about adventures he'd had in the posting inns on the way here, she'd seen *exactly* why he hadn't wanted her staying at any of them.

She'd got to stop looking for signs that he was going to turn out to be just like her father.

'There are some decent rides on the estate itself, but we can hack across country if you like, see a bit of the surrounding area, too. You'll want to know where the nearest town is, get the lie of the land, and so forth….'

'Oh, no,' she said, lifting her chin. 'I cannot ride.'

'You cannot ride?' He looked thunderstruck. And then crestfallen. And then resigned.

Funny, but she'd never noticed what an expressive face he had before. He'd warned her he was blunt, but not that he was incapable of hiding his feelings.

Which gave her food for thought. He might be thoughtless, even inconsiderate, but she would always know exactly where she was with him. And he would never be able to lie to her.

And though she hadn't known she'd been carrying it, she certainly felt it when a layer of tension slithered off her shoulders. She hadn't been able to help worrying about what kind of husband he was going to be.

But so far he'd shown her more courtesy than any other man ever had.

Eventually they drew up in front of a large, and completely dark, bulk of masonry. He muttered an oath and sprang from the carriage with a ferocious scowl. 'Where is everyone?' He strode away and pounded on the front door with one fist while she clambered out of the vehicle unaided.

It was so very like the way her father would have behaved, after a long and tiring journey, that it resurrected a few bad memories that made her feel, just for a moment, the way she had as a girl. That there was always something more important, more interesting, for a man to do than care for his wife and child.

'I wrote to the Brownlows, the couple who act as caretakers, warning them I would be coming down and bringing my bride with me.'

With a determined effort, she shook off the shadow of past experience as Lord Havelock took a step back, craning his neck up to the upper storeys of his house. 'I can't see any lights anywhere,' he said. 'Did you see any lights, perchance, as we were driving up?'

'No.'

'What the devil,' he said, planting his fists on his hips and glaring at her, 'is going on, that's what I want to know?'

'I have no idea.' He *wasn't* like her father. He *wasn't* yelling at her because he blamed her for whatever was going wrong. He was just…baffled, and frustrated, that was all. For all she knew, he might really be asking her what she thought was *going on*.

Well, there was only one way to find out.

'Well, perhaps…'

'Yes? What?'

'Perhaps they didn't get your letter.'

'Nonsense! Why shouldn't they get it? Never had any trouble with the post before.'

It wasn't nonsense. He'd arranged their marriage really quickly. And written dozens of letters, to judge from the state of his desk at the hotel.

'Are you quite sure you wrote to them?'

'Of course I did,' he said, snatching off his hat and running his fingers through his hair.

'Well, then, perhaps, if they were not expecting you… not in the habit of expecting you to call unexpectedly, that is, they may have gone away.'

'Gone away? Why on earth should they want to do any such thing? I pay them to live here and take care of the place.'

'Because it is almost Christmas? Don't you permit your staff to take holidays?'

She had his full attention now. But from the way his eyes had narrowed at her dry tone, she was about to find out how far his temper might stretch before snapping.

'Begging your pardon, my lord,' said one of the post-boys, as he deposited the last of their luggage on the step. 'But since you seem not to be expected here, will you be wanting us to take you to the inn where we'll be racking up for the night?'

Lord Havelock rounded on the poor man, his eyes really spitting fire now.

'I'm not taking my wife to the Dog and Ferret!'

'No, my lord, of course not, my lord,' said the hapless individual, shooting Mary a pitying look.

She supposed she ought not to despise them for turning tail and fleeing. But, really! What kind of men abandoned a woman, outside a deserted house, in the sole charge of a husband whose temper was verging on volcanic?

And then, just when she'd thought things couldn't get any worse, an eddy of wind tugged at her bonnet, sprinkling her cheeks with light, yet distinct drops of rain.

Chapter Eight

'That's all we need,' he said, ramming his hat back on his head. Things had been going so well until they'd reached Mayfield. She'd been warming towards him throughout the day. It hadn't even been all that difficult. She had a generous nature and seemed disposed to try to like him.

But now her face had changed. It put him in mind of the way his great-aunt had looked at him when he'd turned up to one of her ridottos in riding boots. No credit for remembering the insipid event and tearing himself away from a far more convivial gathering to get there. And more or less on time, as well. No. Only disapproval for being incorrectly dressed.

Not that the cases were a bit the same. He couldn't really blame Mary for being cross with him.

He scowled at the carriage as it disappeared round a curve in the drive, wishing now that he hadn't dismissed the post-boys with such haste.

'The Dog and Ferret really is no place for you,' he said aloud, as much to remind himself why he'd had all the luggage unloaded, as to explain himself to her.

'But,' he said, turning to her at last, bracing himself to meet another frosty stare, 'at least it would have got you out of the weather. And now,' he said, shooting the back of their post-chaise one last glare, 'we are stuck here. Can't expect you to walk to the village at this hour, in this weather.' If it had been just him, he could have cut across the fields. But he'd seen the state of her boots the night before. They wouldn't keep her feet dry. Nor was that fancy coat and bonnet of hers cut out for hiking through the countryside in the rain.

'Only one thing for it,' he said, and before she could raise a single objection at leaving the shelter of the porch, he seized her arm and set off round the side of the house.

She shivered when the rain struck them both with full force. When she stumbled over some unseen obstacle, he put his arm round her waist and half carried, half dragged her through what was starting to become something of a storm, under the gated archway that led to the back of the house.

It was much darker in the enclosed courtyard, so that even he had trouble navigating his way to the servants' entrance. But at least it was sheltered from the wind that was getting up.

He rattled the door handle, cursing at finding it locked.

Not that it would be all that hard to get inside.

Couldn't expect Mary to climb in through a window, though. Which meant he'd have to leave her out here while he groped his way along the darkened passages and got a door open for her.

He shucked off his coat.

'Here,' he said, tucking it round her shoulders, 'this should keep the worst of the wet off you while I break in.'

'B-break in?'

He couldn't see her face, it was so dark, but he could hear the shock and disapproval in her voice.

'There's a window, just along here,' he said, feeling his way along the wall, with Mary following close on his heels. 'Ah, here it is.'

He reached into his pocket and found a penknife. 'Never used to fasten properly,' he explained, flicking open the knife blade. 'The footmen used to use it to get in after lock-up, when they'd sneaked off to the Dog and Ferret.'

'That's…'

'Dreadful, I know.' He worked the knife blade under the sash. 'As a boy, I shouldn't have known anything about it. But nobody paid me much mind in those days.' The lock sprang free and he heaved the window up. 'Never thought knowing how to break into my own house would come in so handy,' he said, getting one leg over the sill. 'You just wait there,' he said firmly. He didn't want her stumbling about in the dark and hurting herself. 'I'll come and let you in, in just a jiffy.'

If it had been dark in the courtyard, it was black as a coalhole in the scullery. And yet he had little trouble finding his way past the sinks and along the wall, round to the kitchen door. This place was deeply embedded in his memory. Even the smell in here flung him back to his boyhood and all the hours he'd spent below stairs in the company of servants, rather than wherever it was he was meant to have been.

In no time at all he'd laid his hands on a lamp, which was on a shelf just beside the back door, where it had always been kept.

As he lit it, he pictured Mary, huddled up under the

eaves in a futile attempt to find shelter from the wind and rain, and no doubt counting the minutes he was making her wait. And wondering what the hell he'd dragged her into. All of a sudden he got a sudden, vivid memory of the day his stepmother had first come to Mayfield. How she'd stood—not in the rear courtyard, shivering with cold, but in the imposing entrance hall, nervously watching the servants, who'd all lined up to greet her. She'd attempted a timid smile for him and he'd returned it with a scowl, seeing her as an interloper. A woman who had no right to take the place of his mother.

He couldn't recall her ever smiling again, not while she'd lived here.

He paused, the lighted lantern in his hand, recalling how he'd complained to his friends about how a woman changed a man when she got him leg-shackled. But the truth was that it wasn't just a man who took a huge risk when he got married. When a woman chose the wrong partner, she could be just as miserable. He knew, because he'd seen it with Julia's mother. She'd blossomed when she'd finally married her childhood sweetheart. Only to shrivel to a husk of her former self when shackled to her third husband. Who'd been a brute.

It was all very well protecting himself from hurt, but not at Mary's expense. Theirs might not be a love match, but there was no reason why he shouldn't do whatever he could to make her happy.

He set the lamp back on its shelf by the back door before he unbolted it. And when Mary saw him, and came scurrying over, he caught her round the waist, then swept her up off her feet and into his arms.

'Nothing else has gone right so far,' he said. 'But at least I can carry my bride over the threshold.'

To his immense relief, she flung her arms round his neck and burrowed her face into his chest.

She must be freezing, poor lamb. Else she wouldn't be clinging to him like this.

He set her down gently and shut the door. Turned, and took both her hands in his.

'I haven't made a very good start as a husband, have I,' he said ruefully. 'I must have written a dozen letters yesterday. Thought I'd organised it all so brilliantly. But never took into account the possibility the Brownlows might have already made their plans for Christmas. And...' he squeezed her hands '...I fear you are right. There's nobody here but us. And there's no telling how long they'll be away. I dare say you must be really cross with me, but...'

'No!' She stunned him by placing one hand on his cheek. 'Not at all. There are far worse things for a man to be, than a bit disorganised.'

'Well, it's good of you to say so,' he said gruffly, raising his own hand to cover hers where it rested on his cheek, 'but you do realise we've no option but to rack up here for the night? And that there are no servants, no beds made up for us...'

She gave him a brave smile. 'It will seem better once we can get a fire going,' she said bracingly. Clearly determined to make the best of a bad job. 'And if the Brownlows normally live here, then there's bound to be some provisions in the larder. We can manage.'

'Come on, then,' he said, kissing her hand in gratitude at her forbearance. 'Let's raid the kitchen.'

Pausing only to pick up the lantern, he led Mary along the stone-flagged corridor, his brow knotted in thought. His father had never really appreciated Julia's mother.

He'd treated her as though she ought to have been grate-ful he'd given her his name and title. He hadn't seen it as a boy, but his father had treated his dogs and horses better than his own wife.

The minute he thought of horses, he recalled the hurt look that had flickered across Mary's face when he'd told her how he'd sent his own horses down by easy stages.

Lord, he'd started out as badly as his own father had done! Pampering his horses and pitching his wife head-long into hardship.

'You ought by rights to be ripping up at me for mak-ing such a botch of things,' he growled as he opened the door to the kitchen for her.

She gazed up at him, wide-eyed. Then gave a little sniff and shook her head.

'You were just in a hurry to get things ready for your sister,' she said. 'You were concentrating on getting her to a place of safety. It would have been a miracle if, somewhere along the line, your plans *hadn't* hit a snag.'

'That's very generous of you—to take that attitude,' he said, setting the lantern on the shelf just inside the door, which had always been used for that very purpose.

'Let's just hope this is the worst snag we hit,' she said, untying the ribbons of her bonnet and setting it on the massive table that stood in the very centre of the room. Then she walked across to the closed stove and knelt in front of it.

'Good, dry kindling laid ready,' she said, opening the door and peeking inside. 'And plenty of logs in the bas-ket.' She stood up, and scanned the shelf over the fire-place. 'And here's the tinderbox, just where any sensible housewife would keep it.'

Thank goodness she wasn't one of those useless, helpless females whose sole aim in life was to be decorative. It would be an absolute nightmare to be stuck in this huge, empty house with one of those.

Fortunately, he managed to keep his thoughts to himself rather than blurting them out and provoking an argument. For what woman liked to hear a man think she was useful rather than decorative?

'I'll go and take a look around, then,' he said, going to light another lamp. 'See what I can discover. So long as you will be all right here for a while?'

She glanced at him over her shoulder and nodded, with a look that told him he was an idiot for even asking.

He gave a wry smile as he set out to explore the house. He'd contracted a practical marriage, with a practical, no-nonsense sort of woman. Of course she wasn't going to have a fit of the vapours because he was leaving her alone to get a fire lit.

By the time he returned to the kitchen, it was noticeably warmer. And there were plates and bowls and things out on the sides, which had previously been bare.

'While you were gone I had a good look round the larder, found some tea and made a pot,' said Mary, pouring some into two cups. 'There's no milk to go in it, but we can sweeten it with some sugar.'

'I didn't expect you to have to act like a servant,' he said glumly as he set the lamp on its shelf.

She put the teapot down rather hard.

'Would you rather sit all night in the gloom, with an empty stomach, and wait for someone else to turn up and wait on you?'

'No. I didn't mean that! It's just—I promised you a life of luxury. And on the first day, you're already reduced to this.' He waved his arm round the big, empty kitchen.

'Oh.' Her anger dissipated as swiftly as his own ever did. She shot him a rueful glance as she dumped two full spoons of sugar into both cups. 'I don't mind, you know. It's the biggest house I've ever had to call my own. And I'm sure, come the morning, you will be able to find out what has become of the couple who should be taking care of the place. The state of the larder leads me to believe they have not been away all that long.'

'It looks as though there's been a horse in the stables very recently, too,' he said, taking a seat at the table next to the place settings he noted she'd laid. Then he picked up his cup and braced himself to swallow the sickly concoction without grimacing. She'd been looking through the larder and preparing a meal, when she could have been sitting in front of the fire sulking. Her temper was frayed—the way she'd slammed down the teapot and ladled sugar into his drink without asking whether he liked it or not told him that much. So he'd be an ungrateful oaf to provoke her again, by complaining about such a small thing, when she was clearly doing her utmost to make the best of things.

'Though no sign of any of my own. Nor my groom,' he finished gloomily. Dammit, where was everyone?

'Well, at least we have plenty to eat. Would you like something now? I can make an omelette, if you'd like it.'

'I am starving,' he admitted with a wry smile. 'I suppose we ought to do something about finding somewhere to sleep really, but I could do with fortifying before I can face going upstairs again. The whole place is like an icehouse.'

'We…we could sleep in the kitchen,' she suggested, taking a sip of her own tea. 'It is, at least, warm.'

'Absolutely not,' he said, setting his own cup down firmly on the table—with some relief that he had a valid excuse for doing so without having to endure any more of the noxiously syrupy drink. 'There are a dozen perfectly serviceable bedrooms above stairs. And just because you've put on an apron and have to act like a cook doesn't mean you need to sleep below stairs, as well.'

'I've slept in worse places,' she admitted.

'Yes, maybe you have, but you're married to me now and it is my job to take care of you.' He was going to do better than his own father had done with Julia's mother. He wasn't going to assume Mary should be grateful for the privilege of bearing his name, and his title, no matter what the circumstances.

'Of course,' she said meekly, before rising and going across to a sort of preparation area near the stove and cracking several eggs into a bowl.

She didn't utter a word of reproof, but the set of her back as she grated some cheese into the egg mixture told him he really shouldn't have raised his voice to her just now.

He cleared his throat.

'It's very clever of you to know how to do all this sort of thing.'

'It was necessary,' she said, pouring the egg mixture into a pan where she'd already started some butter melting. 'If I hadn't learned how to cook, once Papa died, we would have gone hungry. We'd never been all that well off, but after he went, we had to move into a much smaller place and let all the servants go.' She frowned as she kept pulling the slowly setting mixture from the edges into the middle. 'Mama did the purchasing and tried to learn how to keep the household accounts in order, while I did the actual physical work of keeping house.'

'Well, I'm glad of it,' he said, and then, realising how heartless that sounded, added hastily, 'I mean, glad you can turn your hand to cooking. That smells wonderful,' he said, desperately hoping to make up lost ground. 'Anything I can do to help?'

She stirred the egg mixture several more times before making her reply.

'It might go down better with some wine,' she suggested as she added some ham to the egg mixture. 'But only if you can fetch it quickly. This won't take but a minute more.'

He didn't need telling twice. Lord, but he needed to get out of the kitchen before he said something even more tactless and shattered the tentative hold she must be keeping on her temper with him. He returned, with a dusty bottle and two wine glasses, just as she was sliding the omelette on to a plate.

'Not the best crystal,' he said, putting the bottle down beside his place setting and pulling a corkscrew from his pocket. 'But you did specify haste, so I got these from the butler's pantry.'

'I'm not used to the best crystal, anyway.'

She startled him then, by looking up at him and smiling ruefully. That she could still muster a smile, any kind of smile, and turn it his way, felt nothing short of miraculous. He dropped into his chair with relief, picked up his fork, swearing to himself he'd praise her cooking to the skies no matter what it tasted like.

But in the event, there was no need to feign appreciation.

'This has got to be,' he said, 'one of the tastiest omelettes I've ever eaten.'

She flushed and smiled again, this time with what looked like real pleasure.

'The…the wine is very good, too,' she reciprocated, having taken a sip.

'Don't go heaping coals of fire on my head. Coming here has been a disaster. All my fault. And you haven't uttered a single word of complaint. You're the only woman I know who wouldn't be ringing a peal over my head.'

'This really isn't so very bad,' she replied, lowering her gaze to her plate, 'compared to some of the things that have happened to me.'

'What do you mean?' He hadn't really learned all that much about her past, now he came to think of it. He'd been in such a hurry to get her to the altar he hadn't taken the time to talk.

'Oh, just…well, it was bad enough after Papa died, but at least Mama and I managed to maintain our independence. Even if it did mean moving frequently, to keep one step ahead of our creditors.' She flushed, and moved the omelette round and round on her plate, before taking a deep breath and plunging on.

'But when she died, her annuity died with her. I really did have absolutely nothing, for a while. Fortunately, I managed to track down the lawyer who'd dealt with Papa's affairs, hoping he would have some solution. But all he did was refer me to Papa's relations. None of whom wanted the added burden of an indigent female. I really was at my wit's end by the time I reached Lon-

don and my aunt Pargetter. I thought…' She looked up
and flashed him a tight smile. 'Well, you can see why
all this…' she waved her hand round the kitchen, much
as he'd done earlier '…doesn't seem so very dreadful. At
least nobody can turn me out into that storm, can they?
And we have food and a fire.' She shrugged and popped
another forkful of omelette into her mouth.

He didn't know what to say. She'd been through so
much. So bravely. And all on her own. And here he'd
been, half expecting her to throw a tantrum like some
spoiled society miss.

He pushed his empty plate to one side.

'Come on, let's go and see about somewhere to sleep.'

'But I need to wash the dishes….'

'Leave 'em. Plenty more about the place, I'm sure. So
we can have clean ones in the morning. The staff can do
the washing up when they get back. That's what I pay
'em for.' He went round the table and pulled her to her
feet. 'I'm glad you've pitched in and put a meal together,
but I draw the line at you washing dishes.'

'I'll just stack them in the scullery, then.'

'Very well.'

'I think,' she said, with a shy smile, 'that I'm going
to like being Lady Havelock.'

'What! After this?'

'I have always hated washing up,' she said, wiping
her hands and tossing her apron aside. 'It's wonderful
to just do the things I enjoy and leave the unpleasant
tasks to others.'

Wonderful? From his point of view, it was wonderful
she could describe *any* part of this evening in positive
terms. 'Glad to hear it,' he said, tucking her arm into
his and leading her up the stairs.

'This way,' he said, tugging her to the left and pulling a bunch of keys from his pocket.

He proudly flung open the double doors at the head of the stairs.

'The master bedroom,' he said. Then reeled back, coughing, at the musty smell that wafted out to greet him.

'It doesn't look as if anyone has used this room for years,' she said, wrinkling her nose.

'About a dozen, I suspect,' he groaned. 'I seem to recall the trustees saying something about only letting the tenants use certain rooms. I should have realised this one would be one of the ones out of bounds.' He ran his fingers through his hair. The Dog and Ferret was looking more appealing by the minute.

'Well, let us find a room that has been in use more recently and is a bit better aired,' she said, stepping smartly back into the corridor.

'What a good job you thought of coming down to look the place over before telling your sister she could come to live here,' she said brightly, after they'd inspected several more rooms and found them in a similar state to the master suite. 'I'm going to have my work cut out, getting it ready for her return.'

Not if he could help it. He'd hire an army of servants to scrub and clean this place from top to bottom. Hang the expense. He wasn't going to have her working her fingers to the bone on his account.

Mary was just beginning to think they would have to go back to the kitchen, after all, when Lord Havelock opened the door to a room that didn't reek of damp and mice.

'It doesn't strike so cold in here, does it?' he said, stepping over the threshold. 'I'll tell you what it is,' he said sagely, as she lifted the corner of a cover that shrouded an item of furniture that turned out to be a bed. 'Right at the end of the corridor, here, the room faces south. It must get the sun all day. Bound to keep it drier than the others, which face west or east.'

'Even so, I'm not too sure we can use this bed,' she said, lifting the cover higher to reveal a rolled-up mattress at the end of the frame.

He sighed. 'The bedding at the Dog and Ferret may have been dirty and damp, but at least there would have been some.'

'We could air the mattress for a while in front of the fire, once we get it lit,' she suggested. 'And we can use our coats, and what have you, for bedding. Just for one night. If…if you wouldn't mind fetching our luggage.'

'I'll do that,' he said. Then, as he passed her, he swept her into his arms and gave her a swift, hard kiss. 'You think of everything.'

Well, in the past, she'd had to. She wouldn't have got as far as Aunt Pargetter, if she hadn't had the sense to track down the lawyer who'd dealt with her father's affairs.

But, only fancy, now she was telling her husband, a peer of the realm no less, how to deal with the situation in which they found themselves. And sending him off on an errand.

She wouldn't have believed it, if someone had told her, even a few weeks ago, that she'd have the courage.

But it came easily to her, with Lord Havelock, she mused, kneeling on the hearth to see if she could get the fire going. In fact, as she set a taper to the wadded-up paper in the grate, she decided she was going to ask him to fetch some more coal, when he came back with their luggage. For there were only a few dusty coals sitting on top of the kindling, and only a handful more in the scuttle. And she really didn't think he'd mind.

Thanks heavens she'd decided to make the best of things, rather than nursing her grievances. What was the point, after all, of dwelling on past mistakes, when he was clearly making such an effort with her now? He'd been an attentive companion during the journey, apologised profusely for the state of the house and even carried her over the threshold—a romantic gesture that had taken her completely by surprise. Not that she was going to read too much into it.

She didn't care that circumstances were far from ideal. They were making a much better job of being married than her parents ever had, with each blaming the other for everything that went wrong and neither of them lifting a finger to do anything about it.

She put her hand to her lips, which were still tingling from his last kiss, a great surge of hope rising up in her heart.

'How are you getting on?' said Lord Havelock as he came back to the room with one of her cases and one of his.

She opened her mouth to thank him for being so even-handed, rather than just bringing up his own cases first. But the moment he'd opened the door a cloud of smoke came billowing into the room instead of going up the chimney, making her cough and wipe at her streaming eyes.

'Now I can see,' he said, shutting the door hastily, 'why this room was never occupied by the family, in spite of the view. It looks as though it has one of those fires that sends more smoke into the room than up the chimney.'

'It doesn't seem to be drawing very well,' she said. 'I just thought the chimney was probably a bit damp.'

'No. I've just remembered something. I never understood it before, but it was so odd, that it stuck in my mind,' he said, striding to the window. 'Nobody ever lit the fire in here without shutting that door and opening this window first.'

He turned the handle and pushed at the casement. It didn't budge.

'Stuck,' he said gloomily. 'Frame is probably warped with damp. Will probably need to get a lot of the frames shaved,' he said, giving it another, harder shove, 'or replaced.'

Suddenly, the window gave. Only not just the casement, but the hinges, too. His entire top half disappeared through the opening for a moment while a gust of wind whooshed in.

The smoke curled in on itself and got sucked up the chimney while flames finally started dancing across the sluggish kindling.

Lord Havelock hauled himself upright and staggered away from the window. He was sopping wet. And swearing fluently at the segment of window frame he was still clutching in his hand.

'You…you…' She pressed her hand to her mouth. But it was no use. She couldn't suppress the torrent of giggles fizzing up inside.

'You are quite…' she managed shakily. 'Quite right, the fire d-does draw better with the window…the window…'

Finally rendered speechless with laughter, she pointed at the frame dangling from his hand.

'You think this is funny?'

She nodded, completely unable to frame any words for the laughter bubbling over.

With a low growl, he spun away from her, wedged the window frame back in place and thumped it home with several strategic blows from his large, powerful fists.

Strange, but she wasn't the least bit intimidated by the demonstration of raw masculine frustration. If that had been her father, now, she would have been crouching lower, keeping her eyes down, her head bowed. Anything and everything to render herself small and invisible.

But Lord Havelock wasn't cast from the same mould as her father. He might be hot-tempered, but he wasn't bad-tempered. And that made all the difference.

As if to prove the point, the second he'd mended the window as well as he could, he strode across the room, dropped to his knees beside her and draped one arm about her shoulders.

'You're a good sport,' he said brusquely, before planting a kiss on her temple. 'I know I've said it before, but you must be the only woman alive who would see the funny side, rather than ripping up at me.'

He took the poker from the set of fire irons and started pushing the coals into more strategic positions.

'So far today you've had to skivvy like a kitchen maid and now you're going to have to sleep in conditions that are tantamount to camping out.'

Whatever must the women in his past have been like, to carp over such trifles as that? No wonder he'd been so reluctant to get married, if that was his expectation of female behaviour.

'All I really asked of you was a room of my own, in whichever of your properties I happened to be,' she countered. 'We never specified it should have fully f-functioning, w-windows…' And suddenly she couldn't quite stifle another bout of giggles as she recalled the look on his face when the whole thing had come away in his hands. 'Or f-furniture of any kind, come to that.'

'Like I said, a good sport,' he said, smiling at her with approval.

'What would be the point of ripping up at you, over something as silly as this? You didn't mean me any harm. It's just…' She reached up and cupped his cheek.

'Oh—you are so cold. You must get out of those wet things at once.'

His smile turned a shade wicked.

'Now that's what a man likes to hear from his bride. An invitation to get out of his clothing and into—' He stopped short. 'Only, hang it, we haven't actually got a bed to get into.'

'It won't take long,' she said, a touch breathlessly, 'to make one up.'

He tossed the poker aside and gave her a look that made her heart leap behind her breastbone.

'In fact, all we need to do…'

'Yes?'

'Is to bring the mattress over here and unroll it in front of the fire.'

'Brilliant notion,' he said, dropping a swift kiss on her cheek.

As she went to open their cases, he ripped off his damp jacket and shirt and tossed them into a corner. Her mouth dried at the sight of his naked torso. Though she was supposed to be selecting the items of clothing most suited to form bedding, she just grabbed handfuls at random, unable to keep her eyes straying from the sight of him wrestling the mattress into submission. In the end, it happened to be a couple of his shirts and her spare petticoat that she spread over the mattress, and heaven alone knew what she had wadded up into makeshift pillows.

They fell to the mattress together, lips meeting and locking in a heated kiss.

She ran her hands up and down the smooth, sleek muscles of his back as he rolled her beneath him. And moaned with pleasure when he grabbed a handful of her skirts and pushed them up out of the way.

'Lord,' he groaned, 'we should slow this down, somehow. You are so new at this.'

No! He couldn't stop now. Not when she needed him so badly.

'We can go slow next time, if you like. But please...' She shifted her hips impatiently.

'Next time, she says,' he growled into her neck. 'Do you know what it does to a man, hearing the woman he's taking, promising him there will be a next time?'

'No....'

'Of course you don't, my little innocent. That's what makes you so adorable.'

Adorable? He thought she was adorable? Well, she thought he was adorable, too. She hugged him hard, on a wave of tenderness.

'And I don't want to wait any longer than I have to, believe me,' he assured her.

'Good.' She half sighed, half moaned, as he slid his hand, and with it her skirts, all the way up to her waist.

'Oh, God,' he moaned, exploring her with his fingers. 'You are so ready for me. I can't believe it. I don't deserve you.' He raised himself up to claw open the fall of his breeches. 'I don't deserve,' he said, thrusting home, 'this.'

It was heavenly. She knew the pleasure he could bring this time, and instead of lying back and letting him do all the work, she became an equal participant, striving to reach the finishing line alongside him. And this time, instead of a soft, gentle burst of pleasure, it was like a thousand rockets going off inside her, all at once. Shattering. Sparkling. Satisfying. So satisfying. She clutched at him, stroking his back as he settled over her, his face buried in her neck.

'Mary,' he growled after a moment or two. 'Mary?'

'Hmm?'

'I know I said you could always have a room of your own,' he said plaintively. 'But I hope you're not going to insist I find somewhere else tonight.'

'You must be joking,' she said. 'I will need you to keep me warm.'

When he would have rolled off her, she clung on.

'Not so fast.'

He half rose up to look down into her face.

'You mean, now I can take it slowly?'

'I didn't mean that,' she protested.

But with a wicked grin, he reached down between them and began to toy with her, just where their bodies were still joined.

She gasped. 'I didn't know… Can you do it all over again?'

'It seems that with you, I can. You are an astonishing woman.'

'Me?' She looked up at him, perplexed. Though she couldn't meet his eye for very long, not when he was doing what he was doing.

'Oohh,' she groaned.

'Oh, indeed,' he agreed. And wrapped her legs round his waist.

Chapter Nine

She didn't know what woke her, but the moment she did so, she knew she was alone. And the place where her husband had been was cold.

She could hear windows rattling somewhere, chimneys moaning as the wind protested its inability to get in. The fire had died down considerably, but it still cast a dim glow over the room. She snuggled down further into the pile of clothing that had become her bed, marvelling that she could feel so calm, that the sounds of the storm raging outside only made her feel more secure.

She'd never known this. This complete faith that she was safe. There'd always been a feeling of dread hanging over her, as far back as she could remember. But it had gone now.

She rather thought it had started to lift the moment Lord Havelock had slid his ring on to her finger.

She heard the sounds of footsteps in the corridor, then, as she turned her head towards the door, she saw her husband, wearing nothing but his breeches and boots.

'D-didn't mean to w-wake you,' he stammered through chattering teeth. 'Had to f-fetch more c-coal.'

He dumped the bucket he'd been carrying and tossed several shovelfuls of coal on to the fire.

'You must be frozen,' she said, noting the goose-bumps all over his back.

'That's p-putting it m-mildly.'

'Why on earth didn't you put your coat on?'

'What, and rob you of your b-blank-kets?' He shook his head, a scowl darkening his features.

It might be cold in the house, but her heart felt as if it was melting. What a perfectly wonderful thing for him to do. She sniffed back a welling tear. He was such a *chivalrous* man.

'B-besides,' he added as he came back to the bed, 'you'll soon warm me up.'

With a growl, he burrowed under the mound of clothing, then wrapped his arms and legs round her as though she was his own personal hot-water bottle.

She couldn't help shrieking as an ice-cold hand slid inside the bodice of her chemise.

'Mmmhh.' He half sighed, half groaned. 'You feel wonderful.'

'Ow! You don't,' she yelped as he ran a cold foot up her calf.

'Is that any way to thank me for going all that way to fetch coal? Come on, Mary,' he murmured, burying a cold nose into her neck. 'Don't you think I've earned a reward?'

He had. He definitely had. But just as she started to tell him so, his cold hands had her dissolving into giggles. He kept on searching for particularly sensitive places, tormenting her until she was begging for mercy.

He ignored her pleas, ruthlessly turning her giggles into moans of pleasure, her wriggling to escape into writhing to get closer. Pretty soon, neither of them felt the slightest bit cold. Together, they stoked up the fires of passion until it consumed them both in a blaze of wonderful completion.

It was daylight stuttering in through the broken window that brought Mary awake the next morning. With a contented sigh, she snuggled into her husband's side and put an arm round his waist.

'Thank God you're awake at last,' he said. 'For the past half hour, at least, I've been so hungry I've even started to wonder what coal tastes like.'

'You are awake?' But he'd been so still. 'You should have woken me.'

He traced one finger over her creased brow. 'You looked so peaceful lying there. So…lovely, with the firelight flickering over your hair. I could quite happily have stayed here all day, admiring you.…'

Why was he saying that, when they both knew she wasn't the slightest bit pretty? He'd even made a point of saying it didn't matter.

Need not be pretty.

She'd been lying there, feeling warm and contented, and grateful that marrying him had brought her into a cosy shelter from the storms of life, and with one careless remark he'd brought that horrid list to the forefront of her mind.

'If only we had someone to bring us breakfast up here,' he finished ruefully.

That was more like it. She preferred honest, even mundane, conversation, as long as he didn't try to…to soft-soap her with the kind of meaningless, insincere flattery that was an insult to her intelligence.

'Since we don't,' she said with a stiff smile, 'we will just have to go down and make it ourselves.'

'By which you mean you will conjure up something, while I am obliged to watch from the sidelines,' he grumbled, sitting up and rummaging through their bedding until he came across a shirt. 'You shouldn't have to do it all,' he said, pulling the shirt over his head, while she reached for the least crumpled item of clothing she could find. 'I may not know my way round a kitchen, but surely I could spare you some of the heavy work? Heaving coal, or hauling water, or something?'

Once again, she was glad she'd kept her brief spurt of annoyance to herself. He might have his faults, but at least he was willing to pitch in and help, rather than leaving her to struggle alone.

And he'd certainly got the muscles for it, she reflected, watching his beautiful back flex and stretch as he thrust his arms into the sleeves.

'If you are sure, then…thank you.'

The smile that blazed across his face had the strange effect of making her want to pull him straight back down on to the mattress.

Just because he'd smiled at her? How…weak and pathetic did that make her? Rather shaken by the strength of the feelings he could rouse, without, apparently, even trying, she pulled on her dress.

Only to feel her insides turn to mush when he took her hand as they ventured out of their room into a corridor that was so cold their breath misted in the air in great clouds. He kept it clasped firmly in his all the way to the kitchen. If she'd wanted to retrieve it, she would have had a struggle. And there didn't seem much point in taking objection to such a harmless demonstration of affection.

Affection! No, it couldn't be that. He'd specifically warned her not to go looking for affection.

'What would you like me to do first?' he asked when they reached the kitchen. 'Fetch more coal? Or wood?'

She'd rather he stopped being so amazing, she thought crossly. So she wouldn't be tempted to forget this was supposed to be a practical arrangement. Or start thinking that gestures such as carrying her over the threshold, or holding her hand, or saying she was adorable, were just the sort of things that went on in a love match.

'Whichever you prefer.' She sighed, going to the stove and kneeling to rake out the ashes. 'The log basket does need filling,' she admitted. The sooner she set him to work, the sooner she'd get back into a sensible frame of mind. Rather than wondering what it would be like if they were really lovers, stranded here alone. Or how romantic it would seem to have a lord chopping wood and hauling water while she sat indoors in the warm…

She shook her head. She needed to stay focused on practicalities, not drift off into stupid daydreams.

'We will need quite a lot of water. This stove has a place where you can pour it, to heat, and then we can draw it off from this tap here, see, whenever we want some.'

'Ingenious,' he said. And then his stomach rumbled.

And she recalled him lying quietly, so as not to disturb her, even though he'd jested he was hungry enough to try the coal.

'There is no rush,' she said, ashamed of constantly getting annoyed with him when, in his own way, he was clearly doing his best. 'There is enough wood to get the fire hot enough to put the breakfast rolls in. Why don't you help yourself to some of that ham we had last night while I fetch them?'

'You're sure?'

'Yes.' She got up, dusted her knees and smiled at him. 'No point in setting you to work on an empty stomach.'

He didn't need telling twice before he'd got the ham out of the larder and carved himself a huge slice.

'I had no idea,' he said, much later, once breakfast was ready and they could both sit down together, 'that so much work was involved in just throwing a bit of breakfast together. And do you know, I don't think I'll be half so impatient about getting served in inns, after this. When I think of some of the insults I've heaped on waiters, when I've come in, sharp set...' He shook his head ruefully, before breaking open a roll and slathering it with butter.

He groaned, half closing his eyes as if in ecstasy.

'That has to be the most delicious thing I've ever tasted. You're a marvel.'

She shook her head. 'I'm no marvel. You are simply very, very hungry. I don't suppose you would think a simple bread roll would be all that delicious if you weren't.'

'That may be part of it,' he agreed, reaching for another roll, a faint frown furrowing his forehead. 'Perhaps I have fallen into the habit of taking such simple things for granted. But I shan't any longer. And as for—'

He'd just reached across the table to take her hand when there came a knock at the back door.

Muttering under his breath, Lord Havelock strode

across the room to answer the knock while she stood up and whipped off her apron.

'Mornin',' said a short, wiry man who was knuckling his forehead.

'Gilbey! Where the devil,' snapped her husband, 'have you been?'

He then, belatedly, seemed to recall she was there. 'Pardon my language,' he said perfunctorily, over his shoulder at her, before waving his arm in her direction.

'My wife, Lady Havelock,' he said to the wiry man, who'd sidled in out of the cold.

Out of habit, Mary dropped a curtsy, causing the wiry man's shaggy eyebrows to shoot up his forehead.

'This is my *groom*,' said her husband with a touch of impatience. 'You don't need to curtsy to such as him. Now, you, explain yourself,' he snapped, turning his attention back to the wiry man too quickly to notice Mary flinch.

How could he reprove her like that? In the man's hearing?

'I expected to find you, and, more important, Lady and Lightning, in the stables when I got here last night,' snapped Lord Havelock.

'Well, when I got here yesterday, me lord, seeing as how there was nobody about, and the stables deserted, I thought it best to take them, and your chestnuts, to the nearest inn, make sure they was taken proper care of, like. And see if I could find out what was afoot here. Brought 'em back as soon as I'd made sure there would be proper provisions for them and knew as you'd arrived yourself.'

'Hmmph,' said Lord Havelock and stalked out into the yard, the groom trotting behind in his wake.

Mary stood looking at the door for a moment or two, her mouth hanging open. Where had his appetite gone? He'd been complaining of hunger ever since they awoke. So hungry he'd even joked about trying the coal. But the moment he heard his horses had arrived they'd driven every other thought from his mind.

He must care about them a lot, she decided, closing first her mouth, then the kitchen door through which he'd just vanished without a backward glance. She should have picked up on the clues the day before, when he admitted he'd had them travel by stages so as not to tire them, though he'd pushed her into making the entire journey in one go. And the way his face had fallen when she'd admitted she couldn't ride.

Which told her two things. First, he must have thought about going out riding with her. Not only thought about it, but looked forward to it, or he wouldn't have looked so disappointed.

And second, that she'd been right about his character. Even though Lord Havelock had looked as angry as she'd ever seen him, the groom hadn't seemed the slightest bit scared of the way he'd shouted. He'd just stood there letting her husband rant a bit, then stated his case clearly.

And her husband had listened.

Just as he'd listened to her, when she'd stood up to him over the matter of their betrothal. He'd scared her a bit, back then, the way his anger had blown up seemingly out of nowhere. But it had blown out just as swiftly.

Not that it excused him rebuking her in front of a third party. Her father had exercised that particular form of cruelty towards her mother, whittling her sense of worth down, insult by insult, until there had been nothing left but splinters.

Well, she wasn't going to let her husband do the same to her. Not that she really thought he was doing it deliberately.

Nevertheless, she needed to take a stand, now, so that he would learn she wouldn't tolerate such treatment.

She strode to the dresser and took down another cup to set on the table. Outside staff generally came into the kitchen for their meals. Since there was nobody else to provide them, she would have to take on the task of feeding the groom.

Even if her husband disapproved of her sitting at table with him.

Well, she didn't care if he did think she was committing yet another social *faux pas* by extending common humanity to the poor wretch, the way he'd done when she'd dropped that curtsy.

Lifting her chin, she strode to the table and placed the cup down firmly before one of the empty chairs. She half hoped he *did* disapprove of her willingness to hobnob with a lowly groom. She went back to the dresser and picked up a plate, a knife and a fork with a toss of her head. For then he'd discover that he had most definitely not married *a mouse*.

She set about preparing such a substantial meal that it was bound to earn his forgiveness, once she'd shown him that he couldn't get away with trying to browbeat her in front of servants.

'You were right,' said Lord Havelock, the moment he came back into the kitchen. She glanced up from the stove to assess his mood, before reaching for the kettle.

'Was I?' She poured water into the pot, noting that

her hands were shaking as she braced herself to stand up for herself for the first time in her life. 'What about?'

She couldn't see any sign of the anger that had driven him out to the stables, which must mean he was pleased with the condition of his horses, and had forgiven the groom for not being on hand the night before. She just hoped he'd be as quick to forgive her.

'About the caretaker and his wife. Gilbey found out— Stop loitering there in the doorway, man,' he barked at the groom over his shoulder. 'Come in and shut it before you let all the heat out,' he said, depriving her of the opportunity of inviting him in herself.

The groom snatched off his hat, shuffled forward and closed the door behind him, while Lord Havelock sauntered over to the stove, holding out his hands to warm them.

'Gilbey put up at the Dog and Ferret last night,' he said. 'The landlord told him that the Brownlows have gone away to visit relatives of some sort for the season. They don't plan to come back until the twenty-eighth. It was a shock to everyone in the taproom to hear I'd come back, expecting to take up residence. God only knows where my letter to them has gone. Still at the receiving office, I shouldn't wonder. Is that a fresh pot of tea? Capital.'

To her intense irritation, he then pulled up a chair at the table and indicated the groom should do so, as well. Where had his insistence on keeping the groom in his place, and she in hers, gone? She was torn between wanting to hug him for being so affable, or slap him for depriving her of the opportunity to take a stand. In the end, all she did was pour both men a cup of tea.

She'd have to find some other way of showing him

he couldn't speak to her like that. Only…if she launched into that kind of speech right now, wouldn't she look a bit shrewish?

'Looks as though my wife has cooked enough to feed an army,' he said. Cheerfully.

He clearly had no idea what he'd done to her.

'And even if you've had something at the Dog and Ferret, you should at least have a couple of these rolls,' he said, putting some on a plate and pushing them over, with what looked suspiciously like…pride. 'They're first-rate.'

No, she definitely couldn't start complaining about the way he'd talked to her when he'd been in a temper, not when he was being so complimentary about her cooking. Lips pressed tightly together, she served both men with eggs and ham, then sank, deflated, on to her own seat.

'Which leads me to the next question,' said her husband, in between mouthfuls. 'What are we going to do until the Brownlows return, my Lady Havelock?'

'I don't understand.'

He wasn't asking her opinion, was he? Men didn't do that. So what was he about now? And why was he addressing her so formally? When all through the night he'd used her given name. Over and over again.

Mary, he'd whispered into her ear.

Mary… he'd growled.

Oh, Mary… he'd moaned.

Oh, it was all so confusing. *He* was confusing!

'Well,' he said very slowly, as though explaining to a child, 'we could go and rack up at the Dog and Ferret. We'll have plenty of food and a proper bed.'

'If'n you don't mind damp sheets and bedbugs,' muttered Gilbey.

'It doesn't sound very…appealing,' Mary agreed.

'Trouble is,' said her husband, 'the only alternative is to remain here. And you've already discovered how uncomfortable this place is, too, without servants.'

He laid down his knife and fork, and gave her a straight look.

Both her husband and groom were watching her intently, she realised after a moment or two.

Heavens, they really were waiting to hear what she thought. Her husband hadn't just told her what the choices were, before telling her what he was going to do. He really was going to let her decide. Well, she'd wanted the chance to take a stand. And though it wasn't exactly the topic she'd wanted to confront him about, it was better than nothing.

'This is my home now,' she therefore stated firmly. 'I would much rather stay here and try to make the place a bit more comfortable, than throw myself on the mercy of a landlord who sounds as though he doesn't care about the welfare of his guests one bit.'

'Capital,' he said, beaming at her as though she'd just said the very thing he was waiting to hear. 'I didn't really want you to have to put up with the rabble that frequent the Dog and Ferret. No offence to you, Gilbey.'

'None taken. I've got no wish to go back there meself,' he said, scratching his neck. 'There's the makings of decent quarters over the stables. Just want a bit of sorting, like.'

'It's the same with this house, I'm sure,' said Mary.

Lord Havelock frowned. 'But you are going to have to do it single-handed. Da—dash it, this isn't the Christmas I'd planned to give you,' he said, slamming his half-emptied cup down on to the table. 'But I will make it up to you, I swear. I'll tell you what I'll do,' he said, his face brightening. 'I'll go into the village and see if I can purchase the makings of Christmas dinner.'

'That's a very…' she'd been going to say, a good idea. But he'd already reached the back door and was striding out into the yard.

'That's his lordship all over,' said the groom, eyeing her astonishment with amusement. 'Get's a notion in his cockloft and don't stop to consider if it's even possible, never mind sensible.'

'R-really?' She hadn't known him long, but, yes, she could well believe that he was the type of man to act on impulse, rather than planning anything in great detail. He was so full of energy. And with the kind of confidence that came from being both wealthy and having a secure position in society. Yes, he could very easily set off into the unknown, assuming that everything would work out well for him.

Except when it had come to marriage. When he'd contemplated marriage, he'd sat down with a group of friends and got them to help him plan it all out down to the last detail.

Which only went to show how hard it must have been for a man who was used to doing as he pleased, whenever he pleased, to shackle himself to just one woman.

She supposed she ought to look upon his making of that list as a symptom of his determination to get it right. She'd seen several examples of that determination. That drive to do his best. Though it still hurt to read herself, the wife, described in such terms.

'I'd best get back to the stables, if you will excuse

me,' said Gilbey, getting to his feet. 'Unless there's anything you want helping with, in the way of heavy work?'

'That's very good of you, but I won't know until I've taken a good look about the place, to see what wants doing.'

'Ah, you're just what his lordship needs,' observed the groom with a knowing air. 'Sensible. And calm. Begging yer pardon for speaking so free, but...' He twisted his hat between his rather grubby fingers. 'You oughtn't to listen to those who will tell you he's wild. Or worry about his temper,' he said knowingly.

'I don't,' she replied firmly. She hadn't been afraid of him since...since...

Actually, she hadn't ever been really afraid of him. Nervous, yes, of the pull he exerted over her. Scared of her reactions to him. But of him, not really ever.

'Sure, he's fought his duels,' Gilbey added. 'But he's a good lad, at heart.'

'Duels? He's fought duels?'

'He didn't mean no harm by them,' hastily put in the groom. 'It's just, he ain't never had nobody, not since his mother passed, to care what he did, one way or another, y'see. 'Twill make all the difference to him, to have someone steady, to be his...well, his anchor, like,' he finished gruffly, before slapping the hat on his head and scuttling off out of the door.

She reached for her cup of tea and took a long, sustaining drink. Now that the initial shock had worn off, she could see exactly how her husband could have stumbled into fighting a duel or two. Not only did he have a hair-trigger temper, but he also had a highly developed sense of his own honour. Only look at the way he'd reacted when she'd assumed he'd been making her an insulting proposition.

He'd calmed down as soon as she'd explained herself, though. Which only went to prove that whoever he'd fought hadn't attempted to apologise. So if he had shot them, it was entirely their own fault.

He was good at heart, the groom had insisted. And gone on to talk about Lord Havelock's mother. Which showed he'd stayed with the family for years, as well as sort of proving his point. Servants didn't stay with cruel masters. She should know. They'd gone through dozens of servants during the time they'd been able to afford to pay their wages.

Besides, she'd seen many instances of his deep-down goodness. Only look at the way he'd set to work hauling water for her. Or going to fetch coal in the middle of the night, shirtless, and come back shivering rather than deprive her of the warmth of his coat. Or let her sleep as long as she wanted, even though he wanted his breakfast.

She drained the cup and set it down on the table.

But what impressed her most of all was the way he'd apologised. And tried to make amends for all that had gone wrong. He'd even gone charging off, just now, to buy food in an attempt to *make it up to her.*

A smile played about her lips as she recalled the look on his face when he'd set off to the village as if he could purchase the answer to all his problems there. It was sweet of him, but she could think of far better ways he could make it up to her, if his conscience was troubling him.

None of which involved him *buying* anything at all.

Chapter Ten

'Duck,' he announced, some hours later, as he came in the door.

'Why, are you going to throw something?'

'Ha ha,' he said. 'Very droll. Though I just might, if you provoke me like that, you minx. Anyway, what I meant is, I've got a duck for Christmas dinner,' announced her husband with pride as Gilbey followed him into the kitchen, carrying a game bag. 'And a meat pie for tonight. There is cake, and fruit, too.'

'All…all in that sack?' Oh, dear.

Gilbey solemnly laid the bag on the kitchen table and opened the tie at the neck. The first thing to come out of it was the pie. The crust was a little the worse for wear, but it was definitely still edible. As were the apples that had done most of the damage, to judge from the amount of gravy coating them.

'Apples in gravy, how…novel,' she said diplomatically. 'Is there gravy on the cake, too? No. Oh, well…' she sighed as she lifted it out and set it to one side '…I suppose I can bear to eat it without.'

'Now look here,' snapped her husband. 'I had the

devil of a job to get hold of this little lot. You wouldn't believe the haggling I had to do.'

'I'm very grateful,' she said soothingly. 'This is the makings of a true feast.' It really was. She'd been worrying, ever since he'd set off in such a hurry, that he'd come back with all sorts of ridiculously inappropriate things. But in the event, the only thing he hadn't got quite right was the method of bringing everything home.

'I shall have no qualms about sending you shopping in future.' Although she might hand him a shopping basket rather than let him snatch up a game bag, as if he was going out shooting.

'Shopping,' he cried indignantly, planting his fists on his hips. 'That was not shopping. That was…foraging.'

'I see. Well, in that case, I have to say I am impressed by your foraging skills. In fact, I think you would make a good soldier.'

He would certainly look good in a uniform. All that scarlet cloth stretched across his broad shoulders, with a sword dangling from his slender hips to complete the very picture of masculine perfection….

'A soldier, eh?'

'Yes.' She sighed, dragging herself out of a brief vision of him pulling a pistol from his belt and shooting some random marauder. 'Actually,' she said with one part of her mind while another was seeing him metamorphosed into the captain of a ship, his hair tousled by an Atlantic gale rather than his restless fingers, 'I think you could be anything you set your mind to.'

Anything he set his mind to? No, surely she didn't mean *anything*. Oh, he had total confidence he could rise to any form of physical challenge. He was a crack shot, a bruising rider and a long-standing member of the Four-in-Hand club. But nobody, in his entire life, had ever expressed any faith in his ability to put his *mind* to work. And so far, surely, he'd demonstrated he was a total dunce when it came to organising anything. Even with the help of his lists, he'd overlooked several important issues that any man who exercised his brain occasionally would have thought of before he set off into the winter weather with a brand-new bride in tow.

Yet she was looking at him as though he'd just done something remarkable. As though he really did have it in him to accomplish…*anything*.

He stood quite still, basking in the completely novel sensation of having a female look at him with wholehearted admiration.

Totally unwarranted admiration, as far as he was concerned. If he hadn't made such a mull of opening up Mayfield, he wouldn't have had to go out on the foraging expedition in the first place.

She'd come to her senses before long. End up wishing him elsewhere, the way everybody always did, eventually.

She lowered her eyes to the spread on the table. Just as though she'd sensed him bracing himself against the day it happened.

'I think—that is, I hope,' she said, darting him the kind of look from under those dark lashes that made him catch his breath, 'that you will be pleased with what I have been about today, as well.'

'I'm sure I shall,' he said. As far as he was concerned she could have been sitting in front of a fire toasting her toes all day, after looking at him the way she'd just done, merely because he'd managed to rectify *one* of the blunders he'd made.

But he couldn't help wondering what kind of treatment she must have been used to, if it took so little effort to get her to look at him as though he was some kind of…hero…stepped straight out of the pages of a romance novel.

Not that he'd ever read any, but a lot of girls seemed to do so, then spent hours sighing over characters with odd names and complaining he wasn't a bit like any of 'em.

'I went exploring,' she said. 'And I discovered that all the rooms in the part of the house that used to be let out are in very good order. It looks as if those caretakers of yours have kept them in readiness for tenants to come in at a moment's notice. So I lit a fire and aired the mattress in the one I liked best,' she said with a slightly defiant tilt to her chin, as though expecting him to object. 'And I ironed the damp out of some sheets I found in a linen closet and made up a bed.'

'That's wonderful news.'

'Oh. I am so glad you don't mind which room we have tonight,' she said with evident relief. 'Indeed, there are so many in a state of near readiness that if you don't like it you can soon choose another….'

'No, no, I shall be glad to sleep in a real bed tonight, thank you.' He went to her, seized her hand and kissed it. She really was a treasure. 'And I don't care which room you picked. I told you this is your home as much as mine. You must do whatever you like in it. But,' he added, 'don't you see what this means? After the window came away in my hand last night I was beginning to think the whole place had fallen into ruin while I wasn't paying attention. But now I can write to Lady

Peverell and tell her that Julia can come here as soon as she likes. I can get her safely out of that man's reach before he has a chance to—'

He shot a look at Gilbey, who was folding up the sack, with the wooden expression of a servant who was listening to a conversation not meant for his ears.

'In fact, I think I shall go and write immediately. Gilbey, instead of hanging around in the kitchen, you can make yourself useful by riding down to the post with it as soon as I've written it.'

'Yes, m'lord.'

Mary sat blinking at the swirl of dust that eddied across the kitchen floor after he'd slammed the door on his way out.

He'd been a bit like a whirlwind himself. Breezing in, delivering his mound of booty, then dashing off to his next task. She couldn't stop smiling as she pottered about the kitchen. The more she learned about her husband, the better she liked him.

She liked him even more when he turned up for supper on time, praised her cooking to the skies and then tried to prevent her from doing the dishes.

'I thought I'd made my views on that sort of thing plain,' he growled when she started to carry a stack of plates to the scullery.

'Yes, you did,' she said. 'But if the Brownlows aren't going to return until the twenty-eighth, every useful surface will be covered with dirty dishes by then. It wouldn't be fair to them to have to come back to that sort of mess.'

'It would serve 'em right for sloping off just when I

particularly wanted 'em here.' He scowled. 'And if you don't want the working surfaces cluttered, why don't you stack the dishes on the floor?'

'I could do that, I suppose,' she said with a shudder. 'If you want the house invaded by rats.'

'Point taken,' he said. 'Dishes need to be done. But I won't have you doing them. I made you a vow.'

For one moment she thought he was going to order Gilbey to do the dishes for her. But then, to her amazement, he stood up, removed his jacket and rolled up his shirtsleeves.

'I shall need instruction,' he said, as he strode into the scullery.

He meant to do the dishes himself?

Well—she'd always thought that it was a man's actions that revealed his true nature. And after seeing him literally roll up his sleeves to perform such a lowly task, she would never make the mistake of suspecting he was anything like her father, ever again.

'Not that it can possibly be all that hard,' he said airily. 'I've never met a scullery maid yet with anything approaching half a brain.'

'Have you met many scullery maids?' she heard herself say, inanely, as she tipped a bucket of hot water into one of the sinks. Still, it was better than blurting out any of the other thoughts swarming round her head. Or simply gazing at him, wide-eyed and slack-jawed in wholly feminine appreciation.

For heaven's sakes! All he'd done was roll up his sleeves and she was practically dribbling at the sight of his forearms.

'I'm sure I must have done,' he said, as she handed him a scrubbing brush. And only just managed to stop herself from running her hand up that enticing expanse of sinewy, hair-roughened flesh.

'On their days off. At fairs and such,' he added, seizing the nearest plate and manfully dunking it into the soapy water. 'And there was definitely one who used to prowl around the stables after the head groom at…well, never mind where. She couldn't have had much in her cockloft to throw herself at him the way she did. Without the slightest sign of encouragement, I might add. Remember her, Gilbey? I can see you loitering in the doorway, so don't bother trying to pretend you aren't listening to every word. Don't you have work to do?'

'Yes, m'lord,' said the groom, before disappearing out into the night to do whatever it was he did for the horses.

Thank heaven she hadn't started stroking her husband's arms. She hadn't been aware the groom was there, so rapt had she been by the sight of a man, her man, cheerfully engaging in what her father would have scathingly described as woman's work.

'The tale of me up to my elbows in soapsuds will spread like wildfire through the taverns,' Lord Havelock grumbled, holding out the plate he'd scrubbed for her inspection.

'Perfect,' she said with a sigh. Then blushed. 'The plate, I mean,' she added hastily. 'At least it will be once you rinse it. Or perhaps I should rinse it.' She went to take it from him.

'Oh, no, you don't,' he said, dunking the plate into the clean water in the next sink over and clasping her about the waist. 'I am quite capable of doing this, you know.'

'Yes, but if you don't want people to talk—'

'I don't care what people might say about me,' he declared, before dipping his head to kiss her. 'They can go hang for all I care.'

She totally lost the thread of what they'd been discussing as he kissed her over and over again, walking her backwards across the room until she fetched up against a wall. The slide of his wet hands up her legs as he impatiently thrust her skirts out of the way, and the thrill of complying as he murmured heated, explicit instructions into her ear.

The joy of having this man want her so much that he couldn't even wait to find a horizontal surface to lay her down on thrilled her.

And the gratitude that came from discovering that for all his impatience to have her, he possessed the self-control to wait until he'd satisfied her, before taking his own pleasure.

It got better every time, with Mary. He'd thought nothing could surpass their wedding night, yet sharing that mattress in front of the fire, the next night, had somehow been even better.

And as for last night...even when they'd eventually finished 'doing the dishes', the fire between them hadn't gone out. They'd raced up the stairs to the room she'd prepared and torn each other's clothes off with such haste they hadn't bothered using the warming pan she'd insisted on filling with embers from the kitchen fire.

He raised himself on one elbow to look at her. Just look at her. How had he ever thought her plain? Not that she had one of those faces that attracted notice at first glance. No, what she had was an attraction that shone from the intelligence in her eyes, or the warmth of her smile.

He couldn't help just sifting her soft, silken hair through his fingers, then fanning it out across his pillow. He liked the fact she didn't wear it in bunches of fussy ringlets. In fact, he wouldn't be surprised if she found it hard to make it take a curl. It was so straight—like her.

He wasn't a fanciful sort of man, not normally, but when it came to her hair, he'd surprised himself by comparing it to all sorts of things that another man, the kind of man who was bookish, might work up into a poem. It put him in mind of hot summer nights when, as a boy, he'd stolen away from this house to go swimming in the lake. Naked, he would float on his back in water that had felt like silk against his skin and gaze up at the stars. Stars whose reflection shimmered in the water that bore him up. There seemed hardly any distance between water and sky. He'd got the notion that if he stretched his hands up, he could have touched them, made them shiver the way their reflections all around him shivered. As though he was floating in sky, and stars, and water, all at the same time.

And when he plunged his fingers into her hair while he was plunging himself inside her, he got the feeling that what he was doing was not just slaking a physical urge, but something more…something almost mystical.

Her eyes fluttered open, fixed on him and…warmed. Welcomed his presence.

There was no pretence about it. There hadn't been a moment of hesitation, followed by the calculated smile he was used to getting from the women he'd taken to bed in the past. She was genuinely pleased to see him when she woke up.

A strange feeling stirred inside. A feeling of acceptance he hadn't felt since… Well, he wasn't sure he'd ever had anyone show such fondness for him, not once they'd got to know him as well as she'd done, over the past few days. He couldn't remember his mother all that well. He'd been too young when she'd died to work out whether those vague feelings of acceptance had truly come from her, or whether he'd just dreamed them up in his childish need for...for something he certainly never got from his father. His father had definitely never been *fond* of him. He'd seen him pet his hounds and horses, but never, not once, had he been anything but brusque with his own offspring.

Things changed a bit when Julia was born. As soon as she could walk she toddled around after him. Wanting him to notice her. Believing he could do no wrong in spite of all evidence to the contrary. Even when she got old enough to develop some discernment, her face would still light up when she first saw him after sufficient time apart.

Which was one of the reasons why he'd been determined to move heaven and earth to keep her safe.

Although, what had it cost him, really? Marriage hadn't turned out to be anything like the irksome chore he'd imagined. By some miracle, he'd found the only woman on earth who could have made becoming a husband a positive pleasure.

And it wasn't just because she matched practically every item on the list his friends had helped him make. It was because, in spite of all the ways he'd gone wrong, she appeared to genuinely like him.

So he kissed her. Well, what else was a man to do when a woman looked at him like that?

'You were looking very serious, just now,' she said

when he broke off to take a very necessary breath. 'What were you thinking?'

He was damned if he was going to upset her by telling her she met every criterion on his list of what constituted an acceptable wife. Or admitting that he'd dreaded the prospect of marriage so much he'd actually sought the moral support and guidance of his friends in compiling it.

And he certainly wasn't ever going to share, with *anyone*, that he'd had that moment of...metaphysical madness...diving into star-studded lakes of black silk to find the road to...some spiritual realm where souls could entwine, or some such rot, indeed!

He'd tell her the first thing he'd thought on waking, instead. Haul his mind back to the arena in which he felt far more at home.

'I was thinking,' he admitted with a rakish smile, 'that every time we change the venue for our...conjugal activities, it gets more enjoyable. Do you know,' he said, shifting over her, 'I have this...craving to...' he nudged her legs apart with his own '...enjoy you in every single room in this house.' He nuzzled her neck. 'Just to see if I'm right.'

For a moment it looked as though she was going to yield. But then her sinuous, responsive movements turned into unmistakable attempts to wriggle out from under him.

'We can't...not now,' she said apologetically. 'There's so much to do this morning. If you want to eat Christmas dinner at a decent hour...'

'Hang dinner,' he said, catching her round the waist just as she was about to leave the bed and pulling her back. 'And hang decency. We'll eat whenever what you make *is* ready.'

'But Gilbey will expect—'

'And hang Gilbey, too. He'll eat when we do.'

'But—'

He stopped her mouth with a kiss. And smiled against her lips when, with a sigh, she wrapped her arms round his neck and kissed him back.

It was the happiest Christmas she'd ever known. And it wasn't just because, at last, she had a secure home, plenty of food to eat and no need to worry about how to pay for it.

It was because of Lord Havelock.

He made Christmas Day pass in a whirl of merriment and lovemaking. Which he topped off by declaring it had been the best Christmas of his own life, too.

'Don't look as though you don't believe me,' he said, a touch belligerently, when she gaped at him in surprise. 'You may as well know, right now, that I *never* lie. Have never seen the point,' he finished loftily.

'I didn't mean to imply you would,' she said, going to the oven and kneeling down to rake embers into the warming pan. 'It is just, well, it was all so… I mean, you must have had far more grand food and all sorts of entertainments, other years.'

'Oh. Yes, I see what you mean. And in a way, you're right. I've definitely been to a great many Christmas house parties where no expense was spared. But you see,' he said, gently taking the warming pan from her as she turned and got to her feet, 'when I was a grubby schoolboy, I always felt I was there on sufferance, wherever I was. And then, when I got older, the same girls who'd been turning their noses up at me all their lives suddenly realised I was a catch and began trying to trap me. Don't care for being hunted down like a…coursed hare,' he finished bitterly.

'I see.' She picked up the lantern, glanced at the kitchen table and smothered a giggle. He'd surprised her, right after dinner, by sweeping the dishes aside, bending her over the table and lifting her skirts. What followed had been wild and wonderful, if a little shocking. 'It has been the best Christmas Day I've ever had, too.' It had been just as well the table was so sturdy. They'd have shattered a less robust piece of furniture.

And probably carried right on, in its splintered ruins, until they'd finished what he'd started.

'I meant what I said, you know,' he said with a mischievous twinkle in his eyes as he followed the direction of her gaze.

'What about?' She'd lost the thread of the discussion while she'd been reliving the way his hands had taken command of her body, while his lips pressed hot kisses into the nape of her neck.

'About wanting to make love to you in every room in this house.' As if to prove his point, when they reached the door of the room they'd slept in the night before, he kept on walking.

'There must be a dozen bedrooms along this corridor alone.'

'They…they won't be very comfortable, though,' she pointed out, hanging back.

He turned and looked at her keenly.

'It isn't fair to expect you to put up with another night on a hearthrug, is it? Very well,' he said with an exaggerated sigh. 'Let's be practical.' He turned back and entered what she'd come to think of as their bedroom.

'For now,' he said firmly, shutting the door behind them. 'But I give you fair warning that once the Brownlows get here, I shall have them make up every bed, in every room, so that we can try out whichever takes ours fancy, whenever,' he said, thrusting the warming pan under the quilt, 'it takes our fancy.'

Whenever? Oh, yes. She liked the sound of that. Funny, but she'd never thought of herself as a spontaneous sort of person. But then she'd never had the chance to find out who she really was, or what she really liked. She'd been too busy just surviving.

But from the moment she'd married Lord Havelock— or at least, the moment he first started to get undressed, she'd decided she liked being able to make love whenever the fancy took them.

'But for tonight,' he said, taking her in his arms, 'I shall make up for the fact we have to stay in here, by showing you...something new.'

'Something new?'

What more could there be? He'd started by teaching her that people could make love in broad daylight. And gone on to demonstrate that they didn't even need to lie down.

Her stomach flipped over in anticipation as he took her hand and led her to the bed. The look in his eyes made her legs tremble.

'What,' she whispered, 'do you intend to do to me?'

'Drive you wild,' he whispered back.

Chapter Eleven

On the morning of the twenty-eighth, while they were still eating breakfast in the kitchen, the back door flew open and a middle-aged couple burst in, bringing with them the inevitable gust of rain-laden wind.

'My lord, I'm that sorry,' the woman began to apologise. 'Had we any idea you was coming, we'd not have gone away. To think of you having to make do, at Christmas of all times.'

'My Lady Havelock,' drawled Lord Havelock icily, 'allow me to present, finally, Mr and Mrs Brownlow. The caretakers of Mayfield.'

She managed, but only just, to follow her husband's lead and not get to her feet and welcome the couple into the home as though they were guests. But she felt most uncomfortable when the one bowed while the other curtsied to her.

'You look as though you've done very well, considering,' said Mrs Brownlow, her eyes darting about the kitchen before coming to rest on Mary, who suddenly became very aware of the shabbiness of her gown and the fact that she'd not bothered taking off her apron when

she'd sat down to breakfast. It felt as though Mrs Brownlow was sizing her up for the position of cook, rather
than lady of the house. And that, given the choice, Mrs
Brownlow wouldn't have granted her either position.

'But now we're back, you won't need to bother yourselves with all this sort of thing any longer,' she added
with a sniff, before going to the stove, opening the doors,
rattling the poker about inside, then shutting them with
more noise than was anywhere near necessary.

'I notice you've decided to make use of the green-
silk room,' said the woman, taking the tea caddy from
the shelf where Mary had left it and restoring it to the
higher one where she'd first found it, but which was so
awkward to reach. 'Saw the smoke from the chimneys
as we was coming up the drive,' she added, which explained how she'd worked out where they'd slept, without anyone telling her.

But then Mrs Brownlow stilled, catching the full
force of Lord Havelock's scowl.

'We was that relieved,' she said, veering from her
display of competence to ingratiating sweetness, 'you
hadn't tried to take over the rooms what used to be his
late lordship's and his wife's. None of the rooms in that
wing have been touched since I don't know when. Need
a real good spring clean before they will be fit for use.'

Mary could have told her, had she paused to draw
breath, that she could tell exactly how competent she
was, from the state of the larder, the kitchen and the
wing that had been let out to raise revenue. And that
she didn't have anything to worry about. Lord Havelock
might have a ferocious scowl, but he wasn't the kind of
man who'd turn someone off for not somehow sensing he
was about to marry and descend on his ancestral home.

'And we'll need to get the chimneys swept before anyone attempts to light a fire in any of the rooms. Probably got several years' worth of birds' nests in them by now.'

At her side, Lord Havelock froze, his cup halfway to his mouth. From the way his face paled, and the muscles in his jaw twitched, she guessed he'd just had a vision of setting the chimney on fire and burning his house down around his ears on the very first night he took up residence.

'Now, you don't need to sit in the kitchen any longer, not now we're back,' said Mrs Brownlow, laying her hand on the teapot, then whisking it off the table with a rueful shake of her head. 'Mr Brownlow will light the fire in the drawing room.' She shot a speaking look at her husband, who scurried off in the direction of the coal store. 'It will be warm as toast in next to no time. And I'll bring you a fresh pot of tea in there.'

Lord Havelock set his cup down and got slowly to his feet.

'See that you do,' he drawled. His attempt at nonchalance was good enough to deceive the Brownlows, but not Mary. She could tell he was still reeling from that casual reference to highly inflammable nests, which often did get lodged in chimneys.

'Lady Havelock,' he snapped. 'Remove your apron and leave it behind. I sincerely hope never to have to see you in it again.'

Well, he had to give vent to his feelings somehow, she supposed. Lowering her head, in token meekness, she untied her apron strings. But she had to press her lips together to stop a smile forming. She kept her mouth firmly shut all the while Lord Havelock led her to the drawing room.

But once they were standing in the middle of the cold, inhospitable room, it struck her that they were behaving more like two naughty children caught out by their governess, than the lord and lady of the house.

And the giggles that had been building finally began to bubble over.

'What are you laughing at?'

Lord Havelock turned to her, his brows drawn down repressively.

'N-nothing,' she managed in between giggles. 'E-everything,' she admitted, dropping on to the nearest sofa and pressing her hand over her mouth in a vain attempt to stop.

'There's nothing funny about nearly burning the house down.'

'Y-you didn't, though. There must not have been,' she said in a vain struggle to both reassure him and bring herself under control, 'any n-nests up the ch-chimney, after all.'

'Don't say that word!' He planted his fists on his hips and glared down at her.

'Which one? Ch-chimneys? Or n-nests?'

She was laughing so hard by now that she had to wipe away the tears that had begun to run down her face.

'Neither,' he snarled, though his eyes had lost that dead, hollow look. 'Both.' As though coming back to life, he began to stalk towards her. 'Do you hear me, woman? You are never, ever, to mention birds' nests, or chimneys, to me again.'

His words were firm, but his lips were starting to twitch, too.

'Or…' she said, gratitude that he was a man who didn't take himself too seriously surging up within her on a tidal wave of joy. 'Or what?'

He was almost upon her now and his eyes were smouldering with such heat it made her want to lean back into the sofa cushions and open her arms to him.

'Or,' he growled, 'face the consequences.'

With a little shriek, she leapt up off the sofa just before he lunged for her. For the next few minutes, he chased her round and round the sofa, uttering dire threats of what he would do if he caught her, which he could have done any time he chose since she was laughing too hard to properly control her movements.

And then the door opened and Mr Brownlow appeared with a full coal scuttle. And came to a dead halt at the sight of his master and mistress playing chase.

'Dashed cold in here,' panted her husband as Mary froze in place. 'Just keeping warm, with a little exercise.'

The look on Mr Brownlow's face, the knowledge that had he come in a few seconds later he would have caught them rolling about *on* the sofa rather than running round and round it, was too much for Mary. With a shocked little cry she darted past the scandalised caretaker and out into the corridor, where she made for the stairs.

She heard her husband's footsteps pursuing her, but this time she wasn't playing. She really did just want to run away and hide. Without thinking, she made for the only room in the house where she would feel safe. The bedroom in which they'd slept the night before. The embers still glowed in the grate, making the room less chilly than any other, except the kitchen.

Lord Havelock reached it only a few seconds behind her. Before she could even turn round, he'd grabbed her by the waist.

'Got you,' he cried, propelling her across the room and flinging her down on to the bed.

'Now, my girl, we'll see how long you can keep on laughing at me,' he growled. Not that she felt like laughing any more. All the humour had gone out of the situation.

'What is it? What's the matter?'

She hadn't realised she'd communicated her chagrin to him. But she'd definitely tensed up and he'd noticed.

'I…I'm sorry,' she said, tears starting to her eyes as he reared up and looked down at her in confusion. 'It was just…' She gulped. 'I can't believe I forgot Mr Brownlow was on his way to make up the fire in there. A few more moments, and he would have found us… He would have found us…' She couldn't go on. Her face flamed though, at the knowledge she'd been about to let her husband catch her and tumble her to the sofa he'd been chasing her round. And let him commence the perfectly thrilling punishments he'd been threatening.

He started to chuckle.

'It isn't funny.'

'But it is, though. Far funnier than almost burning the house down around my ears. And you, madam…' he gave her a squeeze '…couldn't stop laughing about *that*.'

He kissed her brow in a comforting sort of way. And then her mouth, as his fingers sought the ties of her bodice.

'Surely you cannot still be thinking about…about…' Oh, but he most definitely was. And the minute he slipped his hand inside her gown, she was thinking about it again, too. Not just thinking about it either, but wanting it.

'Since we've been married,' he groaned, pushing aside an inconvenient swathe of material so that he could get at bare skin, 'it seems to be damn near all I can think about.'

'B-but we can't.'

'I don't see why not. Mr Brownlow already knows what we've come up here for.'

'Oh, surely not!'

'Of course he does. He almost caught us at it in the drawing room, don't forget.'

'As if I ever could,' she cried in mortification.

'Mary,' he said more gently, stroking the hair from her forehead. 'You don't really want me to stop, do you? Not…now?'

He ran his hand up the outside of her leg, pushing her skirt out of the way. A thrill shot through her, making her heart beat faster, her insides melt and her hips squirm.

'It would be a positive crime to disappoint Mr Brownlow.'

'Oh, don't speak to me of him,' she whimpered, torn between giving way to the delicious sensations he was rousing and the notion that she oughtn't, she really oughtn't, behave like this any more, not now they had indoor servants.

'Not another word,' he agreed affably. 'In fact, I'm sure I can put my mouth to much better use.'

He did. He set about making love to her with such skill that before long her world shrank to the size of one bed, and the only two people left were the two people on it. What had started out downstairs as playful rose swiftly again to a crescendo of desperate need. The urge to scream when her release came was so overwhelming she didn't know how to deal with it. In the end, she pressed her mouth into his shoulder to muffle the cry.

Afterwards, they lay together panting and just looking into each other's eyes in a kind of mirrored awe. She was shocked at herself for responding to him with such ardour, in spite of her awareness that the servants must know what they were doing.

And he must be wondering what kind of a woman he'd married. One minute she'd been saying she felt self-conscious. That she really couldn't...do *that*. The next she'd been tearing at his clothes in a kind of frenzy, wrapping her arms and legs round him, and coming to such a cataclysmic release she'd...she'd bitten him. She could see the teeth marks on his shoulder!

'Oh, what have I done?' She raised trembling fingers to his shoulder. Then pressed penitent lips to the reddening crescent.

She'd made him feel like a god, that's what she'd done. He'd never been with a woman who responded to him the way she did.

'It's nothing.' He shrugged with feigned nonchalance, whilst desperately trying to stifle the unfamiliar, and slightly disturbing, emotions welling up inside him.

'It isn't nothing. I've left a bruise....'

'A mark of passion. Such things happen between lovers all the time.'

He winced at the look on her face. He'd been trying to make light of a moment he was damn sure was going to live in his memory for a lifetime. Instead he'd made her think of her wondrous passion as something...tawdry.

Sitting up, he turned his back on her and thrust his fingers through his hair in annoyance. He should have just admitted he liked it. He could have done so in a teasing kind of way, so that she wouldn't guess how deeply she'd moved him, couldn't he? And then she would have smiled and...

God, but it was damn complicated, being married. The good moments got all snagged up with darker feelings until he couldn't unravel the tangle.

'Look, Mary...' He sighed with exasperation. 'If ever you do anything I don't like, I will be sure to tell you. No need to get worked up over such a little thing.'

'I...I'm sorry.'

The tremor in her voice made him turn to look at her sharply. Her little face was all woebegone.

Damn. Why wasn't he more adept with words? His explanation of how his mind worked had come out sounding more like a reprimand. And he'd hurt her. Which was the very last thing he ever wanted to do.

'Look, I warned you before we got married that I'm a blunt man.' In lieu of smooth words, he reached for her hand and gave it a squeeze. 'So this is the truth. I like being married to you.' Far more than he'd thought possible.

'Oh. Well, I like being married to you, too,' she said shyly, returning the pressure of his hand.

He lifted her hand and kissed it.

'There. That's all right and tight, then.' He got up and reached for his clothes. 'Think I'll go for a ride.' Clear his mind. And let her recover.

Because if he stayed he was bound to end up saying something that would make this awkwardness between them ten times worse.

All of a sudden, it seemed to Mary, the place was teeming with servants. When she'd eventually plucked up courage to go downstairs and face Mrs Brownlow, the woman had told her exactly how many she would need to run a house of this size efficiently, then brought them all in. She didn't even go through the motions of letting Mary interview them. She just hired the people she always hired on whenever Mayfield had tenants.

Not that she could fault any of them. Each of them knew exactly what they were supposed to be doing— and each other, too.

She was the only one who seemed to feel like a stranger here. Who wasn't totally comfortable with their role. She was used to *doing* housework, not ordering others to do it, that was half the trouble.

So, as the spring cleaning commenced, even though the new year had not yet come round, Mary took to walking about the rooms with a rag in her hand, and a scarf tied over her head, desperate to find some dirt, or a cobweb, Mrs Brownlow's team might have overlooked.

While her husband rode out early to avoid, she suspected, all the bustle, even though he muttered vague excuses about tenants. And only making love to her at night, behind the closed doors of their bedroom.

'There's a carriage coming up the drive, my lady.'

Mary looked up from the skirting board behind the sofa—where she'd found a satisfyingly thick layer of dust—to see that Mrs Brownlow herself had come with the news, instead of sending her husband.

'You've got visitors. So I'll take that,' she said, snatching the duster from Mary's hand. 'You shouldn't be doing it, anyway,' she grumbled.

Though what was she supposed to do all day, now that her husband didn't seem inclined to chase her round the furniture any longer? Sit on a sofa and twiddle her thumbs?

'I'll have Mr Brownlow…' who'd taken on the mantle of butler '…show them to the drawing room while you go and change into something more suitable.'

'Yes, yes, of course,' said Mary, fumbling the strings of her apron undone and making for the door.

Change? Into what? She supposed she would look slightly better in a clean gown, rather than one she'd been crawling around on the floor in, but not much. Neither of the other gowns she owned were in all that much better condition, after serving as bedding, then withstanding her time as cook and housemaid.

There was her wedding gown, of course. Only was it suitable for receiving callers?

What did the wife of a viscount wear for receiving callers, anyway?

Oh, what did it matter? Surely the most important thing was to make them feel welcome?

And it was no use, she decided—snatching the scarf from her head and stuffing it into her pocket—trying to pretend she was something she wasn't.

She stifled a pang of guilt as she hurriedly tidied her hair before the mirror. Lord Havelock had said he wanted her to be well dressed when the local gentry came calling. He'd said she would have to buy a lot of new clothes.

Only, somehow once they'd got down here, the topic had never come up again. And she hadn't liked to mention it.

With any luck, whoever was calling on her today would be able to tell her where she could find a reliable dressmaker, locally. In fact, it would be a very good topic of conversation. Anyone who knew her husband would have no trouble believing he'd swept her off her feet, and down here, without giving her a chance to buy any bride clothes.

Feeling much better about her gown now she could look upon it as a conversation opener, rather than a personal failing, Mary made her way to the drawing room.

She had only just reached it and taken a seat on one of the chairs by the fireplace, when Brownlow opened the door again.

'Lady Peverell,' he intoned. 'And Miss Julia Durant.'

'Oh!' She leapt to her feet, her hand flying to her throat. She knew that her husband had written to invite Julia to come and live with them, but as far as she knew, he hadn't received a reply.

Lady Peverell, a stylishly dressed blonde who didn't look much beyond the age of thirty, flicked Mary's crumpled, grubby gown a look of scorn, drew off her gloves and made for the chair she'd just leapt out of.

'Oh. Of course,' said Mary, moving out of her way. 'Do come and sit beside the fire,' she said a moment too late. 'You must be dreadfully cold after your journey. Such weather. I expect you'd like tea.'

It was all she could do to cross to the bell pull and ring for a servant, rather than run down to the kitchen and put the kettle on herself. With one withering look, Lady Peverell had made her feel as though she had no right to be in the room. Let alone pose as lady of the house. And as for presuming to the title…well!

'And you, too, Ju—' She pulled herself up, remembering she had no right to *address* her husband's sister by her given name, just because they'd been used to speaking *of* her that way. 'I mean, Miss Durant.'

She sent the girl a timid smile. Which wasn't returned. Miss Julia Durant remained standing just inside the doorway, scowling at her.

Oh, but she looked so very much like Lord Havelock, when things weren't going his way! She had the militant stance and the determined chin. She had the same-shaped hazel eyes, too. And from what she could see of her hair, which was fighting its way out from under her bonnet, the same thick mass of unruly curls that graced his head, too.

Though, she frowned, he had described her as a beauty. A girl at risk from a predatory older man.

Julia could certainly *become* very attractive, once she'd outgrown the spots that marred her complexion, learned not to pout and glower at strangers, and had her hair styled by a professional.

Julia responded to her smile with a look of scorn and a toss of her head. She flounced over to the window and flung herself on to the sill, turning her shoulder to the other occupants of the room.

'You see?' said Lady Peverell, waving the riding crop she held in one hand in Julia's direction. 'You see what I've had to contend with? I have a houseful of guests, but does she care? No. The minute she gets that letter from her brother nothing will satisfy her but instant removal to this godforsaken pile. Won't even wait till Twelfth Night.'

Well, that was very like Lord Havelock, too. He didn't see the need to wait once he'd made up his mind to do something, either.

'And now she *is* here,' Lady Peverell continued, her voice rising both in volume and pitch, 'she's no better pleased. Not that I'm taking you back, miss, so don't you think I will.'

Julia shot her a look of fury over her shoulder, before folding her arms and glaring out of the window again.

'That is the only thing that made me give in to her badgering. The knowledge that at long last I would be able to wash my hands of her! Even though I can see that we've taken you by surprise, turning up unannounced.'

'Oh, no, not at all….' Mrs Brownlow could have any of the bedrooms in the guest wing ready in a trice. 'It doesn't matter in the least that we didn't know the exact date she would arrive—'

'Stuff,' snorted Lady Peverell. 'And this is how it will *always* be once you have her under your roof. Well, I just hope you have a *very* strong constitution. The girl is a complete hoyden. Selfish and self-willed. Totally impossible.'

Mary didn't believe it for one second. From what Lord Havelock had told her, the poor girl had spent her life being passed around like a parcel. The few weeks during which Mary had undergone such treatment had given her a very good idea of how Julia must feel. Especially since her current guardian was doing what her own relatives had done—talking about what was to become of her as though she had no say, no brains, no will of her own.

And no feelings.

She had just taken a deep breath, to explain, calmly and rationally, that Julia would be a welcome addition to the household, when the door burst open and Lord Havelock strode in.

'Gregory!' With a heart-rending cry, Julia leapt to her feet, flew across the room, flung herself into his out-stretched arms and dissolved into noisy sobs.

'There, there,' he crooned, rocking her in his arms. 'No need to cry. You're safe now. You're home.'

'Oh, for heaven's sake,' muttered Lady Peverell. 'No wonder the girl is so wild. Nobody can ever do anything with her, because she only has to pour out some tale into your ear and you come rushing in to take her side. She's a spoiled madam and it is all your fault.'

Lord Havelock's arms tightened round his sister's heaving shoulders. He glared at Lady Peverell.

'Then you can have no qualms about leaving her in my care, can you?' He jerked his head towards the door. 'Have a safe journey home. I heard you say how busy you are with your house party. Do not let us detain you.'

Mary's jaw dropped. She knew he had a temper. But was he really going to throw Lady Peverell out, after travelling so far, in such horrid weather? She hadn't even had any tea.

But the peevish Lady Peverell didn't appear the least surprised by his attitude. She just got to her feet and gathered her things together with an air of magnificent disdain.

Shooting the siblings one look of sheer loathing, Lady Peverell turned to Mary.

'I wish you luck,' she said. 'Oh, and before I forget, I brought you a small gift. Here,' she said, thrusting the riding crop into the hands Mary had stretched out, impulsively, to implore her not to leave without at least having a cup of tea.

Mary blinked down at the riding crop in confusion. She couldn't ride a horse, so had no need of such a thing. Of course, Lady Peverell couldn't know that. She raised her eyes, trying to form a polite smile of gratitude.

'I've found,' said Lady Peverell, shooting Julia a look of pure malice, 'it's the only way to keep that creature in line.'

With that parting shot, she strode from the room, her nose in the air.

The smile froze on Mary's lips.

There was a beat of silence.

Lord Havelock was looking at her with cool, assessing eyes. And with a start, Mary realised she was still clutching the riding crop in her hands.

With a cry of disgust, she flung it away. It landed on the floor by the window with a clatter that caused Julia to lift her head from her brother's shoulder and look up.

'I would never,' cried Mary, '*ever* use such a thing. Not on an animal, let alone a person!'

'I know,' he snapped.

There was no need for her to say it. She was such a gentle creature—too gentle for her own good, sometimes.

He'd heard Lady Peverell's tirade well before he'd reached the room, her voice was so strident. And though she'd spoken venomously, he couldn't deny there was an element of truth to what he'd overheard. Julia could be...a bit of a handful. She was a Durant, after all, with the Durant will and the Durant temper.

And he could just see her running rings round Mary, given half a chance.

Well, he'd just have to make sure she didn't get a chance.

He stilled as it struck him that Mary's happiness was now just as important to him as Julia's had ever been. Which was ironic, considering he'd only married her so he could provide a home for Julia. Yet now this had become Mary's home, too. She loved it here. He'd watched her blossom in it. Delight in it.

And he didn't want Julia's moods to ruin it all for her. It would be totally unfair to expect her to deal with Julia—in *this* frame of mind, anyway. Not even Lady Peverell could exert any sort of control over his sister, so how could he expect Mary to take her in hand? Why, she couldn't even keep Mrs Brownlow in her place. The dratted woman had promoted herself to the position of housekeeper and was running Mayfield just as she pleased.

'You needn't be afraid of Mary,' he said to Julia. 'She has the kindest heart imaginable. Honestly,' he said when she continued to cling to him, whilst looking at Mary as though she was some kind of ogre. 'I made sure of it before I married her.'

Mary flinched. Made sure of it? How? They'd only known each other a few days before he proposed.

And yet he'd made that list, hadn't he? A list that ensured the woman he picked would provide a home for his beloved, treasured sister. The girl he was holding in his arms. The girl who'd flown to him. Who called him by his given name without thinking, when so far Mary had never dared be so familiar....

She always had to call him *my lord*, or *husband*, or occasionally, when she felt very daring, *Havelock*. Because he'd never invited her to share the intimacy his sister naturally took for granted.

Though she was sure Julia hadn't meant to, the girl had given her a very brutal reminder of what her place in his life really was.

A means to an end.

'She's been very busy,' said her husband to his sister, 'putting this old place to rights, so you could come home.'

'C-can I have my old room back?'

He shook his head. 'Sorry, Ju. The family wing hasn't been used in such a long time it's still a bit of a mess. But there are any number of rooms in what used to be the guest wing you can choose from.'

When she didn't stop pouting, Lord Havelock chucked her under her chin. 'How about coming and having a look? A couple have good views over the stables.'

'The stables?' Julia stopped crying abruptly. 'I…I suppose that would be…' She sniffed and wiped her tear-stained face with the back of one hand.

'And even better,' he went on, before she had the chance to form her thoughts into words, 'I've got something inside the stables that will put a smile back on your face.'

'A new horse? For m-me?'

'Welcome-home present,' he grinned. 'Saw Panther at Tatt's and knew he'd be just the thing to put the roses back in your cheeks. Want to come and meet him?'

Julia shook off her angry, tearful demeanour the way a dog shakes off water after a dunking.

'Oh, yes, please.'

All smiles and arm in arm, brother and sister left the room without a backward glance. As though Mary didn't exist.

And then Mrs Brownlow came in, with a tea tray. Behind her came Susan, who was the chief housemaid, with another tray, laden with cakes and other dainties.

'Where has everyone gone?' Mrs Brownlow looked most put out to find that her efforts to whip up a tray of refreshments for their unexpected visitors had all been for nought.

'Lady Peverell has gone home. And Miss Durant and his lordship have gone to the stables.'

'And what are we to do with miss's luggage?' said Mrs Brownlow, plonking her tray down on the nearest table with a clatter. 'There's boxes and trunks all over the hall. I can't just leave them there. One of my girls will be tripping over them and breaking her leg, I shouldn't wonder. What room shall I have them taken to?'

'You could have them taken up to the guest wing and placed in…oh, I don't know. How about the room that has all that crimson brocaded wallpaper?'

'It's not really suitable for a young girl, my lady. Far better to put her—'

'Well, one of the rooms that overlook the stables, if you please,' she said more firmly. 'And if she doesn't like it, she can pick another one. You needn't unpack anything. Just move her luggage up there, so it is out of your way.'

'Hmmph,' said Mrs Brownlow, before bustling out with Susan in tow.

Leaving Mary in sole charge of an enormous pot of tea, half a dozen cups and more cakes than she could eat in a fortnight.

Chapter Twelve

'Julia, I think you have something to say to Lady Havelock, do you not?'

Julia hunched her shoulders and lowered her head. 'I'm sorry I was rude to you when I got here,' she muttered.

Good grief. Lady Peverell had said Julia was completely unmanageable, but at only a hint from her brother, she'd apologised for her behaviour. Grudgingly, it was true, but it was far more than she'd expected.

And she was very grateful. She hadn't been looking forward to enduring many more dinners like the one they'd just sat through. It had been bad enough getting used to the formality of the immense dining room anyway, and letting footmen wait on her, but having to try to make conversation with a girl who clearly wanted nothing to do with her, whilst grappling with the reminder of her unimportance to her own husband, had been downright demoralising.

'Think no more of it,' she said. 'It sounds as though you've had a perfectly horrid time with Lady Peverell. Frankly, I was appalled at the way she spoke about you as though you weren't even in the room. If it had been me in your shoes...'

She frowned at the recollection that it had been all too easy to picture herself in Julia's place. Though she'd never had the courage to make a fuss, the way Julia had done, or demand her own way. She'd just meekly allowed people to dispose of her as they liked. She'd let them parcel her off like...like a bundle of dirty washing for someone else to launder.

How she wished she had a tithe of Julia's spirit.

'Well, anyway, I just want you to be happy here. It is your home, after all.'

'I don't remember much about when I lived here before,' Julia retorted. 'I was still quite young when Mama married again and we had to move away.'

And yet she'd requested her old room back, reflected Mary.

'We can soon rectify that,' put in Lord Havelock. 'There are some splendid rides to be had in the area. And now you've made the acquaintance of Panther I'm sure you'd like to put him through his paces. Tomorrow I'll start taking you about and introducing you to people.'

Julia's face lit up.

Mary's hackles rose. He'd never offered to take *her* about and introduce her to anyone. He'd never bought her a horse, either. Not that she had any use for one. But that was beside the point. He simply hadn't bothered.

Lord Havelock smiled back at his sister, then turned to Mary with a troubled frown. It was just as well he'd already reined himself in, in an attempt to spare Mary's blushes after that time Brownlow had nearly caught them out. He certainly wouldn't want Julia catching him chasing his wife through the house and tumbling her on sofas. It wasn't the kind of behaviour he wanted his sister to think was acceptable. And, dammit, it wasn't.

He rubbed his hand round the back of his neck, wondering just what had got into him lately. He'd never been one of those fellows who was led by the urgings of his cock. But ever since marrying Mary, he couldn't stop wanting her. Couldn't keep his hands off her.

True, she'd submitted to every demand he made on her and derived pleasure from every encounter, but didn't he owe her more respect?

He'd been a thoroughly selfish sort of husband, so far. He'd promised her she would always have a room of her own, wherever they lived, that nobody else could enter except with her permission. It was pretty much all she'd asked of him. But had he ever honoured that promise? Had he ever knocked on her bedroom door and asked if he could join her? No.

Well, he could rectify that situation tonight. From now on, he'd be the model of decorum.

He still hadn't provided her with the means to purchase her trousseau, either. Nor had she had the time, she'd been so busy putting Mayfield to rights.

Not that she'd complained. Not once. Not about anything. Most women would have nagged him half to death by now, but she just smiled sweetly and made the most of what little she did have.

'You know, it's past time you saw a dressmaker about getting some new clothes,' he said, guilt making his voice a little gruff. 'I know you've been busy, getting the place ready for Julia's arrival, but surely now you can spare the time to spruce yourself up?'

* * *

Spruce herself up? Spruce herself up! Mary took a deep breath and bit back the indignant response she would have given had Julia not been there.

But then that was just it, wasn't it? This was the second time he'd humiliated her by rebuking her in front of someone else. If he had complaints, couldn't he at least show her the courtesy of waiting to make them until they were alone?

It was bad enough feeling that she half deserved it. She'd known from the look on Lady Peverell's face that the way she dressed was letting him down. But did he really have to chide her like this, as though she was a...a...well, someone who wasn't his equal? When she hadn't complained about any of the things he'd done wrong. Not once.

To add insult to injury, neither he, nor his sister, noticed that she was sitting there, quietly simmering with resentment. They were chattering away happily about people she didn't know and places she'd never been.

After what felt like an hour of being comprehensively ignored, Mary'd had enough.

'I am going to bed,' she said, getting to her feet. And then, because she didn't want to be rude, added, 'Goodnight, Julia,' with a forced smile.

'*I'm* not tired,' Julia declared with a toss of her head.

'It has been a long day,' said Lord Havelock, getting to his feet, as well. 'We'll all go up.'

The three of them mounted the stairs in various states of dudgeon. Julia was pouting at being sent to bed before she was ready to go. Mary was still smarting from her husband's cavalier attitude towards her tonight and tallying up all the other things he'd done to annoy her.

And Lord Havelock looked distinctly uncomfortable at being flanked by two women who were in the sulks.

'What do you think of the room Mary chose for you?' he asked with determined cheerfulness as they mounted the stairs.

Julia shrugged.

'You can always move to another if it's not to your liking. What about this one?' He flung open the door to a room they'd slept in only once. Mary hadn't liked it much. The wall hangings were of a cold greyish-blue, liberally spattered with muddy-hued hunting prints.

'I'm in here, for the moment,' said Lord Havelock, to Mary's surprise, 'but I can soon shift if you prefer it.'

Julia peeped inside, wrinkled her nose and shook her head. 'I like the red room better,' she said.

Heavens, Mary reflected sourly. She'd actually got something right today.

'Good. Mary is in here,' he said, striding to the door of the bedroom she had assumed they would be sharing.

'It's rather poky,' said Julia, taking a quick glance round the room that Mary found so cosy that it had become her favourite. It was easy to keep warm, the chimney didn't smoke and the walls were decorated in a very restful shade of green, with sunny little details in gold here and there.

And then, as one, the siblings bid her goodnight and turned away, arm in arm.

She stared at the door they'd shut behind them on their way out.

What was going on?

And then various snippets of conversations she'd had

began to trickle into her mind. The one she'd had with Mrs Brownlow, only the day before, about how lords and ladies always had their own bedrooms, dressing rooms and sitting rooms. About how her husband would have the ones that had been his father's, while she would have the other, prettier set. How she'd sadly accepted that one day, when the rooms were ready, he would move into his and she into hers.

She'd assumed, until that day, things would carry on as they were. But no. He'd stated, quite firmly, that he would be sleeping in that horrid blue room, while she was to sleep alone in here.

The worst of it was she'd look a complete idiot if she voiced a protest. Because she'd said, before they got married, that she *wanted* her own room. That she valued her privacy.

But privacy, she now realised, was the last thing she wanted. She'd got used to sharing her room with her husband. To sharing her life with him.

No—it was more than that.

Why hadn't she seen it sooner?

She uttered a strained little laugh. Over the years, watching her father's brutality towards her mother, she'd feared the power a husband had over his wife. She'd feared the deliberate oppression of a man bent on ruling his household with a rod of iron. And when she'd discovered her own husband wasn't the kind of man to treat anyone with cruelty, she'd let down her guard completely.

And fallen headlong in love with him.

Which meant he now had the power to hurt her without even noticing. The way he'd done today. Showering his sister with all the affection and attention he would never, ever, give her.

'Stupid, stupid,' she muttered to herself as tears welled and seeped down her cheeks.

Why hadn't she guarded herself against falling in love?

Because she hadn't expected to do anything so stupid, that's why. She didn't even *like* men, as a rule. But Lord Havelock had entered her life like a whirlwind, sweeping her off her feet and into his arms. Totally overwhelming her with his generous, open nature. His spontaneity. His beautiful face and muscular body. His incredible lovemaking.

But now, like the whirlwind of a man he was, he was sweeping right on past her. His focus was all on his sister now. And she was left standing here alone, pining for a man who'd been completely honest about what he wanted from her from the start. And that didn't include *affection*, let alone love.

She'd excused him for not chasing her all over the house now that it was teeming with servants. Had told herself she was imagining he was being a bit more restrained when he came to bed.

But he wasn't the type of man to exercise restraint. He did whatever he wanted, whenever he wanted.

He was bored with her, that's what it was. Why else would he have moved into a room of his own?

Unless it was because, from his point of view, the honeymoon was over.

Hadn't he warned her that his ardour wouldn't last very long? Oh, he'd couched it in terms of them going off each other, but that was what it boiled down to.

She was, after all, only a mouse.

She sucked in a great, shuddering sigh, swiping angrily at the tears she'd been weak enough to shed.

She'd never realised how boring he must have found it, spending the evenings alone with her, until she'd watched his face transformed by the amusing little anecdotes Julia could supply.

He chose that very moment to knock on the door. She only just had time to dash the back of her hand across her face, to swipe away the few tears she hadn't been able to prevent from leaking out, before he came in.

The fact that he was grinning, as though he hadn't a care in the world, felt like a slap to her face. He had no idea how badly he'd hurt her.

Well, of course he hadn't. She wouldn't *be* hurt if she'd managed to stick to the agreement to keep their marriage free from emotion. And she wasn't going to admit she was hurt either, by things he'd consider stupidly trivial.

She drew herself up to her full height and dammed up the flood of tears she wanted to shed behind a façade of pride.

'What,' she said coldly, 'do you want?'

His smile turned downright wicked. 'You know perfectly well what I want,' he said, moving towards her.

But he couldn't want it all that much any more, or he wouldn't have decided it was time to have separate rooms.

She held up her hand, stopping him from coming any closer. How long would it be before separate rooms became separate lives altogether? Before they embarked on the second stage of their marriage? The one where they scarcely saw each other any more?

'It's not what I want!'

Her outburst wiped the smile from his face. 'Is something wrong?'

Wrong? Only the fact that she'd just discovered she no longer wanted a room of her own. That she'd be content to live entirely in *one* room, and cook for him, and do his laundry, and, yes, even wash his dishes without a word of complaint, if only she could be sure she mattered to him. Even half as much as his sister did.

In spite of her determination to avoid the humiliation of bursting into tears, she felt her lower lip start to tremble.

'Wrong?' She managed to produce a laugh and a toss of her head. 'What could possibly be wrong?'

He eyed her up and down dubiously.

'I don't know. But I'd have to be blind not to see that something is wrong. You look, ah...'

Suddenly, she became conscious of the frayed hem of her gown and the patches on her petticoat.

'In need of sprucing up?'

Suddenly, it seemed much easier to let him think he'd offended her with the criticism of her clothing, than to admit she'd breached the terms of their agreement. Temper he would understand. But love? No—to speak of love, when he'd warned her it was the last thing he wanted, would only serve to make her seem utterly ridiculous in his eyes.

'Yes,' she therefore said as waspishly as she could manage. 'You've made your point. Don't worry. I will find a dressmaker locally and smarten myself up so that I don't offend your neighbours with my shabby clothing.'

'Look here—I didn't mean to offend you—'

'You didn't!' And wasn't that the truth? But by flinging her head high, and letting some of her hurt flash from her eyes, she could give him the impression that he had.

'Mary...' He came towards her, hands outstretched, an apologetic expression on his face.

She backed away hastily. For once she let him take her in his arms, she wouldn't be able to hold herself together any longer. She'd break down and sob into his chest. Like the idiot she was. And, being the man he was, he wouldn't rest until he'd winkled the truth from her.

And then her humiliation would be complete.

'That's far enough,' she snapped, holding up her hand to halt him. 'I am not in the mood for...for...'

Actually, that was true, too. She most certainly wasn't in the mood for the decorous brand of lovemaking that only went on behind closed doors, not any longer. Not when she knew he was capable of so much more.

Not when she *wanted* so much more.

His face closed up.

'Forgive me,' he said, looking very far from apologetic any longer. 'I have no wish to annoy you. So I'll take myself off.' He turned on his heel and stalked to the door. 'Goodnight,' he tossed over his shoulder as he went out.

The moment the door snicked shut, her legs gave out, her resolve gave out and the tears flooded out.

How could he just turn and walk away, without making even a token protest? Even a few days ago, he would have done his utmost to cajole her into bed.

But then how could she have hoped to hold his interest? She just wasn't an interesting person. She was a mouse, that was all. That was why he'd picked her. Because there wasn't the slightest risk he would ever feel anything for such a creature.

She wasn't anything special, even if he had made her feel as though she was, for those few, heady days. Of course he'd enjoyed the adventure of the situation. Of foraging for themselves, and letting go of all the restraints society imposed on men and women. It was nothing to do with being stranded, alone, with *her*.

The only reason she'd had his undivided attention, when they'd first arrived, was because there wasn't anyone else there.

For the whole of the following week, every time he knocked at her bedroom door and she turned him away, she told herself she was doing the right thing to make a stand. Not letting him walk all over her and treat her like some plaything he could pick up, or set down, as the whim took him.

Yes—she had the satisfaction of sending him away looking disgruntled. But it was a bittersweet kind of satisfaction. She'd much rather he put up more of a protest. Instead, the way he simply turned and walked away convinced her he just wasn't interested any more, and that the only reason he did persist in coming to her room was because he wanted an heir. It was the second most important reason he'd given for marrying her.

Every day, she grew more and more unhappy, as he made it perfectly plain in dozens of little ways that he didn't return a tithe of her feelings.

He was out practically all day, for one thing, galloping all over the countryside with his intrepid sister. They came back full of stories about the people they'd met and the feats they'd performed, all couched in a kind of jargon that was well-nigh incomprehensible to her.

Not that either of them was unkind to her. They just

made her feel like the odd one out, so alike were they. It wasn't just in their looks. They were both happiest outdoors, on horseback, wearing clothes that didn't fetter their movements.

Whereas she didn't like going outside at all in winter. Having known what it was to fear being homeless, she relished being able to sit indoors in front of a blazing fire.

She didn't even need to go into the village to visit a dressmaker. After consulting Mrs Brownlow about who might be suitable, the housekeeper sent for a local woman, who brought fabric samples and pattern books to Mayfield.

The only time Mary left the house was to attend church on Sundays. People flocked round, after the service, for introductions, but Julia was so much more lively that they invariably ended up talking to her, rather than Mary. Especially since they remembered Julia from when she'd been a little girl. Anyway, Mary felt downright uncomfortable when people curtsied to her and called her my lady, when she still felt like an impostor, so tended to hang back, behind her husband and his sister, and let them bear the brunt of local curiosity.

Apart from Sundays, each day fell into the same dreary pattern. She'd drag herself out of bed after hearing her husband and his sister go out and go down to the deserted dining room to eat breakfast alone. She'd listen to Mrs Brownlow's suggestions for meals, have a fitting, or try on a new outfit, then sit in front of a fire, toasting her toes and wishing she could be content with her new, lazy, luxurious lifestyle.

She could have spent ten times the amount of money she'd laid out on her new clothes and didn't think her husband would have flinched. Julia was even starting to return her tentative smiles, once she'd realised Mary had no intention of trying to change a single thing about her. She'd even confided, one evening at supper, when Mary had put on the first of her new gowns, that a lot of the trouble with Lady Peverell had stemmed from her attempts to turn Julia into one of those fashionably demure girls who would have done her credit in a ballroom.

Lord Havelock had laughed. 'You're a hoyden, Ju. A regular out-and-outer. You'd cause havoc in a ballroom.'

He'd had a sort of fond twinkle in his eye as he said it that showed he was proud of his sister just as she was.

And Mary's spirits sank even lower. *She'd* never cause havoc in a ballroom. Why, the first night they'd met, he'd had to virtually drag her out from behind that potted palm.

No wonder he'd thought she was a mouse.

And still did. Because she was acting like one. Putting up with the way he and his sister overlooked her. Putting up with his coolness towards her in the bedroom, too.

What had happened to her determination to make a stand? To her wistful yearning to have some of Julia's spirit? Hadn't she decided, the day Julia arrived, that she ought to cease being the kind of woman who let others post her round the country like a parcel?

Spending the days waiting for her husband to come home, only to endure his obvious preference for his sister, was draining what little self-respect she'd ever had.

What was the point in hanging around, hoping he might, one day, come to return her feelings? He'd told her in no uncertain terms it was the last thing he wanted from a wife. And how would she attempt to go about it, anyway? There was nothing about her to attract him. She sat there, night after night, with nothing to add to the conversation apart from domestic trivia that was bound to bore him.

Eventually he would cease knocking on her bedroom door at all. And then what would she do? It made her feel like a condemned woman, waiting for the axe to fall.

And then one night, it all became too much. While she was waiting in her bedroom, half-convinced this would be the night he gave up, her stomach contracted into a cold knot. Sweat beaded her upper lip. For a moment, she thought she might actually be sick.

Head swirling, she tottered to her dressing-table stool and sank down on to it, shutting her eyes.

When the room stopped spinning, she lifted her head and stared bleakly at her wan reflection. She couldn't go on like this. Enduring his indifference was taking its toll on her health.

And the only way she might, just might be able to recover from this hopelessly painful case of unrequited love would be to remove herself from the situation altogether. Surely, if she spent some time away from him, she'd be able to get used to the idea of living separate lives?

And at least she'd be the one doing the separating. She would be able to leave with her head held high, rather than collapsing in floods of tears if he should be the one to go.

So, when he knocked on the door, she didn't bother getting up from her stool. Taking her brush in her hand, she began to swipe it through her hair, to disguise the fact that her hands were shaking.

'Any point in asking if I may stay tonight?' His face

bore the look of resignation he'd adopted after her very first refusal.

'None,' she said tartly, carrying on brushing her hair. 'Though before you go,' she added hastily, as he turned on his heel, 'I may as well inform you that I plan to go to London tomorrow.'

'London?' He swivelled round, his brows drawing down into a knot. 'What the devil for?'

Did his frown mean he didn't want her to leave, after all? Would he ask her to stay? And if he did, would she do it? Would she carry on trying to endure, just so she could be near him?

'I...' Well, she couldn't tell him the truth, could she? That loving a man who was never going to love her back was destroying her.

'I thought I might buy some more clothes. For...for the Season.'

'The Season?' He looked thunderstruck. 'But you've just bought a whole lot of clothes, haven't you?'

'Yes. But...' She did some quick thinking. 'They have been made by a provincial dressmaker. Society people will know.'

'I wouldn't have thought you would want to mingle with society people. Or take part in the Season.'

No. Because he didn't think she would fit in.

Which was true enough, but, oh, so insulting.

'It isn't just for me though, is it? I shall have to start paving the way for Julia to make her come-out, won't I?'

'I don't see that at all,' he snapped. 'I've plenty of aunts and such who have the entrée into the kind of circles where Julia will find a husband, once she gives any sign of wanting to look for one.'

So, he intended to sideline her even when it came to

Julia's come-out, did he? He was going to get some aunt, with the proper connections, to launch her?

Setting down her hairbrush, she half turned on her stool and glared at him.

'You promised me I could do as I pleased, as long as I don't cause a scandal. And I feel like going to London and buying some fashionable clothes. I don't think that is the slightest bit scandalous. Do you?'

'No. But, hang it, Julia has only just got here. You leaving so soon may well cause talk. Couldn't you…wait a bit? And we can all go up together?'

Together? They wouldn't be together. He would be with Julia and she would be hovering on the fringes. Enduring the pain of being the unwanted, unloved wife in a new location, that was all.

And the fact that he was bringing Julia's welfare into the equation was the last straw. Julia. Julia. It was always Julia who mattered. Not her.

Well, two could play at that game.

'And what sort of state is Durant House in, do you happen to know? Will it be fit for her to move into? I really do think it would be better if I went on ahead and checked. After all, one of the reasons you asked me to marry you was to refurbish the place.'

Hoist with his own petard. He turned and walked over to the fireplace, so she couldn't see the devastation her words had wrought. He'd known this day would come. Every time he'd knocked on her bedroom door and been turned away, he'd felt it coming closer.

Even so, he hadn't expected it to hurt so much. Dammit, he'd taken steps to ensure it wouldn't! He'd deliberately picked a woman who wouldn't expect too much from him, who wouldn't nag him for more than he was willing to give. He'd even sat down and spelled out the terms of their marriage, to make sure neither of them would get hurt.

What he hadn't factored in was that Mary would work her way so far under his skin that hearing she wanted to leave him was like having every single bone removed from his body.

Moodily, he kicked at a smouldering log, sending sparks flying up the chimney, when what he really wanted to do was yell, and rampage up and down, and hit something. But he'd learned his lesson, fighting that second duel. As he'd stood there with the smoking pistol in his hand, watching Wraxton fall to the earth with blood gushing down his neck, he'd known he had to change. Never attempting to keep his temper in check had brought him to the brink of killing a man. He'd grown up, that day. He was no longer a child who might be forgiven for lashing out when people let him down, or hurt him.

Though this was the very reason he had got into the habit of lashing out. His temper had kept people at bay. He'd learned early on that all people did was hurt him, if he let them get close.

Lord, what a fool he'd been to have thought his marriage could be any different, because he'd entered into it with such a cool head and with so little expectation. All marriages ended in misery, one way or another.

Fortunately for Mary, the wave of misery he felt drowned his anger completely. It was no use raging at her and forbidding her to leave. She wouldn't understand. He *had* promised her she could come and go as she pleased. That he would let her spend his money as she liked. That he wouldn't kick up a fuss.

And lord knew, she'd put up with him far longer than any other woman had, before losing her patience.

And none of this was Mary's fault. She had no idea she was wounding him. So he would take her departure like a gentleman, not a savage. He would be cool and calm. Polite.

When he eventually turned to her, he'd got himself under control. So far under control that he felt as though ice was flowing through his veins, rather than warm, red blood.

'Just as you wish, of course.' He could hear the ice that was freezing his insides dripping from his words. 'I will furnish you with the direction of my man of business. You must send all the bills to him.'

He sauntered past her and made it to the door. Hesitated. Swallowed.

He couldn't bear the thought of her travelling alone. Of perhaps running into difficulties and having nobody to take care of her. But since she was so independent, so capable, so used to doing everything for herself, she wouldn't think there was any need. 'You will take one of the maids with you,' he bit out. 'You have an appearance to keep up now you are my viscountess. You cannot go jauntering off all over the place on your own. It won't do.'

Chapter Thirteen

Mary didn't feel as if she'd slept at all. Yet the sound of the maid making up the fire and drawing back the curtains the next morning definitely woke her up, so she must have done.

She almost groaned at the thought of facing the day. If only she could pull the covers over her head and hide. Actually, she supposed she could. She could have a tray brought up here, to her room, rather than going downstairs and facing a deserted breakfast table.

While she waited for it to arrive, she heard the sound of hooves trotting past her window. Two sets of hooves. Just as usual. She clenched her fists. While she felt as if her world was coming to an end, her husband and his sister were going out riding. Without a care in the world.

Lord Havelock had exactly what he wanted. Julia was safely ensconced under his roof. Nobody would think it necessary to investigate her hasty removal from Lady Peverell's care. He'd quashed the potential for rumours by marrying.

Yes, he'd got what he wanted, all right. And now she, his wife, was surplus to requirements. In every single way. He'd even made it plain she wouldn't be of any help whatsoever when it came round to Julia's Season.

And very well, it was true that Mary had never had a Season. Didn't know anyone in society. And had no idea how to handle the bevy of suitors that Julia, with her wealth and vivacity, was bound to attract.

She supposed Julia *would* need someone like Lady Peverell, who had at least mingled with the kind of people Lord Havelock would consider eligible, to steer her through that rite of passage. But had it really been necessary for him to rub her nose in all her shortcomings like that?

She was already dealing with the knowledge she wasn't of any practical use around the house any longer. Mrs Brownlow and her team had everything running like clockwork. Even when she consulted Mary about menus it only served to emphasise that Mrs Brownlow knew what were his lordship's favourite dishes, and what was available locally, and who the best suppliers were. While Mary didn't.

Making Mary fully aware how useless she really was. He'd scarcely notice when she'd gone.

By the time a knock on the door heralded the arrival of a couple of maids bearing her breakfast, her insides were so churned up that the last thing she wanted to do was eat. Throw something, yes, that might have made her feel better. But since the man she wanted to aim the teapot at was probably halfway across the county by now, she couldn't have the satisfaction.

Besides, it hadn't been that long ago when she hadn't known where the next meal might come from. She couldn't squander perfectly good food without suffering a terrible backlash of guilt.

So she accepted the tray, let the maid pour her tea and set a slice of toast on her plate.

And in a cold, leaden voice, instructed one of them to pack her clothes.

'Of course, my lady,' said Susan cheerfully, going to the armoire and lifting down the shabby portmanteau. 'His lordship has said as how you'd be going up to town to buy some new clothes for the Season.'

Oh, had he? Mary took a vicious bite of toast and chewed it thoroughly.

'And I'm to go with you,' she said, setting the portmanteau on the floor in front of the open cupboard. 'Gilbey is preparing the coach,' she added, reaching up for a gown and taking it off its hanger.

Mary's hand froze halfway to her mouth. Gilbey was preparing the coach? 'I'm that excited,' babbled Susan as she draped the gown over the back of a chair. 'I've never been further than Stoney Bottom in my life.'

Mary threw the toast back on to its plate, her stomach roiling. Her husband had given orders to all the servants to hasten her departure, had he? Couldn't wait to get her out of his house and out of his life, in fact.

It felt like a blow to the gut. So real was her pain that she had to fling back the covers and hurry over to the washbasin, over which she heaved for a moment or two before sinking back on to the dressing-table stool, her face clammy with sweat.

'Oh, my lady, are you ill? Shall I cancel the coach? You surely don't want to go anywhere today, if you're poorly.'

Mary shook her head. 'I shall be fine in a moment.' She wasn't ill. Or at least it was only her husband's rejection of her that was making her sick to her stomach.

The nights spent weeping quietly into her pillow. The days spent sitting alone, feeling thoroughly useless.

And she wasn't going to get any better by carrying on in the same way. No—the only way she was likely to find a cure was to get as far away from him as she could and lick her wounds in private.

'Carry on with the packing, Susan.'

'Yes, my lady, if you're sure.'

Rather more soberly now, Susan folded and stowed Mary's new clothes into her old portmanteau while Mary got washed and dressed. Rather shakily.

Her whole body hurt, not just her heart. How could she have let him reduce her to this shivering, quivering wreck of a woman?

Without even trying, that was the most galling thing. He hadn't made any pretty speeches, or given her flowers, or anything. He'd just brusquely told her his requirements, more or less snapped his fingers, and she'd gone trotting after him, all eager to please. Had kept on trying to please him, day after day.

Even though she knew it was pointless.

Because she'd read that horrid list.

A list, she recalled on a mounting wave of bitterness, she'd had to fit, to pass muster. When she'd had to accept him exactly as he was.

Which was completely and totally unfair.

She came to a dead halt in the middle of the floor, pain and resentment surging through her.

If he could measure out her worth according to some stupid list, then why shouldn't she treat him to a dose of his own medicine?

Uttering a growl of frustration, she stormed over to the table under the window where she'd taken to sitting to write her correspondence, pulled out a fresh sheet of paper, trimmed her pen and stabbed it into the inkwell.

What I want from a husband, she wrote at the top of the page, underlining the *I* twice.

Need not have a penny to his name, she wrote first, recalling his stipulation that his bride need not have a dowry.

Can be plug-ugly, she wrote next, recalling how hurt she'd been by his stipulation she need not be pretty, *so long as he will love his wife and treat her like a queen, not a scullery maid.*

Said love will include respecting his wife, being kind to her and listening to her opinions.

Not only will he listen to her opinions, she wrote, underlining the word *listen, he will consider them before he pitches her into a situation she would naturally shrink from.*

Won't deny his wife the right to feel like a bride on her wedding day.

Will appreciate having any living relatives—underlining the word *any* twice.

Need not have a title. But if he has one, it ought to be one he earned. One lieutenant in his Majesty's navy, she explained, remembering her own brother's heroic deeds and his death fighting the enemies of her country, *is worth a dozen viscounts.*

By that time, she'd reached the bottom of the page. And splattered as much ink over the writing desk as she'd scored into the paper.

And had realised what a futile exercise it was.

She wasn't married to a plug-ugly man who treated her like a queen. She was married to a handsome, wealthy lord, who thought it was enough to let her spend his money however she wanted.

She flung the quill aside, got to her feet and went to the bed, on which Susan had laid out her coat and bonnet.

The coat in which she'd got married. With such high hopes.

Before she'd read his vile list and discovered what he really thought of her.

Well, futile it might be, but she was jolly well going to let him know what she thought of him, too. Before she walked out of his house and his life.

Telling Susan she could go and collect her own things, Mary buttoned up the coat and pinned on her hat.

Then snatched up the list she'd just written, stormed along the corridor to the horrid blue room where her husband had taken up residence and slapped the list on to the bed.

And then, recalling the way the list *he'd* written had ended up fluttering across the floor when the door shut, and knowing she was on the verge of *slamming* the one to this room on her way out any second now, she wrenched out her hatpin and thrust it through the list, skewering it savagely to his pillow.

And with head held high, she strode along the corridor, down the stairs and out of his house.

God, but it had been a long day. He'd kept putting off returning to Mayfield, knowing that when he did return, Mary would have gone. But Julia was tired, cold and hungry, and in the end he'd had to bring her back. Had come upstairs to get changed for dinner.

The first dinner of his married life that he'd have to face without his wife at his table.

He had at least the satisfaction of knowing he'd done what he could to make sure her journey would be as easy as he could make it, without actually going with her. She'd been able to use the travelling coach, which had only just come back from the workshop. He hadn't had to hire a chaise, and leave her in the care of strangers. Gilbey was an excellent whip. And she had a maid to save her from impertinent travellers at the stops on the way. He—

He came to a halt just inside the door to his room, transfixed by the sight of a single sheet of paper, staked to his pillow by what looked remarkably like a hatpin.

So she had left a farewell note. He'd wondered if she would. Heart pounding, he strode across to the bed, hoping that she… She what? A note that was staked to his bed with a symbolically lethal weapon was hardly going to contain the kinds of fond parting words he wanted to read, was it?

But it might at least give him a clue as to where he'd gone wrong with her. Why she'd withdrawn from him when, to start with, she'd seemed so eager to please. So eager to please, in fact, that after her first refusal, he'd told himself she must be going through that mysterious time of the month that afflicted every woman of child-bearing age. It had only been when she'd kept on refusing to allow him into her bed that the chill reality struck.

She simply didn't want him any more.

Well, hopefully, this note would explain why.

He snatched it up and carried it to the window, so he could make out the words in the fading light of late afternoon.

Only to see the words *What I want from a husband* scrawled across the top of the page.

With the word *I* underlined.

A chill stole down the length of his spine as he scanned the whole page. Because it wasn't just a damning indictment of all his faults. It was worse, far worse than that.

The way she'd set it out, even the way she'd underlined certain words, the very choice of words she'd used—all of it meant she must have read the damn stupid list he and his friends had written, the night he'd decided he was going to start looking for a wife.

A list he'd never meant her to know about, let alone read.

No wonder she hadn't wanted to sleep with him any more. She must be so hurt....

No—that couldn't be right. Heart hammering, he strode along the corridors to the bureau in his father's rooms, where he'd taken to stashing his bills and letters. And found the list locked away, exactly where he'd put it when he'd moved here. Since he had the key on a fob on his waistcoat and that key had never been out of his possession, it meant she must have read it before they reached Mayfield.

And still done her utmost to be a good wife to him. He shut his eyes, grimacing as he recalled one instance after another, when she'd made the best of his blunders while all the while she must have been trying to overlook *this*.

Well, he'd just have to go after her. Tell her he'd never meant to hurt her...

He got as far as the corridor, before it struck him that he'd never done anything *but* hurt her. Blundering, clumsy fool that he was...he'd watched her growing more and more depressed with every day that passed, wishing he knew what to say, how to reach her.

And now he saw that it had never been possible. There was no way he could defend the indefensible.

No wonder she'd left him. *He* would have left him if he'd been married to such an oaf!

He staggered back into his father's rooms, dropped into the nearest chair and put his head in his hands.

What was he going to do? How was he going to explain this to her? Win her back?

Win her back? He'd never had her to win back. Because he'd told her he wasn't looking for affection from marriage.

And this was why.

When men fell in love, it made them weak, vulnerable. God, he hadn't even realised he *had* fallen in love with Mary, until just now, when he'd read her list and realised how much she must hate him. Felt the pain of her fury pierce his heart the way her hatpin had pierced the soft down of his pillow.

His feelings for her had crept up behind him and ambushed him while he'd been distracted by congratulating himself for being clever enough to write that list and pick such a perfect woman.

Why hadn't he seen that picking the perfect woman would practically ensure he *would* fall in love with her?

Because he was a fool, that was why.

A fool to think he could marry a girl like Mary, and live with her, and make love to her, and be able to keep his heart intact.

Let alone keep her at his side.

She'd gone and he couldn't really blame her.

All he could do was hope she'd find the happiness, away from him, that he couldn't give her himself.

And find some way of coming to terms with it all.

Gilbey informed Mary that the roads were too bad to make the journey all in one stage, so they stopped at an inn that wasn't anywhere near as bad as her husband had led her to believe might be the case.

It probably helped that she stalked into the building, still hurt and angry at her husband, and ready to take it out on whoever happened to cross her next. Susan did her part, too, making up the bed in the best chamber with sheets Mrs Brownlow had provided, with such disdain for the hotel's bedding that all the staff treated Mary as though she was a duchess. But all the bowing and scraping from the landlord and his minions could not quite compensate Mary for the knowledge that when her husband had travelled with her, he'd hired a well-sprung, comfy little post-chaise, rather than put up with the antiquated, lumbering carriage that Gilbey had unearthed from somewhere. When she'd travelled with him, she hadn't ended up aching all over and feeling so sick and dizzy that she would have cheerfully curled up on the rug in front of the fire, just as long as she could get her head down.

And then, of course, thoughts of spending nights on hearthrugs in front of fires had churned her insides up so much that she could have been offered the finest, softest feather bed, and it would still have felt like an instrument of torture.

It was past noon by the time Mary reached London the following day. She heaved a sigh of relief when she

finally alighted outside one of the largest, most imposing mansions she had ever seen.

Gilbey, and the horrid carriage, disappeared round
the side of the house at once. Taking the precious horses
to the warmth of their luxurious stables, she supposed.
Susan, carrying Mary's bag, mounted the steps ahead
of her and knocked on the glossily painted, black front
door.

'Lady Havelock, you say?' The butler who opened the
door raised one eyebrow in a way that implied he very
much doubted it. 'We received no notice of your intention to take up residence.'

This was a problem Mary hadn't anticipated, though
perhaps she should have done. It was just like her husband to have forgotten to inform the most relevant people involved.

'Well, I'm not spending another night in a hotel,' she
snapped. One had been more than enough. And she was
blowed if she was going to write to him and tell him his
servants wouldn't let her into the house he'd promised
she could treat as her own. She'd come to London in
part to prove that she could stand on her own two feet.
Survive without him. She wasn't going to crumble, and
beg for his help, at the very first sign of trouble.

'What's to do, Mr Simmons?'

A stern-looking, grey-haired lady came up behind
the butler, who was obstinately barring the way into the
house, and peered over his shoulder.

'There is a person claiming to be Lady Havelock,'
said the butler disapprovingly.

'Well, the notice was in the *Gazette*, so I dare say his
lordship *has* married somebody.'

While the butler and the woman she assumed was

the housekeeper discussed the likelihood of her being an impostor, Mary's temper, which had been on a low simmer all the way to London, came rapidly to a boil.

She'd had enough of people talking about her as if she wasn't there. Of making decisions for her, and about her, and packing her off to London in ramshackle coaches to houses where nobody either expected or welcomed her.

'It's all very well thinking it is your duty to guard my husband's property from impostors,' she pointed out in accents that were as freezing as the rain that had just started to fall. 'But if you value your positions at all...'

'That's 'er, right enough,' a third voice piped up, preventing her from saying exactly how she would exact retribution. 'Leastaways,' said a small boy, who pushed his way between the butler and the housekeeper, 'she's the one wot was wiv 'is lordship when he saved me from the nubbing cheat.'

'Indeed?' The butler's expression underwent a most satisfying change. At about the same moment she recognised the little boy. The last time she'd seen him, he'd been dressed in rags and her husband had been dragging him out of Westminster Abbey by the scruff of his neck.

'My goodness, but you've changed,' said Mary to the boy. He'd not only filled out, but seemed to have grown taller, too. Of course that might have been an illusion, caused by the fact that he wasn't cowering. Or wearing filthy, ill-fitting clothes. And the fact that his hair was clean, and neatly brushed.

'That's wot plenty of grub and a reg'lar bob ken'll do fer yer,' said the former pickpocket, with a grin.

'He means,' put in the butler, having swiped the lad round the back of the head, 'that he is grateful to his lordship for saving him from the threat of the hangman's noose, taking him in and giving him a clean home where he has regular meals. And though we oblige him to wash regularly, I am sad to say that we are still teaching young Jem to speak the King's English, rather than the dreadful language he acquired in the gutter that spawned him.'

The hangman's noose…

Mary's mind went into a sort of dizzy spin, during which time several apparently random items fell rather more neatly into place. Her husband's assurance to his sister that he'd made sure she was kind-hearted, her inability to work out how he could have done so, the lad's pleading for mercy from Mr Morgan and the verger…

And the clincher—this lad's total lack of fear, even when surrounded by his accusers, threatening him with gaol.

'No real fear of the noose though, was there, Jem?' she said acidly. 'It was just a prank Lord Havelock put you up to, wasn't it?'

The urchin's grin widened. 'No putting anything past you, is there, missus?'

The butler swatted him again. 'It is your ladyship, not missus,' he corrected the boy.

It might have been something in Mary's expression as she realised what a fool her husband had made of her, time after time, or the lad's vouching for her character, or her own veiled threat—but for whatever reason, the housekeeper was beginning to look rather alarmed.

'Your ladyship,' she said, pushing both butler and boy to one side. 'Please come in out of the rain. We are so sorry you have caught us all unawares.'

'Yes, indeed,' said the butler, wresting his attention from the boy to his new mistress and permitting Mary to finally step inside Durant House.

The hall was massive. And dark. So dark she couldn't see to the far end of it. That was due in part to the shoulder-high wainscoting, which seemed to suck up what little light filtered in through the few windows that hadn't been shuttered. She couldn't see the ceiling either, no matter how far she craned her neck. But from the echo to the butler's and housekeeper's voices, she judged it was very, very high. On either side of the hall was a dark and ornately carved staircase, which ran by several stages, interspersed with half landings, up under a series of grimly glowering portraits until all disappeared into the murk above a gallery landing.

She wasn't surprised her husband had likened it to a mausoleum.

'We do not, just at present, even have anywhere for you to sit and take tea while we make your room ready,' said the housekeeper nervously. 'Everything is under holland covers.'

Mary wondered how the housekeeper would react if she simply went down to the kitchens and made herself a pot of tea?

But the poor woman had probably sustained enough shocks for one day.

'I dare say you have your very own sitting room,' said Mary. 'Which I'm sure you keep comfortable enough for my needs, for now.'

'Oh, yes, well, I do. Of course I do, your ladyship,' said the housekeeper, torn between relief that her mistress wasn't going to demand another room be made ready at once and consternation at having her invade her territory. 'It's this way,' she said, pragmatism winning.

When Susan scuttled off somewhere with her portmanteau, Mary did her best to calm down. It wasn't fair to take her hurt and anger out on servants.

'Even if we had known you were coming,' said the housekeeper apologetically as she poured the tea, 'I wouldn't have rightly known what room to show you into. The whole place has got that shabby.'

'I know that there is a lot of work to be done here,' said Mary, reaching for a slice of cake. 'It is, in part, why Lord Havelock married me.' Though the reminder depressed her, it seemed to have the opposite effect on the housekeeper.

'Well, now,' she said, perching on the very edge of her chair, 'I'm that glad to hear it. That agent who acts for his lordship—well, I suppose he thinks he has his lordship's best interests at heart, but—'

It was like a dam bursting. The housekeeper had clearly been storing up a lot of grievances. As they all came pouring out, Mary helped herself to a second slice of cake and turned her chair so that she could rest her feet on the fender. Her appetite had come roaring back now she was at journey's end and there was no risk of getting back into that vile coach again. And met a house-keeper who was actually *glad* she'd come. And had a task to perform that would bring benefit to not only her husband, but to all the souls who lived in Durant House.

'I think,' said Mary, once she felt she simply couldn't cram in any more of the delicious fruit cake, 'that you should show me all over the place. So that I can get an idea of exactly what will be required.'

The tour took them right up to suppertime. Mary had known that titled families often owned houses in the town as well as having country estates, but somehow she'd never dreamed her husband would own such an impressive, if sadly neglected one. Neither he, nor his father, the housekeeper informed her, had taken any interest in the maintenance of what had originally been built as something of a showpiece.

Now every room cried out for attention. No wonder he'd moved into a set of cosy apartments and rented this place out. Not only was the amount of work required daunting for a bachelor, it was just too large for one person to live in alone.

Though living here alone was to be her fate, she reflected gloomily.

She felt even more alone when, at suppertime, the housekeeper came to escort her to the hastily tidied dining room and led her to the solitary place at the head of a table that could easily have seated thirty.

As attentive footmen served her course after course, she recalled her bold words about how a lick of paint and rearranging furniture could make any place feel more like home. She almost snorted into her soup. It would take more than that to make this dining room a comfortable place to eat her meals. But since she had no intention of leaving, she would just have to think of something else.

Perhaps there was a smaller, more convenient room in which she could eat her meals. Straight after the last footman had removed the last dish from the table, she went to see if she could find one. And very soon came across a little drawing room off the back of the entrance hall that overlooked the central courtyard around which the house was built. The fountain, which was on the housekeeper's list of repairs, was just outside the window. It would make a very soothing background noise once she got a plumber in to get it working again.

She rang for the housekeeper at once.

When Mrs Romsey arrived, Mary told her that from now on, she wanted to have all her meals served there. And between them, they decided how best to rearrange what furniture there was, to make such a change of use possible.

And then, having started to put her own stamp on the place, Mary suddenly felt bone-weary.

Though she went upstairs, she wasn't yet ready to climb into the bed where she was going to be sleeping alone for the foreseeable future.

Instead, she went into the sitting room that adjoined her bedroom, where she'd earlier seen a writing desk. Mrs Romsey had told her that the desk contained a supply of paper, should she wish to write any letters. Now that she'd calmed down, she couldn't believe she'd left that note for Lord Havelock to find. By letting him know exactly how upset she was, she'd sacrificed what little pride she might have held on to. She'd hoped to leave Mayfield with her dignity intact. Instead, she'd made herself look utterly ridiculous. Emotional and attention-seeking. Why, she'd always despised women who created scenes in futile attempts to get bored husbands to notice them. And wasn't that more or less what she'd done, staking her list of complaints to his pillow in that melodramtic fashion? Oh, if only she'd ripped it up and thrown it on the fire before she left.

A cold chill slithered down her spine and took root in her stomach as she saw that there were far worse things than being secretly in love with a man who didn't handle sentiment well. Forfeiting his respect, to start with. At least before she'd written her stupid list of complaints, she'd had that much.

But there was no undoing it. She'd written it. He'd no doubt found it and read it by now.

And probably despised her for getting all emotional about what was supposed to have been a practical arrangement.

With feet like lead, Mary went to the writing desk and sank on to the chair. She'd known she'd be alone in London, but now she'd made her husband despise her, she felt it twice as keenly.

She'd write to her aunt Pargetter, that's what she'd do. She needn't admit she'd made a total mess of her marriage. She could focus on all the jobs that needed doing at Durant House and ask her for practical advice on that score. She was, after all, the very person to know where she could find everything and everyone she might need.

She carefully refrained from saying anything about her state of mind, but couldn't help ending with just one sentence stressing how very glad she would be to see her aunt and that she would be at home whenever her aunt wished to call round.

Then she rang for Susan, who said she would give the letter to one of the footmen to take round immediately. It was on the tip of her tongue to say there was no need for the man to turn out at this time of night, when it occurred to her that it might be better to have the servants falling over themselves to impress her. Better than having them virtually ignore her, the way they'd done at Mayfield, in any event.

She'd regretted uttering that veiled threat about dismissing staff, upon arrival, because in truth she didn't have the heart to turn a single one of them out, not when she knew only too well what it felt like to get evicted. Particularly not after Mrs Romsey had told her the peculiar nature of their contracts. When there were no tenants her husband's agent had let them all stay on, for bed and board, rather than go to the inconvenience of laying them all off, only to have to hire a fresh set all over again when the next tenants were due, making each of them regard Durant House as their home.

Eventually they'd realise there was plenty of work for them all, since she meant to restore Durant House to its former glory. They'd probably even realise she was too soft-hearted to carry through on her vague threat of dismissals. But for now, at least, they'd treat her with respect.

So it was with a cool smile that she handed the letter to Susan, then wearily succumbed to the maid's suggestion she help her get ready for bed.

She was exhausted. The past couple of days had completely drained her. And yet, once Susan had left, Mary lay wide awake in her magnificent bed. The harder she strove to relax, the more her mind ran hither and thither, the same way the shadows flickered over the network of cracks in what had once been ornately decorated plaster. What was *he* doing, right now? Chatting away happily with his sister, no doubt. Talking about horses and people she didn't know. *He* wouldn't be aching to feel her in his arms, the way she was aching for him. Wishing she could curl into his big warm body. She'd got used to him rolling her into his side and keeping her plastered to him right through the night. As though he couldn't bear the thought of letting so much as an inch creep between them. It had been bad enough sleeping alone when he'd been just along the corridor.

But it was far worse thinking of him in a different building altogether.

For a moment or two she couldn't even recall why it had seemed so important to leave him. So what if he did prefer his sister? Couldn't she have learned to live with that? Couldn't she have put up with him only visiting her in bed from time to time? At least it would have been preferable to this…this distance she'd created. This vast gulf. A gulf he might never deign to cross, now she'd made such a fool of herself.

The thought that the only person she'd hurt, by writing that list and flouncing off to London, had been herself, was so painful that she curled into a ball and cried herself to sleep.

She'd always hated the months between Christmas and spring, but this year those months were going to be almost unbearable.

Each day she'd have to drag herself out of bed to face yet another seemingly endless day.

But drag herself out of bed she did. By the time Susan came in with her breakfast next morning, Mary was up and almost dressed. No matter how low she'd felt during the night, she was not going to lay about in bed all day wallowing in misery. She had a home, she had the security she'd always craved, more money than she'd ever dreamed of. And a title, to boot.

There were many people far worse off than her. And it would be downright ungrateful to dismiss all she did have because she was hankering after the one thing she could not have.

Anyway, it was bad enough knowing she'd made a

mess of her marriage, without drawing attention to the fact and having people pity her.

It would be far better if nobody could guess, by looking at her, that she felt so dead inside.

In fact, it was a jolly good thing Durant House was such a wreck. Restoring it would be a project that would keep her busy, as well as gain favour from her husband. He'd said he would be for ever in her debt if she could make it more like a home....

She gave herself a mental slap. That was no way to get over him. Planning ways to gain his favour! She ought instead to use this time in London to get used to living without him. It was why she'd come, after all. Without him around, prodding at her bruised heart every five minutes with shows of indifference, it would soon start to heal.

Wouldn't it?

Yes. The longer she stayed away from her husband, the easier it would become to be his wife. Hadn't she always suspected that was the only sort of marriage that could work? She certainly hadn't wanted the kind of clinging, cloying relationship she'd seen destroy her parents. That was what had made her tell him, at the outset, that the only man she might consider marrying would be a sailor, because she'd thought that when a man wasn't around, he couldn't hurt his wife.

Well, she knew now that was a load of rubbish. She still hurt, even though she'd created a distance between them. Perhaps even *because* she'd created a distance between them.

And now she couldn't help recalling that those sailors' wives she'd envied so much in her youth for having charge of a man's income without having to put up with his beastly nature, never had looked as happy as she'd thought they should.

Because they were lonely. Lonely and miserable without the men they loved.

When Susan came to take away her breakfast tray, she also brought the news that Mary had visitors.

'Mrs Pargetter. And her daughters. Say they are some sort of relations of yours,' said Susan as if she wasn't totally convinced. 'Mrs Romsey has shown them to the white drawing room.'

'Oh!' When she'd sent an invitation to call whenever they liked, she'd never imagined they would come at once.

As if they couldn't wait to see her again.

Forgetting all her resolutions to behave like a lady and impress the servants, Mary hitched up her skirts and ran along the corridor to the room Mrs Romsey described as white, but which was in reality a patchwork of twenty years' accumulation of stains.

Her cousins, Dotty and Lotty, were poking rather gingerly at the worn coverings on some spindly-legged chairs that looked as though they'd collapse if anyone sat on them. Her aunt was running her gloved finger along the mantelpiece, with an expression of disgust.

Mary had never been so glad to see anyone in her life.

'Mary, my dear!' Aunt Pargetter smiled with genuine pleasure. And then executed a clumsy curtsy. 'I suppose I should address you as my lady now. Old habits die hard.'

'Oh, no. No, you must never call me anything but Mary,' she insisted. 'I don't feel a bit like a my lady.'

She felt her face crumple.

'My dear girl, whatever is the matter?'

And Mary, who'd vowed that nobody, but nobody, would ever know what a mess she'd made of what should have been the perfect marriage, let out a wail.

'I've left him!'

Then she flew across the room, flung herself into her aunt's outstretched arms and burst into tears.

Chapter Fourteen

'Whatever has gone wrong? Has he been cruel to you?'

Mary shook her head. 'No. He has been very k-kind.' How could she have forgotten the way he'd gone to fetch coal during the night, shirtless, just so she wouldn't get cold? Or the way he'd praised her cooking? And told her she was an angel for putting up with his failings?

'And g-generous,' she wailed, suddenly remembering he'd promised her free rein to decorate this house, to buy as many clothes as she liked and not worry about the bills because he'd pay them all.

'Th-that's why I f-fell in love with him,' she sobbed into her aunt's shoulder.

'But…so…why have you left him then, if he is so wonderful? And you've fallen in love with him?'

'Because he doesn't love me,' she wailed.

'Of course he does. Why, I've never seen a man so smitten. He couldn't wait to get you to the altar….'

'It wasn't because he fell in love with me. It was because he was so sure he *wouldn't*! He only wanted to marry me so quickly because of…because of…'

'What do you mean, sure he wouldn't?'

'He wanted a certain sort of wife. A woman who wouldn't give him a m-moment's bother. He warned me not to expect affection from marriage. *I'm* the one who changed my mind about what marriage means to me. *I'm* the only one who wants more.'

'Well, if that is true, running away isn't going to endear him to you,' said her aunt tartly, though she was still patting Mary's shoulder in a comforting sort of way. 'If you don't believe he can ever love you, you must surely want him to respect you, don't you? It would have been far better to stay with him and show him what a wonderful wife you can be. That your love needn't make him uncomfortable.'

'I know!' Mary sat up and scrubbed angrily at the tears she couldn't check. 'I know that *now*. Only for a while I completely lost my head. Said things and did things he will never, ever, forgive. I've ruined everything!'

While her aunt had been soaking up Mary's tears, Lotty had poured her a cup of tea and now pressed it into her hands.

'Here. Drink this. And we'll help you come up with a plan to win him round.'

Well, if anyone could, Dotty and Lotty could. They were such adept flirts they could probably make a living giving lessons in it.

'I'm so sorry,' said Mary, wiping her eyes with the handkerchief Dotty gave her. 'I can't think why I've become such a watering pot. I'm not usually prone to tears.'

Aunt Pargetter sat bolt upright.

'Is it possible you are increasing?'

'What?'

'Well, every time I have been in the family way, I became a touch unstable. And this sort of behaviour is most unlike you. I always took you for a very sensible, down-to-earth sort of girl.'

'Increasing…' Mary laid her hand flat on her stomach, and did a few sums. 'It…it might be the case. I haven't…'

Aunt Pargetter nodded sagely. 'Well, then. That is a sure way to win him round. Every time I got in the family way Leonard was so pleased with me he couldn't do enough for me. You have only to write and tell your own husband and I'm sure he will come post-haste to your side.'

'No.' A cold, sick feeling knotted Mary's stomach. 'No, that really would be the end. We agreed, you see, that once I was expecting, he would no longer need to… need to—' She broke off, blushing fierily. 'He said that as soon as I gave him an heir, we could go our separate ways.' She buried her face in her hands. 'If I am increasing, he won't think there's any need to see me again. I'll *never* get him back.'

'Well, then, don't tell him.'

Mary's head flew up. 'But I promised him an heir. Wouldn't it be dishonest to keep him in the dark about something he finds so important?'

'Pish,' said her aunt, making a dismissive gesture with her hand. 'The man clearly needs to be brought to his senses. And you're not going to be able to do it unless you can get him here. Unless you would rather go crawling back to him and beg him to love you?'

Since she'd already vowed never to do such a craven, spineless thing, Mary shook her head vehemently.

'I thought not. But anyway, it won't be exactly dishonest. It is far too soon for you to be absolutely sure you are increasing. I know I detected more than a hint of uncertainty in your voice when I brought it up.'

'Yes. I mean, no. I'm not sure...' Although it was far too early to tell, now that her aunt had mentioned it, it *did* explain her tendency to weep and her ungovernable bursts of temper. And why she'd been feeling alternately nauseous, or ravenous. And it was better than going on believing she'd become physically ill simply because she'd fallen in love and had no hope of her feelings being returned.

Besides, there was the matter of a missing monthly flow. And her husband had been so very amorous, at least to start with. Hadn't she always thought how very virile he was? Yes—it must be true. She *was* going to have a baby.

'He sets great store by getting an heir, you say?'

Blushing hotly, Mary nodded her head. Then she glanced at Lotty and Dotty, wondering how much she could confide in her aunt, with them listening. Both of them were staring at her, wide-eyed, with a mixture of concern and curiosity.

'He said that he wanted to get me with child as soon as he possibly could,' she admitted.

'Then it's likely, if you keep him in the dark about your suspicions, that he will have a good excuse to come to town and keep trying.'

Mary shifted uncomfortably in her seat.

'I can't... It must seem odd, but somehow I can't bear the thought of him steeling himself to visit my bed....'

Her cousins giggled.

'Mary. You are such an innocent.'

'What do you mean?'

'Hush, girls,' said her aunt repressively. Then turned to Mary. 'I do not think it is his feelings about the act that trouble you, but your own. Now that you have fallen in love with him, you shrink from permitting an act that has probably up till recently been only carnal in nature.'

The words struck to her very core. She hadn't been in love with him that first night, had she? When she'd been so hot for him she'd practically ripped off his shirt.

'You are right. I want more than just...enjoyment. Is that very selfish of me?'

'Not in the least. I think most women want much more from their husbands than they ever receive, in emotional terms. Men are just not given to deep feelings.'

'Then what am I to do? How can I learn to settle for... for the little he is prepared to give?'

Her aunt patted her hand. 'Perhaps coming to London without him was the best thing you could have done. If he wants a calm, sensible sort of wife, then you can give yourself the time to calm down. And when he does come after you, which believe me, my dear, he will do, then you must show him you can be sensible. Be the kind of wife he wants. And you will regain the respect you believe you have forfeited.'

Mary twisted the handkerchief between her fingers. What Aunt Pargetter was saying was only what she'd thought herself. And what's more, she did know *exactly* the sort of wife he wanted. He'd written it all down on that list.

At least, he'd written what he *thought* he wanted. She'd soon discovered he didn't really want a modest wife. He enjoyed her eager response to his inventiveness.

The delicate handkerchief ripped.

She could tie herself in knots trying to conform to

the things he said he wanted and be totally wasting her time. And anyway, she couldn't—no, actually, she simply *wouldn't* try to be something she was not, just to keep him sweet. She'd watched her mother do that and look where it had got her!

'No,' she said firmly. 'I am not going to start plotting and planning, and embarking on a campaign to alter the terms of our marriage. After all, I agreed to all those terms, didn't I? I told him I wanted a practical, loveless marriage. It's not his fault I went and fell in love with him, is it?'

'I don't see how you could have helped it,' said Dotty. 'He's remarkably handsome and was so attentive to you.'

'And at a time when you must have felt so alone,' added Lotty.

'Yes,' said Dotty indignantly. 'He practically pounced on you when you were at your most vulnerable.'

Like a predator with a mouse.

But she *wasn't* a mouse.

It was heartening to have the girls blame him for everything, the way she'd been doing up till now. But was it fair to say he was a predator and she'd been his victim? Was it even true? She'd just told her aunt she'd agreed to marry him for practical reasons. And at the time, she *had* seen it as a way to help her aunt and cousins. To help Julia. But had she just used that as an excuse to get close to him? To belong to him?

Oh, lord, she thought, perhaps she had. That was why she'd been so devastated when she'd discovered and read that list. He'd already told her he didn't want a woman who would be looking for affection within marriage. But it hadn't really struck home until she'd read it in black and white.

She'd married him under false pretences. Oh, perhaps not deliberately. And she'd been deceiving herself more than him.

'It's *not* his fault,' she said with resolution. 'I cannot blame him for being what he is. And sticking to the terms we agreed. I shall…I shall just have to pull myself together.'

'We'll help you,' vowed Dotty.

'Yes. We'll keep you so busy you won't have time to mope over the stupid man.'

And every day she would grow more accustomed to her lot. She *would*.

'It looks as though there's enough for you to do in this house to keep you occupied until well after the baby arrives,' added her aunt. 'You did say, in your letter, you needed the names of reliable plumbers, and plasterers, and painters, and upholsterers, didn't you?'

'Yes,' said Mary. She was also going to need the name of a doctor she could trust. And a midwife. And she'd certainly have to buy all those clothes she'd used as an excuse to come up to London without him, or she really would look pathetic.

'Do you know which modiste the most fashionable, wealthiest ladies of the *ton* patronise? If I'm going to live apart from my husband, there's no sense in looking as though I mind.'

'That's the spirit,' said her aunt with a smile. 'Spend his money making yourself all the rage and he'll soon sit up and take notice.'

Would he?

Well, whether he did, or didn't, she was going to get on with her life. She was going to start by making Durant House into a comfortable home for herself and her baby. And she had the confidence she could do it, too, with her family, to wit, these women in the room with her right now, on her side.

Yes. By the time Julia was ready to make her come-out, she would have transformed this place.

She didn't know what had come over her at Mayfield. She didn't know why she'd got so low she even thought she had nothing to offer Julia. She had something very wonderful to offer Julia. An introduction to these three women. Her warm, witty and wise aunt Pargetter and her bubbly, generous-natured cousins. They might not be out of the top drawer like Lady Peverell, but they had something that lady lacked. They would never look down their noses at Julia and would accept her just as she was, the way they'd accepted Mary. They'd make friends with her. Go shopping with her. Giggle with her over her conquests and give her tons of practical advice about how to charm men.

Not only would she make Durant House the envy of every other society lady, but she was going to ensure that Julia enjoyed every moment of her first Season.

And only married for love.

Lord Havelock handed his horse over to a young groom he didn't recognise, wondering where Gilbey had got to. He would have felt better if he could have had a few words with him before he went inside. Found out how Mary was, in a casual sort of manner, without making it obvious he was at his wit's end.

He glowered up at the gloomy façade of Durant House as he strode across the stable yard to one of the rear doors. He'd sworn he'd never spend another night under its roof, but what else was he to do? Mary was here.

And he couldn't stay away from her another moment. He'd got to the stage where he'd rather have her rant and rage at him, or even skewer him right through the heart with a hatpin, than spend one more dreary day without the chance of getting so much as a glimpse of her. Or endure one more restless night, reaching out for her after finally succeeding in dozing off, only to jerk wide awake on finding the space at his side cold and empty.

He paused, with his hand on the door latch. He had no more idea now what to say to her, how he could make things right with her, than he'd had the first minute after he'd read her farewell note. He hadn't come here with a firm plan, but...

Hell, when had he *ever* made plans? Only the once. And look how that had turned out.

With a sense of impending doom, he pushed open the door and went in.

The corridor was deserted, but he could hear some sort of activity going on towards the front of the house. A strange clattering, rattling sound, interspersed with what sounded like shouts of encouragement. And the smell of paint hung in the air.

No matter what she thought of him, Mary was obviously keeping her word about doing up Durant House. The noises were probably that of workmen, doing something in the hall. It certainly needed it. There couldn't be a gloomier entrance hall anywhere in town. What had his grandparents been thinking when they agreed to its design?

'The deuce!'

The words escaped his lips involuntarily as he opened the door from the servants' quarters and stepped into a space that he barely recognised.

It was the light that struck him first. He looked up, astonished to see there were so many windows.

But before he could register what other changes Mary had made, he saw two little boys go thundering up each of the lower staircases that rose to the gallery. When they got to their respective half landings, they flung themselves down on to what looked like little sleds.

'Three,' shouted a footman who was stationed at a midway point of the upper landing. 'Two! One! Go!'

The boys launched themselves down their staircases with blood-curdling yells. Explaining what the odd clattering, rattling sound had been that he'd been able to hear from the stable yard.

Seconds after they landed on piles of what looked like bundled-up holland covers, money changed hands between his footman and a stranger in brown overalls. They'd clearly been taking bets on which boy would reach the ground first.

'Strike me down, it's 'is lordship,' cried one of the boys—whose face looked vaguely familiar—struggling to free his legs from the swathes of material that had cushioned his landing. He rather thought it was Jem, although the pickpocket looked vastly different with a clean face and wearing the Durant livery.

He thought he recognised the other boy, too. He only had to imagine him coated in flour and he would swear it was the youngest Pargetter.

While he was eyeing the boys with something that felt very much like jealousy—because he'd never seen the grand staircases put to better use and only wished he'd thought of tea-tray races down them when he'd been their age—the footman sprang guiltily apart from the workman and came dashing forward, buttoning up his jacket.

'May I take your hat, my lord?' he said, red-faced and perspiring nervously. 'Your coat?'

He handed them over.

'Is my wife at home?'

'Yes, my lord. In the ballroom.'

'I will take you up myself, my lord,' put in the butler, who just then came wheezing out of one of the reception rooms. He was swathed in an enormous sacking apron and had cobwebs in his hair. 'I do apologise for not being here to admit you. I did not hear the door knocker over the noise....'

'Didn't use it, since I didn't come in the front way,' said Lord Havelock dryly. 'And I think I can find the way to my own ballroom.' Indeed, now that the boys weren't making such a racket, he could hear the sound of piano music echoing down the stairs.

'Will you be staying here?' The butler regarded him anxiously.

What the devil was going on? Why shouldn't he stay here?

'Where the hell else would I stay?'

'I beg your pardon, my lord. Only it is not usually your habit to... I mean, that is, not that I would question your movements. Only it won't be easy to find a room that doesn't have some kind of workman attending to it. As you can see...' he waved his hand to encompass the workman in brown overalls '...her ladyship has us busy on various projects.'

He was damned if he would slink off, simply because it didn't suit his wife to have him here.

'Of course I am going to stay here. In the same

room as my wife, if there really is nowhere else fit,' he snapped.

Having staked his claim on his house, and his wife, he stepped over the holland covers and stalked up the stairs.

Only to come to a halt in the doorway to the ball-room. Or the rear half of the ballroom, anyway. Mary had left one section screened off by the huge double doors, which could be moved aside entirely to double the area of the dance floor.

There was an elderly woman he would swear he'd never seen before in his life sitting at the piano, playing a country dance tune with some gusto. Mary's cousins were skipping up and down the room with two young men he'd also never seen before in his life. A stringy little man—no doubt a dance teacher—was shouting the figures as he capered alongside them to demonstrate how it should be done.

And Mary was sitting on a sofa, by a cheerfully crackling fire, the low table in front of her almost en-tirely hidden under mounds of various coloured materi-als, notebooks and charts. Her aunt Pargetter was sitting next to her. They had their heads bent over a length of stripy stuff, running it through their fingers and mur-muring to each other.

The pain of her leaving was nothing compared to what struck him now. Here she was, cheerfully getting on with her life as though she hadn't a care in the world. She didn't need him. She wasn't showing even the slight-est sign of missing him. On the contrary, the atmosphere in here was positively festive.

Here he'd been, tying himself in knots trying to think how he could make it up to her, and she'd gone and got over him all by herself.

He must have made some sound, or movement, or something, because her head suddenly flew up and she saw him standing in the doorway.

For a moment her face lit up. She made as if to rise.

And the pain vanished. He wanted nothing more than to go to her, sweep her into his arms and tell her he couldn't bear being apart from her one moment longer. But the room was full of people.

And anyway, her smile had faded now. She'd sat back in the seat, and lifted her chin.

'This is a surprise,' she flung at him.

'Not you, as well,' he growled, stalking across the room, snagging a chair on the way so he could sit down beside her. 'I've already had Simmons complaining about me coming here without giving him fair warning.' He sat down and folded his arms across his chest. 'I don't see why I should have to give an account of my movements to all and sundry.'

'No. You wouldn't,' she responded tartly.

'And what is that supposed to mean?'

'Only that you don't think about the work it takes to prepare a room, or order in extra food…'

'You seem to have a house full of guests eating and drinking their heads off,' he said, pointing to a table under the window that was littered with the remains of what looked like a substantial nuncheon. 'One more isn't going to make much difference. And as for preparing a room, what is wrong with us sharing? That won't give the servants any extra work, will it, if that is what is bothering you?'

He'd barely coped with having her turn him away from her room at Mayfield, but he wasn't going to let her think she could get away with coldly rebuffing him any longer. He hadn't come all the way to London to...to...

Dammit—now he'd made her blush. He hadn't meant to embarrass her. He'd meant to tell her he wanted to put an end to this nonsensical separation and try to find a way back to what they'd had those first few heady days of their marriage. But as usual, his temper had grabbed him by the throat and shaken out all the wrong words.

'Girls!' Mary's aunt got to her feet and clapped her hands. 'Come and pay your respects to his lordship.'

'He's here?' The younger and more forward of the two whirled towards him, leaving her partner grasping for empty air after his own turn.

'So soon?' Lotty was making towards him as well, a huge smile on her face. 'Why, that's wonderful! Isn't it, Mary?'

'I...well, I... Yes, of course it is,' she agreed, looking rather harassed.

His hackles rose. He'd seen girls in the throes of a conspiracy to manage their menfolk often enough to recognise something of the sort was in train.

'What have you been plotting?'

'Nothing,' said Dotty with convincing indignation. At the same time as Lotty, unfortunately, admitted, 'We were hoping you would throw a ball.'

'And of course,' put in the aunt smoothly, while Mary looked as if she wanted to slide under the heap of materials and vanish, 'we could not even consider it while you were not here.'

'Absolutely not,' he said, wondering what they'd really been plotting. Mary couldn't dissemble to save her life. And it was clear that this was the very first she'd heard anything about a ball.

The other girls pouted, however, and started to complain.

'Oh, but surely you want everyone to meet your wife. Isn't that what people do when they get married in your set? Throw parties, and such?'

'Not until she's made her curtsy in the Queen's drawing room,' he said firmly. And then inspiration struck him. She might not think she needed him, but there was one sure way he could make it seem perfectly natural for them to spend time together. Which would give him time to win her round. Somehow.

'That's one of the reasons I've come up to town,' he said airily. 'Need to see to Mary's presentation. Besides, it's not the thing for a wife to come up to town alone, you know. At least not the first time. I shall have to squire you about a bit, Mary,' he said, turning to her fully, so that he could gauge her reaction. 'Introduce you to the right sort of people and warn you off the wrong 'uns.'

'I'm sure I never meant to be so much bother,' she said in a flat, subdued little voice. 'You don't need to… squire me about.'

She couldn't have made it plainer she didn't want him here.

'It's no bother,' he insisted icily. 'It's just one of those things I should have remembered I'd have to do when I took a wife.'

Her shoulders slumped still further.

'Think I'll take myself off to my club until dinner,' he said, getting to feet that were itching to get out of here.

'Will you be dining here?'

She had no need to look as though he'd threatened her with a visit to the dentist.

'Of course I d—dashed well will!' He wasn't going

to fall at the first hurdle. He'd just wait till he could get her alone, so that they could thrash things out properly. Get her to see sense.

Although, he reflected moodily as he left the ball-room, perhaps what he really needed was for her not to have so much. Sense, that is. For no sensible woman would give him what he wanted.

Not when she'd already agreed to something very different.

Chapter Fifteen

Lord Havelock came to a dead halt on the threshold of the dining room. Every stick of furniture was shrouded in holland covers.

'Excuse me, my lord,' said Simmons, materialising at his elbow. 'But her ladyship has requested that all meals be served in what used to be the morning room.'

'Of course she has,' he replied grimly. It was that kind of day. Nothing had gone as expected. Even at his club, the gossip had all been about Chepstow's sudden, and startling, marriage to a girl nobody had ever heard of.

No wonder the ancient Greeks had decided to represent love by a mischievous little chap, shooting arrows at innocent passers-by. A chuckling, chubby child who struck at random. Mortally wounding his victims.

Havelock absent-mindedly rubbed at his chest, where there was a dull ache. An ache that only one thing—or rather person—could assuage.

Mary was sitting on a chair by the fire. She got to her feet, as though startled, when he walked in. Then looked pointedly at the table, which was set for two.

'I'm sorry I kept you waiting,' he said. 'Went to the dining room first. Stupid thing to do, really.'

She frowned at him. Or rather, the frown she'd been wearing already grew deeper. Her lips thinned and she took a breath, as though to utter some tart remark.

'You look lovely, by the way,' he said to forestall her. 'New gown?' He pulled out a chair for her and, after a brief struggle with herself, she swept across to the table and sat down on the chair.

'Yes,' she said, with a toss of her head. 'That is why I came up to town. To buy clothes.'

Yes, that *was* the excuse she'd made. He eyed the short string of pearls at her neck.

'Jewels, too? I should be buying you those.'

'You are,' she said with a lift to her chin. 'I'm having all the bills sent to your man of business, just as you said.'

'Touché,' he murmured as footmen started swarming round the table.

Though the atmosphere between them remained cool, the food at least was hot. Which was a vast improvement on how things had been in his father's day.

In fact, in the short time she'd been here, Mary had transformed Durant House from a dark, repressive display of his forebear's wealth, into the kind of place where boys could hold tea-tray races down stairs and a man could stretch out his legs before the fire while waiting for his dinner.

She'd turned it into a home.

'It was a good idea of yours, to have meals served in here,' he said, as the cloth was removed and a dish of nuts set at his left hand. 'Walnut?'

She shook her head.

'Not hungry?' She hadn't done justice to the delicious meal, merely pushing the food round her plate. And she looked a touch pale. 'Are you unwell?'

She sat up straighter and gave a strange, nervous little laugh. 'Whatever gives you that idea?'

'Mary…' He sighed, setting down the nutcrackers. 'I can't stand this.'

'Stand…stand what?' She looked at him with wide, wary eyes.

'You being in London and me being in Mayfield. I know I said I'd let you lead your own life when you'd had enough of me and I wouldn't cut up rough, but…' He drew a deep breath. 'I'm exhausted. I just can't sleep without you in bed beside me.'

'You were the one,' she said tartly, 'who moved into another bedroom.'

'In other words, I started it?' He smiled grimly. 'That's what I get for trying to be noble.'

'Noble?'

'Yes. All that day I'd been thinking of all the promises I'd made you. Promises I'd failed to keep. And I decided that at least I could keep the one I made you about you having your own room.'

'I…I…I didn't realise. I thought you were just bored with me.'

'Bored? How could you possibly think I was bored when I couldn't keep my hands off you?'

'You'd started managing to keep your hands off me until night-time,' she flashed back at him. 'When at one time you'd pounce on me anywhere in the house, at *any* time of day.'

'Well, that was before the servants came back. You got so upset when Brownlow almost caught us in the drawing room that I thought I'd better rein back a bit. I was trying,' he said grimly, 'to spare your blushes.'

'Spare my blushes?' She pressed her hands to her mouth. 'You are saying it was *my* fault? My stupid fault for being so—'

'Now stop right there,' he said sternly. 'I knew you were shy when I married you. I don't mind only making love to you in a bedroom, if that's where you feel most at ease. I'm only sorry I gave you the impression I was getting tired of you. I don't think I ever could. These past weeks, with you gone…nothing has been right.'

'B-but surely… I mean, you have Julia home now. That was the whole purpose of marrying me, wasn't it? To give her a secure home.'

'Funny, that. The moment she got to Mayfield I realised it was your home just as much as hers. And I didn't want her making you unhappy, by throwing the kind of tantrums that had reduced Lady Peverell to the state she was in. You have no idea how hard I worked to bring her round, to improve her mood, to persuade her to try to make friends with you.'

'You…you did? That was what you were doing with your sister all day and every day? I thought…I thought…' Her face flamed. 'I just thought you preferred her company to mine….'

'Prefer her company? Are you mad?' He looked at her pinched, wary expression and realised it was past time he came clean.

'Mary, don't you have any idea how lovely you are? How alluring? How much I…?' He shifted uncomfortably in his seat. What if he said the words and she took them as a breach of trust? What if she didn't want anything but the cool, practical arrangement they'd agreed on? She was a cool, practical kind of woman, after all. But dammit, if he didn't say anything at all, they'd be right back where they started.

'To tell you the truth,' he said, with a swooping sensation in the pit of his stomach as though he was about to jump a five-barred gate with a sheer drop on the other side, 'it felt as though you'd cut out a part of me and taken it with you when you left.'

She looked confused. Pleased would have been his choice, but at least confused was better than affronted.

'But you said…' she began speaking hesitantly. 'You said you'd only come up here because it was the right thing to do, on my first visit to London as your wife. That you'd come to arrange my Court presentation. To…' she drew in a breath, and looked at him with huge, wounded eyes '…make sure I didn't fall in with the wrong sort of people.'

'Dash it, did it sound as bad as that?' He got up, went round to her chair and dropped to his knees at her feet. 'I warned you I don't have a way with words. Whatever I mean to say always seems to come out wrong, around you. And I didn't want to blurt out the truth with all those people there, anyway. And then I thought you were still angry with me. You didn't seem a bit pleased to see me.…'

'I was. Very pleased. But then you looked so cross, too. And I couldn't forget that horrid note I left. I was sure you must be mad as fire about that. And then you said all that about coming to make sure I wasn't getting in a tangle, and I…'

'Gave as good as you got.' He sighed. 'I know all about going off at half-cock, Mary. I've been doing it most of my life. It's only of late that I've learned it's better to count to ten or so before letting rip.'

'I never even knew I had a temper, until I married you.' She clapped her hand to her mouth. 'Oh! I didn't mean it like that....'

'No, well...' He shrugged and leaned back on his heels. 'You have a lot to contend with, don't you? You made that quite clear in that list you wrote.'

'Please, please don't bring that up! I put some quite dreadful things in it. Things I didn't mean. You *are* kind. Nobody else has ever given me their coat to shelter me from rain. And when I think of you going round the house without your shirt to get more coal, so as not to take a single covering off me...' She leaned forward, and placed one palm against his cheek. 'And you did consider my opinions, too. You asked me if I wanted to stay at Mayfield or remove to the Dog and Ferret...'

'Yes, but you wouldn't have written any of those things at all, if I hadn't made a stupid list of my own first.' He covered her hand with his own. Enfolded it. Drew it to his chest. 'That was my worst offence, in your eyes, wasn't it?'

She shook her head. 'After a while I think I understood why you might have written it. The thought of getting married was so abhorrent to you that—'

'That's another thing you need to understand. *Why* it was so abhorrent. The thing is, you see, it changes people. That was what scared me. Julia's mother, for instance. She was quiet and withdrawn all the time she was married to my father. And then she bloomed with Geoffries. She was like a different woman. Laughing all the time and full of energy. Her third husband turned her into a shell of what she'd been. And so I decided, if I had to get married, it would be to a woman who wouldn't have the power to change me. A woman who'd accept me just as I am and let me carry on living the way I always had.'

'I don't want you to change, either,' she said, gripping his hand hard. 'In fact—'

'Just hear me out,' he said firmly, cutting her off before she had a chance to deflect him from his purpose. 'I never meant you to ever know I'd written that stupid list. It was only a means to help me get my thoughts together. And my friends, seeing how low I was at the prospect of getting married, made it all into a bit of a joke. The thing is...' he raised her hand to his mouth and kissed it '...it was a meaningless piece of nonsense. Whereas the one you wrote...'

Letting go of her hand, he dug into his pocket for the list she'd written.

She gasped when he unfolded it and she saw what it was, her eyes widening in horror.

'You raised some serious points,' he said, getting to his feet. 'Which I fully intend to answer.'

'I really wish you wouldn't! I've already said I was wrong about you being unkind and inconsiderate.'

'We'll skip over the bit about not having any money as well then, shall we?'

Her hand flew to the pearls about her neck.

'I know it was a bit wicked of me to buy jewels as well as the clothes you promised me...'

'You really are the most absurd creature,' he said with a tender smile. 'If you wanted to punish me by squandering money on jewels—and I wouldn't blame you if you did—you should have bought diamonds.' He glanced down at the note. 'I was trying to amend my behaviour, you know. I was trying to think of what you wanted, and to treat you better. I just made a mull of it.'

'Yes, yes, I see that now....'

'And as for the bit about family...' he looked down at her, sorrowfully '...I can see how my original list made it sound as if I don't care about family. It was another stupid, selfish thing we wrote down when we were trying to see if there was some way to make marrying *anyone* slightly less unpalatable....'

He cringed when he thought how crass his behaviour had been when he'd first started to match what he liked about her to the items on his list.

'The thing with family is that you can wish them at the devil three-quarters of the time, but the minute you find one of them in real trouble, you have no choice but to help them out. And not just close family, either. Not even true family, come to that. Take Julia's little brothers, for example. After spending the happiest school holidays in their home, with their father, I'll never be able to turn my back when they need their school bills paying, or when they want sponsorship into their career, will I?'

'Plenty of men could,' she pointed out, a strange expression flitting across her face. 'My own relatives didn't think twice about turning me away.'

'You've been on the receiving end of such shabby behaviour, you've come to expect nothing else. Even from me.'

'Oh, please, please don't take what I wrote so... seriously. I was angry when I wrote it. I didn't mean the half of it.'

'Yes. Well...' He looked down at the scrap of paper in his hand. 'I wrote mine when I was drunk. And before I met you, at that.'

His heart was beating so hard now, because what he said next, how Mary responded, was going to shape his whole future.

'Tell you what I'd like to do,' he said, fishing in his pocket for the list he'd written, before he'd known there could be a woman anywhere in the world like Mary. 'I'd like to tear these lists up, scrap our original agreement altogether and make a fresh start.'

'What do you mean? Scrap our agreement? Don't you want,' she said in a small, scared voice, 'to be married to me any more?'

'Mary. I want to be married to you more than anything. But not in the way we said. When we were both so convinced marriage couldn't work we gave ourselves permission to walk away from it without even trying to smooth things out when we hit our first bumpy patch. Now, if you will just bear with me a minute, I have something I'd like you to consider.'

He reached into his pocket yet again.

'I've written another list,' he said, feeling his cheeks heating and his collar growing tight. 'Setting down what I want from marriage, now that I understand a bit more what it's really about.'

He cleared his throat.

'"My perfect wife,"' he said and glanced at Mary. She was sitting stock-still, her hands clasped on her knees, her dark eyes staring up at him with trepidation.

'"My wife needs to be as tall as my shoulder. She will have straight dark hair that feels like bathing in silk at midnight."'

He heard her gasp. Glanced up. Her hands were still clasped together, but they were at chest height now, not on her lap. And her eyes…

'Brown eyes,' he said, because he'd got this part off by heart. 'That look right to the heart of me and accept me just as I am, because her own heart is so generous,' he said, hoping it was true right now. But just in case it wasn't, he lowered his gaze to the paper again, unwilling to say the rest in the face of any direct opposition.

'"She won't be afraid to work hard. She won't be afraid of being poor. She will be a little shy and uncertain, but so responsive to my kisses that after a bit she will forget where she is and surrender to the waves of passion that break over us, drowning us both. She won't care about my title. She would feel just the same about me if I never had one. She will judge everyone by a yardstick of kindness and generosity. She won't care so much about her appearance that she would rebuff a child." Oh, and one last thing,' he finished, lowering the sheet, and making himself look her steadily in the eye, no matter what.

'Her name must be Mary.'

A little sob escaped her throat. 'I never knew you had it in you to be so…poetical.'

'If I could write poetry,' he scoffed, 'I would have done. Setting all this down so it made any kind of sense took me hours and hours. But the thing is, you're worth it, Mary. I want to court you. Woo you, if you like. Make this marriage one that's full of romance, and…' he gulped '…and love.'

'Love?'

'Yes, love. Don't look so shocked. I don't expect you to fall in love with me, the way I've fallen in love with you. Don't suppose it's possible. But I can stand that,' he said, drawing himself up to his full height. 'I can bear anything, so long as you don't forbid me to love you.'

'Of course it's possible,' she cried. 'I've loved you practically from the very first night I saw you!'

'From the...' He shook his head. 'No. You couldn't have. You didn't give me the slightest bit of encouragement. I had to get your cousins twisting your arm to even get you to come out sightseeing with me.'

'That's because I was afraid.'

'Afraid of me?'

'Not of you. But the way you made me feel. I'd never thought of any man in...*that* way before. I thought those sorts of feelings made a woman weak and vulnerable. It shocked me. Scared me. So I fought it. Tried to deny it.'

'Right up to the altar.' He nodded.

'And after. I didn't admit to myself that I loved you for a while. And even then, I tried to hide it....'

'You did that extremely well. You always kept me at arm's length. You wouldn't even call me by my given name.'

'I didn't know I was allowed to,' she put in, a touch indignantly, he thought. 'You never said.'

'It never occurred to me I had to. But I want you to. It would make me feel so much closer to you.'

'Gregory,' she said shyly. 'I am so sorry.' She got to her feet and closed the distance between them. 'Sorry that I never showed you any sign of my growing affection for you.' She took hold of his hands.

'But then, I had told you not to expect, or request, affection from me,' he groaned.

'But if you do want it to be part of our...our fresh start,' she said hesitantly, 'then...'

He was about to crush her to his chest and shower her face with kisses. But before he could do anything of the sort, she'd stretched up on tiptoe, put her arms round his neck and kissed him.

Kissed him.

For the first time, she'd been the one to initiate an embrace.

'My God, Mary, Mary,' he gasped. 'This feels like a miracle. Can it really be true? Can you love me?'

'How could I not love you?' There were tears in her eyes. 'I am only sorry I was so miserly with my heart before. If I'd been as generous as you said, I would have shown you how I felt, rather than hiding it all, to try to save face. And speaking of hiding things...'

She'd known it was wrong to keep the news of her pregnancy from him. Even when she'd feared it would mean the end of any chance of a reconciliation. But now, after he'd professed his love and his hope they could have a fresh start, it would be tantamount to saying she didn't trust him.

And how could she say she loved him, if she didn't trust him, completely?

She did trust him. He'd never lied to her, not even when the truth had hurt. So if he said he loved her and wanted a different sort of marriage from the one they'd agreed on at first, then he meant it.

'I'm...'

The words stuck in her throat. It felt as though she was about to fling herself off a cliff into his arms, hoping he really would be there to catch her.

'What is it, Mary? Whatever it is, I swear I won't be angry with you.'

It had never been his anger she'd feared. And wasn't now.

Taking a deep breath, she flung herself over the edge.

'I'm increasing.'

His eyes widened. He glanced down at her stomach. Then laughed with what looked like absolute joy. And hugged her. 'You clever, clever girl,' he said, sweeping her into his arms and over to one of the strategically placed armchairs, where he settled her on his lap.

Where he kissed her a bit more.

'It doesn't matter how we started, does it?' she said, after a while. 'We both made mistakes and both hid what we really felt, but we can do better from now on, can't we?'

'Well, I'm certainly determined to do better,' he said. 'From now on, I mean to show you how much you mean to me, every second of every day. I'm going to treat you like a queen.'

'I'm not sure,' she said thoughtfully, 'I want to be treated like a queen.'

'Very well. What would you like, then? Bearing in mind you want me to take your opinions into account whenever I have to make a decision.'

She pulled away from him a bit, her lips pursing. For a moment, he wondered whether he'd ruined the moment by referring to her list of complaints. But then she darted him a distinctly saucy look.

'All I want,' she said, with a glint in her eye, 'is for you to want me so much you can't keep your hands off me. Day or night. I know I'm not pretty. But you made me feel as if I was, to you, when you were so on fire for me you chased me round sofas, scandalising every-one from the butler to the scullery maid.'

His heart seemed to turn over in his chest. And when

it settled, it was pounding like a galloping horse. 'Is that so?' He pushed her off his lap. 'Go on, then,' he said.

'Go on, what?'

'I shall give you a head start.' He leaned back in the chair and crossed one leg over the other. 'I shall count to twenty. No,' he said, 'actually I can't wait till I've counted to twenty. Make it ten.'

'Ten?' She edged away from him, a confused frown on her face.

'One,' he said, or rather growled, leaning forward and eyeing her hotly from head to toe.

'Two...'

She shivered where she stood. An answering heat flared to life in her eyes.

'Three...'

She glanced round the room. At the hearthrug at his feet. At the table. Back at him, a smile playing about her lips.

'Four...'

She turned, and made her way slowly towards the door.

'Five...'

She hesitated, her hand on the latch, and glanced back over her shoulder.

'Six...'

He got to his feet.

'Seven...' He stalked away from the chair.

Her face lit up. With a little shriek of laughter, she fumbled open the door, hitched up her skirts and ran from the room.

'Eight-nine-ten,' he yelled and set out in hot pursuit.

* * * * *

PORTRAIT OF
A SCANDAL

To the ladies (and gentleman) of flat B1.
You know who you are!

Chapter One

'*Madame, je vous* assure, there is no need to inspect the kitchens.'

'*Mademoiselle,*' retorted Amethyst firmly as she pushed past Monsieur Le Brun—or Monsieur Le Prune, as she'd come to think of him, so wrinkled did his mouth become whenever she did not tamely fall in with his suggestions.

'Is not the apartment to your satisfaction?'

'The rooms I have so far seen are most satisfactory,' she conceded. But at the sound of crashing crockery from behind the scuffed door that led to the kitchens, she cocked her head.

'That,' said Monsieur Le Brun, drawing himself to his full height and assuming his most quelling manner, 'is a problem the most insignificant. And besides which, it is my duty to deal with the matters domestic.'

'Not in any household I run,' Amethyst muttered to herself as she pushed open the door.

Crouched by the sink was a scullery maid, weeping over a pile of broken crockery. And by a door which led to a dingy courtyard she saw two red-faced men, engaged in a discussion which involved not only a stream of unintelligible words, but also a great deal of arm waving.

'The one with the apron is our chef,' said Monsieur Le Brun's voice into her ear, making her jump. She'd been so intent on trying to work out what was going on in the kitchen, she hadn't heard him sneak up behind her.

'He has the reputation of an artist,' he continued. 'You told me to employ only the best and he is that. The other is a troublemaker, who inhabits the fifth floor, but who should be thrown out, as you English say, on his ear. *If* you will permit…' he began in a voice heavily laced with sarcasm, 'I shall resolve the issue. Since,' he continued suavely, as she turned to raise her eyebrows at him, 'you have employed me to deal with the problems. And to speak the French language on your behalf.'

Amethyst took another look at the two men, whose rapid flow of angry words and flailing arms she would have wanted to avoid in any language.

'Very well, *monsieur*,' she said through gritted teeth. 'I shall go to my room and see to the unpacking.'

'I shall come and report to you there when I have resolved this matter,' he said. Then bowed the particular bow he'd perfected which managed to incorporate something of a sneer.

'Though he might as well have poked out his tongue and said "so there",' fumed Amethyst when she reached the room allocated to her travelling companion, Fenella Mountsorrel. 'I think I would prefer him if he did.'

'I don't suppose he wishes to lose his job,' replied Mrs Mountsorrel. 'Perhaps,' she added tentatively, as she watched Amethyst yank her bonnet ribbons undone, 'you ought not to provoke him quite so deliberately.'

'If I didn't,' she retorted, flinging her bonnet on to a handily placed dressing table, 'he would be even more unbearable. He would order us about, as though we were his servants, not the other way round. He is one of those men who think women incapable of knowing anything and assumes we all want some big strong man to lean on and tell us what to do.'

'Some of us,' said her companion wistfully, 'don't mind having a big strong man around. Oh, not to tell us what to do. But to lean on, when...when things are difficult.'

Amethyst bit back the retort that sprang to her lips. What good had that attitude done her companion? It had resulted in her being left alone in the world, without a penny to her name, that's what.

She took a deep breath, tugged off her gloves, and slapped them down next to her bonnet.

'When things are difficult,' she said, thrusting her fingers through the thick mass of dark curls she wished, for the umpteenth time, she'd had cut short before setting out on this voyage, 'you find out just what you are made of. And you and I, Fenella, are made of such stern stuff that we don't need some overbearing, unreliable, insufferable male dictating to us how to live our lives.'

'Nevertheless,' pointed out Fenella doggedly, 'we could not have come this far, without—'

'Without *employing* a man to deal with the more tiresome aspects of travelling so far from home,' she agreed. 'Men do have their uses, that I cannot deny.'

Fenella sighed. 'Not all men are bad.'

'You are referring to your dear departed Frederick, I

suppose,' she said, tartly, before conceding. 'But given you were so fond of him, I dare say there must have been something good about him.'

'He had his faults, I cannot deny it. But I do miss him. And I wish he had lived to see Sophie grow up. And perhaps given her a brother or sister...'

'And how is Sophie now?' Amethyst swiftly changed the subject. On the topic of Fenella's late husband, they would never agree. The plain unvarnished truth was that he had left his widow shamefully unprovided for. His pregnant widow at that. And all Fenella would ever concede was that he was not very wise with money. Not very wise! As far as Amethyst could discover, the man had squandered Fenella's inheritance on a series of bad investments, whilst living way beyond his means. Leaving Fenella to pick up the pieces...

She took a deep breath. There was no point in getting angry with a man who wasn't there to defend himself. And whenever she'd voiced her opinion, all it had achieved was to upset Fenella. Which was the last thing she wanted.

'Sophie still looked dreadfully pale when Francine took her for a lie down,' said Fenella, with a troubled frown.

'I am sure she will bounce right back after a nap, and a light meal, the way she usually does.'

They had discovered, after only going ten miles from Stanton Basset, that Sophie was not a good traveller. However well sprung the coach was, whether she sat facing forwards, or backwards, or lay across the seat with her head on her mother's lap, or a pillow, she suffered dreadfully from motion sickness.

It had meant that the journey had taken twice as

long as Monsieur Pruneface had planned, since Sophie needed one day's respite after each day's travel.

'If we miss the meetings you have arranged, then we miss them,' she'd retorted when he'd pointed out that the delay might cost her several lucrative contracts. 'If you think I am going to put mercenary considerations before the welfare of this child, then you are very much mistaken.'

'But then there is also the question of accommodation. With so many people wishing to visit Paris this autumn even I,' he'd said, striking his chest, 'may have difficulty arranging an alternative of any sort, let alone something suited to your particular needs.'

'Couldn't you write to whoever needs to know that our rooms, and yours, will be paid for no matter how late we arrive? And make some attempt to rearrange the other meetings?'

'*Madame*, you must know that France has been flooded with your countrymen, eager to make deals for trade, for several months now. Even had we arrived when stated, and I had seen these men to whom you point me, who knows if they would have done business with you? Competitors may already have done the undercutting...'

'Then they have undercut me,' she'd snapped. 'I will have lost the opportunity to expand on to the continent. But that is my affair, not yours. We will still want your services as a guide, if that is what worries you. And we can just be genuine tourists and enjoy the experience, instead of it being our cover for travelling here.'

He'd muttered something incomprehensible under his breath. But judging from the fact these rooms were ready for them, and that a couple of letters from merchants who might take wares from her factories were already awaiting her attention, he'd done as he'd been told.

At that moment, her train of thought was interrupted by a knock on the door. It was the particularly arrogant knock Monsieur Le Prune always used. How he accomplished it she did not know, but he always managed to convey the sense that he had every right to march straight in, should he wish, and was only pausing, for the merest moment, out of the greatest forbearance for the unaccountably emotional fragility of his female charges.

'The problem in the kitchen,' he began the moment he'd opened the door—before Amethyst had given him permission to enter, she noted with resentment—'it is, I am afraid to say, more serious than we first thought.'

'Oh, yes?' It was rather wicked of her, but she relished discovering that something had cropped up that forced him to admit that he was not in complete control of the entire universe. 'It was not so insignificant after all?'

'The chef,' he replied, ignoring her jibe, 'he tells me that there cannot be the meal he would wish to serve his new guest on her first night in Paris.'

'No meal?'

'Not one of the standard that will satisfy him, no. It is a matter of the produce, you understand, which is no longer fit to serve, not even for Englishmen, he informs me. For which I apologise. These are his words, not my own.'

'Naturally not.' Though he had thoroughly enjoyed being able to repeat them, she could tell.

'On account,' he continued with a twitch to his mouth that looked suspiciously like the beginnings of a smirk, 'of the fact that we arrived so many days after he was expecting us.'

In other words, if there was a problem, it was her fault. He probably thought that putting the welfare of a child before making money was proof that a woman shouldn't be running any kind of business, let alone attempting to expand. 'However, I have a suggestion to make, which will overcome this obstacle.'

'Oh, yes?' It had better be good.

'Indeed,' he said with a smile which was so self-congratulatory she got an irrational urge to fire him on the spot. That would show him who was in charge.

Only then she'd have to find a replacement for him. And his replacement was bound to be just as irritating. And she'd need to start all over again, teaching him all about her wares, the range of prices at which she would agree to do deals, production schedules and so on.

'For tonight,' he said, 'it would be something totally novel, I think, for you and Madame Montsorrel to eat in a restaurant.'

Before she had time to wonder if he was making some jibe about their provincial origins, he went on, 'Most of your countrymen are most keen to visit, on their first night in Paris, the Palais Royale, to dine in one of its many establishments.'

The suggestion was so sensible it took the wind out of her sails. It would make them look just like the ordinary tourists they were hoping to be taken for.

'And before you raise the objection that Sophie cannot be left alone,' he plunged on swiftly, 'on her first night in a strange country, I have asked the chef if he can provide the kind of simple fare which I have observed has soothed her stomach before. He assures me he can,' he said smugly. 'I have also spoken with Mademoiselle Francine, who has agreed to sit by her bedside, just this once, in the place of her mother, in case she awakes.'

'You seem to have thought of everything,' she had to concede.

'It is what you pay me for,' he replied, with a supercilious lift of one brow.

That was true. But did he have to point it out quite so often?

'What do you think, Fenella? Could you bear to go out tonight and leave Sophie? Or perhaps—' it suddenly occurred to her '—you are too tired?'

'Too tired to actually dine in one of those places we have been reading so much about? Oh, no! Indeed, no.'

The moment Bonaparte had been defeated and exiled to the tiny island of Elba, English tourists had been flocking to visit the country from which they had been effectively barred for the better part of twenty year. And filling newspapers and journals with accounts of their travels.

The more they'd raved about the delights of Paris, the more Amethyst had wanted to go and see it for herself. She'd informed her manager, Jobbings, that she was going to see if she could find new outlets for their wares, now trade embargoes had been lifted. And she would. She really would. She'd already made several appointments to which she would send Monsieur Le Brun, since she assumed French merchants would be as unwilling to do business with a female as English merchants were.

But she intended to take in as many experiences as she could while she was here.

'Then that is settled.' Amethyst was so pleased Fenella was completely in tune with her own desire to get out and explore that for once her state of almost permanent irritation with Monsieur Le Brun faded away to nothing.

And she smiled at him.

'Is there any particular establishment you would recommend?'

'I?' He gaped at her.

It was, she acknowledged, probably the first time he had ever seen her smile. At him, at least. But then she had never dared let down her guard around him before. She'd taken pains to question every one of his suggestions and to double-check every arrangement he'd made, just to make sure he never attempted to swindle her. Or thought he might be able to get away with any *attempt* to swindle her.

And he had got them to Paris. If not quite to his schedule, then at least in reasonable comfort. Nor had he put a foot out of place.

She was beginning to feel reasonably certain he wouldn't dare. Besides, she had Fenella to double-check any correspondence he wrote on her behalf. *Her* grasp of French was extremely good, to judge from the way Monsieur Le Brun reacted when he'd first heard her speaking it.

'The best, the very best,' he said, making a swift recovery, 'is most probably Very Frères. It is certainly the most expensive.'

She wrinkled her nose. It sounded like the kind of place people went to show off. It would be crammed full of earls and opera dancers, no doubt.

'The Mille Colonnes is popular with your countrymen. Although—' his face fell, '—by the time we arrive, there will undoubtedly be a queue to get in.'

She cocked her eyebrow at him. Rising to the unspoken challenge, he continued, 'There are many other excellent places to which I would not scruple to take you ladies… Le Caveau, for example, where for two to three francs you may have an excellent dinner of soup, fish, meat, dessert and a bottle of wine.'

Since she'd spent some time before setting out getting to grips with the exchange rate, his last statement made her purse her lips. Surely they wouldn't be able to get anything very appetising for such a paltry sum?

Nevertheless, she did not voice that particular suspicion. Having watched her intently as he'd described what were clearly more expensive establishments, he was probably doing his best to suggest somewhere more economical. He wasn't a fool. His manner might infuriate her, but she couldn't deny he was observant and shrewd. Because she'd made him suffer enough for one day and because Fenella had a tendency to get upset if they quarrelled openly in her presence, she admitted that she rather liked the sound of Le Caveau.

It wasn't long after that she and Fenella had changed, dressed, kissed a drowsy Sophie goodnight and were stepping out into the dimly lit streets of Paris.

Paris! She was really in Paris. Nothing could tell the world more clearly that she was her own woman. That she was ready to try new things and make her own choices in life. That she'd paid for the follies of her youth. And wasn't going to carry on living a cloistered existence, as though she was ashamed of herself. For she wasn't. She'd done nothing to be ashamed of.

Of course, she was not so keen to start becoming her own woman that she was going to abandon all her late Aunt Georgie's precepts. Not the ones that were practical at any rate. For her foray to the bargain of a restaurant that was Le Caveau, she wore the kind of plain, sensible outfit she would have donned for a visit to her bankers in the City. Monsieur Le Brun had just, but only just, repressed a shudder when he'd seen her emerge from her room. It was the same look she would have expected a member of the *ton*, in London, to send her way.

Provincial, they would think, writing her off as a nobody because her bonnet was at least three years behind the current fashion.

But it was far better for people to underestimate and overlook you, than to think you were a pigeon for the plucking. If she'd set out for the Continent in a coach and four, trailing wagonloads of servants and luggage, and made an enormous fuss at whatever inn they'd stopped at, she might as well have hung a placard round her neck, announcing 'Wealthy woman! Come and rob me!'

As it was, they'd had to put up with a certain amount of rudeness and inconvenience on occasion, but nobody had thought them worth the bother of robbing.

And there was another advantage, she soon discovered, to not being dressed in fine silks. 'I can't believe how muddy it is everywhere,' she grumbled, lifting her skirts to try to keep them free from dirt. 'This is like wading down some country lane that leads to a pig farm.'

'I suggested to you that it would be the mode to hire

a chair for your conveyance to the Palais Royale,' Monsieur Le Brun snapped back, whiplash smart.

'Oh, we couldn't possibly have done that,' said Fenella, at her most conciliatory. 'We are not grand ladies. We would both have felt most peculiar being carried through the streets like—'

'Parcels,' put in Amethyst. 'Lugged around by some hulking great porters.'

'Besides,' said Fenella hastily,' we can see so much more of your beautiful city, *monsieur*, if we walk through it, than we could by peeping through the curtains of some sort of carriage. And feel so much more a part of it.'

'That is certainly true. The mud certainly looks set to form a lasting part of my skirts,' observed Amethyst.

But then they stepped through an archway, into an immense, brilliantly lit gravelled square, and whatever derogatory comment she might have made next dried on her lips.

And Monsieur Le Brun smirked in satisfaction as both ladies gaped at the spectacle spread before them.

The Palais Royale was like nowhere she had ever seen before. And it was not just the sight of the tiers of so many brightly lit windows that made her blink, but the crowds of people, all intent on enjoying themselves to the full. To judge from the variety of costumes, they had come from every corner of the globe.

'This way,' said Monsieur Le Brun, taking her firmly by the elbow when she slowed down to peer into one of the brightly lit windows of an establishment in a basement. 'That place is not suitable for ladies such as yourselves.'

Indeed, from the brief glimpse she'd got of all the

military uniforms, and the rather free behaviour of the females in their company, she'd already gathered that for herself.

However, for once, she did not shake Monsieur Le Brun's hand away. It was all rather more...boisterous than she'd imagined. She'd found travelling to London, to consult with her bankers and men of business after her aunt's death, somewhat daunting, so bustling and noisy was the metropolis in comparison with the sleepy tranquillity of Stanton Basset. But the sheer vivacity of Paris at night was on a different scale altogether.

It was with relief that she passed through the doors of another eatery, which was quickly overtaken by amazement. Even though Monsieur Le Brun had told her this place was economical, it far surpassed her expectations. She had glanced through the grimy windows of chop houses when she'd been in London and had assumed a cheap restaurant in Paris, which admitted members of the public, would resemble one of those. Instead, her eyes were assailed by mirrors and columns, and niches with statues, tables set with glittering cutlery and crystal, diners dressed in fabulous colours and waiters bustling around attentively.

And the food, which she'd half-suspected would be of the same quality she'd endured in the various coaching inns where they'd stayed, was as good as anything she might have tasted when invited to dine with the best families in the county.

But what really made her evening, was to see that the whole enterprise was run by a woman. She sat in state by the door, assigning customers to tables suited to the size of their party, taking their money and tallying it all up in a massive ledger, spread before her on a great granite-topped table.

And nobody seemed to think there was anything untoward about this.

They had just taken receipt of their dessert when a man, entering alone, inspired a grimace of distaste from Monsieur Le Brun. Her gaze followed the direction of his to see who could have roused his displeasure and she froze, her spoon halfway to her mouth.

Nathan Harcourt.

The disgraced Nathan Harcourt.

Her face went hot while her stomach turned cold, curdling all the fine food inside it to a churning mass of bile.

And the question that had haunted her for years almost forced its way through her clenched teeth in a despairing scream. *How could you do that to me, Nathan? How could you?*

She wanted to get up, march across the restaurant and soundly slap the cheeks that the proprietress was enthusiastically kissing. Though it was far too late now. She should have done it the night he'd cut her dead, after making a point of dancing with just about every other girl in the ballroom. The night he'd started to break her heart.

He hadn't changed a bit when it came to spreading his favours about, she noted. The proprietress, who'd merely given them a regal nod when they'd come in, was clasping him to her bosom with such enthusiasm it was a wonder he didn't disappear into those ample mounds and suffocate.

Which would serve him right.

'That man,' said Monsieur Le Brun at his most prune-faced, watching the direction of her affronted gaze, 'should not be permitted in here at all. But it is as you see. He is in favour with *madame*, so the customers are subjected to his impertinence. It is regrettable, but not an insurmountable problem. I shall not permit him to disturb you.'

It was too late for that. His arrival had already disturbed her—though Monsieur Le Brun's words had also roused her curiosity.

'What do you mean—subjecting the customers to his impertinence?'

'He does portraits,' said Monsieur Le Brun. 'Quick studies in pencil, for the amusement of the visitors to the city.'

As if to prove his point, Nathan Harcourt produced a little canvas stool from the satchel he had slung over one shoulder, crouched down on it beside one of the tables near the door, took out a stick of charcoal and began to sketch the diners seated there.

'Portraits? Nathan Harcourt?'

Monsieur Le Brun's eyebrows shot up into his hairline. 'You know this man? I would never have thought... I mean,' he regrouped, adopting his normal slightly supercilious demeanour, 'though he is a countryman of yours, I would not have thought you moved in the same circles.'

'Not of late,' she admitted. 'Though, at one time, we...did.'

All of ten years ago, to be precise, when she'd been completely ignorant of the nature of men and from too sheltered a background to know how to guard herself against his type. And from too ordinary a background to have anyone sufficiently powerful to protect her from him.

But things were different now.

Different for her and, by the looks of things, very, very different for him too. Her eyes narrowed as she studied his appearance and noted the changes.

Some of them were just due to the passage of years and were pretty much what she would have expected. His face was leaner and flecks of silver glinted here and there amidst curls that had once been coal black. But it was the state of his clothing that most clearly proclaimed the rumours that his father had finally washed his hands of his youngest son were entirely true. His coat only fit where it touched, his hat was a broad-brimmed affair of straw and his trousers were the baggy kind she'd seen the local tradesmen wearing. In short, he looked downright shabby.

Well, well. She leaned back and observed him working with mounting pleasure. When he'd achieved the almost-impossible feat of becoming too notorious for any political party to put him up for even the most rotten of rotten boroughs, he'd vanished, amidst much speculation. She'd assumed that, like the younger sons of so many eminent families, when he'd blotted the escutcheon, he'd been sent to the Continent to live a life of luxurious indolence.

But it looked as though his father, the Earl of Finchingfield, had been every bit as furious as the scandal sheets had hinted at the time and as unforgiving as her own father. For here was Nathan Harcourt, the proud, cold-hearted Nathan Harcourt, forced to work to earn a crust.

'I shall not be at all displeased if he should come

to my table and solicit my custom,' she said, a strange thrill shivering through her whole being. 'In fact, I would thoroughly enjoy having my portrait done.'

By him. Having him solicit her for her time, her money, her custom, when ten years ago, he had been too…proud and mighty, and…*ambitious* to have his name linked with hers.

Oh, what sweet revenge. Here he was, practically begging for a living and not doing too well from the look of his clothing. While here she was, thanks to Aunt Georgie, in possession of so much wealth she would be hard pressed to run through it in ten lifetimes.

Chapter Two

Nathan stood up, handed over the finished sketch to his first customer of the night and held out his hand for payment. He thanked them for their compliments and made several comments witty enough to hit their mark, judging from the way the other occupants of the table flung back their heads and laughed. But he had no idea what he'd actually said. His mind was still reeling from the shock of seeing Amethyst Dalby.

After ten years of leaving him be, she had to go and invade territory that he'd come to think of as peculiarly his own.

Not that it mattered.

And to prove it, he would damn well confront her.

He turned and scanned the restaurant with apparent laziness, hesitated when he came to her table, affected surprise, then sauntered over.

If she had the effrontery to appear in public, with her latest paramour in tow, then it was time to remove the gloves. The days were long gone when he would have spared a lady's blushes because of some ridiculous belief in chivalry towards the weaker sex.

The weaker sex! The cunning sex more like. He'd never met one who wasn't hiding some secret or other, be it only her age, or how much she'd overspent her allowance.

Though none with secrets that had been as destructive as hers.

'Miss Dalby,' he said when he reached her table. 'How surprising to see you here.'

'In Paris, do you mean?'

'Anywhere,' he replied with a hard smile. 'I would have thought…' He trailed off, leaving her to draw her own conclusions as to where he might have gone with that statement. He'd made his opinion of her very plain when he'd discovered how duplicitous she'd been ten years ago. Back then, she'd had the sense to flee polite society and presumably return to the countryside.

He hadn't allowed himself to dwell on what might have become of her. But now she was here, why shouldn't he find out? He glanced at her hand. No ring. And she hadn't corrected him when he'd addressed her as Miss Dalby, either.

So it didn't look as though she'd ever managed to entrap some poor unsuspecting male into marriage with a pretence of innocence. This man, this sallow-skinned, beetle-browed man whose face looked vaguely familiar, was not her husband. What then? A lover?

'Are you not going to introduce me?' He cocked an eyebrow in the direction of her male friend, wondering where he'd seen him before.

'I see no need for that,' she replied with a stiff smile.

No? He supposed it might be a little awkward, introducing a former lover to her current one. Especially if he was the jealous sort. He gave him a searching look and met with one of mutual antipathy. Was it possible the man felt…threatened? He could see why he might look like a potential competitor. Without putting too fine a point on it, he was younger, fitter and more handsome than the man she'd washed up with. Not that he saw himself in the light of competitor for *her* favours. God, no!

'After all,' she continued archly, 'you cannot have come across to renew our acquaintance. I believe it is work you wish to solicit. Is it not?'

Of course it was. She didn't need to remind him that whatever they'd had was finished.

'I explained to *madame*,' put in the man, proclaiming his nationality by the thickness of his accent, 'that this is how you make your living. By drawing the likenesses of tourists.'

It wasn't quite true. But he let it pass. It was…convenient, for the moment, to let everyone think he was earning his living from his pictures. And simpler.

And that *was* why he'd strolled across to her table. Exactly why.

There could be no other reason.

'*Madame* wishes you to make her the swift portrait,' said the Frenchman.

Miss Dalby shot her French lover a look brimming with resentment. He looked steadily back at her, completely unrepentant.

Interesting. The Frenchman felt the need to assert his authority over her. To remind her who was in control. Or perhaps he'd already discovered how fickle she could be, since he clearly wasn't going to permit her to flirt with a potential new conquest right before his eyes.

Wise man.

Miss Dalby needed firm handling if a man had a hope of keeping her in her place.

He had a sudden vision of doing exactly that. She was on her back, beneath him, he was holding her hands above her head... He blinked it away, busying himself with unfolding his stool and assembling his materials. No more than one minute in her presence and he was proving as susceptible to her charms as he'd ever been. The Frenchman, on whom he deliberately turned his back as he sat down, had every reason to be jealous. He must always be fighting off would-be rivals. What red-blooded male, coming within the radius of such a siren, could fail to think about bedding her?

Even though she was not dressed particularly well, there was no disguising her beauty. As a girl, she'd been remarkably pretty. But the years—in spite of what her lifestyle must have been like to judge from the company she was now keeping—had been good to her. She had grown into those cheekbones. And the skin that clad them was peachy soft and clear as cream. Those dark-brown eyes were as deep, lustrous and mysterious as they'd ever been.

It was a pity that for quick sketches like this, he only used a charcoal pencil. He would have liked to add colour to this portrait. Later, perhaps, he would record this meeting for his own satisfaction, commemorating it in paint.

Meanwhile, his fingers flew across the page, capturing the angle of her forehead, the arch of her brows. So easily. But then she wasn't a fresh subject. Years ago, he'd spent hours drawing her face, her hands, the curve of her shoulder and the shadows where her skin disappeared into the silk of her evening gown. Not while she was actually present, of course, because she'd been masquerading as an innocent débutante and he'd been too green to consider flouting the conventions. But at night, when he was in his room alone, unable to sleep for yearning for her—yes, then he'd drawn her. Trying to capture her image, her essence.

What a fool he'd been.

He'd even bought some paints and attempted to reproduce the colours of that remarkable hair. He hadn't been able to do it justice, back then. He hadn't the skill. And he hadn't been allowed to pursue his dream by taking lessons.

'It's for young ladies, or tradesmen,' his father had snapped, when they'd discussed what he really wanted to do with his life, if not follow his brothers into one of the traditional professions. 'Not a suitable pastime for sons of noblemen.'

He could do it now, though. He'd learned about light and shade. Pigment and perspective.

His fingers stilled. In spite of what his friend Fielding had said, she wasn't merely a brunette. There were still those rich, warm tints in her hair that put him in mind of a really good port when you held the glass up to a candle. Fielding had laughed when he'd admitted his obsession with it and clapped him on the back. 'Got it bad, ain't you?'

He glanced up, his hand hovering over the half-finished sketch. He might well have *had it bad*, but he hadn't been wrong about her hair. It was just as glorious as it had ever been. After ten years, he might have expected to see the occasional strand of silver between the dark curls. Or perhaps signs that she was preserving an appearance of youth with dyes.

But that hair was not dyed. It could not look so soft, so glossy, so entirely…natural and eminently touchable…

He frowned, lowered his head and went back to work. He did *not* want to run his fingers through it, to see if it felt as soft as it looked. He could appreciate beauty when he saw it. He was an artist, after all. But then he would defy anybody to deny she had glorious hair. A lovely face. And sparkling eyes.

Though none of that altered the fact that she was poison.

He looked up, directly into her eyes, eyes that had once looked at him with what he'd thought was adoration. He smiled grimly. It was easier to read her now that he was older and wiser. She was looking at him assessingly, challengingly, with more than a measure of calculation simmering in the brew. All those things she'd taken such care to hide from him before.

Yes, she was poison right enough. Poison in a tantalising package.

From behind him, he heard her current lover shift impatiently in his chair. He probably regretted allowing her to have her way in this. It must irk him, having her looking at another man with such intent, while he was sitting mere inches away. But he was doing so, as though he was powerless to deny her anything.

God, she must be extraordinarily gifted between the sheets…

His mouth firming, he dropped his gaze to the page on his lap, adding a few deft strokes which put depth to the image he was creating.

'There,' he said, taking the finished sketch and tossing it to her lover.

The man looked at it, raised his brows and handed it across the table to Miss Dalby, who snatched at it.

'This is…' She frowned as she scanned the picture. 'It is amazing, considering you did it so quickly.' The expression in her eyes changed to what looked almost like respect. And he felt that glow which always came when people recognised his talent. His gift.

They might say he was a failure in every other department of his life, but nobody could deny he could draw.

'How much do you charge?'

Miss Dalby was looking at the picture she held in her hands as though she couldn't quite believe it. He stood up, folded up his stool and gave the insouciant shrug he always gave his subjects. And gave her the answer he always gave them, too.

'Whatever you think it is worth.'

Whatever she thought it was worth? Oh, but that was priceless! She would have paid any amount of money to have him sitting at her feet, a supplicant. Ten years ago he'd swaggered everywhere, bestowing a smile here, an appreciative glance at some beauty there, with the air of a young god descended to the realms of lesser mortals. It was worth a king's ransom to see him reduced to working for a living, when at one time he'd thought that she, with her lowly background and her lack of powerful connections, could be tossed aside as though she were nothing. And a delightful notion sprang to her mind.

'Monsieur Le Brun.' She beckoned the courier, who leant closer so that she could whisper into his ear. 'I should like this young man to have the equivalent of

twenty-five pounds. In French francs.' It was the annual wage she paid her butler.

'Do you have sufficient funds about you?'

His eyes widened. 'No, *madame*, to carry such a sum
on my person would be folly of the most reprehensible.'

'Then you must draw it from the bank and see that
he gets it. First thing tomorrow.'

'But, *madame*—'

'I insist.'

After a moment's hesitation, he murmured, 'I see,
madame', with what looked, for once, bafflingly, like
approval. And then, 'As you wish.'

He reached into his pocket and produced a heap of
coins, which he dropped into Harcourt's outstretched
palm.

'Please to furnish me with your direction,' he said,
'and I will call to settle with you for the rest.'

Nathan's lips twisted into a cynical smile as he
scrawled his address on the back of the sketch he'd just
drawn. It was obvious this impudent fellow meant to
call round and warn him to stay away from the beauty
he currently had in his keeping. From the sneer about
the fellow's lips, the Frenchman assumed he was penniless. It was the trap so many people fell into where
he was concerned, because he wore old clothes when
he was sketching, clothes that he didn't mind getting
ruined by charcoal dust, or from sitting in the dirt
when there was an interesting subject he simply had
to capture.

This Frenchman planned to make the point that Nathan
need not bother trying to compete. *He* had the wealth to

satisfy her. To keep her. And what did he, a shabby, itin-erant artist, have to offer?

Apart from relative youth, good looks and a rogu-ish smile?

And all of a sudden, he had an almost overbearing urge to do it. To take her away from this slimy excuse of a man. To pursue her, and win her, and enslave her, and bind her to him…and then throw her away.

Because, dammit, somebody ought to punish her, for every single thing he'd gone through this last ten years. If she hadn't set her sights on him and damn near enslaved him, then he wouldn't have been so dev-astated when he found out what lay concealed behind the pretty façade. He would not have agreed to the di-sastrous marriage brokered by his family, or embarked on an equally disastrous political career, from which he'd only managed to extricate himself by committing what amounted to social suicide.

Oh, yes, if there were any justice in the world…

Only of course there wasn't. That was one lesson life had taught him only too well. Honesty was never rewarded. The devious were the ones who inherited the earth, not the meek.

Tucking the pile of coins into his satchel, along with his supplies, he employed the smile he'd perfected during his years in politics, directing it in turn at the Frenchman, at Miss Dalby, and at the mousy woman who was sitting with them at table.

And strode out of the door.

'Goodness,' breathed Mrs Mountsorrel. 'I have heard of him, of course, but I never expected him to be quite so…' She flushed and faded into a series of utterances that could only be described as twittering.

But then that performance was the one he'd used so many times to reduce susceptible females to a state of fluttering, twittering, hen-witted compliance. Having those heavy-lidded, knowing hazel eyes trained so intently on her face would have had the same effect upon her, too, if she hadn't been enjoying seeing him grovelling at her feet quite so much. And then again, there was something about the combination of those aristocratic good looks, and the shabby clothing, that might have tugged at her heartstrings, had she any heart left for him to tug at.

'He has the reputation with the ladies rather unsavoury,' put in Monsieur Le Brun, at his most prune-faced.

'Oh, yes, I know all about *that*,' twittered Fenella. 'Miss Dalby is always reading accounts of his doings that appear in the newspapers. Why, his wife wasn't dead five minutes before the most terrible rumours started up. And then, of course, when he fell from grace so spectacularly, there was no doubting the truth of it. He would have sued for libel if the papers had been making it up. Or is it slander?'

'You sound as though you find him fascinating,' he said, with narrowed eyes.

'Oh, no, not I. It is Amethyst who followed his career in public life so closely. I mean, Miss Dalby, of course.'

He turned to her with a frown.

'Well, *madame*, I…I commend you for wishing to aid someone you have known in the past. And being so generous, it is one thing, but I implore you not to be deceived by his so-charming smile.'

Oh. So that was why, for once, he hadn't argued with her about the way she chose to spend her own money. He thought she was being generous to a friend who'd fallen on hard times.

If only he knew!

'It is rather distressing,' put in Fenella, 'to see a man from his background sunk so low.'

'He brought it all on himself,' said Amethyst tartly.

'And yet you have been so generous to him,' said Monsieur Le Brun.

'Well…' she began, squirming in her seat, and blushing. It hadn't been generosity, but a desire to rub his nose in the reversal of their fortunes that had prompted her to pay him a year's wages for five minutes' work.

'I don't see why you should be so surprised,' said Fenella stoutly. 'I thought you were more perceptive than that, *monsieur*. Surely you have noticed that she doesn't like people to know how generous she is. She hides it behind gruff manners, and…and eccentric ways. But deep down, there is nobody kinder than my Miss Dalby. Why, if you only knew how she came to my rescue—'

Amethyst held up her hand to silence her. 'Fenella. Stop right there. I hired you in a fit of temper with the ladies of Stanton Basset, you know I did. Mrs Podmore came round, not five minutes after Aunt Georgie's funeral, telling me that I would have to employ some female to live with me so long as I remained single or I would no longer be considered *respectable*. So I marched straight round to your house and offered you the post just to spite them.'

'What she hasn't told you,' said Fenella, turning to Monsieur Le Brun who was regarding his employer with raised eyebrows, 'was that she'd never been able to abide the way everyone gossiped about me. But she'd never been able to do much about it apart from offer her friendship until after her aunt died.'

'Well, it was dreadful, the way they treated you. It must have been hard enough, coming to live in a place where you knew nobody, with a small baby to care for, without people starting those malicious rumours about you having invented a husband.'

'For all you knew, I might have done.'

'Well, what difference would it have made? If you had been seduced and abandoned, surely you were due some sympathy and support? What would you have been guilty of, after all? Being young and foolish, and taken in by some glib promises made by a smooth-talking scoundrel.'

Was she still talking about Fenella? Amethyst wondered as she shakily reached for her glass, and downed the last of its contents. Or had it been seeing Nathan Harcourt that had stirred up such a martial spirit? And bother it, but Monsieur Le Brun was leaning back in his chair, his eyes flicking from one to another with keen interest.

They were both revealing far more about themselves and their past than he had any right to know.

'I think we have said enough upon this subject,' she said, setting her glass down with quiet deliberation.

'She always gets embarrassed when anyone sings her praises,' Fenella informed Monsieur Le Brun. 'But I cannot help myself. For she didn't just give me work to support myself and Sophie, she made sure my little girl finally had all that a gentleman's daughter should have had. All the things,' she said with a quivering lip, 'that my own family denied her, because they never approved of Frederick. A nurse, beautiful clothes, a pony and, best of all, an education…'

'Well, she's such a bright little thing.' And it wasn't as if Amethyst was ever going to have any children of her own. At seven and twenty she was firmly on the shelf. No man would look twice at her if it weren't for the fortune her aunt had left her. As she knew only too well.

'So don't you go thinking,' she said, hauling herself up by the scruff of the neck, 'that I'm…a pigeon for the plucking. Put one foot wrong and I will give you your marching orders,' she finished.

'Miss Dalby!' Fenella turned a puzzled, disappointed face towards her. 'There is no need to keep on treating Monsieur Le Brun as if he is working out ways to rob you. Hasn't he proved over and over again on this trip how very honest, hard working and…ingenious he is?'

And he was sitting right there, listening.

'If you must discuss Monsieur Le Brun's many and various skills, please have the goodness to do so when we return to the privacy of our own rooms.'

'I expect it was the shock of seeing Nathan Harcourt that has made her so out of reason cross,' Fenella explained to Monsieur Le Brun, who was by now starting to look rather amused. 'They used to know one another quite well, you see. He led poor Miss Dalby to believe they might make a match of it—'

'Fenella! Monsieur Le Brun does not need to know *any* of this.'

Fenella smiled at her, before carrying on in the same confidential tone. 'He was the youngest son of an earl, you know. Well, I suppose he still is.' She giggled.

And that was when it hit Amethyst.

'Fenella, I think you have had rather too much to drink.'

Fenella blinked. Her eyes widened. 'Do you really think so?' She peered down at her glass. 'Surely not. I have only been sipping at my wine, and, look—the glass is still half-full...'

What she clearly hadn't noticed was the way the waiters kept topping up the glass. And taking away the empty bottles and bringing fresh ones.

'Nevertheless, it is time to go home, Monsieur Le Brun, wouldn't you say?'

It said a great deal for the amount of wine Fenella had inadvertently consumed that it took both her and Monsieur Le Brun to get her into her coat and through the door. Then, when the fresh air hit her, she swayed on her feet. Monsieur Le Brun proved to have remarkably swift reflexes, because he caught her arm, tactfully supporting her before she could embarrass herself. Just to be on the safe side, Amethyst took her other arm, and between them they steered her through the crowds milling about the central courtyard of the Palais Royale.

But she was almost certain she heard him chuckle.

'This is not funny,' she snapped as they ushered her through the archway that led into the street that would take them home.

'She isn't used to dining out like this. Or having waiters going round topping up her glass. And as for that wine...well, it was downright deceitful. It tasted so fruity and pleasant...more like cordial than anything with alcohol in it.'

'It was not the wine. It is Paris,' said Monsieur Le Brun with an insouciant shrug. 'It has the effect most surprising on many people. So we must make sure, as her friends, that we take especially good care of her from now on.'

Her friends? Monsieur Le Brun considered himself Fenella's friend? And what was worse, he was putting himself on a level with her, as though they were…a team, or something.

Well, that would not do. It would not do at all.

And just as soon as she could think of the right words to do so, she was going to put Monsieur Le Brun firmly in his place.

But not until they'd got Fenella safely home.

Chapter Three

'I have let you down,' moaned Fenella.

'Nonsense,' Amethyst murmured soothingly. It had actually been rather cheering to see her friend was not a complete paragon of all the virtues.

'It is just…foreign travel,' she said. 'Or perhaps, as Monsieur Le Brun says, the excitement of being in Paris…'

Fenella rolled on to her side and buried her face in the pillow.

'There is no excuse for what I did…'

'You just had a little too much to drink and became rather more talkative than usual, that is all.'

'But my judgement…' Fenella protested, albeit in a very quiet voice.

'Well, it is not a mistake you will make again,' said Amethyst bracingly, 'if this is how ill you become after partaking too freely. You wince whenever you try to open your eyes. Let me make you more comfortable.'

'I shall never feel comfortable again,' she whimpered as Amethyst crossed the room and drew the curtains, plunging the room into darkness.

'How am I ever going to face Sophie? Oh, my little girl. When she finds out…'

'Why should she find out? I am certainly not going to tell her anything more than that her mama needs to stay in bed this morning, because she is a little unwell. Heavens, she has had to have enough days in bed while we've been travelling to assume that the rigours of the journey have just caught up with you.'

'But to lie to my own child…'

'You won't have to lie. Just not admit to the truth.'

Amethyst strode back to her friend's side and smoothed her hair back from her flushed face. It was an indication of just how ill Fenella really felt that she flinched back from her touch.

'I promised to take her out to see the sights of the city today. She will be so disappointed.'

'No, she won't, for I shall take her myself. You look as though you need to go back to sleep. Don't even think about stirring from this room until after you have had your luncheon, either. Which I shall order the staff to have brought to your room.'

Fenella caught her hand and kissed it. 'You are too good to me. Too kind. I don't deserve your understanding…'

'Fustian! It is about time you stopped being so perfect. I like you the better for it. Makes me feel less of a failure, if you must know.' Usually, she felt like a hard-headed, prickly, confrontational excuse for a woman in comparison to the perfect manners of her elegant and utterly feminine companion.

Amethyst was wealthy, courtesy of her aunt, and she had a good head for business, but she didn't make friends easily and simply could not imagine ever getting married. If a man made up to her, it was because of her wealth, not anything intrinsically attractive about her. She'd learned that lesson the hard way when she'd been too young and vulnerable to withstand the experience. It had scarred her. Wounded her. She'd felt a staggering amount of empathy for those beggars they'd seen so many of, lying by the roadsides of every French town they'd travelled through, for a vital part of her had been ruthlessly amputated in battle and she would never be quite whole again.

Not that it mattered, according to Aunt Georgie. Lots of people led perfectly good lives in spite of what other people thought of as handicaps. So what if she could never trust a man again? Neither did her aunt.

'Useless pack of self-serving, scrounging scum, if you ask me,' she'd sniffed disparagingly, when she whisked Amethyst from the village on what was supposed to have been a therapeutic trip round the Lakes. 'Don't understand why any sensible woman would wish to shackle herself to one. And I'm beginning to think you are capable of being sensible, if only you will get over this habit of thinking you need a man in your life. All any of them do is interfere and ruin everything.'

After what she'd been through, she'd been inclined to agree.

Fenella moaned again, drawing her attention back to the present, and then she flung the back of one hand over her eyes.

Amethyst pursed her lips. She sympathised with Fenella for having a sore head. She sympathised with her feeling embarrassed at having to be helped home. But...

'Good heavens, Fenella, anyone who is not used to drinking might have made the same error. It is not the end of the world.' And there was absolutely no need for all these theatrics.

'I know what you're doing. You are worrying about what people will say. But nothing is ever solved by worrying about what other people think of you. Especially not the sort of people who would love nothing better than to condemn you. They're mostly cowards, you know. Too scared to take life by the scruff of the neck and live it. Instead, they prefer to sit about gossiping in a vain attempt to liven up the boredom of their useless, unprofitable lives. You should never modify your behaviour in an attempt to win the regard of their sort.'

Good heavens. Had she really just repeated one of Aunt Georgie's favourite homilies? In the very tone of voice her aunt would have employed whenever Amethyst had been a bit blue-devilled?

She had.

She wrapped her arms round her waist and walked rather jerkily over to the window. For years, people had been warning her that if she wasn't careful, she'd end up just like her aunt. But she'd told them she didn't care. She'd been so grateful to her for the way she'd stood up to Amethyst's father. From the moment Aunt Georgie had gone toe to toe with him in his library, telling him he'd been a pompous little boy who'd grown into a pompous prig of a man without a shred of compassion in him, her life had begun to take an upward turn. Well, she could hardly have sunk any lower. So she hadn't listened to a word of criticism levelled at her aunt, not from anyone.

But sometimes…

She thought of the single tear she'd seen tricking down Fenella's face, a tear she'd provoked with that heartless little homily, and wanted to kick herself. She'd sounded as callous and unfeeling as Aunt Georgie at her very worst.

'It's different for you,' said Fenella woefully. 'I am a mother. I have to think of Sophie. Whatever I do has an impact on her. And there are certain things a lady should never do.'

'I know, I know,' said Amethyst, going back to her bedside and perching on the nearest chair.

'I'm sorry I spoke harshly. It's just—'

'You are so strong that it is hard for you to sympathise, sometimes, with weakness in others.'

'I wasn't always strong,' she said. 'You know I would have gone under if Aunt Georgie hadn't stepped in to rescue me when she did. It was her example that gave me the determination to do something for you. I knew what it was like to be alone, unjustly accused of something I hadn't done, with nobody to defend me.' It had been hellish. Her whole family had turned their backs on her just when she'd needed them the most. 'You needed a friend, to stand with you against all those wagging tongues. Just as I needed Aunt Georgie to believe in me. Just as you need me to be a friend now, not...not tell you to pull yourself together. Forgive me?'

'Yes, of course, but—'

'No. Please don't say another word about it. I know it must have been distressing to have been helped home, slightly foxed, last night, but I've already told you I do not think the worse of you for it. And who else knows about it? Only Monsieur Le Brun, and if he dares to make you feel in the slightest bit uncomfortable, he will have me to deal with,' she finished militantly.

Fenella pressed her hands to her eyes and whimpered.

'I will leave you now,' she said, far more quietly. It had occurred to her that a loud voice might bring more distress than comfort, no matter what words she actually said, and that Fenella just needed to sleep it off.

'I will look after Sophie today,' she said, tiptoeing towards the door. 'And make sure no word of what you got up to last night ever reaches her ears.'

She shut the door on yet another moan of anguish, only to jump in shock at the sight of Monsieur Le Brun standing in the corridor, not three feet away.

'I beg your pardon,' he said. 'I did not mean to startle you. I only meant…that is…Madame Montsorrel. How is she?'

'She is feeling very sorry for herself. And very guilty.'

Monsieur Le Brun lowered his head. 'I hope you have not been too harsh with her. Indeed, the fault was not hers. It was mine. I should not have—'

'Oh, don't you start,' she said. 'She made a mistake. That was yesterday. And anyone can see how sorry she is for it. But if you think it was at all your fault, then all you need do in future is to make sure the wine we order is not so strong. And that none of us has more than a couple of glasses. We lived very simply in Stanton Basset and never partook of more than one glass of wine or Madeira, and that only on special occasions.'

'The wine,' he gulped. 'Yes, yes, but—'

'No, I don't wish to discuss this any more.' She was getting a most uncomfortable feeling, seeing him look so concerned about Fenella's health. She'd have assumed he would have been irritated, not remorseful. If she wasn't careful, she might stop disliking him. And then where would she be? Vulnerable!

'We have a busy day ahead of us. Have you dealt with Monsieur Harcourt yet?'

He already had on his coat and was turning his hat round and round as she spoke, as though he had just snatched it off. Or was he just about to put it on?

'Yes, *madame*, I went first thing. I could not sleep, you see. I—'

She held up her hand to silence him. If he wasn't going to volunteer any information about his encounter with Nathan she didn't want to know. 'If your accommodation is unsatisfactory for some reason,' she therefore said tersely, 'you must change it. You can spare me the details.' Only yesterday he'd claimed it was his duty to deal with *the matters domestic*. What was wrong with him today? 'What I do want to hear about is any progress you have made with our contacts. Have you managed to reschedule any of the appointments we missed because of our late arrival?'

He straightened up and gave her a brief, if slightly disappointing, account of his efforts on behalf of George Holdings.

'So the rest of our day is effectively free, then?'

'I regret, *madame*, that yes.' He spread his hands wide in a totally Gallic gesture of apology.

'Well, in that case we can devote it to Sophie. The poor little girl has been through torment to get here. The least we can do is make it up to her by giving her a perfectly splendid day. I want to take her out somewhere today that she will enjoy so much it will prevent her from worrying about her poor mama. Any ideas?'

'Yes, *madame*. Of course *madame*. But—'

'We will be ready to go out in half an hour,' she said, turning on her heel. 'And it's *mademoiselle*,' she threw over her shoulder as she stalked along the corridor to the nursery.

'How are you, my little sweet pea?' she said as she strode into Sophie's room. All her irritation vanished the moment Sophie leapt to her feet, ran across the room and flung her arms round Amethyst's waist.

'Feel better this morning, do you?'

'Yes, Aunt Amy! I have such a lovely view out of my window,' she said, tugging her across the room to show her. 'I have seen so many people walking by. The ladies wear the most enormous bonnets so you can't see their faces and their skirts look like great big bells swinging along the street. And the buildings are all so tall, and grand, but the people who go into them are all muddled up.'

'Muddled up?'

'Yes. You can't tell who the house belongs to by watching who goes in. Not at all. I thought that one over there...' she pointed to the *hôtel* immediately across the street '...must belong to someone very important, because a great big coach drew up last night and people dressed up in fabulous clothes got in, but then this morning, some people came out looking as though they were going to work. A man with a leather satchel and a quite poor-looking woman carrying a bundle...'

'I expect it is the same as this house, then,' she explained. 'Each floor is rented out to someone different. The grand people with the coach would have the ground floor and the woman with the bundle probably lives up in the attics somewhere.'

Sophie's brow wrinkled. 'Are we very grand, then?'

'Because we have rented the ground floor of this house?' Amethyst smiled. 'No. We are not grand at all.

Only…quite well off.' Fabulously well off, thanks to her aunt's shrewd business brain. And, lately, to hers. People who knew she'd been her aunt's sole beneficiary expected her fortune to dwindle, now that she was at the helm. Only a trusted few knew that her aunt had trained her in every aspect of managing her vast port-folio, after discovering she, too, had a knack with num-bers. An ability to spot an opportunity for investment that others overlooked, which stemmed, in part, from a refusal to accept the general consensus of opinion in the masculine-dominated world of finance.

'I just wanted,' she explained to the inquisitive child, 'you and your mother to have the best that money could buy for our little adventure.'

'Where is Mama?'

'She is not feeling well this morning. I have told her to stay in bed.'

Sophie's face fell.

'She will not be coming out with us today, but Mon-sieur Le Brun has promised that he will show you a lot of very interesting things.'

'But Mama won't see them. I would rather she was with us…'

'Yes, so would I,' Amethyst replied with feeling. A whole day sightseeing with Monsieur Le Prune, without Fenella's soothing presence to act as a buffer between them, was bound to end in them having words. 'But you can tell her all about them when we come home. And perhaps buy her a little present to cheer her up.'

Sophie's face lit up. 'A monkey. I saw a man with a monkey go past just now, wearing a red jacket and cap.'

'No, sweet pea. I do not think your mama would enjoy having a monkey for a pet.'

Sophie looked thoughtful. 'No, I suppose not. She... likes quiet things, does she not?'

'Yes.' That was very true. Sophie had much more of an adventurous spirit than her mother. She wouldn't be a bit surprised if she didn't take after her rather reckless father in temperament, though she was a miniature image of her mother, with her light-brown hair and soft, smoky blue eyes.

'We could buy her a picture. She would like that, wouldn't she? Are there shops that sell pictures?'

'I am sure there must be.' For there were certainly plenty of artists about. Infiltrating restaurants and invading people's dreams...

She shook herself. He had not invaded her dreams on purpose. It was her own stupid fault for spending the last few moments before she fell asleep savouring the way it had felt to have him come to her and beg for custom. And then imagining all sorts of other ways she could make him rue the day he'd spurned her for that horsey-faced female, simply because *her* father had a seat in Parliament in his pocket, rather than just a modest parish to govern. In her dreams, he'd gone from crouching on that canvas stool, to kneeling at her feet, begging forgiveness and swearing that he'd made a terrible mistake. That he'd been punished, for years, for the callous way he'd broken her heart. And only a kiss from her lips could assuage his torment...

She'd felt most uncomfortable when she awoke. Gracious heavens, she didn't want him to beg her for kisses, or anything else. She was well rid of him. She'd told herself so every time she'd seen his name in print in conjunction with tales of his ineffectiveness, or lack of loyalty to his party and the men who'd sponsored his career. And eventually, when his penchant for sordid sexual scandals got so out of hand that no amount of pressure from his influential family could undo the damage, she had incontrovertible proof.

He was no good.

And she'd had a lucky escape.

'I'm ready!'

She blinked to see Sophie hopping from one foot to the other, her coat buttoned up, her bonnet tied neatly under her chin.

Time to go out.

And push the feckless, faithless Nathan Harcourt from her mind. She had better things to do with her day than think about him. About how much more handsome he was than she had remembered. How much more vital and alive as he crouched with his pencil in his hand in that restaurant than he'd seemed as a young man. He'd strolled through the ballrooms of polite society, in those days, with a jaded air, as though nothing and nobody could possibly interest him. That had been the cynical ploy of a rake, of course. When he'd deigned to pay her a little attention, it had made her feel there must be something special about her to have dissipated the pall of boredom hanging over him. And when he'd smiled at her that first time, in response to some silly quip she'd made, as though it had been something brilliantly witty, she'd felt as though she'd met the one person in the world who completely understood her.

A little grunt of vexation escaped her mouth, which made Monsieur Le Brun, who was waiting for them in the hall, start guiltily.

She didn't correct his assumption that she might be cross with him. It would keep him on his toes.

Besides, before the end of the day, she was bound to be.

Sophie skipped up to him and smiled. 'Aunt Amy says you are going to show us lots of interesting things. Do you know where the man with the monkey lives?'

His face softened. It was amazing the effect Sophie was beginning to have on him. Even though she'd suspected him of lying about his willingness to take charge of a party that included a child, he had never exhibited the slightest sign of impatience with her. He might have fretted about the delay to his schedule, but he'd never taken out his frustration on her.

'I know Paris well, but alas,' he replied with a shrug, 'I do not know everyone who lives in every house. Especially not now, when my city is so full of visitors. But I can show you the best of it. We shall commence,' he said, gesturing with his hand to the hall door, 'with a stroll along the Boulevard.'

Amethyst grimaced. 'Should I have worn pattens?'

Monsieur Le Brun drew himself up to his full height.

'The Boulevard has gravelled walkways along both sides, shaded by trees. You will not need to worry about soiling your gowns when walking there, I promise you.'

'Hmm,' she said, pursing her lips. Well, she would soon see.

But as it turned out, the Boulevard was an utter delight. Not only was it flanked by the most impressive buildings she'd ever seen, beyond the trees which provided welcome shade, but also there were stalls selling everything from lemonade to toys. There were street

entertainers every few yards, as well: jugglers and ac-
robats and even a one-man band. Sophie was particularly taken with the man who professed to be a scientist,
demonstrating the amazing hydraulic capabilities of
water. What he actually did was squirt it at unsuspecting passers-by through a variety of ingenious contrap-
tions, to the delight of his audience.

Eventually, just as her feet were beginning to feel
rather too tight for her walking boots, and Sophie's
energy was visibly waning, Monsieur Le Brun indicated a café.

'Tortoni's,' he said. 'It is, at night, the most fashionable place to be seen after a trip to the opera. But it also
sells the best ice cream in the world. Mademoiselle Sophie will love it.'

Amethyst bit back the urge to enquire how he knew
the ice cream was the best in the world, since she was
perfectly sure he'd never travelled that far, for Sophie's
tired little face had lit up at the mention of ice cream.

And today was all about Sophie. She would do nothing to mar her enjoyment.

She was glad she'd kept her tongue between her teeth
when Monsieur Le Brun promptly secured them a table
in a very good spot, in spite of the popularity of the café.

'This is lovely,' she therefore said, as they took their
places at a table which had a view over the bustling
Boulevard.

He almost dropped his menu.

Amethyst couldn't help smiling. He'd got so used to
her sniping at him over every little thing that he didn't
know how to handle a compliment. She just couldn't
resist the urge to shock him even further.

'You have made Sophie very happy this morning. Thank you, *monsieur*.'

His cheeks went pink.

Dear Lord, she'd actually made the poor man blush.

She gave him space to recover by helping Sophie choose what flavour ice to have.

And when she next looked up, it was to see Nathan Harcourt making his way across the crowded café to their table.

What was he doing here?

She took in his unkempt clothing, the satchel over his shoulder, and put two and two together. Since this was a fashionable place for people to gather, he was bound to pick up custom here.

Yes, that explained his presence in Tortoni's. But why was he coming to her table? What could he possibly want?

And then she noted the determined jut to his chin as he stalked towards them.

Well, she'd wondered how he would react to being given the equivalent of a year's wages for a drawing that had taken him ten minutes, at most. It looked as though she was going to find out.

From the light of battle she could see in his eyes as he drew closer, she'd achieved her aim of humiliating him by highlighting the difference in their stations, just as he'd done to her ten years ago.

Only he wasn't going to crawl away and weep until there were no more tears left, the way she'd done. He looked as though he was going to attempt to get even for the insult.

Well, let him try. Just see how far he could get, that was all. She was no longer some starry-eyed débutante, ready to believe glib flattery and vague half-promises. She was a hardheaded business woman.

And she never, but never, let *any* man get the better of her.

Indignation carried him all the way across the crowded café to her table. How dare she send her lover to his rooms with all that money?

The Frenchman had been every bit as condescending as he'd expected. The only thing that had surprised him was how early he'd called. Nothing would have dragged Nathan out at that ungodly hour if he'd had Miss Dalby in his bed.

Nor would he have stumbled to the door this morning if he'd had any idea he would have come face to face with the sneering Frenchman, rather than one of his neighbours.

And if he hadn't been so fuddled with sleep he would have refused every last sou. Though it had only been after *Monsieur Le Brun* had sketched that mocking bow and he'd shut the door on him that he'd opened the purse and seen just how great an insult the man had offered him. Without having to say one word.

Sadly for him, he'd given himself away. The moment he'd bowed, Nathan recalled why his face had looked so familiar. So now he had the ammunition to make his stay in Paris extremely uncomfortable, if he chose.

He was here to deliver a warning of his own.

Get out of his city, or by God he would shout the Frenchman's secret from the rooftops.

What a pair they were for secrets. Though it didn't look as though she was trying to keep her secret hidden any more. The proof that she'd lied to him ten years before was sitting openly at table with her. Digging into her bowl of ice cream with a rapt expression, her little feet tucked neatly onto the top rung of her chair. Enjoying the simple pleasure with the total concentration of the truly innocent.

He snatched off his hat and thrust his fingers through his hair. She wasn't just 'an illegitimate baby'. She'd grown up, in the years since he'd learned of her existence, into a very real little person.

And no matter how much resentment he bore the mother, only a blackguard would expose a child to danger by telling the world the truth about its mother's lover.

The child noticed him staring at her and looked straight back at him with unabashed curiosity.

He couldn't see anything of Miss Dalby in her features. Nor her colouring. She must take after her father, he supposed.

Her father. He sucked in a sharp breath.

Of course the child had a father, it was just that he'd been too angry, before, to think of anything beyond the way Miss Dalby had deceived him. The night Fielding had told him about the rumour he'd heard about Miss Dalby's having an illegitimate baby, he'd felt as though he'd been robbed at gunpoint. Those words had stolen his whole life from him. The life he'd planned on having with her. The house in the country, the children he'd imagined running about in the orchard where chickens scratched among the windfalls. Gone in the blink of an eye. He'd been incapable of thinking about anything beyond his own loss.

But she hadn't come by a baby on her own. There

had been a man. A man who must have had fair hair and blue eyes.

And no conscience whatsoever.

Damn it all, Miss Dalby had only been seventeen when he'd started to think he was falling in love with her. So she could not have been more than sixteen when...when some rogue had seduced and abandoned her. Nor made any provision for his brat, if she was obliged to hire out her body to men like this one.

He glared at her French lover again, though his anger was veering wildly from one player in the drama to another with confusing rapidity.

Her parents, for instance. They'd brought her up to London for that Season. They must have known. She couldn't have hidden a baby from them. *They* must have told her to pretend to be innocent. At that age, and after what she'd already been through, she wouldn't have dared defy them. Besides, properly brought-up girls did not set up their will in opposition to their parents.

No more than sons of the same age. He'd only been in London himself at the express command of his own father. Forbidden from exploring his talent as an artist, he'd been pretending to think about choosing some other, respectable profession, whilst really trying to work out if there was any honourable way he could break free from family expectations.

For his father wasn't a man to cross, any more than he guessed the Reverend Dalby had been.

It had only been last night that he'd started to wonder what had become of her all these years. Before that, he'd refused to allow his thoughts to stray in her direction. But...it didn't look as though her family had stood by her. Why else would she be sitting here with her daughter in plain sight, a lover at her side and no wedding ring on her finger?

Was her father the kind of man who would wash his hands of his erring child, just because she'd brought disgrace to the family? The way his own father had done? Had her attempt to inveigle him into marriage been her last, desperate attempt to appease them? Had he, Nathan, been her last resort?

No wonder she'd wept when he'd become betrothed to Lucasta instead.

Strange how the years brought a new perspective to the tragedies of youth. There was always more than one side to any story. And before this moment—at least, before he'd watched the child enjoying her ice cream—the only side he'd ever considered had been his own.

'Are you a friend of Monsieur Le Brun?'

He blinked, to find the little girl was smiling up at him, her wide blue eyes full of curiosity.

'No, Sophie,' Miss Dalby hastily put in, while her lover was taking an indignant breath to refute the allegation. 'This is Monsieur Harcourt. He is an artist. He drew a picture of me last night, while we were out at dinner. I expect he is hoping for more custom from us.'

The little girl's face lit up. 'Oh, could he do a picture of me? You said we might buy a picture today. I thought from a shop. But this would be even better!'

'Yes. It would.' Miss Dalby gave him a smug little smile.

And all his sympathy towards her evaporated. She'd found a man who did not care that she'd already borne a child out of wedlock. And she was going to take great pleasure in obliging *him* to sit at her feet and draw the child. The child whose existence had driven them apart.

The child whose existence she'd tried to conceal, so that she could entrap him into a marriage that would have been...

At that point, his imagination floundered into a wall of mist. He had no idea what marriage to her would have been like, with an illegitimate child hovering on the fringes of it. Could it possibly have been any worse than the one he'd actually had? With a wife he couldn't even like, never mind desire, once he'd got to know her? A wife who'd broadcast her contempt for him with increasing virulence.

But one thing he knew. He wouldn't have wanted to stop bedding *her*. Even now, ten years later, with a gut full of aversion for her lies and scheming, he wanted her. The reason he'd been so slow on the uptake that morning had been because of the sleepless night he'd spent on her account, either brooding on the past, or suffering dreams of the kind that bordered on nightmares, from which he had woken soaked in sweat and painfully aroused.

Just thinking about the things he'd done to her, and with her, during those feverish dreams had a predictable effect.

Hastily he pulled up a chair to her table, in spite of her French lover's scowl, pulling his satchel on to his lap to cover his embarrassment.

With quick, angry strokes, he began a likeness of the girl he might have been forced into providing for, had Miss Dalby been successful in her attempts to snare him.

Chapter Four

Grimly determined not to reflect on how handsome her father must have been to have produced such a pretty child, he concentrated instead on capturing what he could see of her own nature. With deft sure fingers, he portrayed that eager curiosity and trusting friendliness which had so disarmed him.

'Oh,' the child said when he handed her the finished sketch. 'Do I really look like that?'

'Indeed you do, sweet pea,' said Miss Dalby, shooting him a look of gratitude over the top of the sheet of paper.

She was many things, but she wasn't stupid. She could see he'd restrained his anger with her so as not to hurt the child.

Out of the corner of his eye he saw the Frenchman reaching for his purse. He held up his hand to stall him.

'You do not need to pay me for *this* picture,' he said. Then turning to the little girl, because he was damned if he was going to let either of the adults know that he would rather starve than take another penny of the man's money, he said, 'It is my pleasure to have such a pretty subject to draw.'

The girl blushed and hung her head to study her portrait. Her mother gave him a tight smile, while the Frenchman openly smirked.

And all of a sudden, it was too much for him. He was burning with an unsavoury mix of frustration, anger and lust as he stowed his materials back in his satchel.

A waiter provided a very convenient diversion at that moment by arriving at the table to ask if they required anything else, or if they were ready to pay their bill. While the Frenchman was preoccupied, Nathan leaned towards Miss Dalby and muttered, 'Is he really the best you can do? You are still young and attractive enough to acquire a protector who could at least dress you in something approaching last year's fashions, couldn't you?'

Her eyes snapped with anger as she opened her mouth to make a retort, but then something stopped her. She subsided back into her seat.

'You think I am…attractive?'

'You know you are,' he growled. 'You know very well that ten years ago I thought you so attractive I almost threw caution to the winds and made an honest woman of you. But now…now you've grown even more irresistible.'

From her gasp, he could tell he'd shocked her. But what was more telling was the flush that crept to her cheeks. The way her eyes darkened and her lips parted.

'You should not say such things,' she murmured with an expression that told him she meant the exact opposite.

'Even though you enjoy hearing them?' He smiled at her mockingly. She wanted him. With a little persuasion, a little finesse, he could take her from this mean-looking Frenchman and slake all the frustrations of the last ten years while he was at it.

And then, because if he carried on muttering to her with such urgency, people would start to notice, he said in a clear voice, 'It will be my pleasure to do business with you again, at any time you choose. Any time,' he said huskily, 'at all.'

Amethyst blinked and looked around her. They were standing in some vast open space, though she could not for the life of her recall how she'd got there.

Did Nathan Harcourt really think she was in some kind of irregular *relationship* with Monsieur Le Brun?

And had he really been on the verge of proposing to her? All those years ago? No matter how much she argued that it could not be so, what else could he have meant by those angrily delivered, cryptic sentences?

The Tuileries Gardens. That was where she was. Where the three of them were.

'On court days,' she registered Monsieur Le Brun say, 'crowds of people gather here to watch ministers and members of the nobility going to pay their respects to the King.'

'Can we come and watch?'

While Monsieur Le Brun smiled down at Sophie and said he would see what he could arrange, Amethyst's mind went back to the day she'd stood in her father's study, trying to convince them that she'd believed Harcourt had really loved her.

'If you got some foolish, presumptuous thoughts in your head regarding that young man,' her father had bellowed, 'you have nobody but yourself to blame. If he had been thinking of marriage, he would have come to me first and requested permission to pay his addresses to you.'

She wished she could stand next to the girl who'd cowered before her father's wrath, bang her fist on his desk, and say 'Listen to her! She's right! Harcourt did want to marry her.'

But it was ten years too late. The girl she'd been had trusted her parents would understand. When they'd wanted to know why she'd been so upset on learning of Nathan's betrothal, why she couldn't face going to any more of the balls and routs they were trying to push her to attend, she'd blurted it out. Oh, not all of it, for she'd known it was wrong the very first time she'd let him entice her into a shadowy alcove, where he'd pressed kisses first on the back of her hand, then on her cheek. She couldn't admit that she had hardly been able to wait for the next time they met, hoping he'd want to do the same. She'd been so thrilled and flattered, and eager to join him when he'd taken her out on to a terrace and kissed her full on the lips. They'd put their arms round each other and it had felt like heaven.

All she'd been able to do was stammer, 'But he kissed me...'

And her father had thundered she was going to end in hell for such wanton behaviour. He'd whisked her straight back to Stanton Basset where, in order to save her soul, he'd shut her in her room on a diet of bread and water, after administering a sound spanking.

As if she hadn't already suffered enough. Harcourt had made her fall in love with him, had made her think he loved her, too, had then coldly turned away from her and started going about with Lucasta Delacourt. She'd been convinced he must simply have been making sport of her, seeing how far from the straight and narrow he could tempt the vicar's daughter to stray.

For a while she'd felt as though her whole world had collapsed around her like a house of cards.

Eventually they'd let her out of her room and told her she could eat meals with the rest of the family again, but she had no appetite. She stumbled through her duties about the house and parish in a fog of misery that nothing could lift. Then her mother, rather than offering her comfort, had rebuked her for setting a bad example to her younger sisters.

Her father might have accused her of being a trollop, but her mother had heaped even more crimes upon her head. She'd accused her of being vain and self-indulgent, of getting ideas above her station...

Which was ironic, because the last thing she had been interested in had been his connections. Others might have simpered and sighed, and tried to capture his attention because his father was an earl, but she'd just liked him for himself. Or the image of himself he'd projected, whenever he'd been with her.

The last straw had been the attitude of her sisters. The sisters she'd cared for as babies, sat up with during illnesses. They'd closed ranks with her parents. Shaken their heads in reproof. Shown not the slightest bit of sympathy.

She understood them doing so when their parents were around. But couldn't one of them have just...patted her hand as she wept alone in her bed? Offered her a handkerchief even?

Surely what she'd done hadn't been that bad? Besides, they could see she was sorry, that she'd learned her lesson. Wasn't anybody, ever, going to forgive her?

She'd begun to sink into real despair. Until the day Aunt Georgie had descended on them. Sat on the edge of her bed and told her, in that brusque way she had, that what she needed was a change of air.

'I shall tell your parents I mean to take you on a tour of the Lake District, to give your mind a new direction.' Though she hadn't, Amethyst recalled with a wry smile, done anything of the sort.

They hadn't been on the road long before Aunt Georgie had been obliged to come clean.

'I've a mind,' she'd said brusquely, 'to buy a couple of factories that some fool of a man ran into bankruptcy.'

Amethyst had been stunned. Women did not go round purchasing failing businesses.

'He's claiming the workers are intractable,' her aunt had continued. 'Has suffered from riots and outbreaks of plague and God knows what else. We'll probably find that he's a drunken incompetent fool. Naturally we cannot let anyone know our true purpose in coming up here.' Aunt Georgie had smiled at her, patted her hand and said, 'Your breakdown has come at a most convenient time for me. Perfect excuse to be wandering about that part of the countryside in an apparently aimless manner. I can sound out people in the know and find out what is really going on.'

'You can't use me as some kind of a…smokescreen,' Amethyst had protested. 'I'm—'

'Getting angry at last. That's the ticket. Far healthier to get angry than mope yourself into a decline. That young man,' she'd said, 'isn't worth a single one of the tears you've shed over him. And as for your father…' She'd snorted in contempt. 'What you ought to do, my girl, is think about getting even with them. If not the specific men who've conspired to crush you, then as many of the rest of their sex as you can.'

Get even. She'd never thought a chance would come for her to get even with Harcourt. Though she'd wondered if there wasn't some divine justice at work on her behalf anyway. It didn't seem to have done him much good, marrying that woman. In spite of all the connections she had, in spite of all the money her family spent on getting Harcourt elected, his career never went anywhere. His wife died childless. And then he'd created a scandal so serious that he'd had to disappear from public life altogether.

She'd crowed with triumph over every disaster that had befallen him, since it seemed to have served him right for toying with her affections so callously.

But now he'd admitted that he had been seriously thinking about marrying her. That he'd almost *thrown caution to the winds*.

Thrown caution to the winds? What on earth could he have meant by that?

Oh, only one of half-a-dozen things! There had been the disparity in their stations, for one thing. He was the son of an earl, after all, albeit the very youngest of them, while she was merely the daughter of an insignificant vicar. Nobility very rarely married into the gentry, unless it increased their wealth. And she'd had no dowry to speak of. Not then.

But that Miss Delacourt had. The one he'd become engaged to so swiftly after he'd given her the cut direct.

She shivered as she cast her mind back to the way he'd looked at her that night. As a rule, she tried not to think about it. It hurt too much. Even now, knowing that he hadn't been simply playing some kind of a game with her, she recoiled from the memory of the coldness in eyes that had once seemed to burn with ardour.

She dragged herself out of the past with an effort to hear Monsieur Le Brun was now telling Sophie a gory tale of an uprising that had been quelled upon the very spot where they stood. He pointed at some marks in the wall, telling the fascinated little girl that they'd been made by bullets.

She shuddered. Not at the goriness of the tale, though she would claim it was that if anyone should question her. But, no—what really sickened her was the thought that Harcourt assumed she was having intimate relations with this stringy, sallow-faced Frenchman.

Why was everyone always ready to assume the worst of her? All she'd done was leave Stanton Bassett to take a little trip. She'd followed all the proprieties by hiring a female companion, yet just because she'd stepped outside the bounds of acceptable female behaviour, just the tiniest bit, suddenly Harcourt assumed she must be a…a woman of easy virtue!

Based on what evidence—that she was with a man to whom she was not married, dressed in clothing that indicated she was relatively poor? And from this he'd deduced Monsieur Le Brun must be her protector?

Didn't he remember she was a vicar's daughter? Didn't he remember how he'd teased her about being so prim and proper when they'd first met?

Although he had soon loosened her moral stance, she reflected on a fresh wave of resentment. Quite considerably.

Perhaps he thought she'd carried on loosening after they'd parted.

Next time she came across Harcourt she would jolly well put him right. How dare he accuse her of having such poor taste as to take up with a man like Monsieur Le Brun?

If anyone had bad taste, it was he. He'd married a woman with a face like a horse, just because her family was wealthy and powerful.

Or so her parents had said. 'The Delacourts wouldn't let one of their daughters marry in haste. If they've got as far as announcing a betrothal, negotiations must have been going on for some time. His family might even have arranged the thing from the cradle. It is the way things are done, in such families. They leave nothing to chance.'

The certainty that they were right had made her curl up inside. It had seemed so obvious. He couldn't have walked away from her, then proposed to someone else the next day. Miss Delacourt must always have been hovering in the background.

But now…now she wondered just how deliberate and calculating his behaviour had been after all. He'd talked about finding her so attractive he'd almost *thrown caution to the winds*.

As though…as though he hadn't been able to help himself. As though he'd genuinely been drawn to her.

But in the end, it had made no difference. He'd married the girl of whom his family approved rather than proposing to the girl he'd only known a matter of weeks.

Though none of that explained why he seemed so angry with her now. Surely, if he had been toying with the idea of proposing to her back then, he should be glad they'd finally met up when both of them were free to do as they pleased?

Only—he didn't think she was free, did he? He thought she was a kept woman.

Oh!

He was *jealous*. Of Monsieur Le Brun.

That was...well, it was...

So preposterous she didn't know whether to laugh or cry. When Monsieur Le Brun shot her a puzzled glance, she realised that, in stifling it, she'd made a very undignified sound, approximating something like a snort.

She made a valiant attempt to form sensible answers whenever Sophie spoke to her, but it was very hard to pretend to be interested in all the things Monsieur Le Brun was telling them about the park through which they were walking and the momentous historical events which had occurred on just about every corner.

When she felt as though her whole life had been flung up in the air and hadn't quite settled into place yet. If she could only get past how angry he'd made her, by assuming she'd sunk low enough to...well, never mind what he thought she and Monsieur Le Brun got up to. It made her feel queasy. What about the other things he'd said? About finding her attractive?

Never mind *irresistible*. Almost irresistible enough to have lured him away from his sensible arranged match, to live in relative poverty and obscurity.

Had he been serious? Not one man, in the last ten years, had come anywhere near kissing her, yet Nathan claimed to find her so irresistibly attractive he immediately assumed she must be making her living as a woman of easy virtue. He had seethed at her and fumed at her, and only stormed off when he was satisfied he'd rattled her.

She stood stock still, her heart doing funny little

skips inside her chest. She'd only ever been sought after seriously by gentlemen *after* they learned she was Aunt Georgie's sole beneficiary.

But Harcourt assumed she was poor and desperate. And he still claimed to want her.

'Are you getting tired, Aunt Amy?'

Sophie had come running back to her and was taking her hand, and looking up into her face with concern.

'No, sweet pea. I am just…admiring the gardens. Aren't they beautiful?'

She hadn't noticed, not until she'd worked out that Harcourt was suffering from jealousy, but the Tuileries Gardens were really rather pretty…in a stately, regulated kind of way, in spite of all the gruesome horrors which the citizens had perpetrated within it. The trees dappled the gravelled walks with shade, the sky she could see through the tracery of leaves was a blue that put her in mind of the haze of bluebells carpeting a forest floor in spring, and the air was so clear and pure it was like breathing in liquid crystal.

It was almost as magical a place as Hyde Park had been, when she'd been a débutante. She could remember feeling like this when she'd walked amongst the daffodils with Harcourt. Light-hearted and hopeful, but, above all, pretty. He'd made her feel so pretty, the way he'd looked at her back then, when she'd always assumed she was just ordinary, that there was nothing about her to warrant any sort of compliments.

That was because she'd always had to work so hard to please her exacting parents. She'd done her utmost to make them proud of her, with her unstinting work in the parish and her unquestioning support of her mother in bringing up the younger girls.

And what good had it done her? The minute she slipped, nothing she'd done before counted for anything. All they could say was that she was self-indulgent and ungrateful, and vain.

Though at least now she knew she hadn't been vain. He must have liked more than just the way she looked, if he'd contemplated marrying her. He'd liked *her*. The person she'd become when she'd been with him. The girl who felt as though she was lit up from inside whenever she was near him. A very different girl from the earnest, constantly-striving-to-please girl she was in the orbit of her parents. He'd shown her that it was fun to dance and harmless to flirt. They'd laughed a lot, too, over silly jokes they'd made about some of the more ridiculous people they encountered. Or nothing much at all.

She'd slammed the door shut on that Amy when he'd abandoned her.

She'd tossed aside the former Amy, too, the one who was so intent on pleasing her parents.

It had been much easier to nurture the anger Aunt Georgie had stirred up. She'd become angry Amy. Bitter Amy. Amy who was going to survive no matter what life threw at her.

'It is time I took you to another café,' said Monsieur Le Brun. 'It is a little walk, but worth it, for the pastries there are the best you will ever eat.'

'Really?' She pursed her lips, though she did not voice her doubt in front of Sophie. There wasn't any point. The proof of the pudding, or in this case, pastry, would be in the eating. So she just followed the pair to the café, let the waiter lead them to a table and sank gratefully on to a chair, wondering all the while which, out of all the Amys she'd been in her life thus far, was the real one? And which one would come to the fore if *he* should come into this café, looking at her with all that masculine hunger?

She reached for the sticky pastry the waiter had just brought and took a large bite, wondering if it might be a new Amy altogether. An Amy who was so sick of people assuming the worst of her that she might just as well *be* bad.

She licked her lips, savouring the delicious confection. She sipped her drink with a feeling that before she left Paris, there was a distinct possibility she was going to find out.

Chapter Five

'How are you this morning?' Amethyst asked Fenella, noting that she still looked rather wan and shamefaced.

'Much better,' she said, sliding into her place at the breakfast table and pouring herself a cup of chocolate with an unsteady hand. 'Yes, much better.'

What Fenella needed was something to take her mind off herself, Amethyst decided. She could not possibly still be feeling the after-effects of drinking too much. She was just indulging in a fit of the dismals. Since offering her sympathy had done so little good, perhaps an appeal to her deeply ingrained sense of duty might do the trick. A reminder that she was supposed to be a *paid* companion.

'I hope you do not think I am being strict with you, but I really must insist you get back to work today.'

Fenella sat up a little straighter and lifted her chin. Amethyst repressed a smile.

'I need you to double-check any correspondence that Monsieur Le Brun may have written regarding the trade opportunities we've come over here to secure.'

At Fenella's little gasp of dismay, she held up her

hand. 'My grasp of the French language is only very basic, so I need you to keep an eye on everything he does. It is bad enough having to rely on him to represent me at meetings,' she grumbled. 'Anyway, I have to spend some time reading the packet of mail which has caught up with me...' she sighed '...before we can take Sophie out anywhere. It shouldn't take me long, but I must just make sure there is nothing so pressing it cannot wait until my return. Jobbings already thinks I am flighty, because I have come *jauntering off to foreign parts*, as he put it. He fully expects me to fail in this venture,' she said gloomily. 'He doesn't think I have a tithe of my aunt's business acumen.'

'You do not have a high opinion of him, either, do you?'

'He is honest and diligent. Which is more than can be said for most men.'

Fenella cut a pastry into a series of tiny squares, her expression pensive. 'What is your opinion of Monsieur Le Brun, now that you have got to know him better? Sophie said that you did not seem so cross with him yesterday as you usually are.'

'Well, although he looks far too sour to have ever been a child, let alone remember what one would like, he did take us to a whole series of places which were exactly the kind of thing that a lively, inquisitive child like Sophie would really enjoy,' Amethyst admitted.

'Yes. Sophie told me all about it,' said Fenella, lifting her cup and taking a dainty sip of tea.

'I confess,' Amethyst continued, 'I had my doubts when he said that he did not mind having a child form part of our party. I got the distinct impression,' she said with a wry twist to her lips, 'that he would have said anything to get the post, so desperate was he for work. Even the testimonials he provided were so fulsome they made me a bit suspicious.'

'So why, then, did you take him on?'

'*Because* he was desperate for the job, of course. I thought if he would say anything to land the job, then he was likely to work harder to ensure he kept it. And so far, my instincts have not failed me. He has worked hard.'

'Then you do not...' Fenella placed her cup carefully back on to its saucer '...dislike him as much as you did to start with?'

'I do not need to like the man to appreciate he is good at his job. So far he has proved to be an efficient and capable courier. And though his manners put my back up they have a remarkable effect on waiters on both sides of the Channel. He always manages to secure a good table and prompt service. I attribute that,' she said, digging into her own plate of eggs and toast, 'to that sneer of his.'

'Oh, dear, is that all you can say? Is that really... fair?'

Amethyst raised her brows, but that was not enough to deter Fenella. 'You *did* make a good choice when you employed him,' she said stoutly. 'He is...' She floundered.

'Arrogant, opinionated and overbearing,' said Amethyst. 'But then he is a man, so I suppose he cannot help that. However,' she added more gently, noting from the way Fenella was turning her cup round and round in its saucer that her companion was getting upset, 'I am sure you need have no worries that he may take his dislike of me out on you. What man could possibly object to the way you ask for his advice? For that is what you do, isn't it? You don't challenge his dominance by giving him direct orders, the way I do, so he has no need to try to put you in your place. You just flutter your eyelashes at him and he does whatever you want, believing the whole time that it was all entirely his own idea.'

To her astonishment, Fenella flushed bright pink.

'I am sorry if that unsettles you. I meant it as a compliment. You handle him with such aplomb...'

Fenella got to her feet so quickly her chair rocked back and almost toppled over. 'Please, I...' She held up her hand, went an even hotter shade of pink and fled the room.

Amethyst was left with a forkful of eggs poised halfway to her mouth, wondering what on earth she had said to put such a guilty look on Fenella's face.

It took Amethyst less than an hour to run her eyes over the latest figures and tally them in her mind with the projected profits. At home, in Stanton Basset, she had always started her day by doing exactly this, and before she'd set out she had seen no reason why she shouldn't keep up with the latest developments as assiduously as ever.

But she'd never felt so relieved to have got through the columns of figures and the dry reports that went with them. She couldn't wait to put on her hat and coat, and get outside and start exploring Paris again.

She'd never enjoyed being in business for its own sake, the way Aunt Georgie had. It had always been more about repaying her aunt's faith in her by making her proud. And as for coming to France to expand the business...

The truth was that the end of the war had come at just the right time for her. Everyone with means was flocking to Paris. It was the perfect time to break away from Stanton Basset and all its petty restrictions. To do something different. Something that was nothing to do with anyone's expectations.

So why had she justified her decision to travel, by telling Jobbings her motive for coming here was to expand the business she'd inherited? Why was she still making excuses for doing what she wanted? Whose approval did she need to win now her aunt had gone? Not Jobbings'. He worked for her.

Was she somehow trying to appease the ghost of her aunt? She'd thought that coming somewhere different would jolt her out of the rigid routine into which she'd fallen and stuck after her aunt had died. But it wasn't proving as easy to cast off the chains of habit as she'd thought it would be. She was still looking over her shoulder to see if her aunt would approve.

She eyed her bonnet in the mirror with dislike as she tied the frayed brown ribbons under her chin. It did nothing for her. She rather thought it wouldn't do anything for anyone.

Well, while she was in Paris, she was going to treat herself to a new one. No woman visiting Paris could fail to come back with just one or two items that were a little brighter and more fashionable than she was used to wearing, would she? It wouldn't exactly be advertising her wealth, would it?

And what was the point of having money, if all you ever did was hoard it?

'I hope,' she therefore said upon reaching the communal hall, where the others were waiting for her, 'that we will be visiting some shops today. Or if not today,' she amended, realising that she had not asked Fenella to make shopping a part of their itinerary, 'tomorrow. I have decided that we should all have new bonnets.'

Fenella flushed and pressed her hand to her throat, but Sophie cheered.

'Monsieur Le Brun has already said he is going to take us to the Palais Royale,' she said, bouncing up to her with a smile. 'He says it is full of shops. Toyshops and bookshops, and cafés like the one where we bought the water ice yesterday. I expect you could buy bonnets, too,' she added generously.

The Palais Royale. Oh, dear. Well, at least she'd already come up with the notion of buying bonnets for all three of them. The prospect of getting something new to wear was bound to help take Fenella's mind off returning to the scene of her downfall.

Though when she took another look at Fenella, it was to find that she still looked rather pink and more than a little uncomfortable.

'A new bonnet,' said Fenella. 'Really, Miss Dalby, that is too kind of you. I don't deserve—'

'Fustian,' she barked as she marched out of the front door. 'You have both been ill. You deserve a reward for putting up so heroically with me dragging you and poor Sophie all the way out here.'

Fenella trotted behind her, twittering and protesting for several yards that the last thing she deserved was a reward.

When they finally reached the Palais Royale and caught sight of the shops by daylight, however, her final protest dwindled away to nothing.

The people thronging the gravelled courtyard were all so exquisitely dressed. It made their own plain, provincial garb look positively shabby.

And the shops were full of such beautiful things.

It occurred to her that Fenella didn't often have new clothes. She couldn't outshine her own employer, after all. But now Amethyst wondered how much she minded dressing so plainly, when she spent so many hours poring over fashion plates in the ladies' magazines.

'Oh, just look at that silk,' sighed Fenella, over a length of beautiful fabric draped seductively across the display in a shop window. 'I declare, it…it glows.'

'Then you must have a gown made up from it,' declared Amethyst. Before Fenella could come up with a dutiful protest, she interjected, 'It is ridiculous to go about looking like dowds when I have the means for both of us to dress stylishly.'

'Oh, but—'

'Neither of us have had anything new for an age. And nor has Sophie. You have to admit, that shade of blue would suit you both admirably.'

'Well…' Fenella bit her lower lip, which was trembling with the strain of knowing quite the right thing to do in this particular circumstance.

'I have made up my mind, so it is no use arguing. Both you and Sophie are going to return to Stanton Basset in matching silk gowns.'

Sophie's face fell, predictably. She knew that visiting a modiste meant hours of standing about being measured and dodging pins.

'But first, where are those toyshops Monsieur Le Brun promised us?'

Sophie's face lit up again and she skipped ahead of

them to a shop she must have already noted, so swiftly did she make for it.

The adults followed more slowly, glancing into all the windows as they went past.

Until they came to a shop that sold all kinds of supplies for artists, at which point Amethyst's feet drifted to a halt. Did Harcourt buy his supplies here? Or perhaps, given the preponderance of tourists milling about, he would frequent somewhere cheaper, known only to locals. Although the money she'd given him for that quick portrait would ensure he could buy the best, for some time to come.

She frowned. She didn't like the way her mind kept returning to Harcourt. It was a problem she'd struggled with for years. Every time his name appeared in one of the scandal sheets, all the old hurts would rise up and give her an uncomfortable few days. It was too bad he'd had to flee to Paris, of all places, when London grew too hot for him.

She heard Sophie laugh and turned to see that the rest of her party were going into the toyshop already. She chastised herself for standing there peering intently into the dim interior of the artist's supplier. She'd actually been trying to see if she could make out the identity of any of the customers. There was no reason he would be there, just because she was.

Sighing, she tore herself away from the window and moved on to the next shop, which was a jeweller's. Once more her feet ruled her head, coming to a halt without her conscious volition. As her eyes roved over the beautiful little trinkets set out on display, she heard her aunt's voice, sneering that women who adorned themselves with such fripperies only did so to attract the attention of men, or to show off to other women how much wealth they had.

'Wouldn't catch me dead wasting my hard-earned money on such vulgar nonsense.'

She bit her lower lip as she silently retorted that it might very well be vulgar to wear too much jewellery, but surely it wouldn't hurt to own just a little?

Her eyes snagged on a rope of pearls, draped over a bed of black silk. She'd worn a string just like it, for the few short weeks her Season had lasted. She'd been so happy when her mother had clasped them round her neck. She'd felt as if she was on the verge of something wonderful. The wearing of her mother's pearls signified the transition from girlhood into adulthood.

Something inside her twisted painfully as she remembered the day she'd taken them off for the last time. They'd gone back in their box when her mother had brought her home from London and she hadn't seen them again for years.

Two years, to be precise. And then they'd been round Ruby's neck.

And her mother had been smiling at Ruby and looking proud of her as she'd walked down the aisle on her father's arm to marry a wealthy tea-merchant she'd met at a local assembly. They hadn't even had to splash out for a London Season for Ruby. No, she'd managed to get a husband with far greater economy and much less fuss. And she therefore deserved the pearls.

Amethyst might not have minded so much if any of her sisters had spoken to her that day. But it was clear they'd been given orders not to do more than give her a nod of acknowledgement. She'd pinned such hopes on Ruby's wedding. She'd thought the fact her parents had sent her an invitation meant that she was forgiven, that they were going to let bygones be bygones.

No such thing. It had all been about rubbing her nose in it. Ruby was the good daughter. She was the black sheep. Ruby deserved the pearls and the smiles, and the bouquet and the lavish wedding breakfast.

Amethyst didn't even warrant an enquiry after her health.

She dug into her reticule, fished out a handkerchief and blew her nose. That was ages ago. She didn't care what her parents thought of her any more. They'd been so wrong, on so many counts. Why should she stand here wasting time even thinking about them, when they probably never spared her a second thought?

And then somehow, before she even knew she'd intended any such thing, her militant feet had carried her into the shop and over to a counter. Her mother had decided she didn't deserve the pearls. And her aunt had held the opinion that wanting such things was vulgar anyway. But neither her aunt nor her mother was in charge of her life, or her fortune, any longer. If she wanted to drape herself with pearls, or even diamonds, she had every right to do so. Why shouldn't she buy something for the sheer fun of splashing out her money on something that just about everyone in her past would have disapproved of?

The shop was a veritable treasure trove of the most beautiful little ornaments she had ever seen. One object in particular caught her eye: a skillfully crafted ebony hair comb, which was set with a crescent of diamonds. Or possibly crystals. Since she had so little experience of such things, there was no way she would ever be able to discern whether those bright little chips of liquid fire were genuine or paste.

But whatever it was, she wanted it. It wasn't as if it was a completely useless ornament, like a rope of pearls would have been. Besides, she sniffed, she didn't want to buy something that would remind her of such a painful episode in her past.

She glanced warily at the man presiding over the shop, who was watching her with a calculating eye. For one fleeting moment she wished she had Monsieur Le Brun at her side. He wouldn't let a shopkeeper chouse him. With that cynical eye and world-weary manner he would put the man in his place in an instant.

She shook the feeling off. She could manage this herself. She might have no experience with jewels, but she had plenty with people. Aunt Georgie had taught her how to spot a liar at twenty paces. She wouldn't let him dupe her into paying more than *she* decided the item was worth.

She took a deep breath and asked how much the comb cost.

'*Madame* does realise that these are diamonds?'

She couldn't help bristling with annoyance. Why did Frenchmen persist in addressing her as *madame*? It made her feel so…old. And dowdy.

And all the more determined to dress a little better.

So she nodded, trying to look insouciant, and braced herself to hear they cost an exorbitant amount, only to suck in a sharp, shocked breath when he quoted her a sum that sounded incredibly reasonable.

Which meant that they couldn't possibly be real diamonds. He *was* trying to trick her.

Like all men, he assumed she must be too stupid to

notice. Her eyes narrowed. She stood a little straighter, but was prevented from saying anything when the door burst open and Harcourt strode in.

'I had almost given up hope of catching you alone,' he said, taking hold of her arm. Somehow she found him drawing her away from the counter and into the darker recesses of the shop, away from the window.

She ought not to have let him do any such thing. But then she wasn't in the mood for doing as she ought today.

Besides, there was something in his eyes that intrigued her. It wasn't the anger he'd displayed during their previous two encounters. It was something that looked very much like...desperation. And his words made it sound as though he'd been following her. Seeking an opportunity to speak to her alone. After the Frenchman's attitude, she could help being just a little bit flattered.

'When last we met, I should have said...that is... dammit!' He ran his fingers through his hair, leaving furrows in the thick, unruly mass.

My goodness, but he was worked up. Over her.

'I can't stop thinking about you. I am in torment, knowing you are here, in Paris, so near and yet so... out of reach.'

A warm glow of feminine satisfaction spread through her, almost breaking out in the form of a smile. Almost, but not quite. She just about had the presence of mind to keep her face expressionless.

She hoped.

'Would you consider leaving your Frenchman?'

Well, that put paid to looking cool, calm and poised. She felt her jaw drop, her eyes widen.

She managed to put everything back in place swiftly, but even so, he'd seen her reaction.

And he didn't like it.

'I know I don't look as though I am a good prospect,' he said, indicating the scruffy clothes he was wearing. 'But honestly, I am not as hard up as these clothes suggest. They are practical for when I am working, that is all. I get covered in dust and charcoal, and…but never mind that. The point is, you could do better than him.'

'You…you said that before,' she replied. And she'd been simultaneously flattered and insulted by his assumptions about what sort of woman he thought she was. Well, she might be flattered, but she wasn't going to melt at the feet of a man who kept on delivering his flattery wrapped up in insults.

'You have the unmitigated gall to stand there and criticise both my morals, and my taste, without knowing the first thing about my circumstances. And then have the cheek to say you think you are a better prospect for me?'

That hadn't come out quite right. What she had meant to say was that Monsieur Le Brun was not, and had never been, her protector and that, even if she did need one, she would most certainly be far choosier about the man in question.

'Try me,' he grated. Then, before she had time to draw breath to make her retort, which would have been good and acidic, putting him neatly in his place, he'd grabbed her by the shoulders and kissed her. Hard. Full on the lips.

She froze, shocked into indignant immobility. But only for a moment. Because, amazingly, hard on the heels of her indignation came a wave of such sheer pleasure it made her want to purr.

Oh, but it had been so long since any man had kissed her. Since this man, her first and only love, had kissed her. And that time it had been nothing like this. Back then, his kisses had been almost chaste. Tentative. As though he hadn't wanted to frighten her.

But just as she was starting to wonder if he was trying to punish her with the force of his kiss, his mouth gentled. He slid his hands down her arms and round her waist, tugging her closer to him. And she could no longer see why it was so important not to melt against him, into him. She'd never experienced anything so seductive as the feel of his mouth against hers, his arms tugging her close, the heat of his entire body pressed all along the length of hers. He kissed like a man now, she realised. That was the difference. He was an experienced man, not an untried boy.

But the most seductive thing about his kiss was his eagerness. The intensity of his yearning for her flowed off him in waves, making him shake with it. It was his passion, not his skill, which was so very irresistible. Because it made her feel so desirable.

When, too soon, he pulled back, she opened her eyes, stunned to discover that she'd shut them.

'You see?'

What? What was she supposed to see? She hadn't been aware of anything but him, for the entire duration of that embrace. An entire troop of Cossacks could have invaded the shop and she didn't think she would have noticed.

'You still want me.'

Her pleasure dimmed. Was he just trying to prove

something by harking back to their shared past? And if so, what?

'Why deny yourself, Amethyst? Come to me.'

Why deny yourself? He was talking as though taking a lover was nothing more significant than purchasing a bauble to decorate her hair.

When it clearly wasn't. Not even for him. He was standing there, shaking with the force of wanting her.

It was flattering. But she wasn't that kind of woman.

She shook her head.

His face hardened. 'What are you afraid of? What hold does that man have over you? Tell me.'

'He doesn't have any hold over me,' she said indignantly.

'Then prove it.'

'I do not have to prove anything to you.'

'So, I repeat, what is holding you back?'

'Can you not think of anything?' Like the fact she might have some morals, for instance?

A look of complete exasperation flitted across his face.

'Explain it to me.'

She glanced over his shoulder towards the door. At any moment Fenella might come in, looking for her, worrying about what was keeping her.

His face softened. 'I forgot. The little girl. Very well. Make an excuse to get away from the others and meet me somewhere where we can talk. And you can tell me exactly why you are reluctant to yield to the passion that is burning between us.'

Talk. She supposed she could agree to that. And, oh, but she did want to see him again. Hear him say such things again. It was almost like the dream she'd had on her first night here, where he'd grovelled at her feet for a chance to kiss her and to beg her forgiveness for the way he'd treated her.

'We are planning to visit the Louvre,' she said. 'I could easily break away from the others...'

'I go there as often as I can,' he said. 'Can you arrange to be there tomorrow?'

'Yes.' Easily. 'Then I will be waiting for you.'

He seized her by the shoulders, kissed her again, then turned and strode out of the shop.

She raised one trembling hand to her lips. What had she done? Agreed to meet him and let him attempt to talk her into having an affair with him, that's what.

She was shaking so much she needed something to lean on for support. Tottering to the counter, she laid both palms on it and took a deep breath. When the contents of the shop eventually swam back into view, she noted the proprietor pushing the comb, now nestled in a little box lined with silk, across the counter towards her.

She glared at him.

He promptly reduced the price by a further two francs.

With the pragmatism of the typical Parisian, he was continuing to haggle as though there was nothing untoward about men storming into his shop, grabbing potential customers, kissing them until their knees turned to jelly and then storming out again.

All of a sudden she felt like laughing.

'I shall take it,' she breathed. It would always remind her of this day, this moment. And the kiss that had tumbled her back to the kind of breathless wonder she'd felt as a girl, whenever he'd stolen a kiss from her in some secluded nook.

She didn't know what tomorrow would bring. But every time she tucked it into her hair, the fire of the gems sparkling from the darkness of their setting would always remind her of the sparks that had flared from this brief moment of twisted, thwarted passion. And she would remember how desirable he'd made her feel.

Amethyst woke the next morning with a smile on her face. Somewhere in this city, Harcourt was stomping around in fury at the erroneous belief she was a kept woman and wishing he was the one to have her in keeping. For the first time in ten years, she felt as though she was an attractive woman—in one man's eyes at least. And since she didn't much care what any other man thought about her, it was enough to make her feel like skipping down the Boulevard, hand in hand with Sophie, laughing with sheer joy.

'Where do you plan to take us today, Monsieur Le Brun?' she asked with bated breath when he came to report to her, after breakfast. 'I hear the Louvre is well worth a visit.'

'I can arrange for a viewing of the works of art for you, *madame*, of course,' he said.

'Oh, but you promised to take me to see the animals in the menagerie,' cried Sophie.

'We can go another day,' put in Fenella hastily, ever the peacemaker.

'No, no,' said Amethyst, making a play of looking out of the windows. 'The weather may not favour a trip out of doors another day. You must take Sophie to see the animals. Especially since she seems to feel you have given your word. Though I rather think I should like you to arrange for my own admission, Monsieur

Le Brun. Once I have finished my paperwork for the day, I shall not want to sit about twiddling my thumbs.'

Since Sophie had been so determined to go and look at the animals, Fenella had put up very little resistance to her scheme. And not two hours after they'd departed for the Jardin des Plantes, where the menagerie was to be found, she was walking through the maze of statues on the ground floor, then mounting the stairs which led to the gallery where she'd agreed to meet Nathan.

She gripped her parasol tightly. There were so many other people here, studying the paintings. How was she going to find Nathan amongst them all? And did she really want to? What was she going to say to him?

She hadn't thought this through. Her pulse jumping to her throat, she turned blindly toward the nearest painting, which happened to be Titian's *San Pietro Martire.*

'He looks as though he's taken great pride in the kill, I always think,' said Harcourt, who'd somehow found her in the crowd and managed to approach her without her noticing.

She didn't turn round. She didn't think she could look him in the face without blushing. She'd spent far too many hours, since she'd last seen him, reliving the sensations he'd aroused by kissing her. And then, because he'd made it plain he wanted so much more than kissing, imagining what the rest of it might be like as well. It had left her heated, shaky sometimes, and at other times with a delightful sense in all her limbs as though she was floating a few inches above the muddy streets of Paris, in a kind of hazy-pink romantic cloud.

Which was ridiculous. There was nothing the least bit romantic about what he wanted from her.

Nevertheless, she couldn't help feeling…feminine—that was the only way to describe it—in a way she hadn't since she'd been a hopeful débutante, dreaming of veils and orange blossom.

She was feeling decidedly feminine now, at the rush of his breath against her cheek when he'd leaned close to murmur into her ear. He was standing so close that she could feel the heat of his body along her back and smell the aroma of smoke emanating from his clothing, as though he'd recently been standing near a bonfire.

In an attempt to shake off the spell, she resorted to a challenge.

'Is that any way to greet me?'

'No, I suppose not. It's just that you seemed to be studying it so intently. And as I've already told you, I spend a lot of time here, admiring the works of true masters. I cannot help but admire beauty when I see it. Which is why I am drawn to you, every time I see you about the city with your companions, in spite of knowing better.' Just as she was drawn to him, too, in spite of knowing better.

'Perhaps I should not have come…'

Only, he'd reached another Amy, one she tried the hardest not to let anyone see. The Amy who'd lain in bed, night after lonely night, wishing someone, anyone, would come and put their arms round her and tell her she wasn't a disappointment. Not to them.

That Amy couldn't resist getting as close to Nathan as she could. To feel the warmth of his body all along her back. The whisper of his breath on the nape of her neck as he murmured into her ear, 'I am glad you did.'

They stood quite still for a few moments, pretending to gaze at the painting, whilst really enjoying the feeling of being so close. At least, that was what she was doing. And if he wasn't, then surely he would move away, instead of standing there, breathing in such a way that her insides were turning liquid with longing?

'You…you spend a lot of time here, you said.'

'I am an artist,' he said abruptly. Was he annoyed she'd deliberately broken the sensual mood that had been shimmering between them? 'Of course I want to study the works of the greats, and see how they managed to produce works like this, when all I…' He paused. 'I have little talent, not compared with men like these. It can be frustrating.'

'Then why continue?'

'Because being an artist is not something you choose. It is something you are. I cannot simply admire a view without wondering how I could capture something of its grandeur on canvas. Any more than I can look at an interesting face and not itch to sketch it. And as for your hair…'

'My hair?' At that she did turn her head to look up at him over her shoulder. He was staring at the few curls that inevitably escaped her bonnet with a kind of fascination.

'I have never seen another woman, anywhere, with hair quite the same shade. It defies analysis. Fielding always used to say it was just brunette,' he scoffed. 'He never glimpsed the rich ruby lights that shone from its depths when you passed under a branch of candles…'

When she gasped, he looked straight into her eyes. They were standing so close that it felt as though they were breathing the same air. He would only have to bend his head, just a fraction, and they would be kissing.

As though the same thought had just occurred to him, his gaze dropped to her lips. For a heartbeat or two they just stood there, looking at each other's mouths and breathing. Heavily.

'If you are really too afraid to risk losing the protection of that Frenchman,' he said harshly, 'then do you think he might give me permission to paint you? Just head and shoulders. I can't sleep for thinking about your hair. And if I could get you up to my studio, then perhaps—'

'Monsieur Le Brun is not my protector,' she said, cutting him off. He might say he only wanted to paint her, but she knew what he really wanted was so much more than that.

And she wanted it too.

Great heavens, she wanted it too. It was wrong. Perhaps even wicked. But it was far too late in her life to dream of romance and wedding bells. And here stood a man who was burning with desire for her. Genuine desire. It must be, for he had no idea how wealthy she was. He even thought she might be in the keeping of some other man. But it hadn't stopped him…lusting after her. To some women it might not seem like very much, but whatever it was that flared between them was real.

'If you want to paint my portrait, you have only to ask me.'

Harcourt's eyes blazed with an intensity that made her heart skip a beat.

'You will have to come to my studio,' he said.

'Yes, of course.'

'You know where it is?'

'Yes.' She flushed. Since the day he'd scribbled the address on the back of that sketch, she'd found out exactly where he lived, by pretending an interest in the layout of the streets through which they walked or drove. She'd even managed to drive past the *hôtel* where he had his lodgings and tried to guess behind which of the many windows his rooms lay.

'Can you come alone?'

Her heart thudded against her chest. She knew it. He wasn't asking her if he could paint her portrait at all, but whether she was willing to become his lover. A thrill of wicked excitement shot through her. Could she really do it? Take a lover?

It would mean an end to any hope of securing the trade agreements she'd ostensibly come to Paris for, if anyone found out.

And as for Fenella—she would be scandalised.

'You will have to paint my portrait, if I do,' she said. So long as he produced some kind of painting by the time they returned to England, she might be able to convince Fenella that nothing untoward had gone on.

And she wanted him so much. Not in the same way she'd wanted him as a girl. It hadn't been marriage she'd been dreaming of as she lay in her lonely, empty bed.

'I *could* come alone...'

He gripped her hand, though they were in full view of dozens of other tourists and might easily be noticed.

Yet she made no attempt to withdraw her hand, for she was held by the gleam of satisfaction that shone from his eyes.

'Tonight?'

'Tonight?' All of a sudden what she was considering became a bit too real. A kiss was one thing, but all the rest? And straight away?

She might be a virgin, but she knew what men and women did in the privacy of their bedrooms.

Her aunt might have sneered at girls who 'lifted their skirts to oblige a man's beastly desires'. But then her aunt had never been in love. If she had, she would know that sometimes you could look at a man and just swoop inside. And melt. And feel as though you would do anything if only he would put his arms round you again.

Not that she was in love.

She just wanted that feeling she'd got when he'd put his arms round her. And have his lips touching hers again. And...when he wanted more, as he surely would, then she—yes, she wanted to find out what that was like too. She'd overheard servants gossiping and giggling about what their menfolk got up to between the sheets. It had sounded as though they thoroughly enjoyed it.

And if she didn't like it, then she needn't ever do it again. She would have found out the truth for herself. As her aunt had always said—never take anything on trust.

And she'd spent so many years trying to be good. Trying to win approval from people who kept on assuming the worst of her. She'd paid dearly for sins she had never committed.

So what was the point in not committing them?

She lifted her chin and met his look full on.

'Not tonight.' It was too soon. There were preparations she had to make. The one thing she did not want to risk was having a baby, outside of wedlock. And she wasn't going to trip naïvely into his studio assuming he would take care of that aspect of things, let alone trust him to take care of her, should the worst come to the worst.

She didn't need him to take care of her—that was not the point. She was wealthy enough to take care of both herself and any number of children she might have. The point was she did not want to be responsible for burdening some poor innocent child with the terrible stigma of illegitimacy.

'When, then?'

'Tomorrow night', if she could find an apothecary who spoke English well enough to understand what she needed to purchase and for what purpose, because the last thing she wanted was to have to take Monsieur Le Brun along to interpret for her! 'Or perhaps the one after', if it proved difficult to find such an establishment.

He dropped her hand and took a step back, his face hardening.

'I might not be there,' he said.

He might not be there? She'd just taken the momentous decision to fling herself off the precipice of respectability, into the unknown sea of carnality, and he could just shrug it off, as though it was nothing?

Well, she could shrug too.

She did so, then said, with as much insouciance as she could muster, 'Then I will have had a wasted journey.'

She turned to walk away from him. She wasn't going to beg him to change his mind, or show a bit more enthusiasm. She wasn't going to let him see how badly his casual attitude towards becoming her lover hurt her, either.

'Wait,' he said, coming up and falling into step beside

her. 'Make a definite appointment, give me a fixed time, and I will be there.'

The way he looked at her calmed her ruffled feathers instantly. He wanted her. He really wanted her. He was just too proud to beg.

'Saturday, then,' she said. Because in part, he was right. If she didn't set a definite date, she might never work up the courage to go through with it. 'And if, by any chance, I cannot keep our...'

'Assignation,' he supplied, putting paid to any last lingering doubt they might be talking about painting her portrait.

She swallowed. 'I will get word to you, so you will not be disappointed.'

'I will be disappointed if you do not come,' he grated. 'But—' he flung up his chin '—neither will I pursue you. It must be your choice. Come to me freely, or not at all.'

With that, he turned on his heel and stalked away, leaving her frowning after him. That last speech hadn't sounded like the kind of thing a seasoned seducer of women would say at all. In fact, if she hadn't known better, she might have thought his pride might be wounded if she didn't go through with what she'd promised.

Which was absurd. She was only another conquest. Just one more in a long line of women he'd enjoyed and then discarded.

She meant nothing more to him than any of the others. Of course she didn't.

And she'd better not start looking for signs that she might.

Chapter Six

Two nights. She'd made him wait two whole nights.

What kind of game was she playing? What was so important she could put off this raging inferno that blazed between them for two whole nights?

She was letting him know that she was not as desperate to take him as her lover as he was to become hers. He raised his hand and stabbed his brush at the canvas on which he was currently working—the back view of a woman, her head tilted to one side as she tried to make sense of the picture before which she stood.

So be it. Let her play her little games. It was what women did. Lucasta was never happier than when she had some poor victim dangling on a string. But he wouldn't be anyone's puppet, then or now. However long she made him wait, he would do whatever it took to break free of the obsession that had taken hold of him since the night she'd shown up in Paris. And the one sure way to do it would be in bed. Once he'd slaked his lust, there would be nothing left. Wasn't that always the way with women?

Once he'd done with her, perhaps he would be free

of the bitterness that had steadily grown throughout his twenties, the rage that made him cruel to his friends, callous towards women and so reckless of his reputation even his father had been forced to agree there was nothing for it but to send him abroad.

Not that he'd minded coming to Paris. Almost as soon as he'd arrived, he'd started to find a measure of... something in his life that had always been lacking before. It wasn't just the fact that he'd broken free of his family's stranglehold, ceased the pretence and the posturing, and was finally doing what he'd always wanted to do. It was more than that. It was the feeling that he could be anyone he wanted here. Nobody thought him odd for tossing aside his entire lifestyle. After all, they'd just overthrown an entire regime. The whole country was making itself over into something new, not just him.

And if a people could depose their own king, a man could conquer his obsession with the woman who'd sent his whole life into disarray. Yes, he could. He put down his brush and picked up the canvas. The romantic aspirations he'd had as a callow youth had long since charred to ashes. And what was left was something he could handle. He carried the painting to the far corner of his studio, where he put it down, facing the wall.

It was lust, that was all he felt for Miss Dalby. All she was good for was bedding. And he knew, from experience, that once he'd bedded her even the lust would pass. He would finally know, in his heart, as well as in his head, that she was...nothing.

'Are you quite sure you know what you are doing?' Fenella was practically wringing her hands as Amethyst tied the ribbons of her new bonnet in a jaunty bow under her chin. She'd been unhappy from the moment Amethyst had admitted she'd met Harcourt in the Louvre and commissioned him to paint her portrait.

'It isn't really...proper...to be alone with a man, you know. And I am supposed to—'

'Do not worry, Fenella,' said Amethyst briskly, giving her reflection one last assessing glance in the mirror. 'I know exactly what I am doing. And since nobody in Stanton Basset will ever know what we choose to do while we are in Paris, unless we tell them, there is no fear of them criticising you for allowing me to behave with impropriety.'

'I cannot help worrying. You are so innocent. If you are alone with a man...even if he says he is only going to paint your portrait...the intimacy of the situation might well lead to—' Fenella broke off, and bit down on her lower lip. 'I am not casting aspersions on your character, please believe me. It is just that you do not understand how very tempting some men can be. And I know that you do find Monsieur Harcourt tempting. Forgive me for speaking so bluntly, but he has hardly been out of your mind for years and years. And now that he is showing an interest in you, I am afraid it might be turning your head.'

Until she'd said those fatal words, Amethyst had been prepared to ignore Fenella's little homily. She was only doing her job after all, which was to protect her reputation. But to hear the very words her own father had used against her, when she'd needed understanding...

'I have no intention of letting any man *turn my head*,' she snapped. 'I am not some silly girl who is still holding out for marriage. Let alone love.' It was passion she wanted to experience. Just passion. And Harcourt was the perfect man to experience it with. 'There is nothing he can do, or attempt to do, for which I am not completely ready.'

She had no dreams for him to smash, this time. Not that marriage was her dream any longer. She'd come to value her independence. She'd first earned it, then fought for it. And she had no intentions of surrendering it to the likes of Nathan Harcourt, of all men.

Anyway, he'd made it clear, both ten years ago and in the last couple of days, that all he wanted was an affair. Which was exactly what she wanted, too.

'Oh, dear,' said Fenella. 'I can see there is nothing I can say to make you reconsider.'

'Not a thing,' she replied cheerfully. She'd done all her arguing with herself, during the long, sleepless nights she'd spent recalling how wonderful it had felt to be in his arms. Or just having him stand close to her. Her whole body ached to get that close to him again. In vain had she tried to build up a case for abstinence, warning herself of all the potential pitfalls of getting involved with Harcourt again. There was only part of her that was still sensible, cautious Amy. That Amy stood no chance against rebellious Amy and lonely Amy's clamouring for fulfilment.

She was set on her course. And was fully prepared to face the consequences, whatever they might be.

Of course it was easy to say that with a cushion of vast wealth behind her. She couldn't help but compare her own situation with that of the many girls who gave themselves to men who didn't deserve them and paid a terrible price. If the precautions she was taking proved ineffective and she ended up pregnant because of this affair, she would still have a comfortable lifestyle. Even if she was no longer welcomed in the homes of the narrow-minded, morally superior, leading ladies of Stanton Basset, she could simply retire from society and become a recluse. It would not affect her ability to run her businesses. She already did so from behind a screen of companies, with which Jobbings communicated on her behalf. Only…it would be a shame if Fenella felt obliged to withdraw from her employ. Having to work for a woman who had actually committed the crime of which she'd so often been accused might prove too much for her delicate sensibilities.

'I will be discreet, Fenella,' she promised as she went to the door. 'I wouldn't want to do anything to make you uncomfortable.'

As her carriage drew up outside the *hôtel* where Harcourt lived, she raised her eyes to the top floor where he had his rooms and reminded herself she could still turn round and go home, before things went too far.

Only, why should she? She wanted to have this experience. She'd chosen it. He hadn't seduced her into it, which had annoyed her at one point, but now she was glad of it, or she might have felt as though she'd let him weaken her. Broken down her resolve. Instead, coming here like this, flouting all the rules, taking a risk for once in her life, made her feel brave and adventurous. And more of an equal partner in this venture than she'd ever been in any other relationship in her life.

Fate had given her the opportunity, finally, to lie naked in his arms. To have him the way a wife should have a husband. And she'd never forgive herself if she didn't take it.

With her mouth set in a grim line she entered the house and began to climb the stairs.

But both her trepidation and her excitement at the prospect of finally achieving something of her only girl-hood dream had worn off completely by the time she'd climbed all the way to the top floor. All she felt was cross. Oh, yes, and don't forget breathless.

Why on earth hadn't she ordered him to attend her in her own rooms? He could have brought his easel and paints, and…and…

And then she pictured Sophie innocently dancing into the room to see how things were progressing. And finding them locked in a clinch, semi-clothed, on a sofa…

The door flew open just as she imagined Sophie shrieking in shock to see Harcourt doing something unspeakably wicked to her and blushed right down to the soles of her boots.

'I thought you would never get here,' he breathed, fiery-eyed.

'It's your own fault…for living up five…flights of stairs,' she panted. 'Are you going to ask me in, or shall I just expire on your doorstep?'

'My, but you are prickly tonight,' he said with a smile.

Well, that was what came of arguing with herself all the way here—and ever since Harcourt had made his wicked proposition.

He swept her an ironic bow. 'Pray, do come in.'

'You may as well know that I'm nearly always prickly,' she said, moving past him and into his rooms. It was all pretty much as she might have expected a bachelor apartment to look like. The furniture was functional rather than pretty and there was a general air of disorder that was strangely welcoming. There were books piled up on the mantelshelf, interspersed with bottles and glasses. Gloves and a hat tossed carelessly on a side table by the door. Bills bursting from the drawers of a small writing desk and cards of invitation stuck at crazy angles in the frame of the spotted mirror propped up on it. And, permeating through the familiar dusty smell that rented rooms always seemed to have, the distinctive aroma of linseed oil.

'You never used to be,' he said as she drew off her gloves and tossed them on the table next to his. They landed in a kind of tangle, which looked peculiarly intimate, almost as though they represented two invisible people, holding hands.

'When we knew each other in London, I always thought you were…sweet,' he said with a wry twist to his mouth, as though he was mocking himself, or the memory of her.

'You couldn't have been more wrong,' she replied tartly, as she tugged the ribbons of her bonnet undone. 'My sisters always used to call me Thistle.'

'Thistle?'

At least the revelation had wiped that sardonic look off his face. He was openly curious now.

'A variation on Amethyst. I always wanted people to call me Amy, but they invariably ended up following my sisters, and calling me Thistle, or Thistly, because of my prickly nature.'

It was probably why they'd all been so thrilled when she'd come back from London in pieces. She'd been strict with them, coming down hard on their faults because her mother had stressed that, as the eldest, she had to set them all an example and she'd been flattered and pleased, and done her best to make her mother proud. What a waste of effort that had been!

She tossed the bonnet aside in the same way she was mentally tossing aside all the expectations her family had ever had of her. With determination. She'd stopped feeling repentant by the time she'd returned home after her trip 'round the Lakes' with her aunt. Ever since then she'd been angry. The most she'd been guilty of had been *naïveté* where this man was concerned. Had it really been such a terrible sin?

But now she jolly well was going to sin. She'd already been punished for crimes she hadn't committed, so there really was no point in not committing them.

'What would you like me to call you?' His face looked quizzical as she scanned the room, looking for somewhere to sit down.

'I don't really care,' she said. 'I just want to sit down and get my breath back.'

'Then come through here,' he said, indicating a door to his right. 'To my studio. I would like to capture your features as they are right now, all flushed and breathless.'

He hurried through and went straight to a table from which he selected paper and charcoal.

'Sit, sit,' he said, waving his free hand towards a couch under one of the many windows which she could tell would flood the room with light during the day.

She sat, rather disgruntled at his very far from lover-like behaviour. He hadn't offered her any refreshment, he hadn't paid her any compliments and now he was scurrying round, adjusting lamps and candles around the sofa. Then he went back to his stool and started sketching her without saying a word and only looking at her with the dispassionate eye of a workman.

Had she got it wrong? He had said he wanted them to become lovers, hadn't he? Or had she imagined it? Got herself all worked up and gone through that agonisingly embarrassing interview with the apothecary—much of which had to be conducted in signs and gestures—for nothing?

He tossed the sheet on which he'd been working aside and got abruptly to his feet.

'Now for your hair,' he said and stalked towards her. 'I want it loose, tumbling round your shoulders.' Before she could protest, he'd yanked out half-a-dozen pins and was undoing her tightly bound braids. She clenched her fists in her lap. It was beyond infuriating, the way she felt at having him so close. Her heart was pounding, her breath kept catching in her throat and her lips felt full and plump. And he hadn't said or done anything to produce this reaction. He was treating her as though she was just…a subject. An interesting subject he wanted to draw.

But then, as he started to fan her hair out, spreading it like a cloak around her shoulders, something happened to his eyes. They sort of…smouldered. And the lids half-lowered. His fingers slowed in their task and, instead of just arranging her hair to catch the light, he kept on running the strands through his fingers, as though he was getting the kind of pleasure she'd got from stroking the barn cat when she'd been little.

'It's so soft,' he murmured, never taking his eyes from it. 'So beautiful, and lustrous and soft. It's a crime to bind it up in braids and shove it under an ugly bonnet the way you do. You ought to have it always on display.'

'Don't be ridiculous,' she said, her cheeks heating. To think she'd felt hard done by because he wasn't saying anything lover-like. Now he'd gone to the other extreme, uttering such absurdities. Besides, her bonnet wasn't ugly. Not any longer. It was brand new and quite the prettiest article of attire she'd ever owned.

Nathan quirked one eyebrow at her petulantly clenched mouth. It was as though she felt uncomfortable with his flattery. He looked at her plain jacket, recalled the positively dowdy way she dressed and wondered if she was deliberately hiding her beauty. He supposed being seduced and abandoned when she'd been so young had taught her a harsh lesson.

So why had she decided to come to him like this? He studied her face, the tense set of her shoulders, the way her mouth seemed to settle naturally into a bitter line, and wondered again how she had lived these last ten years.

It couldn't have been easy, with an illegitimate child to care for. Society was harsh upon unwed mothers, while the men who'd seduced them got away scot free, for the most part.

She hadn't been the real villain of the piece at all, he suddenly perceived. She'd been damaged by what had happened in their youth, too. It had made her treat him badly, but then perhaps her experience had soured her against men. Perhaps she hadn't known that he had a heart to break, having been used and tossed aside by some rake.

On a pang of sudden sympathy, he said, 'One day, I'd like you to tell me about that little girl's father.'

'Sophie?' Her eyes widened. Then she frowned. 'Why?'

She clearly didn't want him to pry. Perhaps it was still too painful to speak of, even after all this time. Perhaps she was reminded of the man who'd fathered her, every time she looked at that abundance of fair hair, or into those intelligent and rather mischievous blue eyes.

'Forgive me. You are correct. *That* has nothing to do with *this*, does it?'

'No.'

'Then why not take off your coat?' he suggested with a smile.

'My coat,' she repeated, looking down as though she'd entirely forgotten she was still wearing it.

'Here, let me help you,' he said, when her fingers fumbled at their task. He knelt on the floor beside the sofa, deftly slipping the buttons from their moorings. She tensed at first, but made no move to stop him. And when he went to slide the sleeves down her arms, she leaned forwards, helping him speed the process.

'And now your gown, I think.'

She sucked in a sharp breath as he reached behind her for the tapes that held the bodice fast. She blushed and he could see a pulse beating wildly in her throat. And her eyes darted away, looking anywhere but at him as he slid the loosened gown from her shoulders.

If he hadn't known better, he would have thought she had no experience with this sort of thing at all.

Perhaps she hadn't. Perhaps her seduction and ruin at such a young age had put her off men altogether. He'd already discovered she wasn't being kept by that

Frenchman, but was it too much to hope that after that one youthful indiscretion she'd had nobody else?

Her hands went up to her bodice when he went to bare her breasts. And that little show of reluctance made her seem so shy and nervous that he could almost believe he meant something special to her. Whatever had happened to her in her past, whatever had driven her to come to him tonight, she clearly wasn't finding this easy. She didn't seem to be the kind of woman who changed her lovers with as much ease as she changed her gown. She didn't seem to know how to flirt, or tease, or arouse. The fact that she'd got herself here at all made him feel as though she was taking a chance on him, in a way she'd never done with any other man.

And something hot and primitive and possessive surged up within him as he leaned forwards to place a kiss on the pulse that beat so wildly in her neck. For a moment, he felt like a conqueror.

But then he went cold inside.

By God, she was dangerous. All he had to do was get a glimpse of that milky skin and his wits had gone wandering. He was building up a picture in his head of someone he'd once wanted her to be, not looking at the reality of where they both were now.

'Don't move,' he grated, drawing back. He had to get things in perspective. 'Stay exactly as you are, so I can capture that dazed look before it fades,' he said, dashing back to his stool and grabbing hold of a pencil as though it was a lifeline.

Amethyst couldn't believe it. He'd started to undress her, had her practically swooning with desire and then he'd darted away and started drawing her again.

When he finally deigned to speak to her again, it was to make a complaint.

'You are frowning again.'

'You would frown,' she retorted, 'if someone half-undressed you, then shot across the room to do something more interesting instead.'

He smiled in comprehension.

'My apologies. Had I known you were so impatient to share my bed I would have tumbled you first and sketched you in the afterglow.'

He set his sketching pad aside and got to his feet.

'In fact, I think that would probably be for the best.' He stalked slowly towards the sofa. 'I have a feeling you will be a much more co-operative subject once I've released you from all that tension you're carrying around with you.'

Harcourt smiled a wicked smile, then leaned down and scooped her into his arms. She let go of her bodice, briefly, to balance herself in his arms, and the material made an attempt to slide all the way down to her waist, revealing more of herself than anybody had seen since she was about ten years old. Mortified, she grabbed at it again, just as he swung her sideways to manoeuvre through a narrow doorway and into yet another room. His bedroom. Her gaze fixed on the bed, which was in the very centre of the room. The sloping ceilings made that the only sensible place to put it, if he didn't want to brain himself every time he got in or out of it.

She swallowed nervously as he laid her on it, but he didn't give her time to express any last-minute qualms by following her down and showering her cheeks, her neck, her shoulders with brief, tantalising little kisses. They had the effect of stopping the breath in her throat so that she was incapable of speech. Not that she could think of anything to say at such a moment. Except she was making breathy little moans and squirming all over the counterpane, which expressed exactly what she felt far more clearly, to her way of thinking.

She didn't want to protest at all when he went to pull her bodice down again, because he was making little noises expressing his own delight too. And then he proceeded to make her feel as though she was made of some delicious substance, the way he licked, and nibbled at her breasts, before swirling his tongue round her nipples. She had never, in all her life, experienced anything so indescribably wonderful.

When he moved off her, quite suddenly, she wished she'd been bold enough to put her arms round his neck, instead of clutching at the covers, so that she could have held him in place and made him carry on doing what he'd been doing.

But he'd only stood up from the bed to yank his shirt off over his head, slip off his shoes and remove his breeches.

She supposed she ought to avert her gaze, but he didn't seem to mind her looking, so why shouldn't she look? Anyway, she didn't think she could have prevented herself. He was so very much more pleasingly put together than all those cold marble statues she'd glimpsed that day in the Louvre. In fact, the sight of her first naked, adult, flesh-and-blood male just about stole the breath from her lungs.

But before she could catch much more than a

glimpse, he was back on the bed beside her, determined to dispense with her clothes.

If he'd paused to stare at her, once he'd got her naked, she didn't think she could have coped with it. But he seemed far more interested in touching and tasting what he was uncovering. And his blatant hunger for everything about her put paid to most of her shyness. Besides, his caresses and kisses were making it just about impossible to think at all. He was reducing her to a molten mass of delightful sensation which drowned out intellect. There was no longer any place on that bed for shyness, or hesitancy, or logic.

She was reacting to his caresses with instincts as old as time, her hips straining towards him, telling both him and her that they were ready for the act she knew almost nothing about.

When he came over her and nudged her legs apart with his own, she found herself flexing up towards him in a way that must have been purely instinctive, because she had certainly never imagined herself doing anything so...unseemly.

And then he began to prod at her.

And then there was a searing pain.

'Ow!'

He pushed into her again.

'Ow, ow, owww!'

All the pleasure had gone. Instead of wanting to flex up towards him, she cringed away from the painful invasion.

'Stop it,' she cried, getting her hands between them and pushing at his chest. 'You're hurting and I don't like it!' How could she ever have thought this was a good idea? It was horrible.

'Stop it, stop it, stop it!'

'What the devil?' He pulled out of her, rearing back so that he was kneeling between her splayed legs. She couldn't have been a virgin. She had a child.

But there was a smear of blood on her inner thigh. He'd been dimly aware of the barrier even before she'd cried out with pain.

She *had* been a virgin.

How the hell was this possible?

A black miasma swirled up before his eyes, which he shut, to blot out the sight of her curling up on her side, thrusting her hands down between her legs, her face crumpled with anguish.

But he could still see exactly how it was possible.

The bastards had lied to him.

Chapter Seven

Ah, God! He placed his fists over his eyes, barely suppressing a cry of anguish as keen as her own had been.

How could his father have done this to him?

And it had to have been his father who'd told Fielding that Amethyst had secretly given birth to a child. He'd known it from the moment his friend had said he'd been told in confidence and hated to have to be the one to break it to him. He'd recognised his father's style of setting up a dupe to do his dirty work.

But he hadn't really questioned the veracity of the tale. He couldn't quite believe even his father would stoop so low as to deliberately blacken a respectable woman's name, just because she stood in the way of his plans, not back then.

He'd naïvely thought his father—with great tact and forbearing—was trying to deliver a warning that he'd strayed into a potential minefield. Giving him a chance to extricate himself from it, rather than just wading in and throwing his weight around, the way he usually did. He'd felt as though his father was finally giving him a chance to prove that he could do the right thing. That he was offering him an opportunity to go to him, and say he was ready to settle down, to stop resisting his family's efforts to match him up with Lucasta, without either of them having to speak of the disaster he'd almost made of things when left to his own devices.

He'd thought it was that important to his father—their relationship. He'd thought all the subterfuge was about trying to avoid coming to a confrontation between them, which might have resulted in a complete breach.

His insides hollowed out as the truth smacked him in the teeth. It had been the alliance with the Delacourts that had been important to his father. His determination that all his sons should cut figures in society. Even his youngest.

No matter what it cost.

Or who paid the price.

She groaned, then, struggled into a sitting position and shot him a look of loathing.

'I might have known all you'd bring me was pain,' she said, jolting him out of his own agony of mind and reminding him that, right now, she was in actual, physical pain. Pain that he'd caused.

'That you'd lead me halfway…somewhere, then let me down.'

Was that the way she'd seen it? It must have been. She couldn't have had a clue why he'd suddenly turned so cold. For he'd cut her out of his life with brutality. And in public. Her face that night—oh, God, the wounded, bewildered look she'd given him as he'd given her the cut direct. The way she'd crumpled when he'd danced with one girl after another. What had he done to her?

Why hadn't he questioned it? Why hadn't he gone straight round to see his father and demanded proof?

Because he'd finally seen a way to win his father's approval, that's why. Having Fielding carry him that tale had told him the old man was vehemently opposed to the match with Amethyst. He had plans for his youngest son. Plans that did not include him marrying a nobody and settling down in the countryside to live a life of contentment in obscurity.

So he had played along. Hardened himself against her tears. Told himself they were evidence of her guilt. That she was upset at being found out.

But he'd known, deep inside, that he was watching her heart breaking.

He'd known, God dammit!

Just as he'd sensed her innocence tonight. But just like before, he'd thrust the truth aside, preferring to believe the lie. Because it exonerated him from blame. He didn't want to be the man who'd broken her heart. So he kept on telling himself she didn't have a heart to break. That she was manipulative and deceitful.

But he had been to blame for destroying her. He had indeed *led her halfway somewhere, then let her down*, not once, but twice.

He squeezed his eyes shut on the devastating truth— she'd loved him.

And he'd let one lie destroy it.

All those wasted, miserable, hellish years…years during which he'd believed in a lie. A lie so base it had warped his entire outlook on life.

She hadn't had a child in secret. She hadn't come to London to ensnare a man with her practised wiles. She'd been innocent. Innocent!

She moaned again and struggled to sit up.

And he wondered how long he'd been kneeling there, reeling in horror at the terrible mistake he'd made. Too long, however few seconds it had taken for the truth to strike him right between the eyes the way it had. Because she was suffering, shocked at the painfully brutal invasion of her body, and she needed comfort. Not some oaf, kneeling there, so many miles and years away in his head that he might just as well have left the room altogether.

In his mind, it was the hurt he'd dealt her years ago that was the biggest issue, but for her, it was the hurt he'd dealt her tonight.

And that was what he had to deal with. He had to put *this* right, he had to tend to the pain he'd caused her, right now, prove that he wasn't the uncaring, fickle disappointment of a man who'd brought her nothing but grief.

There was no need to bring up what had gone wrong between them ten years ago. Not as far as she was concerned.

He blenched when he thought how close he'd come to quizzing her about the little girl he'd seen her with—the one he'd assumed was hers. And the man he'd thought had fathered it on her. The man he'd thought of as a vile seducer.

But it was him. *He* was the only seducer of innocence she knew. *He* was the man who'd callously, clumsily, ripped her virginity from her. As if shattering her hopes ten years ago hadn't been bad enough. What effect had it had on her? He hadn't stopped to consider that, not before. But she'd fled London at the height of the Season. And she hadn't ever married…

'I will never let you down, or bring you pain again,' he vowed.

'No, you will not,' she said firmly, grabbing the corner of the quilt to cover her breasts as she swung her legs over the edge of the bed. 'Because I won't let you.'

'Hold hard!' He gripped her shoulders and, when she wouldn't look at him, spoke to her rigidly averted profile. 'Do not leave, not as you are. Let me get you…a drink. Yes, a drink. I should have hot water to bathe you and soothe you, really, but it would take too long to fetch it and heat it.'

He winced as the words came tumbling out of his mouth. He was practically gibbering. But then what kind of man would be able to stay calm after discovering that, ten years earlier, he'd spurned the only woman he'd ever loved, because he hadn't had the guts to question a pack of the most dastardly lies about her? And only finally learned the truth of her complete innocence of any kind of wrongdoing because he'd treated her like the veriest lightskirt?

He darted from the bed, out of the room and over to the table where he kept a decanter of good brandy. For a moment or two he could see the attraction of becoming a Papist. It must feel wonderful to be able to go to a priest, confess, and have your guilt absolved through the muttering of a few prayers.

Sloshing a generous measure into a glass, he hurried back to the bedroom, to find, to his relief, that she was still sitting hunched up on the edge of the bed, clutching the quilt round her shoulders and not, as he had feared, hunting round the room for her discarded clothing.

He handed her the glass, which she took from him with a scowl.

'I...I'm sorry it hurt.' *Mea culpa.* 'The first time often does, I believe...'

'I'm amazed anybody ever does it a second,' she said, screwing up her face as she took a gulp of the brandy.

'Perhaps...other men are not as clumsy about it as I just was,' he admitted, running his fingers through his hair. 'If I'd known...' No, he couldn't tell her that, could he? Or he would then have to explain why he'd made such an assumption. 'I misunderstood. That is...I thought you seemed impatient.'

No, that wasn't good enough. He couldn't try shifting one iota of the blame on her. His was the fault. And it was up to him to make amends.

And there was only one sure way of doing that. He took a deep breath.

'We must marry, of course,' he said. It was the appropriate penalty to pay for all he'd done to her. The ultimate sacrifice to atone for his sin.

But her scowl only grew deeper.

'We will do no such thing!'

'We have to, Amy, don't you see?' He sat down on the bed next to her. 'I have taken your virginity, ruined you...'

'You didn't *take* anything. We were sharing a moment of what I'd hoped would be pleasure. What a stupid mistake to make,' she said bitterly.

He flinched. Had he asked her the same question ten years ago, she would have been overjoyed. She'd loved him, back then, just as he was.

Now he'd become as big a disappointment to her as he'd always been to everyone else.

'It is a mistake, however,' he persisted, 'that can soon be rectified.' He wouldn't be a disappointment to *her* as a husband. He would cherish her. Stay loyal to her. Make up for all the hurts she'd ever suffered on his account and defend her from anyone who ever attempted to do anything similar in future.

'Not by marrying,' she retorted. 'I agreed to your proposition because I believed you were the one man I could trust *not* to want to go all…respectable. You made it quite clear that you had no intention of marrying me, not ten years ago, and not now. You made me,' she said, jabbing him on his arm with her forefinger, 'believe it would be *safe* to take up with you. Oh, why do I never learn? I should have known you would be nothing but a disappointment. To think I hoped that because you had the reputation for being a rake, that you would be able to make this…' she waved the hand holding the brandy glass wildly, indicating the rumpled bedding '…enjoyable! And not only was that the stupidest mistake I've ever made where you are concerned, but now you are talking about trapping me into matrimony.'

She slammed the brandy glass down on his nightstand and got to her feet.

He had to think of something fast. He couldn't let it end like this. If she left now, he would never get her back. Never be free from the guilt. He went cold inside.

Think, man, think!

Firstly, he got the impression that the tighter he clung to her, the harder she would struggle to break free.

And she'd just said she'd wanted to feel safe with him—which meant free to come and go as she pleased.

And finally, she'd said she wanted pleasure.

Summoning every last ounce of his ability to dissemble, he leaned back into the pillows and folded his hands behind his head as she struggled to get off the bed with her dignity intact, which wasn't easy given all she had to preserve it was a rather moth-eaten quilt that revealed as much as it covered whenever she made an injudicious movement.

'Very well,' he said with feigned insouciance, 'you don't want to marry me. I can understand that. For as long as I can remember, there has been somebody telling me I'm no good.' Except for a few heady weeks ten years ago, when a young girl, fresh from the country, had hung on his every word. Her face had lit up whenever she saw him. Nobody had ever made him feel as though he could be enough for them, just as she was, until he'd met Amethyst.

His calm voice, his apparent nonchalance, had an instant, and highly satisfactory, effect on her. Just as a skilled groom would gentle a skittish, badly broken mare, his retreat roused her curiosity. She stopped scrabbling round on the floor for any item of clothing she could find and looked at him fully for the first time since he'd withdrawn from her body.

Though there was still wariness mingled in with the curiosity.

'What do you mean, no good? You are the son of Lord Finchingfield.'

'He was always my sternest critic. I've never had any ambition, you see, which in his eyes is the greatest sin a member of the Harcourt family can commit.'

It was some consolation that he'd taken a stand and broken free of his father before tonight. Otherwise, he'd have had to go and tell him that he'd never forgive him for what he'd done to Amethyst. For what he'd made *him* do to Amethyst. For making him an accomplice in her heartbreak.

Meanwhile, Amethyst had found a shoe, sat down on the edge of the bed with it and was sliding it on to her foot.

He pulled himself together, sat up, slithered closer and slid his arms round her waist.

'You don't really want to leave, do you?' he murmured the words into her ear. She shivered, but didn't pull away. 'I won't mention marriage again,' he breathed, before nibbling his way down her neck, 'if the prospect of being legshackled to a man of my calibre is really so offensive to you.'

'It isn't you,' she huffed, arching, probably involuntarily, to grant him better access. 'I don't want to marry anyone. Ever.'

He wondered why not. It was generally the height of every woman's ambition.

His mouth flattened into a grim line. He had a sneaking suspicion *that* might be his fault too.

'I can understand that,' he said. 'Having gone through the misery of being chained in a bond of mutual antipathy, I would not lightly enter into the state again.'

'But you said…'

'It was the shock, my sweet,' he said, sliding one hand inside the quilt, to cup a breast, 'of finding you a virgin.' Well, it was true, up to a point. 'But if you really don't want to get married, we can forget all about it.'

'There is no *if* about it,' she said vehemently. 'I did not get into your bed in an attempt to extract a marriage proposal from you.'

'Oh?' He nibbled round the outer edge of her ear. 'Perhaps you would like to tell me what you did want to achieve, then. Because you aren't the kind of woman who routinely has affairs, are you?'

'Well, obviously not. You've just discovered that! I…' She faltered into a sigh as he slid the quilt from her shoulders and started kneading at both breasts at once.

'Then tell me,' he urged her. 'Tell me what you want from me.'

'I don't know, exactly,' she protested. 'I just…wanted to know what it would be like.'

'Curiosity? Is that all that drove you here? I don't believe that,' he reproved her by nipping hard at her earlobe.

'Well, no, that wasn't all,' she confessed, her eyes drooping half-shut. 'It is…it has all been building up for some time now.'

'Building up, yes,' he agreed, sliding his hand down her torso until it rested just above the soft downy hair at the juncture of her thighs.

'I'm so sick of people telling me how I ought to behave,' she said, her head lolling back into the crook of his arm. 'Of how to think. And never ever being… happy. I wanted…' She ended on a whimper as he stroked lower.

'You wanted to break free. To be yourself. Even if you're not sure who that is, just yet.'

'Yes,' she moaned. 'Ooh, yes…but how did you…?'

'How did I know? What do you think I'm doing in Paris?'

'I don't know. I don't know what you're doing. But…'

'But it feels good, doesn't it. No pain now. Only pleasure, I promise.'

He pulled her back down on to the bed and shifted so that he was beside her. And kissed her.

She kissed him back for a while, but then stiffened

and pulled her mouth away, and said, 'What are you doing?'

'I'm giving you what you want. I'm going to be your lover. For as long as you're in Paris, we are going to keep on coming back to this bed—'

'You must be joking!'

He lifted one leg over hers when it looked as though she was going to struggle out of his arms, pinning her down while he kissed her again. Until she stopped struggling and kissed him back.

'This is too important to joke about,' he said grimly. 'I hurt you. And made you want to run away when I should have given you the greatest pleasure you have ever known.'

'It wasn't all your fault,' she conceded. 'I knew you'd assumed I was being kept by Monsieur Le Brun, and even though I did tell you he wasn't, I did nothing to discourage you from thinking I was the kind of woman who might. And then, when I agreed to your proposition and came straight round here, just as though I was used to doing this sort of thing...'

'Even if you were an experienced woman, I should have been more considerate. But I wasn't thinking straight. I was...' His arms tightened round her convulsively. He'd never, ever, been so insensitive to a bed-partner's needs. He hadn't cared whether she enjoyed the coupling or not, that was the sordid truth. He had been angry with her when he'd carried her to this bed. He had still been blaming her for everything. 'I wasn't thinking about much of anything at all. Only counting the seconds until I could make you mine,' he finished lamely. He couldn't tell her the truth, or anything that might hint at it, because it would only hurt her more. And she didn't deserve more hurt.

She hadn't deserved any of it, ever. Her only crime had been winning his heart and thereby falling foul of his powerful, manipulative, cold-hearted father.

Well, this was where the hurting would stop. From now on, he would only bring her pleasure.

'I may not be good for much,' he said, 'but one thing I am most proficient at is making love.'

She didn't look as though she believed him. He couldn't blame her, considering the way things had gone so far tonight.

'Give me another chance, Amethyst,' he said, sliding his fingers between the legs she'd clamped shut. 'Just see how it goes, hmm?' She was already damp down there. Her body was responding to his kisses and caresses. It was only her mind that was still resisting. 'You can stop me any time you want to. But I don't think, this time, you will want me to stop.'

He nuzzled her neck as he slid one finger inside her. She gasped and tensed. His heart lurched. But as he continued to caress her and nibble at her neck, she slowly relaxed, until he was able to slide another finger inside her.

'Nathan,' she moaned, half-plea, half-protest. 'I really don't think I want to do this...'

'Hush,' he murmured into her ear. 'You don't know what you want. You cannot, because you have never experienced any of this before, have you?'

He groaned into her neck as another wave of anguish assailed him. They'd been on the brink of something, ten years before, which would have resulted in them both becoming very different people. He wouldn't have become the cynic, or the rake he was, if he'd married her. And she... Well, he didn't know what she'd become since they'd last met. But she didn't look any happier than he was. She had that mean, pinched look about her mouth common to impoverished spinsters. She dressed dowdily, as though she had no pride in her appearance.

Well, that was all going to change. While she was in Paris he would show her a new world. A world of sensuality. She'd said she wanted to break free and find out who she really was, who she was meant to be. And he'd be the man to show her. He'd peel back the layers of hurt and caution that shrouded the girl who'd once made his heart dance, as surely as he'd peeled away her clothes tonight. He'd kiss the meanness from her mouth and teach her to love what her body could make her feel.

Starting right now. She might not want to marry him any longer, but she did want him to show her the kind of pleasure most spinsters could only dream of. And... he wanted to give her the wedding night they should have had ten years ago.

For once he was glad he'd had so much experience. In gaining his reputation as a rake, he'd learned a lot about what brought a woman pleasure. Now he could apply it all to Amethyst.

Her neck had proved to be particularly sensitive, so he kept on kissing her there, while toying with the damp folds between her thighs. He dipped and teased, nipped and nuzzled, until her hips began to squirm in a rhythmical response.

And then, when he was sure she'd got to the point where she wasn't going to tell him to stop, he began a leisurely exploration of the rest of her body, paying close attention to anywhere that provoked a gasp, or a shiver, or made her fingers curl a little more tightly round his neck.

She shivered with pleasure when he lapped at the indentation of her waist, moaned when he nipped at the soft flesh on the outside of her hips and squirmed when he trailed his tongue further down, and inward, to the insides of her thighs.

Since she was a total innocent, he hesitated before bestowing the most intimate kiss of all. But had this been their wedding night, he would have made sure she came to orgasm before he made any attempt to enter her. And this was the most reliable way, he'd discovered, of pleasuring a woman.

And he wanted to give her pleasure. Such unimaginable pleasure that she would want to come back to him again and again. He couldn't make amends for every single hurt he'd caused her, but by God, while she was in Paris he could give her pleasure unlike anything she'd known before. Or would ever experience again.

It would be no penance, no penance at all. It wouldn't wash away his guilt. That would stay with him to his dying day.

But at least she wouldn't think of him as the biggest disappointment in her life.

Chapter Eight

Amethyst could not believe the things he was prepared to do with his tongue. Part of her wondered whether she ought to stop him. But it was making her feel so...blissful. And she'd got the idea he wanted to do penance, in some way, so who was she to demur? Besides, when he slipped first one finger, then two inside her, she lost the ability to think anything at all. It was all melting heat, and rivers of delight, and then a kind of starburst that shattered her, yet made her feel completely whole for the first time in her life, all at the same time.

And then he was above her and sliding into her before she'd even recovered her wits enough to tense, or make a protest that she really didn't want him to try again.

And this time it didn't hurt a bit. In fact, it brought another wave of pulsating pleasure shivering through her, making her flex her hips upwards in an instinctively welcoming gesture.

He kissed her on the mouth. Gently, tenderly. A different kiss from any he'd bestowed on her before. He encouraged her to open her mouth, so he could drive his tongue inside. It was almost more shocking than having that other part of him driving into her, though equally as delicious. After a bit, she wondered if he was trying to distract her from the gentle, yet insistent rhythm he'd set up with his body, by teaching her lips to part, her tongue to duel with his.

If so, it was rather…sweet of him.

And then he broke away from her mouth, to pay attention to that sweet spot just beneath her ear, which sent shivers skittering all the way down her spine. And his movements became more insistent, demanding a response from her. And her body gave it, of its own volition. She'd just discovered that touching and kissing a certain spot between her legs resulted in almost unimaginable pleasure. Now, awakened, that place was clamouring for more sensation, more pressure. And the only way to get it was to grind upwards against his pelvis as he thrust down.

She wouldn't have believed that after the pain she would ever permit a man inside her again, let alone want him to go deeper, and harder, but she did. She wouldn't have believed he would be so sensitive to her needs, after the clumsy way he'd started, but he was. It was as though he was completely in tune with her body now, giving it exactly what it needed, a split second before she knew it herself.

So there was no reason for her to thrash about under him, or claw at his back, or wind her legs about his. Not that he seemed to mind. Not to judge by the way he kept on saying, 'Yes, oh God, yes.' Or the way he moaned and shuddered, and showered kisses all over her face and neck.

But then, once again, her mind took leave of her body as delight broke over them both in a great wave.

'Amy,' he cried as she splintered apart. And there was something in his voice that sounded almost as though...

No. It wasn't tenderness. It was just...passion.

And yet the tone of it had plucked at some long-suppressed emotion deep inside her, which made her want to weep.

Which was ridiculous, she panted, as she drifted back to shore. She'd cried enough tears over this man in the past. His purpose in her life now was to teach her about pleasure.

And he had. Once he'd realized just how inexperienced she was, he'd applied his considerable skill with gentleness.

She should have told him, before they got started, that she hadn't a clue about what went on between a man and woman in the bedroom.

So why hadn't she?

It wasn't just that she'd been flattered he thought her so attractive she could make her living in this way.

No. The truth was much more muddied. He'd accused her of tempting him to marry unwisely in his youth. If he'd known she was a virgin, she'd feared he might have thought this was a renewed attempt on his freedom. And she'd wanted him too badly to allow anything to make him reconsider.

All of a sudden, panic clawed its way to the surface. She wanted him, yes, but not enough to sacrifice her own freedom. Any more than she expected, or wanted, him to sacrifice his.

'I really didn't expect you to propose to me,' she bit

out, 'just because I was a virgin. That is not why I chose you to become my first lover.'

'Your first?' He rolled off her and raised himself up on one elbow to glare down at her. 'Do you mean to tell me you now plan to make a habit of taking lovers?'

No, she hadn't meant that at all, but she could see why her words might have made him think so. But he had an infernal cheek to look so disapproving, with the reputation he had!

'I don't know. I might one day, I suppose. After all, I'm not going to stay in Paris for ever. And I most certainly am not going to marry you.'

'You've already made that crystal clear.'

He was positively glaring at her now.

'There's no need to look at me like that, for heaven's sake. You don't want to marry me either! Don't let's spoil this by quarrelling. I was only trying to reassure you that I have no designs on you, just because you happened to be the man to whom I gave my virginity.'

'No, I…no, I see that.' He pursed his lips in a way that, had he been a woman, she would have described as a pout. 'But I cannot help wondering why you did choose me for this singular honour.'

Irritating man! She was trying to reassure him that his precious freedom was not in jeopardy and he was twisting her words to make it sound as though…as though…well, into an insult, anyway.

'There is no need to be sarcastic,' she huffed, reaching down blindly for the quilt. Or a sheet. Or anything to cover herself up with.

He shifted, releasing a swathe of quilt which he tucked up over her breasts.

'Thank you,' she said stiffly.

'You're welcome,' he said drily. 'But for your information, I was not being sarcastic. I do feel that you paid me a great compliment in coming here tonight and permitting me to initiate you into the joys of lovemaking.' He looked troubled when he added, 'I only wish I had done better...'

Her immediate reaction was to try to console him.

'Oh, no, you were very good. Really.' What was the matter with her? Trying to make him feel better? He was a man, for heaven's sake. A fully grown man. Just because he'd pouted like a sulky boy, then looked a bit hurt, that was no reason to pander to his vanity.

'Except to start with,' she therefore reminded him and, feeling a twinge of conscience, hastily added, 'And that was partly my own fault.'

He gave her a lazy smile. 'Thistle,' he said, and kissed her shoulder. The one bit of her that was peeping out from under the quilt. 'You really are prickly, aren't you? Most women would be purring like a contented kitten after that.' But she wasn't most women. And he'd hurt her so badly before, of course she was going to throw up a shield of sarcasm, from behind which she could jab at him with her sharp little tongue. It was all the protection she had.

'Well, if that's going to be your attitude...'

He held her tight when she would have rolled away from him and clucked his tongue.

'I am not criticising you, not at all. It was merely an observation. And a note to myself that I need to do better next time.'

'Next time?' Her eyes were wide, her lips parted, her knuckles white as they clutched the quilt to her chin.

'But you will have to give me a little respite,' he said, rolling on to his back and tucking her into his side.

'Respite? What do you…oh! Well, I didn't think we'd be doing that again. Not now.'

'No, not now,' he said amicably. 'In just a little while.'

'No, really, I…'

'Don't be so demanding, woman,' he said. 'I have told you I need a little rest before the next round.'

'That wasn't what I meant! I…oh…' she glanced up at him when he started to chuckle '…you're teasing me.'

'Has nobody ever teased you before?'

She shook her head. 'Not since…well, you.'

'You must have mixed with some very dull people since we last met then. Want to tell me about them?'

'Not particularly.'

'Well, what would you like to talk about, then?'

Her fingers clutched at the quilt a bit more tightly. Her eyes narrowed warily. If he wasn't careful, she would retreat behind her protective shield and he wouldn't be able to find out anything about her. And he had this burning need to find out what had happened to her after he'd abandoned her. He couldn't bear to imagine her life being as miserable as his had been. If he could just find out that she'd found some contentment in her spinster state, it might assuage his guilt. A tiny bit.

He shrugged one shoulder, as if her next words weren't going to matter to him one way or another.

'If you don't want to tell me anything personal, then…you could recite some poetry, I suppose.'

'Poetry?'

'Yes. To get me back in the mood. I don't suppose you know anything naughty, do you?'

'Of course I don't!'

'Been living a pure and simple life, have you? Tucked away in that rectory with your parents?'

'No. Far from it,' she huffed.

'Oh?' He permitted himself to show curiosity now. 'Then you've been…travelling the world, posing as a lightskirt, perchance? Using the man who calls himself Monsieur Le Brun as…cover for your work as a spy?'

'Now you really are being ridiculous.'

'It is worth it to see that smile return to your eyes.' He cupped her jaw and turned her face up to his. 'Come on,' he said in a cajoling tone. 'Tell me one thing about yourself. Satisfy my curiosity. Otherwise I am going to imagine all kinds of wild and inaccurate things about you.'

'Such as, for instance, that I have such poor taste that I would sell my body to a man like Monsieur Le Brun?'

'Well, if you cannot give me a better excuse for travelling with him, what else am I to think?'

'That my friend and I hired him, perhaps? To act as courier and guide, since it isn't the done thing for two single ladies to travel without protection?'

Her voice had an acid tinge to it that made him think of tart, ripe berries. Which in turn led to him thinking about puckered, pink nipples. How did she do this to him? Get him roused simply by sniping at him?

'You hired him?'

She tensed again. She really didn't want to let him know anything about her life, which made him all the more determined to find out all there was to know about her. Everything she'd done since she'd vanished so completely from London.

He slid his hand under the quilt and toyed with one of

her breasts until the nipple formed into a tightly furled, mouth-watering little berry.

'Who is this friend of yours? How do you know her?'

'What is this? Why are you interrogating me?'

He rolled over, pinning her beneath him.

'Because you won't tell me anything. Tell me just one fact about you. Satisfy my rampant curiosity.'

Her eyes widened at his deliberately suggestive tone. She'd also registered that it wasn't only his curiosity that was rampant.

'One fact,' he growled.

'Very well,' she sighed. 'Fenella and I...' She gave a little wiggle. 'Fenella is a widow, with a small child and no income. I have inherited a house, from a rather eccentric aunt, with whom I lived in the latter years of her life. We have...an arrangement.'

'That's...' his brow furrowed as he tried to concentrate '...seven facts. Very generous of you.' He dropped a kiss on her brow. 'I think that deserves a reward.'

He nudged her legs apart.

'You really are the most arrogant, conceited, infuriating man...'

'Don't forget irresistible,' he said, sliding into her. 'And before you claw my eyes out, remember, I think you are irresistible too.'

Her eyes widened. Her muscles relaxed.

'You do?'

'Utterly irresistible.' He kissed her jaw, then her neck as her head rolled to one side.

'How can you doubt it? I pursued you all over the city, even though I thought you belonged to another man.'

'Oh! Hmmm. You...'

'Yes.' He pulled the quilt down, and started the slow assault on her senses all over again.

It was a long time before either of them spoke again.

Amethyst opened her eyes to find him standing over her with a tray bearing glasses, some cheese, some fruit and a hunk of bread.

Wearing nothing but a lazy grin.

'Refreshments, my lady,' he said, putting the tray down on the bedside table and perching on the edge of the bed. 'Cannot have you fainting away from hunger on your way home.'

And she would have to get up and go home soon, she realised. She wasn't sure how long she'd dozed, but they'd already spent several hours in this bed.

'When can I see you again,' he asked, as he poured wine from a carafe into one of the glasses and handed it to her. 'Soon, I hope?'

The eagerness in his voice soothed some of the sting that his less-than-subtle hint it was time for her to leave had inflicted.

'Tomorrow evening, I should think. I shall tell my... friend, Fenella, that since we won't be staying long in Paris, you need to work on my portrait as often as possible.'

He frowned briefly, turning away to pull some grapes from their stalk.

'I had hoped perhaps we could meet during the daytime, too,' he said, popping one into her mouth. 'I should like to show you something of Paris. The real Paris. Not the one your hired guide will show you. The one that the citizens inhabit. And tomorrow is Sunday.'

He turned back to her, an eager, open expression on

his face that reminded her of when they'd both been so much younger and they'd talked about…anything and everything.

'I could take you outside the *barrière*, perhaps to the Jardin de la Gaieté. The locals get paid on Saturday and they tend to go outside the *barrière* to spend their money, where goods don't incur Paris custom dues. It's like a huge open-air party, with feasting and dancing all day.'

Something seemed to turn over and flip inside her. He had no idea how wealthy she was. He'd looked at her clothes, listened to her story, which had made it sound as though she and Fenella were pooling their resources, and come up with an entertainment that would make what little money he supposed she had go as far as possible. It meant he really wanted to spend time with her.

'I am sorry,' she said, surprised to find that refusing his invitation really had caused her a pang of regret. 'But I have already made plans.'

'You could break them.'

Yes, she could. The trouble was that she wanted to do just that far too much. It felt wonderful to have him look at her like that as he asked her to spend the daylight hours with him, as though he really wanted to be with her. But then he'd made her feel like this when she'd been younger, too. And just look how that had ended!

No, it was more honest to just limit their relationship to what it was truly all about. If they started to behave like a…well, like a courting couple, then she might start to slide into feeling something for him besides the physical fascination she couldn't deny he exerted over her.

'No. I don't break my word,' she said firmly. Besides, it would be much healthier to spend time with her friends, friends who would still be there for her when this *affaire* with Harcourt had burned out. As it surely would. By all accounts he was incapable of sticking to one female for much more than a week.

'What about the evening, then? I have an invitation to a soirée you might find amusing. We could go together.'

She frowned up at him. 'I'm not sure that would be a good idea.' She didn't know what kind of circles Nathan moved amongst these days. It was just possible she might get introduced to one of the merchants with whom she was trying to do business. And then if they spotted her with Monsieur Le Brun, who was acting for her, they might put two and two together. It was only a slight possibility, but still…

He sucked in a sharp breath. 'You want to keep our affair secret. I can understand that.' He shrugged, and smiled, but it was a cynical smile that made her sorry she'd spoken so sharply. 'But you will come to me again?'

Oh, that was better. Much better. He found her so irresistible that he would accept any terms she chose, so long as she returned to his bed.

She had hugged the sensation to herself all the way home and woken up the next morning with a smile on her face.

She wasn't unnatural and unfeminine, as her father had decreed she must be, for preferring to stay with her aunt and work at her ledgers rather than crawl home to the vicarage and…stultify. She was a desirable woman. Nathan Harcourt, the man who had once spurned her, wanted her. *Her.*

Without knowing a thing about her fortune.

She stretched her arms above her head, wincing as she felt the pull of muscles left tender from all those hours of lovemaking.

No, not *love*making. She wasn't going to mistake his enthusiasm for her body as affection, not this time round. Nor was she going to fall for him, or anything silly like that.

He wasn't anything special. He was just here. At a time in her life when she was ready to explore new possibilities. To find out what she really wanted from life. She'd known it wasn't the cloistered, cramped existence that was all Stanton Basset had to offer. She'd wanted to break free of its petty restrictions, it's narrow-minded parochialism. And she'd thought visiting Paris would do it.

She'd been wrong.

Taking a lover had been what she needed.

They would say she was wanton, if they knew what she'd done last night, the town tabbies. And wicked, to boot, for turning down Harcourt's guilt-induced proposal.

It had surprised her, that proposal. It was the kind of thing an honourable man would do and she'd long since ceased to think of him as anything more than an out-and-out scoundrel.

But he wasn't all bad. He had wanted her, truly wanted her, when he'd been a young man. And if he'd been the villain she'd believed, the rake that the scandal sheets had branded him, he could have taken her virginity then and left her sullied as well as broken-hearted.

But he hadn't bedded her when she'd been a girl. He might have cut her out of his life quite harshly when he'd decided to marry for gain, rather than…well, she hesitated to use the word love, but it really did look as though he had felt *something* for her. But he had left her in such a way that she *could* have married someone else.

If she hadn't been so shattered.

If her parents hadn't added to her misery by heaping all the blame upon her.

If her aunt hadn't swooped down and taken her under her wing. And fostered her poor opinion of the male species until she, too, had grown to dislike them all on principle.

Well, that was all water under the bridge now. It was Sunday and, instead of trudging to church and listening to the moralising of plump and priggish Parson Peabody, she was going out on an excursion of pleasure. Monsieur Le Brun had organised a carriage to drive them out to the Bois de Boulogne. It sounded rather tame, she sighed as she got out of bed, in comparison with the all-day ball that Nathan had invited her to attend. But as she washed and donned her clothes, she reminded herself that it wouldn't do to let him monopolise her time. He was already monopolising her thoughts.

He would have to be content to have the access to her body that no other man had ever known.

Listen to her! Planning to keep her lover at arm's length. She giggled at her newfound confidence in her attractiveness. Oh, if only she'd known how good making love would feel, she would have taken a lover years ago.

Or at least she might have considered it.

Though…actually, she hadn't ever felt the slightest curiosity about what it might have been like to so much as *kiss* a man, until she'd run into Nathan again.

But then, she hastily reminded herself, she hadn't been in Paris, either.

She had just about convinced herself that it was something about the revolutionary atmosphere lingering in Paris that had given her the courage to defy all the rules by the time she went through to the main salon.

And got the shock of her life.

Chapter Nine

'Dare I ask,' said Nathan when he strode into her salon that evening, 'what made you change your mind about accepting my invitation to the Wilsons' soirée?'

'Not here,' she said darkly. 'Wait until we are in the carriage.' So saying, she swept out of the front door and into the street, where the hired carriage he'd come to collect her in was still waiting.

'You look divine, by the way,' he said as he handed her in.

He made her feel divine, too, the way his eyes devoured her as he climbed in beside her.

She was glad she'd succumbed to the urge to dress up for him. She'd briefly wondered whether he would feel more comfortable if she dressed plainly, the way she usually did. But she hadn't been able to resist putting on the prettiest of her new gowns. And tucking the diamond—or possibly crystal—aigrette into her hair had been an act of pure self-indulgence. Just once, she wanted to look her best and have him look at her exactly the way he was looking at her right now. As though she was beautiful. Desirable.

'You look quite…appealing yourself,' she murmured, looking him up and down with appreciation. It was a relief to see he still had some clothes fit to be seen in, in any company. In fact, they looked as though they'd scarcely been worn at all. He must have had quite an extensive wardrobe when he'd been married to his wealthy, well-connected wife. And he clearly hadn't pawned it all yet.

'Thank you,' he said, taking her hands and kissing first one, then the other.

Her toes curled up with pleasure. Oh, but she had been right to seek the solace that only he could give her tonight.

'So what is it that has driven you from your friends this evening? And made you hint at some mystery? I am all agog.'

'I could not stomach one more minute of their billing and cooing, if you must know. And I heartily regretted my decision to turn down your invitation to spend the day with you not half an hour after departing for the Bois de Boulogne. At least if I'd been dancing with you, you would have noticed I was there!'

'Billing and cooing? The stringy Frenchman and the mousy widow?'

'Yes,' she said in disgust. 'Though they do say that love is blind, I had never before considered how very accurate that statement is until today.' She shot him a sharp look. 'But Fenella is not mousy. She is elegant and poised. Perhaps she is a touch reserved, but—'

'Nondescript,' he said dismissively. 'The kind of woman you barely notice. It amazes me that she managed to produce a daughter so vibrant as that…'

'Sophie,' Amethyst supplied. 'Oh. So that is why you asked about her father.'

He didn't contradict her.

'I've often thought Sophie must take after her father, myself.' She smiled up at him. He couldn't return her smile. Her pleasure in assuming they were of like mind about the girl made him feel so guilty he couldn't even look at her.

'Because Fenella is a quiet person, though neither nondescript, nor mousy. I always think she is a perfect lady, actually.'

'She is not perfect,' he said bluntly. 'She pales into insignificance when next to you. When first I saw you here in Paris, I hardly even noticed she was at the table. But I could not get you out of my head, no matter how hard I tried. I thought of you practically all day. And even in my dreams, there you were, your wonderful hair spread across my pillows, your naked—'

'Did you?'

She loved hearing him say things like that. And even if it was merely the practised patter of a seasoned rake, it was close enough to what she'd felt to be convincing. She hadn't been able to stop her thoughts returning to him either. And he'd infiltrated her dreams too.

'But I am being remiss,' he said. 'To distract you from whatever it was you were going to tell me about your friends. You were so annoyed with them you looked as though you really needed to make a clean breast of it.'

His gaze dropped to the bodice of her gown. And all of a sudden she could imagine him baring her breasts, right there in the carriage, and suckling on them the way he'd done the night before.

'It was all your fault,' she said resentfully. She had decided to get out tonight and risk taking a peek at the glittering whirl that was Parisian society after all. But one heated look and all she wanted was to tell the coachman to take her to his studio, remove every stitch of clothing, slowly, while he watched, and then have him do all the things he'd done to her last night.

Over and over again.

'Mine? I cannot be held responsible for every love affair that springs up in Paris, just because I happen to live here.'

'Oh, that's not what I meant. It was what you said, last night. About, *the man who calls himself Monsieur Le Brun.* I've always thought there was something suspicious about him.' That was not quite true. It was more that she was suspicious of all males as a matter of course.

'But this morning, only he was in the salon where we gather before going out. And although we have been in rooms on our own before, he just looked so…uncomfortable. He could not meet my eyes. Well,' she huffed, her eyes narrowing, 'naturally not, the sneak! It turns out he—' but just then the carriage lurched to a halt. They had arrived at the *hôtel* hired by the minor politician who was throwing tonight's informal rout.

'He what?'

'Are you not going to open the door and help me alight?'

'No. I want to hear what *the sneak* has been getting up to.'

'I will tell you inside.'

'But anyone might overhear.'

'So? I care not. Besides, if we just sit here with the door closed, people will think we are…'

'So?' He grinned at her, echoing her own words. 'I care not.'

'You have to be the most annoying man I've ever met.'

'Worse than Monsieur Le Brun?'

'Far worse,' she said darkly. 'Because I suspect you annoy me on purpose.'

'You should not look so utterly captivating with your eyes flashing fire, then.'

'Captivating? Don't you mean shrewish? That's what most men say.'

'Ah, but I'm not most men. And you warned me about your prickles before you let me get too close. If you were really a shrew, you wouldn't care whether you hurt me or not.'

He leaned forwards, and planted a hard kiss on her lips just as she was parting them to give him a piece of her mind. He kissed her until she'd forgotten what she'd been going to say to him. And then, just as she relented and started to kiss him back, he pulled away and sprang out of the carriage.

Only to lean back in, extending his hand to her with a broad smile, which she somehow found herself returning.

'You are incorrigible,' she said, shaking her head.

'That's me,' he agreed cheerfully. 'But you wouldn't have me any other way, would you? You've needed to find a man who is strong enough not to bleed when you try to sharpen your claws on him.'

'And you think you are that man?'

'I'm man enough for you,' he husked into her ear,

just at the moment when a footman stepped forwards to take her coat. Which made her blush. And want to do something to make him squirm, the way he'd just made her squirm. Only she couldn't think of anything that wouldn't make her look a fool as well.

'God, will you just look at this place?' Nathan tucked her hand into the crook of his arm almost absent-mindedly as he stared up at the queue of people snaking halfway down the stairs. 'They must have rented the whole building, not just one floor.'

She took note of the disdainful twist to his mouth. In spite of growing up in exalted circles, in spite of having married into another wealthy family, it looked as though he didn't like people flaunting their wealth either.

'So...' he jerked his eyes away from the marble pillars, the ornate chandeliers, the liveried, bewigged footmen, and turned his attention back to her. 'You were about to tell me what your French hireling said when you told him you knew he wasn't being honest about his name.'

Was she? Oh, yes. She'd been really annoyed about it too.

'That was what started it,' she agreed. 'But then he had the nerve to demand I tell him who had been talking about him, rather than just give me an honest answer.'

'What cheek,' said Nathan with mock horror.

'Yes, it was, actually. He acted as though I had no right to question him, when I am employing him in a position of considerable trust. And I was just pointing out that if he wished to remain in my employ he had better come clean, when Fenella burst into the room and flew to his side. Saying it was all her fault. Well, he tried to silence her, saying that I didn't know the truth, but she just said she couldn't keep it a secret from me any longer and it all came tumbling out. Not about his real identity, not at first, but about how she and *Gaston* were going to marry as soon as we return to England.'

For one terrible moment she'd thought they'd hatched up some plot to swindle her. After all, they had spent so much time together poring over the correspondence from French firms it would have been easy. The thought of Fenella betraying her trust in that way had felt like a knife-blow. Like her sisters all over again. She'd wondered why it was that no matter how much she did for people, nobody had ever stood by her.

It had been a tremendous relief to find out that what they were hiding was merely a romance.

'But why,' he said as the queue shuffled further up the stairs, 'did they need to keep their betrothal a secret from you?'

'It was because he'd seduced her,' she told him grimly. 'The very first night we arrived in Paris. Oh, Fenella said it was all her own doing. She'd had too much to drink and was lonely. And they'd become such good friends during the voyage and had so much in common. And then she said she had missed the kind of closeness a woman can only find with a man. Which, by her blushes, I took to mean in bed.'

And because of the time she'd spent in Nathan's bed, she could actually see why Fenella had succumbed to temptation, when only the day before, she would have been horrified. Sickened.

'Suddenly, a lot of things made sense. Such as the way neither of them could quite look me in the eye any more. And the way he'd gone from being as sarcastic as he dared to being positively ingratiating.' And the way Fenella blushed when she'd made what were, on the face of it, perfectly innocuous remarks.

'And all the while he kept trying to shush her. But when he groaned and covered his face and sort of collapsed on to the sofa, Fenella finally realised we hadn't been arguing about *that* at all. But it was too late. The cat, as they say, was well and truly out of the bag.'

'I wish I had been there,' he said, his lips twitching with mirth.

'It wasn't funny.' Could he take nothing seriously?

'I beg your pardon, but it sounds highly entertaining. When you have a middle-aged couple behaving like some latter-day Romeo and Juliet, with you cast as both sets of disapproving guardians. It's preposterous.'

'To be fair, they were both afraid I would try to part them.'

'Why on earth would you want to do that?'

'Because,' she said, grasping the banister rail with such force it looked as though she was considering wringing someone's neck, 'he'd taken advantage of her. If I'd found out the morning after, when she was so upset about it, you may be sure I *would* have turned him out!'

'But you said Fenella was as keen as he was.'

'I know you don't think there's anything wrong with jumping into bed with people on the slightest pretext,' she said coldly, 'but Fenella was racked with guilt. So much that she couldn't bring herself to confide in me. And he worked on those fears. And seems to have convinced her that they're experiencing some grand passion that will end in marriage.'

She didn't see him flinch when she assumed he had no morals. That he would, as she put it, jump into bed

with any woman, on the slightest pretext. It took an effort, but he managed to carry on with the conversation
after only the slightest hesitation.

'And you don't think it will?'

'I...'

He watched the fire go from her. Her shoulders
slumped.

'This morning, I would have said not. But having
been obliged to watch them...'

'Billing and cooing,' he supplied helpfully.

She shot him a brief, narrow-eyed glare.

'Precisely,' she said bitterly. 'He is certainly very
convincing in his role.' Once they'd gone out and
Fenella and Gaston no longer felt the need to conceal
their relationship, they'd become remarkably demon-
strative. Smiling at each other and laughing at silly
little jokes that made no sense to her whatsoever. And
looking at each other as though, given half a chance,
they would dive into the nearest bushes and rip each
other's clothes off.

And yet somehow they'd managed to include Sophie
in their happy little love bubble. They were bonding into
a family unit, right before her eyes.

Leaving her trailing along behind them. Excluded,
as usual. She'd felt almost as lonely as when her family had closed ranks against her.

She'd grown increasingly resentful of the fact that
she'd stuck to the arrangement she'd made with this
pair, thinking it would be bad form to abandon them
in order to spend time with her new lover, when they
could think of nothing but each other.

As soon as she got home she had sent word that she
was ready to accompany Nathan to the party he'd men-

tioned, to be thrown by some minor politician of whom she'd never heard. If Fenella was going to be wrapped up in Gaston for the duration of their stay in Paris, then she might as well spend every moment she could with her own lover.

'I can see why Fenella believes him to be in earnest,' she admitted. 'But what still worries me is the fact that Fenella really has fallen for him. She was almost weeping when she told me she never thought she'd find love at her time of life, but that Gaston had made her feel like a young bride again.'

And because she'd just spent the earlier part of the day feeling exactly the same, in relation to Nathan, she hadn't been able to utter one single word of rebuke.

'He got to his feet at that point, put his arm round her and claimed that the only reason he did not wish Fenella to tell me of their so-called plans until we returned safely to England was because he was afraid I would turn—' She bit back what she had been about to say, unwilling to let Nathan know that Fenella was also in her employ, rather than just travelling with her as a friend, which was what she'd led him to believe.

'Turn against her, for having loose morals,' she finished lamely.

Monsieur le Prune—and she might as well call him that now, since Le Brun wasn't his real name either—had pointed out that since she'd employed Fenella to give her an air of respectability, now that her own morality was in question, poor Fenella was terrified she would lose her job.

And then had come the only bright spot in her otherwise disastrous day. Fenella had looked up at him with reproach and declared that Amethyst would never abandon her in a foreign country, let alone Sophie. Even when he'd muttered that perhaps she did not know her employer as well as she thought, Fenella had been unshakeable. Fenella had stayed true to their friendship.

No matter what happened next, whether the romance blossomed into marriage, or whether Monsieur Le Brun turned out to be some kind of ageing Lothario, Amethyst was not going to lose her friend.

'I think he had been trying to turn her against me for some time. He's worked on the guilt she felt for actually doing what all the ladies of Stanton Bassett accused her of doing—'

'Hold on. Now you have lost me. What, exactly, have the ladies of Stanley Basset accused her of doing?'

'Stanton. It's Stanton Basset. Well, when she arrived with a baby, but no husband in evidence, rumours started to fly. You can imagine the sort of thing that provincial, narrow-minded women with too much time on their hands can invent. They're always ready to believe the worst of people, without a shred of evidence to support it. Particularly if that person has nobody to vouch for her,' she said indignantly. 'And it was all the more unfair because Fenella is really a very moral person. Well, until she started misbehaving with Monsieur le Prune, I would have said she had never put a foot wrong in her life. Apart from marrying a plausible rogue the first time round. Honestly,' she huffed, as they moved up yet another place in the receiving line, 'you would have thought she'd have learned her lesson where men are concerned.'

Although had she learned anything from her experience with Nathan? Here she was, seeking him out and confiding everything to him as though he was her closest, most trustworthy friend. Just as she'd done before.

What right had she to question Fenella's judgement when it came to men? At least Fenella had gone for a man she swore was completely different from the feckless charmer she'd eloped with as a girl. Gaston was clever, she declared, and hard working and capable, and he never, ever lost his temper.

After that description of his merits, she saw that he was exactly the kind of man Fenella would fall for. She'd confessed she wanted a man to lean on. Someone dependable and patient. His looks were irrelevant.

She might find the thought of getting amorous with him totally repellent, but he'd managed to put a bloom on Fenella's cheeks. He was making her feel like a desirable, vibrant woman. Just as Nathan—

Nathan, she suddenly realised, had gone awfully quiet. When she darted a glance up at him he was staring fixedly at the back of the stout man in front of them in the receiving line, a forced tightness about his lips.

He was probably getting bored with her stupid prattle. Desperately, she strove to find some other topic of conversation.

'You never did tell me,' she said with determined brightness. 'What is your connection to these people and why they have invited you tonight?'

He turned to her then, his face twisting into a mask of harsh cynicism.

'I know Wilson from my days as a Member of Parliament. We both, at that time, had very ambitious wives. They got on well together.'

He didn't look as though that fact pleased him. And when she frowned her confusion at him, he continued,

'You seem to think that if she is so ambitious for her husband to succeed, they would have done better to stay in England, don't you? Open your eyes, Amy, and look at the people they have attracted to their home.'

As they were almost at the head of the stairs, by peering round the stout man in front of them, and his partner's flounces, she could easily have caught glimpses of the glittering crowd thronging a large salon beyond.

'Not that I am likely to recognise any of them,' she retorted, stung by his patronising attitude.

'Much better you don't,' he said harshly, tucking her arm firmly into his as they reached the landing. 'But I will tell you the kind of people she is gathering about her in Paris. Influential people. She is using this trip to cement friendships she could never have forged in London. When Wilson returns to England, she will continue to use the connections she has made here to push him up the greasy pole.'

'That's not strictly true, though, is it? She invited you, even though…' She trailed off.

'Even though she was my wife's friend, rather than mine, and my career is currently at such a low ebb it would be nothing short of miraculous for me to resurrect it?' He raised one eyebrow, his tone challenging.

'I was going to say,' she replied, 'that you cannot be of use to her any more, since you are no longer involved in politics.'

He looked at her steadily for a few moments, then appeared to relent towards her.

'It isn't easy to understand this world until you've been a part of it. I certainly didn't look beneath the glittering surface to the lethal undercurrents before I plunged in. I was even foolish enough, when I first got elected, to think I needed to go to the House upon occasion and listen to debates.' His mouth twisted into a harsh sneer. 'And that was even though I knew that Lucasta's father had bought the votes of the potwallopers in my borough. But I soon learned that isn't how a man succeeds in politics. He needs to ingratiate himself with the right people. Do deals in secret. Be prepared to perjure his soul in return for promotion.'

'But...'

'You cannot see how I can be of use to these people, is that what you were going to say? Oh, Amy...' he laughed, bitterly '...have you forgotten? My father is, and always will be, the Earl of Finchingfield, and he wields enormous political influence. Who knows but that one day he might forgive me? If I find favour in his sight again, those who have supported me at this... low tide...might find him grateful. And prepared to be generous.'

'That's a horribly cynical way to look at life.'

'I prefer to say realistic. Amy, I spent years amongst these people. I know how they operate. Believe me, the more cynical you are about them, the less likely you are to be hurt by them.'

She frowned. 'I wonder you bothered to come tonight, then. They all sound perfectly horrid.'

'They have their uses,' he said darkly. The most urgent being to send a message to his father. Somebody, from this gathering, was bound to return to England with the news that his reprobate youngest son had taken up with the very woman he'd done his utmost to separate him from. And, for once, *he* would taste defeat. Know that all his machinations had been in vain. Amethyst had found her way back to him.

'Uses? What do you mean?'

Nathan rubbed his nose with his thumb. He couldn't admit that he wanted to flaunt her in his father's face. That he was using her.

She didn't deserve to become a pawn in his ongoing battle with his father. Pawns got hurt. His father certainly hadn't hesitated to blacken her name ten years ago. To him, she was nothing. A mere inconvenience to be swatted aside like a pesky fly.

'I shouldn't have brought you here,' he said, a cold knot forming in his stomach. He could have taken her anywhere. Why had he exposed her to the possibility of getting hurt all over again?

'You are no match for these sort of people. It is like throwing a lamb to the wolves.'

'Nonsense,' she snapped. 'Do you think I am a country bumpkin with straw for brains?'

'No! That is not what I meant at all. You are just too…straightforward to know how to survive in this kind of environment. You have no idea how to smile while uttering a threat, or make someone believe you are their friend whilst plotting how to stab them in the back.'

Simple. He thought she was simple. Not up to cutting it in his world.

Well, why should she be surprised? It was what he'd thought ten years ago, too. Well, she'd show him.

But before she had the chance to work out exactly how she was going to prove that she was not the simpering, weak-willed kind of ninny that needed a man to protect her from all the big bad wolves in the world of politics, the stout couple in front moved away and she and Nathan were finally standing face to face with their host and hostess.

'Oh, Mr Harcourt, what an unexpected pleasure to see you here,' gushed the bejewelled woman, flashing a lot of teeth and bosom in his direction. Though how it could be unexpected, since she must have sent him an invitation, Amethyst couldn't imagine.

'I would have thought our sort of gathering would be much too tame for you,' she said archly, before going off into a peal of shrill laughter.

So why invite him, then? *Because my father is, and always will be, the Earl of Finchingfield and he wields enormous political influence.*

'And who is this delightful young lady you have brought with you? I don't believe I have seen her about anywhere, have I?'

Nathan paused, only very slightly, but the woman promptly leapt to her own conclusion.

'Oh, how very naughty of you,' she said, flattening one hand to her impressive bosom. 'To bring your latest *chère amie* into such a gathering. Oh, but isn't that just like you!' She rapped his arm with her fan. 'Always courting scandal one way or another. But I shall not be cross with you. This is Paris, after all, so what does it really matter? Algernon, dearest,' she rattled on, while Nathan seemed to have turned to stone at her side, 'look who it is. Mr Harcourt and his lovely young…French friend.'

'Harcourt, you dog.' He grinned. 'Still the rake, I see! But do you have a name, you lovely young thing?' Mr Wilson, who looked exactly as she'd imagined a minor politician with delusions of grandeur would look, seized her hand and pressed a wet kiss on the back of it.

She flashed Nathan a swift, challenging glance from under her eyelashes, dropped Mr Wilson a curtsy and, summoning up what little French she knew, said, in a little, breathy, voice, *'Moi, je suis Mademoiselle D'Aulbie.'*

Nathan let out a choking sound and turned to her with a look of complete shock.

'It is such the honour to meet the very important man of whom I hear so much,' Amy simpered, batting her eyelashes up at her host, the way she imagined a woman of pleasure, who did not know when she was being insulted to her face, would do. 'And Monsieur 'Arcour, he does not want to attend at all, but I did so want zis treat.'

'Did you, my dear?' Mr Wilson puffed up to almost twice his not-inconsiderable size. 'Don't suppose young Harcourt could resist, eh? Don't say I blame him.' He winked at Nathan over the top of her head.

'But what is zis rayk you say of eem?' she said, her execrable accent getting thicker by the second. 'He is the artist, *n'est-ce pas*? Not some kind of gardener.'

At that point, Nathan abruptly came back to life, grabbing her elbow and tugging her into the room, whilst muttering something to their hosts about making room for the next couple in line.

'What the hell,' he said through gritted teeth, 'has come over you? Putting on that ludicrous accent and letting them think…'

'Oh, I don't know,' she said airily, beckoning a waiter who was circulating with a tray of champagne. 'Perhaps I just couldn't resist showing you that I could very easily disguise not only what I am thinking, but also my very nationality, if I put my mind to it.'

He snagged a glass of champagne himself and knocked it all back in one go.

'But why would you want to do any such thing?'

She sipped her champagne whilst considering how to answer him. And then decided to plump for the truth.

'Do you know, I'm not entirely sure. But I've felt on the verge of…revolution ever since I arrived in Paris. I have the strangest feeling that I can be anyone I want to be here. And just for a moment, I rather fancied the idea of letting that stupid woman think I was your *chère amie*. You have to admit it was rather amusing to see the judgemental, pompous, narrow-minded bladders of wind both run to the lengths of their boorishness, wasn't it? Far better than having to explain that actually I am—'

'No. You don't need to say another word.' He'd frozen in horror when Mrs Wilson had expressed curiosity about her. He'd hesitated to give her real name, knowing it could signal the eruption of another battle between him and his father, with Amy at risk of getting caught in the cross-fire.

He'd been relieved, if a little stunned, when Amy had started to poke fun at their hosts. And now that they'd escaped the danger that people who still had connections to his father's world might find out who she was, he had to admit that he would have found her performance amusing if he hadn't been frozen solid with horror at the danger he'd so foolishly exposed her to.

It reminded him of the rather tart sense of humour she'd displayed ten years before. The perceptive and witty comments she'd made about people they met that had chimed so exactly with his own feelings that he'd felt as though he'd found the perfect partner.

And her remark about being anyone she wanted to be here in France was another case in point.

'I know exactly what you mean about the atmosphere of Paris,' he said. 'The moment I got here, something about the attitude of the people made me feel as though I really could make a fresh start. As though I could wipe the slate clean and be whoever I wanted to be. Or perhaps to find out who I was meant to be—yes, that sums it up more neatly. Because none of them assumed I had an inherent value just because of who my father is,' he said, shooting a dark look towards the doorway, where the Wilsons were gushing over the next arrivals.

Amethyst followed the direction of his gaze.

'In fact, they would be as likely to think of that as an impediment, since they have taken such a dislike to anyone connected to the aristocracy.'

'Hasn't it made you feel a little…scared?'

'No. The revolution is over. They've done with executing people just because of their ancestry,' he said.

'I have sometimes felt a little concerned, though,' she said. 'It is as though there is some sort of charge in the air. Like you get just before a storm. And there seem to be soldiers everywhere, loitering in packs, looking mean and hungry.'

'Yes, well I can't blame them, can you? They've had a taste of power. They've overthrown one corrupt regime and spent years forging a military empire. It won't be easy for them to settle back into the kind of lives they had before, if that is all the Bourbons mean to offer them.'

'What do you think will happen?'

He grinned. 'Who knows? Certainly not the Parisians. Everyone has a different opinion about what should happen to their country next, from the lowliest street vendor to the deposed aristocrats who've come flocking back demanding they have their estates restored, and they aren't afraid to voice it. Nobody here accepts the status quo. They feel they have the power to change just about everything. It's…invigorating.'

'I…suppose it is,' she said.

'*I* think it is. Nothing is set in stone here any more. And apart from that, Parisians don't care that I caused such a scandal in London, that no political party would ever back me to stand for them ever again. It makes me feel that the past is gone. Done. I've broken free from my family's expectations, my reputation, everything. It's as though I've been given a blank sheet of paper and what I draw on it is entirely up to me.'

A new start. Yes, she could see why he would want that after the mess he'd made of what should have been a glittering political career. Hadn't she also left Stanton Basset because it was what she was looking for herself? A chance to break free from the expectations of others, the obligations that weighed her down?

'The trouble is,' she said, putting on a frown, 'that since I've come to Paris, people keep on mistaking me for a woman of easy virtue. What do you suppose,' she said, shooting him a coy look from under her lashes, 'that means?'

'I think it means,' he said, setting his empty glass down carefully on the nearest available surface, 'that it is time you fulfilled your potential.'

'Oh, yes?'

'Decidedly yes,' he said, taking her arm and leading her to the nearest exit. 'If you are determined to play the part of my…*chère amie*,' he husked into her ear, 'then it is about time you put in a bit more practice.'

'Does this mean what I hope it means?'

'Yes,' he replied firmly. 'I'm taking you back to my rooms. I've let you see ze most important man, and all zees so important people. Now you need to pay for me giving you zis treat,' he said playfully, imitating her dreadful French accent.

'Ooh,' she breathed. 'You are a hard taskmaster.'

'Hard is the word,' he agreed. 'And these breeches simply don't disguise a thing.'

She blushed. And then began to giggle. And kept on giggling as they pushed their way back through the throng climbing the stairs, as they made their way down.

Chapter Ten

They hurried back to his rooms as fast as they could.

'I'm not going to have any breath left for lovemaking by the time we've climbed up all these stairs,' Amethyst grumbled as they reached the first landing.

'You won't need to do a thing,' he promised her. 'Just lie back on the bed and let me do all the work.'

And he did.

Amy had never had so much attention devoted to her. So much care lavished on her body. Even before he entered her and took her to the heights, it felt really meaningful. What they were doing together was so incredible, so wonderful, so much *more* than anything she'd ever known she could experience that, yes, if she was a naïve, young, uneducated female, she might have mistaken it for love.

Especially since he gave himself to it with such… enthusiasm.

'Amy, Amy, oh God, Amy!'

Nathan's whole body shuddered as he groaned his release. He slumped to one side of her, gathered her in his arms and buried his face in her hair.

No wonder, she sighed, turning and wrapping her arms round his neck, women so very often mistook the attentions of a passionate lover for something deeper. He had made her feel loved.

And for the first time in her life, she hadn't had to do anything to earn it, either.

'Why so solemn?'

He'd opened his eyes and was watching her, she discovered. When she didn't know what to answer, he smiled and gently traced the fullness of her lower lip with one finger.

'You are full of contrasts, are you not? Nobody, seeing you so solemn after giving yourself to me, would believe you are the same woman who was so playful earlier tonight, when most people would have been trying to impress.'

'What are you trying to say?'

He shrugged. 'Just that there are so many sides to you I never knew existed when…when I knew you before.'

'I am not the same person I was back then.' In fact, she could scarcely recognise herself any more. She'd certainly never suspected she had it in her to mimic a French accent and play-act at being a lightskirt, for the sheer fun of it. She'd always been sober and serious, even as a girl. Getting her heart broken, having her family roundly rebuke her, then spending years living with her embittered, man-hating aunt had only made her more inclined to look on life as a dull, dreary grind that had to be endured. Her only fun, thus far, had come from pulling the rug out from under self-important people like Mrs Podmore, or giving people private nicknames, as she'd done to Monsieur le Prune. It was as if a new Amy was emerging, day by day, the further she got from Stanton Basset and all its petty restrictions.

What else might she discover about herself as she broke free from the habits she'd acquired without even knowing they were stifling her?

'I know,' he sighed. 'And I'm sorry.'

'Sorry? You don't like me as I am now?' She'd just been likening herself to a butterfly uncurling its wings from a crusty chrysalis and he'd preferred her as she was?

'No. I do. I mean, I am sorry for how things ended between us back then. I was cruel to you. I hurt you,' he said, kissing her forehead gently. 'I wish I hadn't. I wish it were possible to go back to a time before everything went wrong. I let you down very badly. Can you... could you ever forgive me, do you think?'

A few days ago she would have said no, she would never forgive him. She'd been so full of rage and bitterness. But she must have started to forgive him without any conscious effort, or she wouldn't be in bed with him now, would she? And those same few days ago, she would never have imagined running down the stairs, hand in hand with Nathan Harcourt, giggling like a schoolgirl after the mischievous trick she'd played on their hosts, either.

Had letting go of her anger with him been what had made such a difference? Was that why she felt so much lighter of heart now?

'Forgiveness...is a strange thing to be talking about while we are naked,' she said, reaching for the sheet. It was funny, but she was more aware of her nudity now they were starting to discuss feelings.

'For instance, my parents were adamant that there

was nothing to forgive.' And perhaps there hadn't been, not really. He might have toyed with her affections, but he'd drawn the line at seducing her. Given the reputation he'd since gained, it was amazing he'd behaved with such restraint. She'd been so infatuated with him he could very easily have talked her into bed. Well, it hadn't exactly taken much to persuade her into it now, had it? A few smouldering looks, a couple of invitations, one hard kiss and she'd climbed five flights of stairs for the privilege.

'They were quick to point out that you never proposed to me, so I had no right to complain, or even to feel hard done by.' And for the first time, she could see their point. He'd stolen nothing beyond a few kisses. And he could have taken so much more. He could have ruined her before tossing her aside.

He reared up on his elbow.

'What rot! I can't let you shrug off my apology, saying the way we parted didn't matter because I hadn't actually made a formal declaration. I *know* I hurt you. I can still see the look on your face the night I cut you, then danced with every other girl in the place. Admit it. You were in love with me.'

He'd known how badly he'd hurt her that night? She'd shown it on her face? Well, she wasn't an infatuated girl any longer, to wear her heart on her sleeve.

'Why should I admit,' she said haughtily, 'anything of the kind?'

'Because I was in love with you, too, that's why. I did want to marry you.' He rolled on to his back and stared hard-jawed at the ceiling. 'We would have been perfect together,' he said, in a voice that quivered with suppressed emotion. 'My deepest wish, back then, was to live the life of a country gentleman, dabbling with my painting, raising a pack of happy children...'

Her stomach swooped. No matter how many people had told her she'd been mistaken, no matter how often she had told herself that she didn't care, either, to hear him actually admit she'd been right all along gave her a tremendous surge of something that see-sawed between triumph and anguish.

'So,' she said coldly, 'why didn't you?' What possible excuse could he give for ending it the way he had, if he'd really been dreaming the same dreams she had?

A muscle bunched in his jaw.

'Because I was an idiot. A young idiot. I had no confidence in my own judgement. I believed...I was persuaded...that it was better to pursue a career, than to live my life in obscurity.'

Persuaded...

Her anger ebbed. Just a touch.

'I know what it's like to have an implacable, domineering father,' she said, reaching for his hand. 'And since we parted, I learned a great deal more about yours than I'd ever guessed when we were...' She couldn't quite bring herself to use the word *courting*, even though she now knew that was exactly what they'd been doing. 'It is obvious, with hindsight,' she said bitterly, 'that he wanted better for you than a virtually penniless clergyman's daughter from an obscure parish. He forbade the match, is that it?'

He groaned and flung up one hand to cover his eyes. He only wished it had been that simple. 'It wasn't exactly like that,' he admitted 'But if it's any consolation to you, I definitely got my just desserts for not keeping faith with you,' he said with a hollow laugh.

His breathing grew laboured as he considered flinging himself off the precipice of a total confession.

But as he lowered his arm and looked at her pinched expression, he took a mental step back from the edge. He hadn't earned her trust yet, even though she was claiming she'd forgiven him. And if she knew it all...the thought of how she might react made his insides freeze.

'I shouldn't have brought it up, should I,' he said ruefully. His selfish urge to salve his conscience had spoiled what had been a beautiful moment between them. 'It is just,' he said, rolling his whole body to one side to stare down at her, 'that I want to get to know you again. The woman you are now. And we don't have long, do we? You are only spending a short time in Paris.'

'So there is little point in trying, is there?' She swung her legs over the edge of the bed, struggling to keep the quilt covering what modesty she had left, and began to search for her scattered clothing.

As she attempted to fumble one stocking on to her foot without letting go of the quilt, he rolled off the bed and reached for his breeches.

'Would you prefer me to leave you in privacy to dress?'

'Yes. I would, thank you,' she said, flushing, for it seemed foolish to feel shy after he'd had his hands and mouth all over her.

But he didn't mock her sudden attack of shyness. He just smiled at her and walked to the door. Though he hesitated on the threshold, leaning his arm on the jamb.

'I can see you are determined to leave,' he said. 'But I hope I can persuade you to spend tomorrow with me.'

'Oh, and just how do you propose to do that?'

He chuckled. 'Not the way you seem to think.'

'I don't know what you mean,' she said crossly.

He raised one eyebrow. Then straightened his face. 'Of course you don't. So I will just point out that the mouse and her Frenchman will be so wrapped up in each other that they will drive you to distraction. What's more, they won't even notice whether you are there or not. So you need have absolutely no qualms about spending every moment you have left in Paris with me.'

Which was all true. She had no stomach for trailing around behind Fenella and Gaston. And there was going to be an awful lot more time to endure in Paris, while Monsieur le Prune attempted to strike a deal with the contacts she'd made. Time she might as well spend with Nathan, rather than moping about the changes she'd have to make to her life once Fenella married.

Because she couldn't deny she did enjoy being with him. Tonight, before they'd started talking about the past, and what had gone wrong, she'd enjoyed his company tremendously.

Yes—as a distraction from the prospect of potentially having to spend a bleak lonely future with one hired companion after another, he would be perfect.

'And I still need you to sit for your portrait,' he reminded her. 'That could take hours,' he said, stalking back to the bed and cupping her face before placing his mouth firmly on her own.

Her knees went weak at once. And after only a little longer, she was wriggling out of the quilt and winding her arms round his neck so that she could pull him back down on to the bed. Only the aggravating man drew back, gave her naked body a scorching look and said, 'Hours and hours.'

The portrait. He was talking about the hours he

would spend painting her portrait. Not the hours and hours she could have with him in bed.

Or was he?

That was the trouble with men like Nathan. They could say one thing and mean another. They called it flirting.

Well, no matter. As long as she didn't believe his apparent eagerness to spend time with her was something on which she could base her life, the way she'd done when she'd been younger, she would be fine.

She returned his smile with a brittle one of her own.

'Well, I'd better come for a sitting tomorrow then, hadn't I?'

'It occurred to me after you left last night,' said Nathan as he handed her into the fiacre he'd hired to take her…well, he hadn't told her where he was going to take her, yet. Aggravating man, 'that you never finished telling me about those two.' He jerked his head towards the window from which Fenella and Gaston were watching them drive away. 'And there was something you wanted to rebuke me for, specifically,' he said, folding himself into the seat next to her. 'I think you should get it over with now, don't you? Then I won't have to live in terror of the moment when you decide to bring it up.'

'Are you deliberately trying to provoke me?'

'Is it working?' He leaned back in his seat and spread his arms wide in a gesture of surrender. 'Come on, do your worst. I can take it.'

She breathed in slowly through her nostrils, then lifted her chin and turned her head to look out of the window on her side of the carriage.

'Not in the mood for fighting yet? Very well,' he

said, sitting up again and nudging her with his elbow. 'But you really do need to finish the tale from which I...distracted you last night.'

'I don't see why. And anyway,' she said haughtily, 'I cannot recall exactly how much I told you.' And she didn't want to bore him by repeating a story that hadn't been able to hold his attention the first time.

'Just that they saw themselves as Romeo and Juliet, with you as both sets of parents. And how you grappled with your very natural desire to turn him off because he'd not only seduced your friend while she was foxed, but because he was trying to come between you, persuading her you would judge her for falling from grace.'

Goodness. He had not only been listening to her prattling on, as they'd made their way slowly up the Wilsons' staircase, but had committed the whole thing to memory.

'I was waiting with bated breath for you to get to the part where he confessed his real name, since you accused me of alerting you to the fact he's currently using an alias.'

'You knew, all along, that Monsieur Le Brun is in reality the Comte de...' she frowned. 'Well, he rattled off a very long list of names and honorifics, but I was so stunned that I cannot recall any of them now. It was the last thing I expected to learn about him.'

'What did you expect?'

'Why, that he was wanted by the law for some crime or other...'

'In a way, he is, or was. His parents went to the guillotine, you know. And he only narrowly escaped with his own life.'

'How did you know that?'

'At one time, I played a very minor role in an attempt to make sure that the very many French *émigrés* who cluttered up London were actually who they said they were and not spies.'

'Goodness,' she said, looking at him properly for the first time since he'd made that jest about doing her worst. 'I knew you'd got into Parliament, but I never imagined you ever doing anything useful. I thought you'd been one of those who used their position to cut a dash in town and treated the House of Commons as nothing more than a highly select sort of gentlemen's club.'

'Oh, no, I wanted to use my position to make a difference,' he said bleakly. 'It just…didn't work out that way.'

She decided not to press for reasons why it hadn't worked. It wouldn't be very pleasant for him to talk about his total failure as a politician, even in such a junior role.

'Did you find out much about my Monsieur Le Brun? It is just that he claims to have property in England and the means to look after Fenella, as well as having a string of unpronounceable titles and a claim on some land in France. If he is lying, it would be tremendously useful to know about it now.'

'I cannot recall much about him, to be honest,' he told her. 'It took me some time to work out where I'd seen him before, because I met him at only one or two gatherings thrown for *émigrés* claiming to be friends of England.' And he'd done his best to blot out as much of that portion of his life as possible. If he didn't dwell on it, he'd hoped it would all fade into the mist, rather than remain fixed at the foreground in lurid detail.

'He was only one of many that were under subtle investigation. What has he told you?'

She pouted. 'Well, he *says* that he is using his work as a courier as cover to enter France and see how the land lies. See whether it is possible to have some of what was confiscated from his family restored, now that the Bourbons are back in power. He *claims* he dare not move about openly under his true name, in case there are still enemies lurking in wait for him.'

'It could all be true,' he said. 'There are a lot of people attempting to reclaim land and titles that were once theirs. And he was certainly introduced to me in London as the dispossessed Comte de...somewhere or other. It was what made me refer to him as *the man who calls himself Monsieur Le Brun.*'

'It would certainly account for his excessive arrogance,' she huffed. 'There are times when I can quite understand why French peasants wanted to teach the aristocrats a lesson—though not, of course, quite such a brutal one—whereas Fenella finds his tale wildly romantic. Which was what made the rest of that outing almost unbearable.' Her lips curled in disgust. 'She would keep looking up at him as though he were a hero stepped straight out of the pages of some rubbishing novel. But,' she concluded, 'whether he really is a dispossessed French count, or just a mountebank, makes no difference, I suppose.'

'How so?'

'Well, if he is a mountebank, and has no real intention of marrying Fenella, it will break her heart. And if he is what he says he is and does marry her, it will break up our happy little household.' For no man, particularly not a member of the aristocracy, could stomach the thought of his wife living anywhere but in his own home. 'Neither of which outcome,' she said glumly, 'particularly appeal to me. I suppose that sounds selfish, doesn't it? And it's not that I don't want Fenella to be happy. If anyone deserves to marry a title, even a French one—even a French one that might not actually exist any more—then it is Fenella. For she is a lady, you see. A lady born. She has been obliged to live with me only because her family cast her off when she married against their wishes. They really should have taken care of her,' she added crossly, 'once she was widowed. Yet they refused to have anything to do with her just because she'd married a man she loved, rather than one they approved of.'

He went very quiet for some time, before clearing his throat and saying, 'She sounds like a very courageous woman. I was wrong to say she was mousy just because I couldn't tear my eyes off you.'

She flushed and shifted, avoiding his gaze. She clearly wasn't comfortable accepting compliments. Any more than he was to hear that a woman he'd dismissed as mousy had done what he'd not had the sense to do: defy his family and marry the woman he wanted.

Not that he'd ever got to that point. His father had tricked him into withdrawing before he'd come up to scratch.

The fiacre lurched to a halt.

'Here we are,' he said, leaning over to open the door.

She stepped out of the carriage, to see they were in front of a church that reminded her just a bit of St. Paul's Cathedral.

'The Pantheon,' he said, having paid off their driver. 'After we'd talked about the way the very air of Paris seems full of revolutionary ideals, I thought you might like to come and see the tomb of the man responsible for so much of it.'

'You've brought me to look at a tomb?'

'Not just any tomb. The tomb of Voltaire. Besides, there's much more to see in here than tombstones. Have you ever seen anywhere quite so awe-inspiring?'

She had to admit the building was impressive, with its soaring pillars and multiple domes. They wandered about, admiring the place for some time before coming to a halt before the tomb Nathan had said he'd brought her here to see.

'There was a girl,' she said, 'selling lemonade from a stall on the Boulevard, who had a copy of the *Henriade* in her pocket. I so wanted to ask her what she thought of it, but Monsieur Le Brun wouldn't let me stop.'

'Well, he probably doesn't approve of peasants having any education. Or they wouldn't have risen up and thrown his class out.'

'Your class, too,' she reminded him.

'Ah, but not in Paris. Didn't I tell you, now I'm in Paris I can be whoever I want to be?'

'Do you think…no, never mind.'

'What? You can ask me anything, Amy.'

'You won't like it.'

'How do you know, unless you try me?'

'Because you're a man,' she said with disgust. 'Men don't like women to have their own ideas.'

'Ouch.' He pretended to flinch. 'That is a little unfair, even for you.'

'Very well, then,' she said, flinging up her chin. 'I will tell you what I wanted to ask that lemonade seller, shall I? I wanted to know if women here in France really do have more freedom than the English. Because everywhere I look, there are women presiding over the cash desks of bars and businesses. Clearly the ones in charge. And it isn't just because they've had to, because the men have all gone off fighting. The men are coming back. And instead of taking over their old jobs, they're hanging around in packs, in their uniforms, letting the women carry right on running everything.'

He stroked his chin with one hand. 'I hadn't really noticed it. But you are right.'

She blinked. 'I am?'

'Don't sound so surprised. You are clearly an intelligent woman. And you are looking at this city with a woman's eyes. You are bound to see things I've missed.' When she continued to gape at him, he chuckled. 'Has nobody ever paid you a compliment before?'

'Not about my intelligence,' she said. 'Not men, anyway. Most men want a woman to stay quiet, or agree with everything they say.'

'No chance of that with you, is there?'

'Not any longer, no. Not after the way—' She bit back what she had been going to say.

'The way I let you down?'

She shook her head, frowning. 'It wasn't so much what you did, Nathan. It was how my family treated me. I was…well, there's no point in trying to deny it, since you claim you knew how badly you hurt me. I was devastated. I needed them to comfort me, but instead they…they turned against me.'

He took her arm and started strolling towards the door. 'I'm so sorry. I wish I hadn't treated you so badly. It was inexcusable. Did I put you off men for life? Is that why you never married?'

'What makes you think I had a choice?' She didn't want to make it sound as if she'd been wearing the willow for him all these years. She had her pride.

'Because you are so beautiful,' he said bluntly. 'Men must have been queuing up to pay their addresses to you.'

She snorted in derision. 'Far from it. The only men who have ever shown an interest in me were…' She'd been about to say tempted by her aunt's money. But she didn't want to go into that. 'Let's say they were put off by the claws I've developed over the years.' She wasn't the dewy-eyed débutante she'd been when she'd gone up to London for her Season. She was as far removed from that open, trusting girl as a domestic cat was from a caged lion. She trusted nobody these days, particularly not if they wore breeches. 'When I see right through their empty compliments, they accuse me of being a harridan.'

'Perhaps not all their compliments are empty, have you ever considered that? Just because I let you down, that doesn't mean all men would.'

There were bound to be men out there, somewhere, who could match her. Who wouldn't be put off by her defensiveness.

He rubbed at his stomach, wondering at the queasy feeling that came from picturing some other man courting her, marrying her and making her happy. Instinctively he made for the open air, where he would be able to breathe more easily.

'It is nothing to do with you, whether I've married or not, you arrogant… Ooh, you make me so angry!'

'Yes, it is,' he said, stopping under the great portico

and pulling her into his arms. 'Just a little bit, anyway. Admit it. I ruined you for all other men.'

'You conceited—' But he cut her words off with a kiss. A kiss that started out fiery with her rage and quickly turned heated with passion.

'Nobody else will ever kiss you like that,' he husked, drawing back just far enough that he could speak. But his lips were still so close to hers she could feel their echo. 'No other lover will ever make you feel the way I do.'

When she opened her mouth to make a pithy retort he silenced her with another kiss. A kiss that she felt right down to the core of her being. By the time he finished it, she'd forgotten what they'd been arguing about.

'I think we've done enough sightseeing for one day, don't you? Let's go back to my studio and work on your portrait.'

'In broad daylight?' He wasn't talking about painting her portrait at all.

'The light in my studio will be perfect, about now,' he said, glancing up at the sky, 'to capture…' he cupped her face with his hand, caressing her jaw as his words caressed her other senses '…all those subtle flesh tones.'

For the next few days they didn't bother with the pretence they were going to explore Paris together. Amy went to his studio at first light and let him capture her subtle flesh tones. With his hands, his mouth, and then, later, when she was too sated to bother protesting, she let him arrange her on his couch so he could paint her.

'What are you thinking?' He'd stopped working, and was looking at her steadily from round the edge of the canvas he refused to let her so much as catch a glimpse of.

'Nothing much. Nothing that would interest you, anyway.'

He pursed his lips. 'Amy, how many times do I have to tell you that every single little thing about you fascinates me?'

When she snorted in derision, he shook his head at her. 'It is true. Why would you think I'd bother to lie about it? I can still get you into bed any time I want. I only have to look at you like this…' and he waggled his eyebrows at her suggestively '…and you turn wild.'

Only a few days ago she would have been furious at the suggestion he had any influence on her, but she'd got used to his teasing ways now. Besides, he might joke that he only had to give her a heated look for her to go up in flames, but nine times out of ten she'd done something to provoke the heated look in the first place. Such as lick her lips in a certain manner, or merely twine one of her curls round and round her finger meditatively.

He came across to the couch, knelt beside it and dropped a kiss on her exposed shoulder.

'I will be able to paint a much better portrait if I know your innermost thoughts. I will be able to capture your essence. What makes you uniquely you.'

'Oh, I see, it is for your art.'

'If you like.' He buried his face in her neck to kiss her throat. And breathe her in. And commit her fragrance to memory. The more time he spent with her, the more he regretted letting her go so easily when they'd been young enough to have forged a life together. He couldn't help thinking that if he'd even had the courage of the mousy Fenella, they would have been together for ten years by now. Not that he wanted to get married again. It was just…if he had married Amy, it wouldn't have been hell, that was all. From the things she'd said, he could tell that if he'd gone into politics from choice, rather than drifting into it because he'd stopped fighting his father, and if Amy had been his wife, she would have supported his wish to make a difference. *She* wouldn't have sneered at every opinion he expressed that didn't align exactly with her own. He might even have become a halfway-decent politician. Oh, nothing to compare with a Wilberforce, or a Hunt, but a man who would have been able to look at his own reflection in the mirror without despising what he saw.

But these few days she was in Paris would be all he'd ever have of her, now. He had to make them count. He had such a short time to create a lifetime of memories.

'Well, I was thinking…'

'Yes?' He nuzzled the sheet she'd been using to preserve her modesty to one side.

'About how unfair it is.'

'What is unfair?'

She speared her fingers into his hair as he sucked one nipple into his mouth.

'That the same rules don't apply to men that so restrict women. A single man can take a lover and nobody much cares. But if a woman does so, she runs the risk of becoming a social pariah.'

He looked up at her sharply. 'Are you afraid that there will be repercussions because of our affair, Amy? We've been discreet. I've deliberately kept you out of the public eye as much as possible. Well, after the Wilsons', anyway.'

'Have you?' It hadn't occurred to her that his reluctance to leave the studio for much more than the occasional glass of beer in the nearest café, which was frequented by locals, was anything more than a wish to keep her as near to a convenient bed as possible.

'Of course I have. I have the devil of a reputation. And the last thing I want is for you to be subject to salacious gossip because you've been seen being a bit too…intimate with me.'

'You seem to forget, I am a nobody. I don't move in the kind of circles where a little gossip could ruin my reputation.'

'That's just where you're wrong,' he said fiercely. 'I mean,' he amended, reining himself back with what looked like a struggle, 'just think what it would do if tales about you having a wild affair with the scurrilous Nathan Harcourt got back to Stanton Basset. They would drum you out of the…the sewing circle.'

They could try, she thought. If she'd ever been a member of such an insipid group. But there wasn't all that much they could do. If anyone did try to make her life in Stanton Basset uncomfortable, she would just move away.

In fact, that might not be a bad idea anyway. Nothing would be the same if Fenella really did marry her middle-aged French Romeo. And it was looking increasingly likely. And she did not have any sentimental attachment to the modest house her aunt had bequeathed her, nor the quiet and rather stuffy little town itself. She could buy a much more commodious property elsewhere. Somewhere by the sea, perhaps.

Nathan startled her by getting up and stalking moodily back to his easel. Well, he'd already startled her by sounding so protective of her reputation, when he'd never given a fig for his own. From the things she'd read about him, particularly in the last weeks before his spectacular expulsion from his party, it was almost as if he'd courted scandal for its own sake.

She would have to be careful she didn't start thinking he cared for her. Just because he hadn't seduced her when she'd been a girl, and had proposed to her when he discovered she'd been a virgin, that did not mean she was anything special to him. It only meant he had a conscience. That he wasn't the hardened rake the newspapers made him out to be.

Not that he might be falling in love with her.

She had to remember that he was a master of this game. He'd had plenty of other lovers. He was probably as charming and apparently tender with all of them. She mustn't lower her guard with him, not even for an instant. Or he would wound her. Oh, he wouldn't mean to. He clearly regretted having hurt her before. It was part of what made him so irresistible.

'You said,' came his disembodied voice from the other side of the easel, 'that your family turned against you after I...married Lucasta. Can you tell me about it?'

'Why do you want to hear about that?'

'Maybe I want absolution. You said that your reasons for not marrying were not my fault and implied other things were far more important than just my abandonment. Besides, I have this insatiable curiosity about you. I want to know every little detail of your life.'

'So you can paint a better portrait of me,' she sighed. 'Yes, you said that before.'

'You don't sound as though you believe me,' he complained. 'If it isn't for that, then what other reason could

I possibly have for wanting you to divulge your innermost thoughts?'

She sighed again. 'You are in one of those moods where you won't give up, aren't you?'

He grinned at her from round the edge of the canvas. 'So, surrender. Tell me something. You will only doze off if I don't keep you talking. And I don't want to hand you a portrait of yourself snoring. It won't be flattering.'

Ah. That was a bit more believable. She could easily have dozed off, after the amount of energy they'd expended making love that morning. And at least having a conversation with him would keep her awake.

'You told me you inherited a house from some aunt,' he said. 'Which made me wonder...'

'What?'

'Well, it is a bit unusual for you to throw in your lot with a friend, rather than return to your family after her death, that's all, if marriage wasn't going to be on the cards.'

'Returning to my family was the last thing I'd ever do, after the way they treated me,' she said mutinously. 'They were so awful, when I...broke down after we parted.'

'Saying you had nothing to make a fuss about, I remember you saying so. Are they all idiots? You were obviously broken-hearted.'

She huffed out a surprised laugh. 'I can't believe you are the one person who can understand, and sympathise, when you were the cause of it all.'

'A moment ago you said I was not.'

'Don't be pedantic,' she snapped. 'You started the chain of events and you know it. Only then they were all so...righteous, and mealy-mouthed, and unkind...'

'As I said, idiots.'

'All except my Aunt Georgie. Though, to be honest, I think she may have sided with me simply to spite my father. They'd clearly been at loggerheads for most of their lives. Anyway—' she shrugged '—I went to stay with her for what was supposed to have been a short visit and ended up living there permanently. She…she was a bit of an eccentric. But we got on.'

'So, I'm guessing that staying with her, your father's arch enemy, didn't endear you to your family?'

'You could say that. Although, to be fair, when Aunt Georgie died, my father did come to the funeral holding out an olive branch. Of sorts.' She sighed. 'He said that in spite of my refusal to show any penitence over our estrangement, he was prepared to take me back into his home and care for me.'

'Oh…oh dear.'

'Are you laughing?' It was infuriating not being able to see his face, but there was a definite trace of amusement in his voice.

'Not exactly. I was just picturing your reaction when he more or less ordered you to surrender, since he thought you had no option.'

'Not only that,' she said indignantly, 'he tried to make sure I *had* no options. As soon as he found out Aunt Georgie had left everything to me, he tried to overturn the will. He told me, in the presence of a lawyer, that since I was merely a woman it would be much safer if he was to handle it all for me.'

Her father had been stunned to discover how much Amethyst was suddenly worth. He'd only been aware that his sister owned a house and a modest amount of capital. He'd assumed that because she lived so modestly, she was just eking out an existence on the interest. Instead she'd invested it in all sorts of ventures that, had he known how risky some of them had been, would have turned his hair white.

'Had he held the position of trustee for his sister, then?'

'No! Which was what made it all so...'

'Humiliating? Infuriating? Unfair?'

'All of those things. But why is it that you seem to be able to understand exactly how I felt?'

'Well, my own father placed no confidence in my judgement, either. Even though I *am* male. Which is possibly even more humiliating, infuriating and unfair.'

'So...you do not blame me for refusing to beg forgiveness and surrender my independence?'

'How could I? Have I not done the very same thing?'

'You mentioned, at the Wilsons', that your father has...'

'Washed his hands of me, yes.'

'But what of your brothers? Do you have any contact with them?'

'Not really. They are all very successful in their own professions and don't want to risk ruining their reputations by being too involved with the black sheep of the family.'

'Same here...' she sighed '...with my sisters. I got invitations to their weddings, but they were too scared of what my father would say to come anywhere near me. It's as if I don't exist for them any more.'

Her only value for them, she'd discovered, was her wealth. Not one of them had contacted her, in all the years she'd lived with Aunt Georgie. It was only after her father had discovered how much wealth she'd inherited that Pearl wrote, telling her that she'd just given birth to a boy, and would be honoured if Amethyst would consent to be his godmother.

She'd very nearly thrown the letter in the fire. It was obvious that having a wealthy godmother far outweighed the risk of drawing down the wrath of an impecunious country parson. If she became Pip's godmother, they would feel entitled to ask her for help with his education and sponsorship in his chosen career. Perhaps even make him her heir, since by then her father would have told them she'd become as confirmed a man-hater as Aunt Georgie and would therefore never marry and have children of her own.

No wonder Aunt Georgie had gone to such lengths to conceal the extent of her wealth from absolutely everyone.

Fortunately, Fenella had pointed out that even if it was from mercenary reasons, at least one of her family had made contact. And that she would regret it, once her anger cooled, if she hadn't taken the opportunity to mend fences.

'So…what will you do if Fenella does marry her French Count?'

She rubbed at her forehead with one forefinger. 'I will have to find someone else to come and live with me, of course, to give me a veneer of respectability. In a way, it won't be all that hard, since I dare say there are any number of single, educated ladies in dire straits. Except…well, none of them would be Fenella. And I will miss Sophie quite desperately.'

'Or,' he said casually, 'you could do something utterly radical. You could marry me. Take me home to live with you.'

'What?' She couldn't believe he'd repeated that idiotic proposal he'd made the first time they'd made love. They were different people now, couldn't he see that? They couldn't go back in time and recapture the youthful feelings they'd had before they'd both had to grow up.

Not that he'd ever mentioned wanting to recapture those feelings. He'd admitted he had been in love with her and wanted to marry her, then. But of how he felt today? He'd said nothing.

So she feigned a laugh. 'Oh, yes, very funny. The answer to all my problems.'

'Well, not all, but possibly some, don't you think? I don't like the thought of you having to live all on your own. Or having to hire a stranger to live with you, for the sake of propriety. It is one thing to invite a widowed friend to live with you, but quite another to have to deliberately hire someone to stay in your home.'

'Well, bringing you home from Paris to live with me, like some...overlarge souvenir is certainly not going to answer. Certainly not the part about propriety, anyway. I can just see the stir it would create, amongst the ladies of Stanton Basset, to have a disgraced politician of your notoriety come live among them. The resulting panic would be akin to shutting a fox up in the henhouse.'

He went very quiet. And still. He wasn't even dabbing paint at the canvas any more, just standing there.

'Nathan?' She sat up and tried to peer at him round the canvas. He was staring at the painting, his jaw hard, his lips compressed into a thin line.

'You were joking, weren't you? A man like you... well, you don't really want to marry anyone, do you? Certainly not to save her from facing loneliness.'

'And you are certainly not that desperate, are you?' he said.

No, she wasn't. But then she looked about the dingy rooms and wondered if perhaps he was. He didn't seem to know exactly how much she was worth, but it was highly suspicious that he'd made that casual proposal just after she'd told him she had a house and admitted to an income of sorts. He would have a roof over his head, guaranteed. And if the sum total of his ambition was to spend the rest of his days messing about with paints...

She shivered.

'You are cold,' he said, flinging his brush aside and coming across the room to drape a blanket over her. 'I'm sorry. I know these rooms are a touch basic, but the light up here is so superb, during the day, that I didn't care about that when I rented them,' he said ruefully.

'Of course,' she said with a tight smile, though if he thought to fool her into believing he was living like this by choice then he'd seriously underestimated her intelligence.

If he was angling for a wife to provide for him, he wasn't going to admit it straight out, was he? And even if he wasn't deliberately trying to deceive her, he was just typical of his class, who refused to admit they were in want. They'd leave bills unpaid, even flee lodgings at dead of night, rather than openly admit their finances weren't in order.

She pulled the quilt up to her chin, but the cold feeling in her stomach wouldn't go away.

'I think it is time I left,' she said in a small voice that didn't sound a bit like her.

'Why? You cannot want to go back to your apartments and have to watch Fenella and Gaston billing and cooing all day, can you?'

'No, but…well, I have to go back some time, don't I? I cannot simply move in with you just because the way they carry on is making me a bit uncomfortable.'

'I wouldn't mind if you did,' he said. 'Though I could wish the place was a bit more comfortable, for your sake.'

That was even worse than proposing marriage. Though it dealt with his earlier assertion that he was being careful of her reputation. A man didn't ask a woman to be his mistress if he really cared about her, did he?

'Hmmph,' she said and stalked to the bedroom to retrieve her clothes. A wave of sadness washed over her as she was pulling her crumpled chemise over her head. If they'd married ten years ago, she was sure they would have been happy. She hadn't any ambitions beyond the kind of life he'd described, after all. She certainly wouldn't have minded him filling up his leisure hours with painting. It was clearly a very large part of who he was. And she would have wanted him to be happy.

But as she swiftly donned the rest of her clothes, she reminded herself that the years had changed them both. She wouldn't be content nowadays to live in some cottage, doing nothing more than raising *a pack of children* and seeing to a man's domestic comforts.

And he'd got used to sampling a different woman whenever the fancy took him. Why, he'd thought nothing of asking her to move in with him, so lax had his morality become.

He didn't really want to marry her.

Any more than she wanted to marry him.

They'd had their chance, ten years ago. And lost it.

By the time she'd tidied her hair in the mirror, and felt ready to leave the room and face him, she'd drawn right back into the crusty cocoon that had kept her heart safe for so many years. Even the grin he sent flashing her way could not pierce it. It just reminded her that Nathan was dangerous.

Because when he smiled at her like that, he could make her say yes to almost anything.

Chapter Eleven

Nathan flung his brush down and plunged his fingers through his hair. Oh, there was nothing wrong with the portrait itself. It was undoubtedly the best work he'd ever done. The trouble was that it was almost finished. Just like his affair with Amy. Only a few more days and she would be leaving Paris, going back to England. And he was going to lose her all over again. And this time it was going to be far worse, because this time round it wasn't all vague dreams of a possible future he would lose. This time he knew exactly what he'd be missing.

Because he'd gone and fallen in love with her, all over again, prickly as she was. He understood why she'd become so defensive. Life had dealt them both some hard knocks, which only made them more compatible, if anything, than they'd been as youngsters. He wouldn't be interested in some shy, naïve young vicar's daughter, straight from the country—not any longer. Tainted by his years in politics, corrupted by the sordid means he'd sunk to in order to obtain his freedom, he'd find such a girl insipid.

But this older, more experienced Amy, the cynical

wary woman she'd become, matched him just as he was now. He wouldn't change a thing about her. Not one thing.

Except her opinion of him.

Moodily he stared at her image, staring back at him from the canvas. He'd caught a look in her eyes that…

He flung himself away from the stool and strode to the window. He'd painted her as he wanted her to look at him, that's what he'd done. With love in her eyes, longing expressed in every line of that sleek, lush body.

Which was the height of absurdity. She might enjoy seeing the sights of Paris with him. Might enjoy casting off the restraints imposed on single women, to indulge in this passionate affair. But once it was time to leave, he didn't fool himself that she was going to experience much more than a tiny pang of regret. She would be sorry to have to return to a life of dull respectability, but would she be sorry to bid him farewell?

He didn't think so.

She'd told him at the outset all she wanted was a fling. And he'd thought he'd be content with that. He'd certainly never thought he'd contemplate marrying anyone, ever again. And yet when she'd turned down his guilt-induced, sacrificial proposal, he hadn't felt so much relieved as…a bit insulted. And as the days had passed he'd begun to find the thought of her being with anyone else unpalatable. At about the same rate he'd seen that being married to her wouldn't have been the ordeal it had been with Lucasta.

And now…well, now he wanted her so desperately, he couldn't stand the thought of her leaving. He leaned his forehead on a pane of glass and gazed out blindly over the rooftops of the city he'd started to think he could call home. It wouldn't feel like home once she'd gone. It would just be one more cold, inhospitable place where he would be merely existing.

So what was he to do? Just let her walk away? Or risk all on one last desperate throw of the dice?

He was definitely going to lose her if he did nothing.

But if he stood any chance at having a future with her, he'd have to tell her everything. He squeezed his eyes shut as panic clawed at his stomach. She'd been incensed with the citizens of Stanton Basset for listening to and believing unsubstantiated rumours about her friend Fenella being an unmarried mother. How much more angry would she be with him, when he told her he'd believed pretty much the same of her?

And then there was her attitude towards his reputation. She'd made it plain she thought he was the kind of man who would take any woman to bed, under any pretext. He hadn't yet found a suitable opportunity to explain the bitter battle he'd ended up fighting with his father, or how he'd seen that only by taking the most drastic measures would he ever win his freedom. Once or twice he'd very nearly confided in her when she'd told him things about her past that echoed his own battles for independence.

But at the last moment his courage had always failed him. Given all that he'd done, all that he'd become, it was a miracle he'd managed to get even this close to her. He didn't deserve her, not one bit. His father was right about him. Had been right all along. He was no good.

So he'd kept quiet and kept on taking what crumbs she was prepared to throw him. At least for the moment she was sharing his bed. Enjoying his company. But once she knew the depths of him, he'd forfeit even that.

He ran his fingers through his hair again as he reached his decision. It was time he owned up. It might make her hate him, but that would only be what he deserved. Punishment. For not standing by her. A lifetime of knowing she despised him would be a just sentence, wouldn't it? For betraying her. For betraying their fledgling love.

He owed her the truth, so that she could understand what had happened, even if he lost her because of it. Well, he was going to lose her anyway, wasn't he? She was leaving. And she'd made it crystal clear she didn't want him cluttering up her tidy, respectable existence by going with her.

He drew in a deep, shuddering breath and let his hands fall back to his sides.

Nothing he'd done so far had helped him to breach those invisible, but very tangible walls behind which she hid. So what did he have to lose?

Perhaps it would take the shock of hearing what had really gone wrong between them, ten years ago, to bring them tumbling down. It had, after all, taken the shock of discovering the truth to jolt him out of his own emotional prison cell. And it was beginning to look as though nothing less would set her free, either.

Amethyst had just picked up her bonnet, a frivolous article she'd bought from a milliner who catered to the needs of tourists, rather than Parisians, when there came a timid knock on her door.

Fenella peeped round it. 'Oh, you are…going out,' she said as Amethyst set the confection of straw, lace and silk flowers at a jaunty angle on her head.

They had not seen all that much of each other since

the day of the trip to the Bois de Boulogne. Though Amethyst had made a point of seeing Sophie every day to hear what she'd been doing, she'd deliberately avoided spending time with Fenella alone. And up till now, Fenella had done much the same.

They were both tiptoeing round the fact that though Fenella and Gaston were courting, Amethyst was just having an affair. If they talked in private, one of them might speak rather too frankly.

'With…with *him*, I suppose.' Fenella's face creased into anxious lines.

'Yes, with him,' Amethyst agreed calmly, tying the ribbons under her left ear in a manner that looked positively flirtatious.

'I…I know that you say it is better not to be seen about with Gaston and me, in case someone you want to do a deal with recognises you and starts to ask awkward questions, but…' She tiptoed into the room and shut the door behind her.

Amethyst sighed. Fenella had apparently decided that she wasn't going to avoid speaking frankly any longer.

'I cannot help worrying,' she said, clasping her hands at her waist, 'about the amount of time you spend closeted with Mr Harcourt in his lodgings. And I know that it must sound a bit hypocritical of me, given the way I have behaved with my Gaston, but I fear that…' she took a deep breath and plunged in '…I fear that Mr Harcourt's intentions are not honourable.'

'Well, of course they are not honourable.' Amethyst would have spared Fenella's sensibilities if she'd just carried on pretending she didn't know what was going on. But since Fenella had broached the topic, she wasn't going to be mealy-mouthed about it.

'That was the whole reason for choosing him to become my lover. You know I have no intention of ever getting married.'

'Oh, dear. Oh, dear.' Fenella tottered to the nearest chair and sank down onto it. 'Your...your lover.' She clenched her hands together again so tightly the knuckles went white. 'I blame myself. I have been so caught up with Gaston that I have completely failed to do my duty by you as chaperon.'

'Nonsense.'

'No, it is not nonsense. I have set you a bad example by allowing my feelings for Gaston to—' She broke off, going pink in the face. 'If ever word of this got out in Stanton Basset, you would be quite ruined. Why, even if people only heard that you have been going all over Paris with a man of *his* reputation, there would be no end of talk. And I...I really don't want you to have to suffer as I did. Even though I was still a completely respectable widow, then, they had no mercy. It will be worse for you, a single lady, if once they get a hint of...of this.'

'Do you know, I don't really care if my reputation does get a bit tarnished,' she replied, pulling on her gloves. 'If I was a young girl looking for a husband, or even a poor person, dependent on the goodwill of others, I might pay more heed to what other people may say of me, or think of me. Besides, you, of all people, must know how good it can make you feel to have an attractive...' She swallowed on the word, as an image of Monsieur Le Brun's sallow face swam into her mind. Well, there were obviously different kinds of attractive. Fenella saw something beneath the unprepossessing exterior Monsieur Le Brun presented to the world which *she* found attractive. 'An attractive man,' she repeated, 'paying me so much attention. I am enjoying having my portrait painted and I am enjoying going out with a man with no sense of decorum whatsoever. He makes me feel...' She paused. She had been about to say he made her feel like a girl again, but on looking back, she rather thought she'd been a bit priggish as a girl. It hadn't been until she'd met Nathan for the first time that she'd discovered she even had a sense of humour. And she'd never just had fun, the way she had fun with Nathan. He'd introduced her to a whole new world of experience and not just in bed.

They'd talked and talked, as she'd never talked to anyone before. He was genuinely interested in her opinions. He didn't always agree with them and sometimes their discussions grew quite heated. But he never seemed to think less of her for disagreeing with him. In fact, if she grew too angry, he would get a wicked gleam in his eyes and tell her she was at her most alluring when she got angry, and then defuse all her irritation by flinging down his brushes, stalking to the couch on which she lay and making her come, over and over again, until she lay limp and sated in his arms. And had totally forgotten whatever it was they'd been arguing about.

'For so long,' she said to Fenella, 'I have felt that I have no appeal as a woman whatsoever. And now the most experienced rake in two countries is hanging on my sleeve.'

Not trying to change her, or form her opinions, or punishing her for disagreeing with him, but allowing her, for the first time in her life, to be herself.

'Do you think worrying about what people might say,

if they were to find out, is going to prevent me from making the most of it, while it lasts?'

'No. I suppose not. But…you will be careful, won't you? I don't want you to get hurt.'

She spun round, on the verge of asking Fenella what she thought it was going to do to her when she left her to marry her French Count, and took Sophie away, if not wound her to the core? Sophie had become almost like a daughter to her, while she'd never had a friend as close as Fenella. If Fenella really didn't want her to be hurt, she wouldn't be obliging her to return to Stanton Bassett and bear the brunt of all the talk there would be, and suffer the pitying looks, the moralising and the unsolicited advice—alone.

But she bit her tongue. She mustn't let self-pity or jealousy ruin what they could salvage of their friendship.

Jealousy? She couldn't possibly be jealous of Fenella, having Gaston, could she? No the notion was absurd. She didn't want a husband. She didn't want any man to have the power over her that a husband would have, by law.

'Thank you Fenella, for your concern,' she said stiffly. 'But I can assure you that I have no intention of getting hurt. This is the man who led me on, then changed his mind once before, don't forget. I know not to trust a single word that comes out of his mouth.'

She'd taken great care not to let Nathan touch her heart. Her body, yes, and her mind. She'd found it liberating to be free with both. But she'd kept her heart safely encased in a block of ice which no amount of passion, no matter how hot, could melt.

'Oh, dear,' Fenella said again. 'That sounds so

very...' She shook her head. 'So very sad. To have no hope that things might develop...'

'It is not the least bit sad. It is practical. I am not going to marry some man and let him wrest control of my life from me.'

'Marriage is not like that. I'm sure Gaston will never attempt to *control* me.'

'And has he informed you yet where he plans to set up home, once you are married?'

Fenella flushed and her face fell. 'Actually, he has. He has a little property near Southampton which he says will suit me and Sophie very nicely.'

'Southampton! The opposite end of the country from Stanton Basset. About as far away from me as he can take you.'

'It isn't deliberate. It isn't as if he bought the place on purpose to keep us apart. He knew nothing about either of us when he bought it.'

Amethyst drew a deep breath. 'I will make quite certain he does not keep us apart,' she said grimly. 'I had already toyed with the idea of moving away from Stanton Basset. After this trip, going back there would feel like going back to a cage. So I had thought about taking a place by the seaside. Southampton will be as good a location as anywhere.'

It eased all the hurt of hearing Fenella was going to live on the south coast when her face lit up.

'Oh, that will be wonderful. I was a little worried,' she admitted, 'about how I would cope in a new town, all on my own. Because Gaston is going to be away quite a lot.'

'Is he?'

'Well, yes. He's...he's hoping to continue working

as a courier for English tourists. So he can return to France again and again, until the matter of his estates is settled. You will give him a good reference, won't you?'

'Is that why he sent you to speak to me this morning?' A cold sliver of uncertainty snaked through her middle.

'Oh, no! He is convinced that you hate him. He is even a bit worried you might try to take some form of revenge on him for stealing me away from you.'

'But you don't?'

Fenella laughed. 'Of course not! I know you better than that. You haven't a vengeful bone in your body. You are all that is good,' she said, pressing Amethyst's hand affectionately. 'Otherwise you couldn't have let that man…Mr Harcourt…back into your life, could you?'

All of a sudden Amethyst felt like crying. Fenella's faith in her was so touching. She was the one person who always chose to see some good in her, even when everyone else chose to think the worst.

She delved into her reticule for a handkerchief and blew her nose.

'I suppose I shouldn't mention him, should I?' said Fenella. 'It must be so difficult for you, having to bid him farewell and never be able to hope you will see him again.'

It was going to be a wrench, she couldn't deny it. Nathan had made her feel…so alive.

'I will always have the portrait to remind me of this time, though,' she said, putting her hanky away.

'You mean there really is a portrait?'

'Yes. I'm going to view it today. And I'm going to buy it,' she said decisively, 'even if it is a bit of a daub.'

'That is so like you,' said Fenella, almost worshipfully.

'Fustian! I won't be doing it for him.' Though she'd already decided she would find something complimentary to say about it, because he cared so greatly about his art. More than he cared about anything else in his life, if she'd read him aright. He'd told her, rather wistfully, when they'd first known each other, that he wished being a painter was an acceptable profession for a gentleman. But it wasn't until these last few weeks that she'd realised that it was all he'd ever really wanted to do with his life. And now that his brief career as a politician had ensured nobody could possibly think of him as a gentleman any more, he was finally free to live the life he'd always dreamed of.

No, after all he'd done for her these past weeks, the way he'd made her feel, she wasn't going to be the one to tell him he didn't have the talent, if that was the case.

'It is just that the painting is a bit, shall we say, *risqué*. I have to ensure that it cannot fall into the wrong hands.'

'Oh, my word. Did he paint you...?'

'Without benefit of clothing, yes,' she said, checking her appearance in the mirror one last time. 'I shall most probably have to shroud it in holland covers and hide it away in the attics.'

She walked briskly to the door. 'I hope you and Sophie enjoy your day. I shall see you...later.' And with that, she left.

She was glad she'd gone prepared to speak with tact, rather than total honesty, when she saw how on edge Nathan appeared the moment he opened the door to her.

As she followed him through to the studio, she wondered at her decision to keep the painting, rather than simply burn it the moment she had the freedom to do so. She wasn't normally prone to making decisions based on sentiment.

Although...it would be pleasant to have a tangible reminder of this heady month, spent in a foreign country, in a handsome man's arms. When she was old and grey, she could creep up to the attic, pull off the covers and warm herself at the memory of having, for one month of her life at least, had a man who found everything about her utterly feminine, and deliciously desirable, to boot. Or even before then. Whenever her father made one of his sporadic attempts to assert his will, she could remind herself that she'd been right and he'd been wrong about Nathan's intentions. And by extension, everything else about her.

That wasn't being sentimental. It was...providing herself with armour against the life she was going to have to live once Fenella left and she stood alone against a harsh, judgemental world.

Nathan paused in the doorway to the studio for a moment or two, before stepping aside and letting her enter. Before he let her see the finished portrait, which he'd turned on its easel to face the door.

'Oh,' she said, coming to an abrupt halt as the full impact of it hit her squarely in the chest.

Not that it was dreadful. She didn't know why she'd ever thought it might be, given the skill he'd demonstrated when producing those swift pencil sketches. There was no problem with perspective, or the way the light shone on the drapery which made it look as though it flowed over her body, or anything like that.

There was no mistaking that the woman in the picture was her, either.

Nevertheless, this painting was most definitely going to be consigned to the attics. She couldn't possibly risk letting anyone see her portrayed like this. And it wasn't just because he'd depicted her reclining on a couch, strategic folds of linen preserving her modesty, whilst advertising the fact that she was naked beneath it. It was the expression on her face that she daren't let anyone ever see. He'd made her look like…like a woman in love. She was gazing out of the canvas as though she adored the man who was painting her. He'd made her look… She swallowed back something that felt very like tears. Younger. Less cynical. Vulnerable, even.

Yes, that was what she objected to. She didn't mind a reminder that she was capable of being feminine, but he'd gone too far. There was not a trace of the hard-headed businesswoman she'd become. Let alone the rebellious daughter, who was the despair of her father, or the shrew from whom Monsieur Le Brun had thought he needed to protect his gentle, ladylike Fenella.

'You don't like it.' His voice was flat.

She shook her head. 'Nathan, you have real talent. I can see that. You have made me look…beautiful. Which is very flattering. But it is not me, that woman there. It makes me feel as though you don't really know me. Or as though you have been looking at me through a… through a prism.'

'That is the most perceptive thing I have ever heard you say.' He turned her round when she couldn't tear her eyes from the vision of womanly submission on the canvas, obliging her to look directly into his face. 'In a way, I have been looking at you through a kind of prism. I have been looking at you through the eyes of a man in love. Desperately in love.'

Something coiled in her stomach and slithered its way up her spine. The hairs on the back of her neck stood on end.

There was only one thing that could account for him saying such a thing. Somehow he must have found out how wealthy she was.

'Love?' She shook her head. 'Do you take me for some kind of fool? You don't love me. You don't even know me,' she cried, waving her hand at the portrait of a woman who was a far cry from the person she knew herself to be.

'But I do know you, Amy. I know better than anyone else how badly you were hurt as a girl and that it made you close yourself off from the possibility of ever getting hurt again. I understand why you have become a cynic. I also know you don't want to hear what I'm going to say next, but I'm going to say it anyway. I don't know what I'm going to do with myself when you leave here and return to England. I can't bear to lose you again. Marry me, Amy.' He went down on his knees. 'Please. I asked you before if I could come back to England with you because I couldn't bear the thought of you being lonely. But now I can't bear the thought of you finding someone to save you from that loneliness, if that someone isn't me.'

She drew back.

'I am not going to be taken in by you,' she hissed. 'I won't let you deceive me. You chose your last wife for what you could gain and I—'

'No! That is not true.' He got up. 'I'm not going to let you believe that lie for one second longer.' He clenched his fists. 'I did not marry my first wife for gain.' His face leached of colour. 'I married her to wound you.'

'You…what? But why? Why would you want to wound me?'

'I was deeply in love with you, Amy. Well,' he hedged, 'as deeply as a boy of that age could be. I've already told you that I wanted to marry you. I confided as much to one or two people, one night, at one of my clubs. They'd been teasing me about what a stranger I was becoming there and how I seemed to be spending all my time mixing with, forgive me for repeating their words, but they described your set as the shabby-genteel.'

She flushed. It was true that he'd seemed out of place at most of the gatherings she'd attended. That she'd always known he was way above her own more humble station. But that was no excuse for doing what he'd done.

'You stopped courting me because your friends teased you about marrying below your station?'

'No! How could you even think I'd do something so…shallow?' He turned away, took a few paces away from her, then turned back, his face implacable. 'I'm just trying to help you see how it must have all come about. I paid no attention to the teasing, knowing it was nothing compared with the opposition I'd have to face from my father. And probably yours. I was plucking up the courage to approach him and ask for your hand in form, knowing that I had little to recommend me. If I could get him to look favourably on my suit, I would have been more than capable of braving my own father's displeasure. I had reached a crossroads in my life. I'd always been something of a disappointment to him, whereas my brothers had all made him proud. So I stopped asking his permission to travel to Italy to study art. I'd agreed to spend that Season in London considering professions he deemed suitable for a man of my background. And then I met you. And—'

He broke off, paced away, paced back again.

'Well, before I got round to approaching either of them, one of my friends told me he'd heard something that made it impossible for him to stand back and let me throw myself away on you.'

He was shaking, she noted with surprise. Actually trembling. He licked his lips, with what looked like nervousness, before saying, 'He told me that he'd heard, from a reliable source, that you were no innocent. That you'd actually borne a child out of wedlock and had come up to town for the sole purpose of luring some poor unsuspecting male into the trap of providing for you and your child. Preferably a man with a title, a man powerful enough to protect you from the scandal.'

She gasped. 'But that's absurd! You know it is. Why, I was a virgin when we…'

The edges of the room seemed to blur and darken. There was a roaring sound in her ears as her mind flew back to his shock, the night he'd first taken her to bed. How his attitude towards her had gone from scornful and aggressive to remorseful and caring.

'You believed it,' she whispered. 'You believed I would be that wicked.' Now her own legs were shaking. For a moment, she wondered if she was going to faint. But then fury surged through her veins, giving her strength to stand and speak her mind, instead of crumpling under the weight of hurt and shock.

'You didn't even demand proof from this so-called friend of yours. You couldn't have done. You didn't confront me with the tale either. You just…you just spurned me!' Why had everyone, at that period in her life, been so ready to assume the worst of her?

'I was devastated, Amy. I was so angry and hurt to think you could deliberately set out to deceive me that I lost my head.'

'Because you believed it. How could you?'

'Because Fielding, the friend who plucked up the courage to come to me with the tale, had been well chosen,' he said bitterly. 'He was the one friend I had who I knew would never tell a deliberate lie. He was not only too honest, but also not bright enough to spin any kind of yarn. He'd never have been able to keep all the threads straight. And he was torn, Amy. He hated having to speak ill of a lady. He only did so because he was convinced someone had to do something to save me from the clutches of an ambitious schemer.' He huffed out a strange, bitter laugh. 'That was what made him so convincing. The fact that he believed it so completely. The poor sap was such a slow-top that he couldn't imagine anyone inventing a deliberate lie about a lady. He was so gullible he genuinely believed that if my father had breached the gentleman's code by repeating such a foul tale about a lady, it could only have been from the best of intentions.'

'You have a nerve to describe him as a slow-top,' she breathed. 'You fell for exactly the same lie he did.'

'Did I? I'm not so certain any more. Deep down I think I always knew my father was behind it. I knew what my father was like. I should have known he would thrust a spoke in my wheel, if he were to discover I'd decided to marry you, rather than tamely submit to the plans he'd started making for me. He must have been livid when his spies brought back tales of me planning to marry a nobody, and settle down in obscurity, just as he thought he'd finally got me to knuckle under. And even if it wasn't true, about you…but I told myself it must be. It made sense, you see.'

'What do you mean? How could it make sense? What had I ever done to make you think I was…that kind of woman?'

'You'd appeared to fall for me practically at first sight,' he said bleakly. 'When everyone else knew there was nothing special about me. I was only the youngest son of four. The runt of the litter. The one with no ambition. The one whose only talent was for drawing, a subject more suited to women than to real men.'

'That's utter nonsense.'

'It was what I felt, at the time. That you couldn't possibly have seen anything in me to admire, apart from my susceptibility to your charms. I could believe you might have seen me as a pigeon ripe for plucking. And then there was the matter of your behaviour.' The corners of his mouth pulled into something very like a sneer. 'You were the daughter of a vicar. At first you seemed so prim and proper, but in no time at all you were letting me lure you into secluded places. Nay, you encouraged me to lure you into secluded places so that I could kiss you, Amy. So you could set my blood on fire. And I was always the one to call a halt. I got the feeling you would have let me do whatever I wanted…'

Yes, she would have done. Because she'd loved him. Loved him! And all the time…

Something inside her snapped. She flew at him, pounding at his chest with her fists. He grabbed her wrists to hold her at a distance, which so infuriated her she kicked out at his legs, twisting and hissing like a cat.

But Nathan was far stronger than her. He just held her at arm's length until, exhausted, she would have collapsed into a sobbing heap at his feet if he hadn't scooped her up into his arms and carried her to the sofa where he cradled her on his lap, rocking her as she carried on weeping.

'I hate you,' she said, when she could at last find the breath, and the control, to form words.

'It's no more than I deserve.'

'You…you…destroyed me…'

'My father destroyed us both. The last ten years have been sheer hell, Amy—'

'No. *You* destroyed us. You had no faith in me. Not even when we met again. You deliberately seduced me, for…for revenge, I suppose.'

'Yes.' There was no point in denying it. That was exactly what he'd done. 'At first, I did want revenge. Until I discovered the truth. And then all I felt was remorse. I wanted to make reparation for all the misery I caused you. I wanted to wipe out the misery by making you happy instead. By giving you one perfect month. A month where you had all you'd ever wanted. But somewhere along the way I fell in love with you all over again.'

'You don't love me. You never loved me. You couldn't, to have believed such foul lies.'

'I did love you, Amy. Not enough, it is true. But I love you more now. For knowing that you were innocent. For growing into the woman you are now. Strong, and independent, and wary, and fiery…'

'You don't know me any better now than you knew

me then,' she cried, wriggling off his lap. 'Not if you think I'm going to have anything to do with you ever again, after learning what you did to me.'

'Amy, please...'

He reached for her, but she darted away from him, towards the door.

'Don't leave like this,' he begged her. 'Not while you are so upset. You shouldn't be alone...'

'I have been alone,' she breathed, 'for the last ten years.' She dashed a tear from her cheek with an angry swipe of her hand. 'And alone is exactly how I like it. If you don't let anyone near you, then nobody can hurt you.'

'That's true. But it's going to be a lonely life, if you cling to that belief and never let anyone near.'

'No. It won't be. Lonely is when you are surrounded by people who betray you. And despise you. And only pay you attention when they want something. *That* is loneliness.'

She flew to the door and ran out.

Oh, God, she was so angry she couldn't see straight. He should know. He'd been in just such a fury on the night Fielding destroyed his hope in the possibility of marrying for love. So he plunged straight after her. He couldn't bear it if some harm befell her on the crowded streets.

He didn't try to stop her, for he knew she was in no fit state to listen to reason. He just kept her in his sights, ready to intervene should she run into danger, until he'd seen her reach her lodgings safely. And then he went to find her friend, and her French lover, to tell them that she needed them. She wouldn't tolerate him anywhere near, for a while, but she must not be alone.

Eventually, the first flood of her anger would recede, and then, by hook or by crook, he would make her listen to him again.

That was the one advantage he had now, which she had lacked the last time this same lie had driven them apart. She'd had no weapons with which to defend herself. No idea she'd even needed to prove her innocence. She'd been completely in the dark.

But this time, they both knew exactly where they stood. And he wasn't going to give her up without a fight. He was no longer an insecure youth, torn between staying loyal to his family and taking a chance on love. He was a man now. A man who'd learned that love was worth fighting for.

Whatever it took. No matter how long it took.

Chapter Twelve

She had to get the portrait from him.

She couldn't believe, now, that she'd been stupid enough to pose for it. Naked. She pressed her hands to her cheeks, which were burning with mortification.

If he was desperate enough for security to ask her to marry him, he'd have no compunction about selling it if she left it behind in Paris. Or deliberately displaying it somewhere if he decided to take a more humiliating revenge for her refusal. He had a reputation for not being particularly kind to former lovers. And she had turned him down in the most insulting terms. She'd called him a slow-top, she'd accused him of being shallow and marrying his first wife for her money, of being faithless and worthless and she didn't know what else.

Oh, yes. She'd told him she hated him, and then, when ten years of repressed rage had swelled up, the dam had burst and she'd physically attacked him.

Not that he didn't deserve every name she'd called him, but it hadn't been a wise move to make an enemy of him all over again. Only look what lengths he'd gone to the last time, when he'd only *thought* she'd betrayed him. He'd coldly, deliberately done the very worst thing he could have done to her. He'd flaunted another woman—a rich, titled woman—in her face. Even gone so far as to marry her to make doubly sure he inflicted the maximum hurt he possibly could.

Not only that, but he'd held on to his anger for ten years. He'd admitted he started up their affair because he wanted revenge.

No. Nathan Harcourt wasn't a man to cross with impunity. He'd get his own back on her somehow.

Well then. Her mouth compressed into a hard line. She'd just have to force herself to go and see him, one last time, before she left Paris. Offer him whatever he wanted to release the portrait to her.

Any sum of money, that was, no matter how steep. She would pay it.

And if his demands were not of the financial kind?

Well, he would be wasting his time trying to blackmail her into anything other than monetary payment. Marry him she would not. Nor let him touch her again.

Anything but that!

She'd just risen from her chair to get ready to go and tell him so when Fenella knocked timidly on her door.

'I know you said you wanted to be alone this morning, but I thought I'd better let you know…that is…he's here. Mr Harcourt.'

Amethyst dropped back down into her chair.

'I tried to turn him away,' Fenella continued apologetically, 'but he's most insistent…'

She'd just bet he was. He'd already worked out that he had a valuable bargaining chip in that portrait and was clearly determined to start negotiations for it before she left.

Her fingers clawed round the arms of her chair
'Show him in.'

'Are you sure?'

'Quite sure. His visit has saved me the bother of going out and seeing him, actually, which I had planned to do later on. He and I have a few matters we need to settle before I leave France. Private matters,' she added, giving Fenella a stern look that sent her scuttling away just like the mouse Nathan had so disparagingly likened her to.

She took a deep breath as soon as the door shut behind her companion, suddenly wishing she'd taken a bit of care over her appearance when Fenella had persuaded her to roll out of bed this morning. She hadn't bothered looking in a mirror, but since she'd scarcely slept last night, and spent most of the day before weeping, she must look a fright. Had she even brushed her hair? She raised a shaky hand to her head and confirmed her suspicion that she had not, when they met with a riot of tangled curls.

She let her hand drop to her lap where she clenched it into an impotent fist. She should have told Fenella to make him wait while she tidied herself up. She didn't want to give him the satisfaction of seeing how low he'd managed to bring her.

For the second time in her life.

But it was too late to do so much as reach for a comb. There was a scuffling sound from just outside the door, then it swung open and Nathan slid in sideways, his movements hampered by a huge, square package done up in brown paper.

A package that was the exact size of the portrait.

She shot to her feet. 'Is that what I think it is?'

He propped up the package against the wall to the right of the door before looking her way. He seemed tense, but defiant, turning his hat round and round in his hands.

'Thank you for agreeing to see me,' he began.

'Never mind all that.' She made a dismissive gesture with her hand as she strode across to what might be her portrait.

'I was hoping you would want to keep it,' he said. 'So I took the chance that it might be my ticket in to see you.'

She shot him just one suspiciously wary glance before tearing at the wrapping with her fingers to find out exactly what it was he'd brought with him. Who knew what kind of trick he might be trying to play on her? She cursed under her breath when she broke a fingernail. Where were the scissors when she needed them?

'Here,' he said, handing her a pocketknife.

She took it from him with an indefinable noise, halfway between the words thank you and a snarl, and severed the string.

It was the picture. Of her. Half-naked and looking at the artist as though she wanted to devour him.

With a shiver, she twitched the slashed wrappings back in place, then dragged the whole thing across the room and tucked it safely behind a sofa.

'You may be able to hide that away,' he observed, 'but you can't hide from what has passed between us this past month.'

'Can you blame me for wanting to?'

'Not if this was just some tawdry affair, no. But it is so much more. I've asked you to marry me, Amy—'

'And I have said no.'

'You said it when you were angry with me for discovering what an idiot I'd been before.' The corners of his mouth tilted into a rueful, yet hopeful smile. 'I was hoping your temper might have cooled somewhat since then.'

'Oh, I'm perfectly cool today,' she assured him haughtily. 'You might say, to the point of chilliness. Why, towards you, I feel…positively frigid.'

'Do you, though?'

He tossed the hat aside, strode across the room, hauled her into his arms and kissed her.

And even though she was still furious with him, especially since he had the nerve to try smiling at her, her body melted into him the moment he took her in his arms. Her own arms went round his neck. Her foolish lips parted for his and kissed him back. Only her pride stood apart, shaking its head in reproof.

'You want me, Amy,' he breathed, breaking their kiss. 'Even though I'm no good, you want me. Don't pretend you don't. Don't be a liar. That kind of behaviour is beneath you.'

'Who are you to tell me how to behave?' Injured pride had her pulling out of his arms. She managed to take two steps away from him, spied her chair and took another two steps, so that she'd put it between her and him.

'The man who loves you,' he said.

'Oh, don't start that again. You never loved me. You couldn't have.'

'Are you saying that because of the way I behaved, or because you believe there is something in you that makes you unworthy of love?'

'What?' She flinched. 'I don't know what you mean.'

His eyes narrowed. 'Oh, I think you do. I think you know exactly what I mean. I recognise that aspect of you, Amy, because I have it, deeply ingrained in me, too. Like me, I think you've always had to try to prove yourself to parents who expect more from you than you are capable of being. Who want you to be someone you will never be. And I wouldn't be a bit surprised to learn that, since we parted, you've carried on living the kind of life where people around you always measure you by a different set of standards from those that matter to you.'

She gasped and pressed one hand to her chest. It was as if he'd looked right into her soul and divined every last one of her secrets.

So she had no choice but to fight back. She reached for the cruellest weapon she had at her disposal.

'You said it yourself, Nathan,' she sneered. 'You are no good. I can't depend on a single word you say. You made me fall in love with you, then decided I wasn't good enough. And now you talk about marriage, when all the world has seen what a dreadful husband you can be…'

'I've already told you it wasn't because you weren't good enough! I confessed my darkest shame to you. You know why I spurned you, Amy, so don't give me that excuse…' He stalked up to the chair, stopping only when his knees touched the upholstered cushions. She gripped the back, but he was so close it scarcely formed a barrier between them at all now.

'And as for being a dreadful husband—I'll tell you about my first marriage, shall I? How I fell into it because I'd ceased caring what happened to me? There was great gaping hole in my future, a void where my dreams of being *your* husband had once been. My father was telling me that I had exhibited poor judgement and that it was better to let him organise my life. And I believed him. I thought I'd made a terrible error of judgement by falling for you. I had only two things left: a chance to redeem myself with my father, of making him proud of me by going along with his plans, and a burning desire to wound you the way you wounded me. Marrying Lucasta achieved both those ends. She was the perfect weapon. To prove to you that I didn't care. To show you that I would rather marry a girl with a pedigree, and a fortune, than one with a pretty face.'

Amethyst flinched. She'd known it. She'd known he'd done his utmost to wound her. That he wasn't the kind to turn the other cheek.

Any more than she was. Hadn't she just said the very worst thing she could think of, with intent to wound him?

'Father had chosen Lucasta for me because she was intelligent and ambitious, and of course well connected. He'd picked the same kind of wife for each of my brothers. Women who would be a help to them rising through the ranks, in whatever career they'd chosen. He matched Freddy to the daughter of an archbishop, the moment he chose to take holy orders. And Berty got the granddaughter of both an earl and a general when he joined the army. The only difference was that others had decided I ought to go into politics, rather than me showing any inclination for it. But nobody thought it would matter. Unlike any other profession, a man doesn't need any aptitude to have a successful career in politics. He only needs the right connections.

'The terrible irony of it all was that initially I fell

in with my father's scheme, because I thought he was showing faith in me. But it was the very opposite. He was putting his faith in Lucasta. He thought she would make me a success, no matter how inept I was. She was the one with all the ambition. She wanted me to reach the top by fair means or foul, whereas I...'

Something he said came back to her. 'You wanted to make a difference.'

He snorted in derision. 'She just wanted me to vote the way I was told. She was furious when she discovered I wasn't the shambling, indolent wastrel my father had persuaded her she could push into doing whatever she wanted. I started to wake up, you see, not long after the nuptials were over. And stopped dumbly agreeing with everything that everyone told me. Voiced a few opinions of my own. Once or twice I even had the unmitigated cheek to vote according to my conscience. A young pup like me, who had no experience, no brains, no *judgement*... They kept telling me I shouldn't think for myself. That I should let older and wiser heads guide me. Which had the opposite effect. I made a couple of dramatic, rebellious gestures that made me look more of a fool than ever.'

In spite of her determination not to believe one word he said, this rang so true she couldn't help it. Hadn't she made the dramatic, rebellious gesture of going to live with her spinster aunt rather than back down when her family had told her she hadn't known her own mind, that she'd misunderstood his intentions?

'And as soon as Lucasta saw she'd been sold a pig in a poke, as she put it, she started to try to punish me.'

He gave a bitter laugh that tugged at a place deep

inside her that had long lain dormant. She swallowed it back down, nervously.

'Her opening gambit was to start spreading tales about her disappointment with my prowess between the sheets. I suppose in a way she had cause to complain. I'd never had that much enthusiasm for her, and what little I managed to muster waned remarkably swiftly once I realised what she was like. But still, I had this stupid, unfashionable notion that what went on between a husband and wife was private. She didn't. She wanted a life lived in the public eye. And when I refused to employ the kind of tactics she wanted me to take in order to start climbing the greasy pole, she took her revenge in public.'

His cheeks flushed dull red as she recalled some of the things she'd read about him in those days. The hints that he wasn't much of a man. The cartoons depicting him as a sort of wilting flower, blowing about with every breeze as he voted not according to the party line, but with the prevailing wind of public opinion.

'Even the fact that I wouldn't break my marriage vows made her despise me more. I made it a point of honour, you see, to show the world that I wouldn't sacrifice my integrity for my own comfort, let alone her ambition. But she even managed to twist that into something…foul.' His mouth twisted with bitterness.

'When, eventually, I suggested we might both be happier if I retired to the country, out of her way, she reminded me that her family had paid a great deal of money for me and I owed it to them to at least go through the motions. Even if I couldn't be a husband she could be proud of, I had no right to make her forfeit the life she loved. Hosting political gatherings, being in the thick of all the intrigue...

'She was right, of course. I stayed in London and... endured. My God, but I was relieved when she died. That makes me sound heartless, doesn't it? But you have no idea what it's like to live with that level of contempt, day in, day out.'

Actually, she rather thought she did. She'd had a taste of it from her family, before her aunt had swooped in and rescued her. Only she hadn't had to endure it for years. Only a few months.

'I wasted no time in embarking on a very public affair with a notoriously rapacious widow,' he said with a touch of defiance. 'A notoriously gossipy, rapacious widow, who was not averse to telling anyone who showed any interest that I was most definitely not a disappointment between the sheets. And after her, I went a little mad, I suppose. Taking whatever was on offer, proving Lucasta a liar, over and over again. Nobody has any doubt about my masculinity, not any longer.'

'Oh,' said Amethyst faintly. That made perfect sense. She could see exactly why he'd gone out and proved his manhood, over and over again, in as flagrant a way as possible. He hadn't let her leave his bed that first time, until he'd demonstrated his ability to take her to the heights of pleasure. He took pride in his prowess as a lover.

'That's right. Your sexual career made all the papers.'

His face darkened.

'Yes. All of it. I made sure it all got published, even though my father tried his damnedest to suppress it. It was my way out.'

'Your way out?' She injected as much cynicism into

her voice as she could muster. She couldn't believe that
in a few short minutes he'd practically demolished beliefs she'd held firmly for ten years. But she wouldn't let
him convince her he had any excuse for being involved
in that Season's most lurid scandal. Lifting her head,
she looked down her nose at him. 'The way I heard it,
they threw you out.'

'Precisely! If I hadn't done something that drastic,
my father would have picked another girl, from another political dynasty, and it would have started all
over again.'

Dammit! She knew he'd come up with something to
make even the end of his political career seem justified.

'So, those last affairs you had, with…'

'Two of the most influential women I could seduce,'
he agreed with a cold, hard smile. 'At the same time,
too, so that even if their husbands could overlook the
affairs, the offended wives could not. If there is one
thing a certain type of woman will not tolerate, it is
infidelity in her lover.'

'Indeed?' She'd thought he would at least tell her that
the stories about that last scandal had been exaggerated. Instead he was confirming them. She shuddered.

The thought of him coldly seducing two women,
married women at that, concurrently, made her feel sick.

His face shuttered.

'You didn't question a single word of it, did you?
You read it in print, so you thought it must *all* be true.'

She glanced up at him as he huffed out a bitter laugh.

'But you've just told me that it was…'

'And you were ready to condemn my behaviour without knowing what lay behind it. Or considered there

might have been people whose sole aim in writing the stories was to blacken my name.'

She drifted blindly away from the chair behind which she'd been cowering and sank down on to the nearest available sofa she could reach without having to walk past him.

'I can excuse you for not seeing my true motives for the way I've behaved,' he said. 'Because you knew nothing of my misery, my sense of utter failure. So now, will you have the honesty to think about my earlier failure to believe in you? Remember, all I knew of you was that although you professed to be from a very strict background, you never protested when I crossed the line. You did not put up even a token protest that first time I kissed you. You wanted me to kiss you. You didn't seem to care if we got caught, either.'

'But that was because…'

'You loved me. I know that now. And I should have believed in it at the time, too. But what Fielding told me put a very different complexion on your behaviour. It was all just credible enough to make me wonder. So before you condemn me for not being able to somehow discern that you were totally innocent of all the charges laid at your door, let me ask you this: When the situation was reversed, did you believe in me?'

No. She hadn't. She'd been so angry with him for the way he'd cast her aside that she'd wanted to believe the worst of him. Stoking up her hatred had given her the strength to go on living. She'd pored over those newspaper stories, believing the very worst of him without a shred of evidence to back any of it up.

So how could she condemn him for believing what a true, honest, good friend had told him, from the best of motives? Especially when, now she looked back on it openly and honestly, her own behaviour might have made the accusations against her seem plausible?

She'd been so bowled over when the handsome, charming young son of such a notable family had paid her attention that she'd forgotten every principle she'd ever had. She had encouraged him, as much as she'd dared. When he'd snatched that first kiss, a hasty peck on the cheek, she hadn't protested. She'd blushed and giggled, and let him engineer situations where he could do it again. They'd rapidly progressed to kisses on the lips. Then heated kisses on the lips.

She caught her lip between her teeth.

'What a pair we are,' he said. 'Neither of us can quite believe in love. I couldn't believe you loved me ten years ago and you cannot believe I love you now. Or perhaps you are just looking for excuses to escape me. I'm not much of a catch, am I? You've made it clear that I'm good enough for a fling, but not a lifetime.'

He walked over to the window and stood with his back to her for some time, in complete silence. When she darted a glance in his direction, it was to see his shoulders hunched in an attitude of defeat.

She wanted to cry out that she'd been too hasty. That, perhaps, if he gave her time to think it over, she might be able to…

To what? Believe in him? Trust her entire future to his hands? When by his own admission he'd proved himself capable of the vilest kind of behaviour?

'I may as well go,' he said, whirling round and making for the door. 'Forgive me for haranguing you. I hope your voyage back to England will be uneventful and that your memories of your stay in Paris are…sweet.'

And with that, he walked out.

Leaving his hat lying on the floor where he'd dropped it.

Amethyst stared wide-eyed at the closed door through which he'd gone. He'd given up. He'd seen that she couldn't ever trust him fully again and he'd given up. And gone.

Just like that.

She got to her feet and ran to the window. One last look. She would take one last look at him as he walked away until the crowd in the street swallowed him from sight. She laid her hand flat on the window pane, as though she could reach through it and touch him. Knowing she couldn't.

She'd blamed him for destroying what they'd had, before. But this time, he was right, *she* was the one who'd destroyed it. She hadn't been prepared to trust him. To forgive him. Worse than that, she hadn't even tried.

She could justify ignoring that first proposal. The night he'd discovered she was still a virgin and guilt had reared up and slapped him round the head for what he'd done. But the subsequent ones? If he didn't know about her wealth, if he was really trying to get her to marry him because he loved her...

She shook her head, tearing herself away from the window and returning to her chair.

Where her eye fell on the portrait that he'd brought to her. For no other reason, according to him, than that he thought it might be a way to get to speak to her again. Was that true? He certainly hadn't attempted to use it against her, the way she'd expected.

A shaft of cold dread speared down to her stomach.

What if he'd meant it? What if he really did think he was in love with her?

No. She took a deep breath, pushing the possibility to the back of the sofa where she'd stashed the portrait. It couldn't possibly be love. He probably thought marrying her would mean returning to a time before his life had gone so catastrophically wrong. To a time when he'd thought he could just marry a simple country girl and live in a sort of bucolic idyll.

But she wasn't that girl any more. She ran businesses. She could never retreat to the country and live the way he'd said was his own fantasy.

It just wasn't possible.

He wasn't the rather dreamy boy he'd been either, who talked about the beauty of nature, and how wonderful it would be to visit Italy and see the works of art on display in so many cities. He'd become a rake. A man who was capable of carrying on affairs with two women at the same time, to deliberately wreak as much destruction and pain as he could.

That wasn't a man she could love, was it? If she was capable of loving anyone at all.

And anyway, why was she sitting here arguing with herself about it? He'd gone. Defeat in every line of his body. He'd realised it was over between them. That it had been destroyed ten years ago and there was no putting it back together.

So that was that.

Chapter Thirteen

Men were good at saying all the right things, but actions spoke louder than words.

Nathan had said he wanted to marry her, that he loved her, that he couldn't bear to think of her leaving Paris. But after one rebuff, he'd disappeared. If he'd really meant what he said, he would have called, every day, begging her to reconsider.

But he didn't call.

Though what would be the point, she didn't know. It had been one thing having an affair with him here, but to make a new life with him in England? Impossible. Even if he still wanted her, which, apparently, he didn't.

Or he would have called.

And since he hadn't, it meant that he'd lost interest.

He was probably painting another woman right now. Telling her she had glorious hair as he sifted it through his long, supple fingers.

Telling her whatever was most likely to get her into bed.

She straightened up from the trunk she was packing, welcoming the flare of anger that had just flowed through her. Anger was what had kept her going for so many years. Without it, she didn't know what might.

She certainly didn't want to return to Stanton Basset looking as if she'd had all the stuffing knocked out of her, which is what she'd felt like after that final scene with Nathan.

Only she couldn't seem to get a solid grip on it. It was as if she didn't have the energy to sustain a decently solid bad temper.

She slumped on to a chair, looking at the belongings strewn across the room. They'd acquired so much stuff since arriving in Paris. It would be no use trying to travel home the way they'd come. It was a symptom of her state of mind that she hadn't raised even a token protest when Monsieur Le Brun decided to hire a wagon to carry all the trunks that contained both hers and Fenella's new wardrobes. And a second carriage to contain the maid he'd insisted on employing for Fenella. A French woman, naturally. He didn't consider English domestics worthy of a place serving his wife.

Amethyst picked up a scarf and absentmindedly rolled it into a ball. Far from being annoyed with Monsieur Le Brun for taking over all the arrangements that had at one time seemed so important, she'd been grateful. Left to herself, she wasn't sure she'd have managed to leave Paris at all. Because once she did, then it really was over.

A peremptory knock on the door heralded Monsieur Le Brun's entrance. He never waited for permission to enter a room these days. Since confessing that he was a French aristocrat, he'd dropped any pretence at servility.

'We must speak,' he said sternly. 'About my Fenella. And Miss Sophie.'

She sighed and waved to the chair opposite. As a gentleman, he had at least waited until she indicated he might sit, she would give him that much credit.

'What do you wish to say?'

'I know that you do not like me. That to start with you would have done all in your power to prevent me marrying her if you had not seen it would cause the rift of permanence between you. But I tell you this—' he leaned forwards, glaring at her '—if you had tried to keep us apart, or given me to lose my employ with you, I would have followed you both back to England and stolen her away in marriage.'

Oh, but that hurt. Here was this man, prepared to follow his lady love across the ocean—well, the English Channel at least—because Fenella was the kind of woman who deserved to find love. She was a good, kind-hearted creature. Not a cold unfeminine shrew without an ounce of trust in her nature. Fenella had trusted Gaston. Given him her heart along with her body. And this was her reward. This determined, dogged devotion.

If she'd been able to trust Nathan, he wouldn't have walked away from her. They might all be going back to England together and arranging a double wedding.

And so what if he was only after her for her money? Or trying to recapture a fleeting moment of their youth when they'd had hope and trust, and belief in goodness? Did that really matter? It wasn't just her money he liked. It wasn't the memory of a girl he'd talked to and danced with, and argued with and made love to, either. It was her, as she was now. He'd enjoyed every minute they'd spent together. She knew he had.

But she'd pushed him away. Once too often.

'I know,' continued Monsieur Le Brun belligerently, 'so you have no need to say it, that she deserves a better man than me. That I cannot provide for her in the way I would wish. But I have hope that one day the estate of my family will be restored and that then she will come to live with me here, in France, as my countess.'

A lump formed in her chest as she contrasted his determination to win Fenella against all obstacles, with Nathan's swift defection.

'And why, exactly,' she said, tossing the balled-up scarf into an open trunk, 'do you feel the need to tell me all this?'

He gripped the arms of the chair, his jaw working.

'She tells me that you plan to move to Southampton to be near her.'

'What of it?'

'Only this. I am a proud man, *mademoiselle*, as you are well aware. Fenella is to be my wife. Sophie will be my daughter. Mine is now the task of providing for them and ensuring their happiness. I give leave to inform you I shall not tolerate your interference in the way I run my household or permit you to do anything that will make either of them question where their loyalty must now lie.'

'I have no intention of *interfering*,' she replied coldly. 'But have you given any thought to how lonely Fenella is going to be while you are away, pursuing your dream of getting your château back? She will have nobody to support her. No family, no friends in that area. I didn't think you disliked me so much that you would seriously wish to deprive Fenella of the one friend she does have.'

His scowl deepened. 'This is what she has told me, too.' He thrust his bony fingers through his hair, then slapped his hand down on the chair arm. 'That only you stood by her in her darkest hour. For that, *mademoiselle*...' he swallowed, as if something painful lodged in his throat '...I have to thank you,' he bit out through gritted teeth. 'And I do not wish for her to be left lonely. But...'

Amethyst held up her hand. 'I don't like you any more than you like me. The only thing upon which we will ever agree is that Fenella deserves better of both of us. I propose, for her sake, that we come to some kind of...truce.'

'A truce?'

'Yes. I will agree to keep my distance when you are at home. But I will be purchasing a property near enough so that I can support Fenella while you are away.'

'That sounds reasonable. Though she will not like it, I think, if you never visit while I am home. She will want us to become friends...'

'Oh, I have thought of the perfect way to calm her fears on that score. And that is to offer you employment.'

'I beg your pardon?'

'Well, unless you have a burning desire to carry on working as a courier to English tourists, I had thought you might prefer a permanent position within George Holdings. As my French agent. There are bound to be outlets for my wares wherever in France you need to travel in pursuit of your quest, so you can fit in my business around your own agenda. It will surely be better for you if you don't have to dance attendance on demanding tourists all day long?'

'It would, but...'

'I know I haven't been an easy person to work for, but I've been most impressed by your tireless energy and efficiency, not to mention your patience. Besides, Fenella loves you…'

'I do not want you to give me work as a favour to my wife! We both know that I have had very little success in procuring for you the new outlets for your goods.'

'On the contrary, you managed to secure two contracts, under almost impossible conditions.' Whilst acting as tour guide, and sweeping Fenella off her feet. 'I propose paying you a small basic wage and meeting your expenses while you are travelling in France. Plus a percentage of any profits my companies make through your efforts.'

'You would really put me in a position of such trust?'

'Without hesitation. You have plenty of sterling qualities. Not least of which is your devotion to Fenella.'

'I…I suppose I could say the same of you,' he said grudgingly. Then his mouth twisted into a wry grimace. 'I think since I have seen what that pig of a man has done to you—both now and when you were just a girl— that you think you have cause to distrust men. And that is perhaps why you have treated me as though I am a worm. And also…you wish not to see your friend hurt, the way you have been hurt.'

'Who says I have been hurt?'

He shook his head reprovingly. '*Mademoiselle*, ever since he came here to give you the *congé*, you have been a shadow of yourself. You do not eat. You do not speak. And most telling of all, you do not assert your will over mine.'

It was all true. There didn't seem to be any point in

anything. It was as if a grey pall hung over her now, which she couldn't ever see lifting.

'Do not,' said Monsieur Le Brun in alarm, 'be so upset. I did not mean to make you weep. *Merde!*' He pulled out a handkerchief and thrust it at her. Only then did she realise that tears were streaming down her cheeks.

'It is not your fault,' she said through his handkerchief as she blew her nose.

'Fenella will never forgive me if she learns I have made you cry. Please cease.'

'I just told you, you have not made me cry. No man will make me cry. I won't let any of you,' she said defiantly, though tears still streamed down her cheeks.

'Now go away,' she said, burying her face in his handkerchief. 'And leave me…alone.'

Alone. As she would be now for the rest of her life.

She had travelled back to England in the second carriage with Sophie, her nurse, Francine, and the new French maid. She'd realised she would much rather hold the child's head over the bowl as she vomited than watch her former companion and courier makings sheep's eyes at each other all the way to Calais.

Both she and Monsieur Le Brun were on their best behaviour whenever Fenella was watching, though she couldn't resist taking one last swipe at his masculine pride by insisting on paying all the wedding expenses and then making it as lavish as she possibly could. She met the groom's objections by pointing out that Fenella had been robbed of a society wedding the first time round and she deserved the best.

There was more than a hint of retaliation in the way

he promptly invited a veritable crowd of remarkably well-connected people to both the church and the wedding breakfast, since most of them looked down their aristocratic noses at her. But she shrugged it off. She'd been mean to him, so...

Or perhaps it wasn't anything to do with her at all. Perhaps he really was responding to what she'd said about Fenella deserving a society wedding and was just doing his utmost to provide it?

Fenella had thoroughly enjoyed her day, which was the main thing. Though she was very tearful when it came time to part on the morning after.

'I hate to think of you going back to Stanton Basset all on your own,' she said.

'I do not plan to stay for very long. I will just see that my aunt's house is cleared for sale, or rent, and then come to join you. Not in your marital home, I hasten to add,' she put in when Monsieur Le Brun looked distinctly alarmed. 'But in some nearby hotel, while I view the properties on offer.'

'Still, I don't like the thought of you travelling all over the country by yourself,' persisted Fenella.

'I do not like it myself,' put in Monsieur Le Brun, to her surprise. 'You hired me to act as your courier from Stanton Basset to Paris and home. London is not your home.'

'If you think I can stomach the sight of you two fawning all over each other in a closed carriage for the next three days you are very much mistaken,' she retorted. 'And I am quite certain that the last thing you want is a former employer joining you on your bride trip.'

The newly married couple blushed.

'Besides, it is not as if I shall be travelling alone. I have employed a woman to act as escort and chaperon.'

Fenella and Monsieur Le Brun both glanced across the inn yard at the nondescript wisp of a woman Amethyst had hired from an agency not two days earlier.

'She doesn't look as if she will provide you with much company, though,' said Fenella with an anxious frown.

'Believe me, I shall not pine for conversation after that last trip with the two French maids jabbering away incessantly like a pair of magpies. Peace and quiet will suit me very well.'

'*Ma chère*, Mademoiselle Dalby has clearly made up her mind. Have you ever been able to sway her, once she has done so?'

With one arm round Fenella's waist, and Sophie's little hand clasped in his own, Monsieur Le Brun firmly ushered his new little family into the coach that stood waiting for them.

A swell of resentment surged through Amethyst as she boarded her own carriage. If it wasn't for him, they would all be going home together. She would still be smarting from losing Nathan, but at least she would have…

She shook her head, angry at herself. When had it ever done her any good relying on others? She was stronger than this.

She consoled herself, for the first few miles of her own journey, with visions of Monsieur Le Brun's discomfort, shut up with a child whose reaction to the bouncing and swaying of their coach was going to be inevitable. Served him right for breaking up her happy home!

Except…Fenella loved him. And if he felt anything

like she did about those two, he wouldn't be finding it a trial. Caring for each other was part of being a family.

Or it should be. It was what she'd always wanted, deep down. She knew herself so much better since being with Nathan. He'd let her express her opinions, rather than trying to form them, and the more she'd done so, the more she understood what she really thought and felt about everything.

And she'd seen that, all her life, she had just wanted to have somebody love her. It was what had made her strive so hard to please both her parents, and then her aunt.

And what had made her fall into Nathan's bed. It hadn't been just adventure she craved. It wasn't just about rebelling and proving that a woman could do anything a man could do. She'd wanted him to love her. Yet when he'd claimed he did, she hadn't been able to believe it. Why should he love her? Nobody else ever had. They'd made her believe there was something intrinsically unlovable about her. And so she'd pretended she didn't care. Hardened herself against hurt. Pushed people away before they had a chance to make so much as the slightest dent in her defences.

But it did hurt, knowing that Nathan didn't love her, any more than anyone else ever had.

She slumped into the squabs, that grey pall making the mere act of breathing feel like an effort.

England was such a damp and dreary place. People scuttled about, heads bowed into the drizzle, as though they were the nation that had just been defeated, rather than the French.

Or was it just the air of defeat hanging over Amethyst that made the rest of the world look so bleak?

The woman she'd hired from an agency to lend her respectability on the journey very soon gave up attempting to converse with her taciturn employer. And no doubt gave thanks, reflected Amethyst on one of the stops to change horses, that her employment was only temporary.

Amethyst gave her a generous tip when at last they reached their destination.

'I hope your return trip is more pleasant,' she said to the startled woman. 'It couldn't have been very comfortable for you, having to travel so far with an employer who had only roused from her depression to make acid remarks about the deficiencies of any stray male unfortunate enough to cross her path,' she said self-deprecatingly.

'I...I don't like men any more than you, madam,' said the woman, with just the hint of a sympathetic smile, before dropping a curtsy and scuttling off towards the town square and the coaching inn where she would rest overnight before taking the stage back to London the next morning. Amethyst half-wished she was going with her. She had to brace herself before walking up the path to Aunt Georgie's front door. After the glorious freedom she'd known on her travels, setting foot inside the house would be rather like putting on a stiffly starched collar. The minute she crossed the threshold, she got the urge to fling open all the windows. Only, since it was raining, all it would achieve would be to make her cold, as well as depressed.

'There is a fire in the morning room, Miss Dalby,' said her butler, a long-suffering individual she'd inherited from her aunt along with the house.

'Thank you, Adams,' she said, suddenly wondering why he'd borne the brunt of her aunt's displeasure for so many years. He wasn't paid much more than the average for his position. 'But I would rather take tea in the study.'

'Of course. I had the fire lit in there, too, thinking you might like to cast your eye over the correspondence awaiting you.'

'That was very thoughtful of you,' she said with real gratitude. 'Thank you.'

He dipped his head in a kind of truncated bow, swiftly, but not before Amethyst had caught a startled look on his face. Good grief, had she really been so lacking in manners towards the man that a mere 'thank you' could surprise him?

She went to the study while Adams made his stately way in the other direction to see to the tea things. There was quite a pile of correspondence piled up on her desk. Hours' worth of work.

She sighed and went to the window, which looked out over her garden. She hadn't come in here because she was keen to put her nose back to the grindstone. It was just that she'd made this room her own, since Aunt Georgie's death. She'd moved the desk so she could see out over the gardens by merely lifting her head. She'd had the walls painted a light, creamy colour, pretty new curtains hung and even put up some watercolours she'd purchased herself, whereas she hadn't got round to doing anything about the gloom that pervaded the morning room. And she'd got the strangest feeling that the room would disapprove of her jaunt to the Continent. That it would gloat at her, too. What good had it done her to go abroad? The solid, heavy furniture would imply. Or buying new clothes, and going dancing and taking a lover? She'd still ended up having to come back alone. More alone than before, since even Fenella had abandoned her. Fenella, the nearest thing to a friend she'd ever had.

And yet…all those ledgers lining the shelves and the correspondence stacked neatly on the desk reminded her that her life still had some purpose. Within those reports lay the livelihood of hundreds of workers. The decisions she made regarding them would affect the prosperity of swathes of Lancashire and the Midlands.

It was probably coincidence that at that moment the sun managed to break through the heavy pall of cloud hanging over the scenery, making the damp shrubbery glisten as though covered with hundreds of tiny jewels. At that exact same moment Amethyst saw a ray of light of her own.

Towards the end of her aunt's life she'd begun to liken her to a dragon, zealously guarding her hoard. She'd accumulated great piles of money simply for the sake of having it. But it had never made her happy. On the contrary, she'd grown increasingly fearful that someone would find out about it, then try to steal it from her, one way or another.

She turned round and stared at the piles of paperwork lying on her desk. She didn't need to follow blindly in Aunt Georgie's footsteps. She didn't need to carry on amassing more and more wealth, for its own sake. She might remain a spinster, secretly running a vast financial empire, but she could do it in her own way. She'd already made a start, she realised, by expanding into France, which would mean increasing output in the manufactories she had, rather than extracting as much profit from one, in order to raise capital to buy the next one, the way her aunt had. Which meant she could start looking after the workers a bit better. She could found schools for the workers' children and organise some kind of welfare fund for the sick, and—

Adams interrupted her train of thought by knocking on the door and informing her that she had a visitor.

'Already?'

'Mrs Podmore,' he said as though that explained it.

'Oh, dear lord,' she groaned, laying her forehead against the window.

'Shall I tell her you are too tired to receive anyone just yet,' ventured Adams, 'having so recently returned from such a long journey?'

'It is tempting, but, no.' She sighed. 'The wretched woman will only call back, again and again, until she's said whatever it is she wants to say. Or ambush me in the high street, or on the way back from church. So I may as well get it over with by taking the tea you were going to bring me, with her.'

If Adams was surprised to be on the receiving end of such a frank speech, he betrayed no sign of it. Merely nodded his head and offered to take the tray she'd been awaiting into the front parlour.

Into which she had not wanted to go, not just yet.

Two birds with one stone, Amethyst muttered to herself as she opened the door to the formal gloom of the parlour and walked in.

'My dear, is it true?'

Trust Mrs Podmore to ignore the convention of commencing a visit with polite enquiries after her health, and so on, and launch straight into the matter that really interested her.

'I heard that dreadful Mountsorrel woman has run off and left you. After all you have done for her. The ingrate!'

'How on earth has such a rumour managed to reach your ears?' Amethyst went to the chair opposite Mrs Podmore and reached for the teapot. 'I have only been back five minutes!'

'But she hasn't come back with you, has she? I had it from…the most impeccable source that it was quite another person who alighted from the carriage with you outside your doorstep earlier. A quite inferior-looking person—yes, thank you, I will have one of these cherry slices—who promptly got on the very next stage back to London. You simply must have your cook give me the receipt for my cook. Not that she will make them half so moist, I dare swear. She *will* leave everything baking until it's done to a crisp. But is it true?'

Though Amethyst was sorely tempted to say she could not possibly know if it was true that her cook burned everything to a crisp, she refrained. She knew exactly what Mrs Podmore wanted to find out.

Which was what had happened to Fenella.

'The rumour that Mrs Mountsorrel has run off? Absolutely not.'

'But she is not here, is she?' Mrs Podmore looked round the room as though she might spy Fenella lurking in some shadowy corner, the way she'd always done when one of the doyennes of Stanton Basset had come calling.

'Indeed not,' replied Amethyst calmly, adding a dash of milk to both their cups.

'Well, where is she, then? Not—' Mrs Podmore sat

forward, her eyes brightening '—not suffered some terrible accident, I hope?'

'Oh, no,' replied Amethyst, dashing Mrs Podmore's hopes. 'In fact, quite the reverse.'

'The reverse?'

Amethyst took a sip of tea, deliberately leaving her visitor trying to work out what could be the reverse of a terrible accident. Only when Mrs Podmore's face betrayed a state of complete bewilderment did she relent.

'She has remarried.'

'No!'

'Yes. The Comte de Quatre Terres de...' She wrinkled her brow in concentration. How irritating. The one time his titles might have come in useful, she could only recall a small part of one of them. 'Well, I forget quite where. A French count, anyway.'

'Well, I never.' Mrs Podmore set her cup down in its saucer with a snap. 'However did a person like *her* come to rub shoulders with a French count?'

'Oh, didn't you know?' She widened her eyes in mock surprise. 'Fenella is very well born.' Though she hadn't welcomed Mrs Podmore's visit, now the wretched woman was here, she might as well put her to good use. To set the record straight.

'She made a poor choice of husband the first time round, it is true. A man who left her destitute and estranged from her family. But she is *exactly* the kind of person who should be rubbing shoulders with a French count. Not that we knew he was anything of the sort when we met him. I...'

She'd been about to say she'd hired Monsieur Le Brun as their courier. But once Mrs Podmore knew of it, it would be all over Stanton Basset, and from there the county, and who knew where else, within days. And he hadn't wanted anyone to know about his mission. He'd taken her into his confidence. And she didn't, she realised, want to break faith with him. It would be… well, a perfectly horrid thing to do. He'd probably exaggerated the danger he might be in, should anyone know who he really was, but she couldn't contemplate exposing him to even the possibility of coming to harm. And it wasn't just because she couldn't bear to think of Fenella being widowed a second time. Especially not through something she'd said, or done.

It was for his own sake.

Good heavens. To cover her consternation at discovering she'd somehow started to care about offending a man she'd thought of for weeks as Monsieur le Prune, she took a defensively ladylike sip of tea.

'Well, it makes no difference,' said Mrs Podmore, bristling with annoyance. 'Even if she was high born, it wasn't her place to go taking up with some Frenchman while she was supposed to be working for you. Putting herself forwards, no doubt, with those airs and graces she had.'

Amethyst thanked providence that Mrs Podmore had lost interest in probing any further into the identity of the French count Fenella'd had the temerity to marry. And was revealing, at long last, just what had been at the root of the townswomen's malice. It sounded as though they'd resented her for behaving like the lady she truly was. Assumed she'd thought herself too good for the likes of them and decided to take her down a peg or two.

'I have never observed Mrs Mountsorrel *put herself forwards*,' she said icily. 'In fact, I think it was her very reticence that brought out all the protective instincts in…her new husband. And I am pleased for her. She deserves some happiness, don't you think, after all she has been through?'

Mrs Podmore pursed her lips and shifted in her chair. 'What I think,' she said, setting her teacup down with a snap, 'is that you are too liable to get the wool pulled over your eyes by people who are out to take advantage of you, that's what I think. I can't say I'm sorry she's gone. But what I am sorry for is what people will say about you now. Why, you had to come back here all on your own. Which is not the thing, you know, not the thing at all.'

'I hired a person from an agency in London for the journey home—'

'Well, we all know how unsatisfactory she must have been, or you wouldn't have sent her packing the moment you got here.'

'No, that wasn't why—'

'A woman in your position must have a decent female companion, as I am sure I have told you before.'

'Yes, you have,' admitted Amethyst drily. 'Many times.'

'Well, then, you must see that the sooner you engage a proper, unimpeachable chaperon, the better. Oh. I think I may know just the person.' She got to her feet. 'I must hurry, or I might miss her. I do apologise for making this visit so brief.'

There was no need for an apology. Amethyst couldn't believe how easily she'd got rid of her.

'But I am sure you are tired after your journey.'

Not that it had prevented her from calling in the first place.

'I can call again another time and fill you in with all the latest news of our little town. Not but what you will probably find it all terribly dull after the adventures you must have been having.'

Oh dear. Her lack of interest in whatever gossip Mrs Podmore wanted to share must have shown on her face. She really must take care to guard her expression better.

'No, no, dear, I insist. Though I must say,' she said tartly, 'that travelling doesn't seem to have agreed with you. You look positively wan. What you need now is a good wholesome English meal, followed by a good night's sleep in your own bed. That will soon bring the roses back to your cheeks.'

They were returning already. Mrs Podmore couldn't possibly have meant anything by that comment about sleeping in her own bed. It was only her conscience shrieking that everyone could tell she was a fallen woman now, just by looking at her.

Fortunately Mrs Podmore had already turned her back on Amethyst as she hurried to the door. Keen to get out and spread the news of Fenella's marriage to a French count, no doubt. And if that weren't enough of a coup for her, she'd also got the notion she was going to be able to interfere in some indigent female's life by obliging her to come and work for Amethyst as a companion. If she was in such a hurry to find her, the poor woman must be attempting to escape Stanton Basset at some point today.

She hoped she made it.

Though she wasn't sorry Mrs Podmore would be out and about disseminating the truth about Fenella. There had been enough unpleasant and unfounded gossip about Fenella doing the rounds of Stanton Basset.

At the mention of unfounded gossip her mind flew back, as it did so often since he'd told her, to the scurrilous rumour that Nathan had heard about her. About her having a child out of wedlock.

There had been something niggling at the back of her mind, something about those days, that she hadn't been able to put her finger on, until this moment, when she'd seen how keen Mrs Podmore was to spread her bit of gossip. Right after she'd kept her own mouth shut about Monsieur Le Brun, out of consideration for his feelings.

The kind of story that Nathan had heard about her was meat and drink to people like Mrs Podmore. If it had reached the ears of someone like that, people would have been twitching their skirts aside as she walked past.

But they hadn't. She'd had no idea what she was supposed to have been guilty of, until just a few days ago.

It meant that Nathan couldn't have repeated the story, not to anyone. Nor could his friend, Fielding.

But Nathan had been furious. He'd wanted to hurt her. He'd told her as much. So, why hadn't he taken the final step and destroyed her completely? He'd had the power to do it. All he would have had to do was repeat what he'd heard and, even though it wasn't true, the damage would have been done. People would always wonder. 'No smoke without fire.' How often had she heard that, in connection to rumours, particularly salacious ones?

What had made him hold back from taking that final step?

One answer came to her mind immediately. It was the conclusion her aunt would have leapt to. That he wouldn't have wanted anyone to know he'd been deceived by the kind of woman he'd thought she'd been. That it was all a matter of preserving his pride.

But from deep within rose another reason to account for his reticence. A reason that made just as much sense. That he'd done it to shield her from the punishment society would have meted out, had the story been made public. He hadn't wanted to be responsible for blackening her name and ruining her reputation.

'Aunt Georgie, I don't think all men are completely bad,' she said out loud. The room seemed to frown at her. Every item in it was deeply ingrained with memories of her aunt, that was the trouble, and every stick of furniture now reproved her for speaking such heresy.

Though she was trembling, she said it again.

'Men aren't necessarily bad, just because they're men. I think they make mistakes, and get hurt and lash out, just the same as we do. And some of them,' her voice dropped to a whisper, 'some of them…might even be *good.*'

Chapter Fourteen

The sooner she left this place and rejoined Fenella and her family in Southampton, the better.

When he'd come in to collect the tea tray, Adams had interrupted her informing her aunt's chair that she thought Fenella was jolly lucky to have found a man like Monsieur-le-Compte-de-Somewhere-Brown. 'Fenella brought nothing to the marriage but a whole pile of obligations,' she'd been insisting. 'But not only did he not seem to mind, he'd actually fought for her. And Sophie, too. You should have seen his face the first time she called him *Papa*. He loves that little girl. He really does.'

Adams had looked round the room, as though searching for whomever she'd been talking to, though he must have known Mrs Podmore had left, or he wouldn't have come in to clear away.

He'd probably come to the conclusion that she was well on the way to becoming as odd as her aunt had been, walking round the room haranguing the furniture.

No, she sighed, her aunt's house was not a healthy

place for her to live. She'd already begun to talk to herself. What next would she do?

Well, it wouldn't come to that. She walked briskly back to her study, drew out a fresh sheet of paper, trimmed her pen and set the process of the move in motion.

There had been many decisions to make. What to sell? What to put away in storage? What to take with her? And how was she going to implement her plan to improve the lot of her workforce from Southampton? Without anyone knowing that she was the one doing it? Practical issues such as these had kept her fully occupied for the next couple of days. During the hours of daylight, at least. But at night, as she had lain in bed, she could not ignore the creeping sense of loneliness and failure that only frenetic activity could keep at bay.

By the end of the week she'd begun to suspect Adams was developing a sort of fatherly concern for her. Or perhaps *fatherly* was not the right word, she grimaced as she tied up the ribbons of her Sunday bonnet. Her father had never shown *concern* when she'd been downcast. He'd always berated her for not displaying proper Christian gratitude, for not always giving thanks in everything. He'd never brought her tea and biscuits at regular intervals, which Adams now did if she lost track of time whilst working her way through the backlog of reports stacked on her desk. Or looked at her with such grave concern when she sat staring into space during meal times, forgetting to keep on raising the fork to her mouth, then nudged a favourite dish towards her, suggesting that cook would be disappointed if she didn't at least try it.

'Adams,' she said as she tugged on her gloves, 'I've come to a decision. I shall be leaving Stanton Basset as soon as I possibly can. But I wondered if you would like to carry on working for me.'

He opened the door for her without betraying any emotion whatever.

'It will be a bigger house, more responsibility, better wages,' she said as she preceded him out of the house.

'And to where, may I ask, are you planning to move?'

Did he have good reason for wanting to stay in the area? She frowned. She had never wondered about his private life before. Or considered he had a right to one. He'd always just been there. A servant. Not a real person.

She'd slipped into the habit of treating him exactly the same as her aunt had always done.

Well, those days were over.

'Somewhere near Southampton. To be close to Fenella.'

'And Miss Sophie,' said Adams, his face softening in what looked like sympathy.

'Yes. Of course, I will understand if you have…ties to this place and do not wish to move away. But I shall be sorry.'

He gave her a nod as he opened the garden gate for her. 'I shall give the matter serious consideration,' was all he would say.

Well, it was a big decision for anyone to make. He'd been here ever since she could remember. And not everyone liked change. Particularly not when they got to his age.

'If you don't come with me and would rather retire,' she said, 'I will make sure you have a decent pension.'

'That is…generous of you,' he acknowledged. 'I had hoped, when your aunt passed, that she might have…' He trailed away. But he had no need to elaborate. Her aunt had not left any of the servants anything.

She shook her head at the slavish way she'd moulded her behaviour to please her aunt. More evidence of her desperate need for approval, she sighed. Well, it had to stop. She wasn't going to live to please anyone else, ever again. She would live by her own beliefs, act according to her own principles and stand on her own two feet.

Her own two feet carried her all the way to church without her mind having to direct their way. They carried her to the pew where she'd always sat without her having to think about that either.

The service commenced. She got to her feet, then dropped to her knees in all the appropriate places, but she was only going through the motions.

Because she couldn't get over the fact that she'd been such a fool. She'd lost Nathan because she'd listened to her aunt's warped views, rather than her own heart.

She'd been happy, in Paris, with him, she sighed. He'd helped her to unfurl, like a tightly defensive blossom in the warmth of spring sunshine. He hadn't tried to dominate her, or change her. He'd just made her feel… first beautiful, then intelligent, and then as though she had an interesting personality. Oh, why hadn't she remembered any of that when he'd said he loved her? Why hadn't she been brave enough to take that leap of faith? Why had she listened to the nasty, suspicious voice in her head telling her he was only interested in her wealth?

She screwed her eyes shut as she repressed a groan.

The whole point of travelling to Paris in the first place had been an attempt to...to break free. Hiring Fenella had been her first act of independence and defying her father over the will had been her second.

It was harder to break free from patterns of thought, she realised, than outward behaviour. She could leave Stanton Basset, buy fine clothes and even take a lover. But inside she was still the bewildered child who'd been denied unquestioning love so often that she'd grown the equivalent of a hedge of thorns round her heart.

She sank on to the pew, shutting her hymn book with a chill certainty. She was going to shrivel up and die alone because there would never be, had never been, any other man for her but Nathan.

Even now she knew the very worst of him, it made no difference. As soon as she'd calmed down and had time to reflect, she could see exactly why he'd done every bad thing he'd done. He'd tried, for years, to please his exacting father and then to maintain his honour whilst chained to a woman who despised him. Until he'd got to breaking point and lashed out in rage and pain. Just as she'd done when her own father had demonstrated his lack of faith in her.

But when he'd come to make a clean breast of it, to ask if they could make a fresh start, instead of reaching out to grasp at the chance of happiness, she'd scuttled back behind her hedge of thorns. Which no man could penetrate, without risking getting cut to ribbons.

There wasn't a man alive who could possibly love her enough to do it.

The congregation was stirring, moving towards the door. She could scarcely believe that the service was over without her having taken in one word of it. But everyone else was already streaming out into the church-yard where they would mill about and gossip for at least half an hour.

She fumbled in her reticule for a handkerchief to blow her nose as tears stung her eyes. How on earth was she going to be able to endure the collective inquisition the citizens of Stanton Basset were bound to subject her to, when she was so raw she felt as though someone had been scouring her insides with a scrubbing brush?

The same way she always had, she supposed. With a series of terse, cutting words that would make them all retreat lest she turn the rapier sharpness of her tongue in their direction.

Oh, God—she *deserved* to end up alone!

'My dear Miss Dalby, do excuse me, but there is someone I would love you to meet.'

All but thick-skinned Mrs Podmore, she sighed. Her unshakeable belief in herself rendered her impervious to even Amethyst's barbs.

She stuffed her handkerchief back in her reticule and prepared herself to meet the poor woman Mrs Podmore had no doubt cajoled and bullied into applying for the post of her companion. She didn't want to frighten the poor creature by unleashing her own pain in a display of venom.

Besides, it was herself she was cross with. If she'd had her wits about her she would have been first out of the door and marched straight down the path for home before anyone could waylay her. But it was too late now. She was well and truly trapped, with only her-self to blame.

'I did not have time to tell you our most interesting news,' panted Mrs Podmore, 'when I visited you the other day. But now I should like to introduce you to the newest resident of Stanton Basset.' She stepped aside and waved her hand to summon the person who'd been hovering behind her, rather in the manner of a conjuror producing coins from thin air.

'Allow me to present Mr Brown,' she said, as Nathan stepped forwards.

Nathan? Here in Stanton Basset? Amethyst could not have been more stunned if Mrs Podmore had conjured up a unicorn from behind her velvet-and-bombazine bulk. She was glad she was still seated or her legs might have given way.

'I am pleased to meet you, Miss Dalby,' said Nathan suavely. 'I have heard so much about you.'

'Mr...Brown?' She gazed at him in bewilderment. And excitement that warred with trepidation.

'Mr Brown is an artist,' said Mrs Podmore, completely oblivious, as usual, to the effect she was creating in her current victim's breast. She was far more interested in having just trumped Amethyst's foreign count, who nobody would ever see, with a genuine, visible, novelty. 'He declares he has fallen in love with the charm of the place and intends to make a stay of some months, capturing it all on canvas.'

'An artist,' said Amethyst weakly. So he wasn't trying to conceal everything about himself.

'Oh, you need not be alarmed. Mr Brown is quite the gentleman. He has taken a lease on old Murdoch's place.'

'Indeed?'

Amethyst's brain finally emerged from the state of shock that seeing Nathan standing in the aisle of St Gregory's had induced, and started coming up with questions. Why had he hired such a massive old mausoleum? How had he been able to afford it? And why was he going by the name of Brown?

And, more importantly, why was he here?

Her heart skipped a beat. Monsieur Le Brun had declared that he would have followed Fenella to England, to continue courting her. Was this what Nathan was doing?

Or was she clutching at straws?

'How…how long have you been here?' It was the one question she could safely ask. The kind of thing one stranger might say to another upon their first introduction. For if he was going by the name of Brown, and getting Mrs Podmore to introduce him to her, then he clearly didn't want anyone to guess they already knew each other.

'Almost a month, now,' said Nathan.

A month? That meant he must have left Paris almost immediately after she'd turned down his proposal. No wonder he hadn't called on her. He'd been on his way here.

But why? Not that she could ask him that, not here.

Nor could she sit staring at him like this. It wasn't seemly.

'If you will excuse me,' she said, getting to her feet. 'I really must be getting home.'

'Perhaps you will do me the honour of permitting me to call on you some time,' said Nathan. And then, with a swift sideways glance at Mrs Podmore, continued, 'You have a very interesting face. I should like to paint you.'

'And I have told him that if anyone in this town is likely to be able to afford such an extravagance, it is you, Miss Dalby. From what I hear,' said Mrs Podmore with a twitch of her brows.

Her stomach roiled in reaction. The whole town had buzzed with the tale of her father fighting the lawyer over her inheritance. And though nobody knew for sure how much was at stake, they'd definitely overheard him prophesying she'd fritter her entire fortune away within a twelvemonth and have to crawl back to him for forgiveness. Because he'd done so in the voice he normally employed for booming hellfire sermons from the pulpit.

'And I am sure you will agree that we should do what we can to support burgeoning talent, the kind that Mr Brown possesses.' Mrs Podmore leaned forwards and confided, 'He is a most interesting addition to our town, my dear. Quite the gentleman. Much more preferable as a tenant of the Murdoch place than some we might be unfortunate enough to get.'

'Yes, yes, of course,' she said, making for the door as fast as she could.

She didn't feel as if she could breathe properly, even once she'd got outside. She wasn't going to let Mrs Podmore's assumptions spoil whatever chance there might be with Nathan. He couldn't have known about her wealth before he'd come here. He'd come here because he'd meant what he said.

He had.

And anyway, even if he had since found out about her money, hadn't she already decided she didn't care? If Nathan had come here to try to win her, then she wasn't going to let any consideration keep them apart. She'd just spent the most miserable weeks of her life berating herself for not accepting any of his proposals. She most certainly wasn't going to turn down any more.

If he'd really come here to propose again.

Yet why else would he be here, if not to offer for her hand again?

A cold, suspicious voice, that sounded very much like her aunt, whispered, *He could be planning to black-mail you.*

She bowed her head into the sleet, which had started some time during the service, and marched doggedly on, though every breath she took made her chest ache, it had gone so cold.

No—she wasn't going to believe Nathan would do such a thing. Why, he'd had her portrait, which he could have used to attempt to coerce her into marriage, or even blackmail her for money, but he hadn't. He'd just handed it over without making any demands at all.

He'd had the chance to blacken her name ten years ago, too, and hadn't taken it. He was too decent.

Nathan Harcourt? The man whose career was punc-tuated by scandal and failure?

Yes, him. He was a decent man. Deep down, where it mattered. He'd had good reasons for acting so badly. He'd been devastated by the lies they'd told him. He'd drifted into a career he hadn't wanted and a marriage that had been like a prison. No wonder he'd broken free the only way he could.

You're making excuses for him.

Perhaps she was. And perhaps that made her a fool-ish, lovestruck woman.

But she didn't care. She was done with assuming the worst of everyone.

She would wait until he'd called, before deciding anything. Hear what he had to say, and then...

Then what?

She didn't know, God help her. She'd just spent the week deciding how she was going to cope without him. Made all sorts of resolutions about striking out in a new direction.

If he really was here to make her another offer, she would gladly toss every single one of her plans out of the window.

And if he wasn't…

If he wasn't, then she'd just have to deal with it.

She barely slept a wink that night.

And it took her an age to dress the following morning. She'd never found her choice of clothing so important before. Pride wouldn't let her wear something that would make her look too eager, just in case he *hadn't* come here to propose again. But she didn't want to dress so soberly that he would take one look at her and think she was going to turn him down, again, either.

In the end, she donned the gown she'd bought for Fenella's wedding. Since he had never seen her in it, it wouldn't have any associations which might put ideas into his head. And it was both suitable for the current weather, being made of fine merino wool, and having long sleeves, yet pretty enough, with its scalloped hem and embroidered detail round the neckline, to make her seem approachable. She hoped.

She had barely nibbled on her toast at the breakfast table, yet she'd managed to bite her nails to the quick by the time Adams came to her study—where she'd been pacing up and down rather than making even a token pretence at shuffling papers round her desk—to inform her that she had a visitor.

'A gentleman,' he said, with a slight inflection on the word which suggested he very much doubted it. 'He claims to have made an appointment. And says his name is Mr Brown.'

How perceptive Adams was. No wonder her aunt had kept him on when she could have saved a fortune by hiring a female as housekeeper to do more or less the same job.

'You are correct upon all counts,' she said, causing one of his eyebrows to quirk, just a fraction. 'He was introduced to me, at church yesterday, as Mr Brown and I did agree to see him.'

The eyebrow rose just a fraction more.

'And, no, I do not think he is a gentleman either.'

His face returned to its proper state of butlerish blandness.

'Shall I bring refreshments to the morning room? I took the liberty of showing him in there, rather than leaving him cluttering up the hall.'

In spite of her nerves, Amethyst couldn't help smiling at this restrained display of humour.

'Yes, please,' she said. 'Tea would be most welcome.'

Her mouth had gone very dry. And going through all the ceremony of pouring and serving would at least give her something to do if the interview didn't go the way she hoped.

'Tea. Of course, miss. He looks just the sort of man,' said Adams with a perfectly straight face, 'to enjoy drinking tea in the middle of the day.'

And with that last caustic comment upon the character of a man who had come calling upon a single lady when everyone knew she didn't have a chaperon, he bowed himself out of the room.

And then, since there was no mirror in the study she hastily checked her fractured reflection in the multiple panes of the glass-fronted bookshelves, one last time, before going to meet Nathan. Although she'd checked it every few turns of the room, so knew exactly what she looked like. It was just that it was hard to credit she looked so neat and tidy when inside she felt as though she was coming unravelled.

He'd dressed with great care too, she noted the moment she entered the morning room, in immaculate breeches and topcoat, his pristine neckcloth foaming from a damask silk waistcoat. He truly was a sight for sore eyes.

He got to his feet and took a step towards her, then stopped, as though unsure of his welcome.

She smiled, or at least tried to. She was so nervous that it felt a little wobbly and yet tight at the same time.

'Please, won't you sit down?' she said, waving to the seat on the other side of the fireplace as she took her aunt's chair.

Some of the stiffness left his face at her tentative gesture of welcome.

'I wasn't sure if you would even let me in,' he said, resting his arms on the arm of the chair and leaning forwards.

'I shouldn't have done,' she replied. 'It is not the thing to receive a single gentleman when I am without a chaperon. The whole town will be scandalised.'

A frown flickered across his face.

'The last thing I want to do is plunge you into a scandal. That is why I decided it would be better if I got here well before you came back, so it wouldn't look as if there was already anything between us. You made it so obvious that my notoriety would be an issue, here in this little town, that I have done all I can to prevent anyone knowing exactly who, and what, I am.'

Oh. That made perfect sense.

And was incredibly sweet of him.

'That is why you are using an assumed name?'

'Of course. You made it so clear you weren't interested in marrying a man of my notoriety, that I was sure you wouldn't want anyone knowing you'd had a liaison with the notorious Nathan Harcourt. So I took a leaf out of your courier's book. He successfully managed to court your companion under the name of Brown. I hoped it might be as lucky for me.'

'C-courting?' Her breath hitched in her throat. He'd come all this way to court her. In spite of the way they'd parted, her conviction she'd driven him away for good. He must have meant every one of those proposals which she'd discounted, for varying reasons.

'Yes. Courting.' He gave a wry smile. 'And I'd better warn you that I've spent my time in this town learning as much as I could about you—surreptitiously, of course—in the hopes that I might find a chink in your armour.'

'B-but you love Paris. You were so happy there...'

'It would have been a wasteland without you in it. Don't you realise, yet, that I cannot be happy anywhere, unless you are with me?'

He did love her, then. Enough to abandon the work he loved and the home he'd made for himself. Assume a false identity and put up with Mrs Podmore taking him under her wing.

Nobody had ever exerted themselves to such an extent on her account.

'Y-yes. Actually, I think I do,' she admitted shyly. 'Because I have been utterly miserable since our last meeting. I was such an idiot to drive you away.' Tears sprang to her eyes. 'I was so scared I'd driven you away for good.'

He left his chair to kneel at her feet. He seized her hands.

'Does this mean what I hope it means? I've been telling myself that once your temper had cooled and you could think things over rationally, you would be able to forgive me. And give me another chance.'

'I will give you as many chances as you want, so long as you are able to forgive me for being so...' She screwed up her face in disgust as she thought of how narrow-minded and judgemental she'd been. 'For being such a...'

He placed one finger over her lips.

'I've no right to condemn you for anything you've done, or thought. Not with my record.'

He tugged at her hands and drew her to her feet.

'Miss Dalby, once and for all, will you forget all the past mistakes we've both made and marry me?'

'Oh, yes.' She sighed. And then, because her legs went limp, she leaned forwards, rested her head on his chest and said, 'Yes, please.'

'Thank God,' he muttered fervently, putting both arms round her and hugging her tight.

And it felt like coming home. No, better than any home she'd ever known. He was the only person who'd ever accepted her, liked her, loved her, just as she was. Everyone else had tried to change her. Sway her opinions to match their own. But not Nathan.

And then just hugging him wasn't enough. Amethyst

raised her face hopefully and he obliged her by meeting her halfway in a kiss. A kiss that went on and on, as though they both needed to drink the other in.

It was only Adams, scuffling against the door as he prepared to bring in the tea tray, that made them break apart, smiling ruefully.

By the time he placed the tray on the table, they were both seated in the chairs that flanked the fireplace, looking perfectly respectable, if a little flushed and breathless.

Adams glanced from one to the other. His face went more wooden than usual and, without a word, he made a swift exit.

Amethyst's hand was shaking too much to pour the tea.

'Never mind that,' said Nathan with a smile. 'It wasn't to drink tea that I came here today. I had this great long speech planned.'

She darted him a shy smile. 'Should I apologise for stopping you making it?'

He grinned back at her. 'Not in the least. It was just… well, I have a few things I do need to tell you, before I make an honest woman of you. I'd thought I would need to prove to you that I could at least appear respectable if I stood a chance of persuading you that I was husband material, rather than only being good enough for a temporary liaison…'

A pang of guilt shot through her. Had she really made him feel like that? It was so typical of the way she'd been—never giving a thought to what her actions might make other people feel like.

'Which is one reason why I hired the biggest house I could find to rent in this area. Which, coincidentally, happens to be the nearest one to yours. I wanted to demonstrate, you see, that I have the means to support you. I realised, in Paris, that I might have given you the impression that I haven't a feather to fly with—'

'Oh, that doesn't matter one bit, Nathan, you see—'

'Please, hear me out. I need to explain why I was living the way I was when you found me. I was doing it to prove a point. I wanted to demonstrate that I was good enough to make a living from my work alone. And I did. But I have independent means, as well. I can keep you in tolerable comfort, Amy. You don't need to fear that we'll ever have to worry about where the rent will come from.'

'No, we won't. Because I have money, too. Quite a lot of it, actually. Which was one of the reasons I was so suspicious of all the proposals you made to me before. I thought you must have found out about it somehow and was trying to…'

His face froze. 'Yes? Trying to what?'

'I'm so very, very sorry. I know it was nothing of the sort, now. It is just that my aunt, the one who took me in and left me this house, would keep on about how important it was to keep the extent of our fortune a secret, or we'd become targets for fortune hunters. I was convinced that no man would ever show an interest in me unless it was because he wanted to get his hands on my money. It became second nature to me to conceal the fact that I'm a wealthy woman.'

'A wealthy woman.' He frowned. 'Exactly how large is this fortune?'

She cleared her throat and then, in a matter-of-fact tone, told him exactly how large, and in what it consisted, and that moreover she had plans to expand into France now trading there was legal again.

By the time she had finished he was looking at her as though she'd become a total stranger.

'So you are not some simple country girl, eking out your existence on a modest little windfall from the spinster aunt you cared for in her last days. And what of Mrs Mountsorrel? Was she really just a widowed friend with whom you threw in your lot?' He flung the words at her as though he was accusing her of something.

Amethyst shook her head. 'I hired her as my companion so that I could continue living in this house and run the business interests my aunt had taught me how to govern. Nathan, why are you looking at me like that?'

'Can you not imagine?'

She shook her head again, her insides turning into a cold, solid lump as his gaze turned downright scornful.

'I thought I knew you. I thought that in spite of the hard veneer you'd acquired, deep down you were still that girl who so enchanted me with her simple, direct approach to life. But you're not her at all, are you?'

'Yes, I am. Just because I'm rich, too—'

He got to his feet, his eyes suddenly blazing with contempt. 'It's not just being rich that is the problem though, is it? You run businesses. You own factories and mills and mines and God knows what else. And you sit here, in this stuffy little town, hidden away like some…spider, spinning a web. Aye, an invisible web, at that. For nobody is supposed to know that it is a woman at the heart of all this enterprise. I never saw it before, but the whole purpose is to make fools of men, isn't it? You delight in making fools of us all. Well, you've certainly made a fool of me.'

'No, I haven't. Truly I haven't. I've explained why I didn't want you to know about it, at first.'

'Not just at first. Even after we'd become lovers. Even when you spurned me, you never admitted the true reason. And it is what you thought, isn't it? That I'm some contemptible fortune hunter. Little things you said to me, your attitude whenever I touched on making our relationship permanent, they should have warned me.'

'Yes, but—'

'Do you think I could want to marry a woman for her money, again? After what I went through last time? Do you know what it does to a man's pride to be labelled a fortune hunter?'

She hadn't. But she was beginning to get an idea.

'The last thing I want is to get leg-shackled to another woman who sees nothing wrong with telling lies to get what she wants. Who has so little integrity she has to buy friends and can only keep them with promise of advancement.'

What?

'Nathan, you don't mean that,' she managed to gasp through the fingers of dread that were squeezing her throat. 'I wasn't lying to you…' His face shuttered.

'Not exactly…'

With a muttered oath he turned and strode for the door.

'You were right all along,' he said coldly, as he set his hand to the door latch. 'We can't go back. We aren't the same people we were when we first met. I…' His face twisted. 'I thought I'd fallen in love with you, all over again, in Paris. I thought you'd got over the pain I put you through and had grown into a strong, admirable woman. A woman I would have been proud to call my wife, and bear my children. I thought…'

He closed his eyes, and shook his head.

'I might have known it was too good to be true. It wasn't real, was it? None of it was real. I've been chasing after a dream. Like some…'

He straightened up and opened his eyes. Eyes which had gone dead and hard.

'Forgive me for taking up your valuable time. I will leave you now. And will not bother you again.'

'Nathan…' She tried to tell him to stop, but her words got tangled up in a sob. She slumped down on to her chair, all strength gone from her legs, as she heard the front door slam behind him.

Oh, why hadn't she said yes, when she had the chance? If she'd said yes to him in Paris, and then explained about her money, he wouldn't have flown into a rage like this, would he?

Would he?

Chapter Fifteen

Shock had taken her legs out from under her. She could no more have run after Nathan and begged him not to go than she could have flown to the moon.

One minute she'd thought all her dreams had come true. Next moment she'd descended into a hellish nightmare. She'd thought Nathan loved her just as she was, but then he'd said he'd never really known her. That he couldn't marry her. That they weren't the same people who'd fallen in love with each other in their youth.

Was he right? Was it too late?

She shut her eyes and bowed her head.

Had they only imagined they'd fallen in love again, in Paris, because they'd both been pretending to be something they were not?

No…no! It was real. She'd had all these long, lonely weeks to ponder it all and she knew it was real. Nathan hadn't had time to think it through, that was all. She dashed a tear from her eye. He'd lashed out—the way she'd done when he'd shocked her with that confession about why they'd broken up the first time.

She leapt to her feet. He'd come after her when she'd

lost her temper with him. When her habit of being suspicious had made her afraid to believe in their love. Now it was her turn to go after him and talk some sense into him.

She was halfway across the room to ring for a maid to fetch her coat and bonnet, when she decided she hadn't the patience to wait that long. Far quicker to run upstairs and plunge her arms into her coat herself. Stuff her bonnet on her head as she hurried down the stairs and tie the ribbons as she trotted down the garden path.

She was in such a hurry to catch Nathan and tell him that he was wrong that she didn't see Mrs Podmore coming up the front path until she almost barrelled into her.

'Oh, good. I have just caught you,' said Mrs Podmore, tilting her umbrella to one side to make room for Amethyst. 'I can see you are in a hurry, but this won't take a moment—'

'I'm so sorry, but I haven't time to stop and talk today.'

She tried to step round Mrs Podmore, but the path was narrow, and her visitor determined.

'Wherever you are going, it cannot be so urgent that you have forgotten your umbrella.'

'It is that urgent,' she countered. 'And I hadn't even noticed it was snowing.' Only tiny specks of it, but the first real snow of the winter, nevertheless.

As she looked up in wonder, she had a brilliant idea. She stopped trying to sidestep Mrs Podmore's substantial bulk and looked her straight in the face with what she hoped was a confiding air.

'You see, everything you have ever warned me about has come to pass.'

'Oh?' For once Mrs Podmore didn't seen to know what to say.

'You have been right to warn me, so many times, just how dangerous it is to be without adequate chaperonage.'

'Was I? I mean, of course I was. But—'

'Yes. You see, while Fenella was preoccupied with her own courtship, and there was nobody to make me behave…' she lowered her voice '…I did something quite scandalous.'

Mrs Podmore instinctively leaned closer to hear the whispered confidence, her eyes wide with curiosity.

'I went to Mr Brown's studio, the one he had in Paris, quite alone, to have my portrait painted.'

'No!' Her eyebrows shot up and disappeared into the ruffles under her bonnet.

'Oh, yes. We were alone in his studio for hours at a time. And worse, he persuaded me to pose for him… naked.'

'Naked?' Mrs Podmore screeched the word, her shock temporarily robbing her of discretion. The baker's boy, who'd been walking past, jumped and dropped his tray of rolls, which went tumbling all over the street.

'And, of course, you must know what inevitably followed.'

Mrs Podmore's eyes grew rounder still. Amethyst could see her mind racing.

'I cannot bring myself to say what I fear you are alluding to.'

'Well, I can,' said Amethyst cheerfully. 'We embarked upon a wildly passionate affair.'

'A what?'

The baker's boy's head popped up over the hedge, his eyes wide with glee.

'And now he's pursued me all the way to England. Don't you think that's romantic?' She pressed one hand to her chest. 'I do.' She sighed theatrically. 'And so I've decided to run off with him.'

'Run off with Mr Brown?'

If he'd have her. And if not, she already had plans to move to Southampton, so nobody would know any different when she disappeared.

'Yes. I enjoyed travelling so much that I can't wait to set off again. We might return to Paris, where we were so happy. Or we might go and see what Italy is like. He's always wanted to go to Italy. And,' she put in before Mrs Podmore could accuse Nathan of latching on to her because of her money, 'I can afford to take him there.'

'No! You must not. Only think what people will say...'

That was exactly what she was doing. Between her and the baker's boy, the news would be all over town within minutes.

'I don't care what anyone says,' she declared. 'I cannot live without him.'

She beamed at Mrs Podmore, who was opening and closing her mouth like a landed trout.

'Good day,' said Amethyst and managed to nip past Mrs Podmore while she was trying to untangle her umbrella from the overhanging branches of her cherry trees. Past the gaping baker's boy, who'd abandoned any pretence at retrieving the spoiled rolls. Up the hill and through the market square she sincerely hoped she'd never have to set eyes on again, before much longer, and along the lane that led to the Murdoch place.

It wasn't long before she caught sight of Nathan in the lane ahead of her, because he was walking really slowly, his head bowed. Impervious to the snow, which was settling on his shoulders and the crown of his hat.

Hope surged. He couldn't look so sad if he didn't still love her. Didn't regret having left her the way he had.

'I have just one thing to say,' she said as he reached his front door.

He spun round. For a moment she caught a glimpse of the carefree young man who'd argued with her about the Rights of Man over a bottle of beer in a Parisian dance hall. But then his face changed. And the cynical, embittered, disgraced politician stood in his place.

'I have nothing further to say to you, madam,' he said coldly.

'Well, you can just listen then,' she said, pushing past him into the house as an unsuspecting butler opened the door.

'I have had longer to think about...us. Knowing all about the discrepancy in our wealth. And do you know what I have realised?'

'You clearly mean to tell me,' he said wearily. 'You had better come in here.' He pushed open the door to a sparsely furnished parlour and ushered her in.

'Well, let's start with why I've been afraid, for so many years, that no man could ever love me.'

He flinched and walked away from her to stare out of the window.

'Exactly. You hurt me so badly that I lost my ability to trust men. Well, actually, it wasn't all your fault.

My father's attitude played a large part in it, too. And then my aunt fostered that suspicion. Because she really, really hated men. She said I'd had a lucky escape anyway, because marriage was nothing but a trap for women. A cage in which some despotic male would lock her. I could understand why she thought like that, but I never wanted to end up like her. She was so…so miserable! She had so much money, but it never did her any good. It didn't make her happy. It didn't compensate for whatever it was that had set her off on her quest for revenge on the entire male sex.

'When she died, I almost slid into the trap of becoming like her. Partly because I had to fight the men around me to hang on to what she'd left me. And I enjoyed winning. I won't deny that I liked it a lot. I liked seeing bullies having to back down, rendering them powerless and sending them away with a flea in their ear.

'But it wasn't enough. It wasn't enough to sit here like—well, you said it—like a spider in my web, holding all the threads together. I didn't want to shrivel up inside, like she had, just because things hadn't turned out the way I wanted.

'Which was why I went to Paris in the first place. I needed to…break out. Find out what I wanted to do with my life. And then I met you.'

She walked across the room to stand behind him. Tentatively she placed one hand on his shoulder.

'I thought you were a penniless artist. And believing that of you was what gave me the courage to take you as a lover. If I'd known you were still comfortably off and only taking a sort of…holiday, I would never have been able to open up to you the way I did. Your privileged background had come between us before. It would have felt like an unbreachable barrier if you'd been swanning about Paris, trading on your right to be treated with the deference due to the son of an English earl. When you started making advances I would have been afraid you were only toying with me, the way I believed you'd toyed with me in the past.'

He made a sort of growling noise and, though he didn't turn round, she could see his cheeks flush. He might accuse her of lying, but he hadn't been completely honest with her either.

'And you wouldn't have pursued me at all, had you known the extent of my wealth, would you?'

'I thought I'd just made that perfectly clear.'

'It wasn't just my wealth that would have kept you away, Nathan. You didn't know I was a virgin, either. You jumped to the conclusion that because I was with a man, I must be his mistress. You most definitely wouldn't have got so jealous of poor Monsieur Le Brun if you'd known I was innocent of everything they told you about me. I suppose you might have still wanted to paint my portrait, perhaps as a memento of the girl you once loved, before I broke your heart and shattered your dreams, but not the rest.'

'I—'

'No, Nathan. Don't you see? If we hadn't both been trying to conceal some aspect of our lives, we would never have got together at all. There were too many obstacles. Too much hurt and suspicion on both sides. The way we got together was the *only* way it could have happened.'

'But—'

'But none of the things that would have kept us apart

mattered one jot when we became lovers, Nathan, and don't you dare try to say they did! We were just a man and a woman, rekindling a love we'd both mourned as lost. And it was a deeper, more meaningful love than the naïve, tentative relationship we started the first time round. Because we were both free to spend every moment with each other, untramelled by chaperons, or restrictions imposed by class. You cannot give up on it, just because you've found out I'm wealthy. It's…stupid. And I know exactly how stupid because I did it first. I rebuffed you in just such a welter of suspicion that you are suffering from now. And I've spent the last few weeks working out that I'd been wrong to cast you as the villain of the tragedy I endured as a girl. You were as much a victim as I was.'

'That was then,' he growled. 'This is different,' he said harshly, spinning round so abruptly that it knocked her hand from his shoulder.

'No, it isn't,' she said firmly. 'We fell in love with each other in Paris and that hasn't gone away. It cannot. Ten years and gallons of suspicion weren't able to drown it. The moment we set eyes on each other again, neither of us could rest until we'd come together, in the fullest sense possible.'

'It is no use, though,' he said. 'It cannot work.'

'Of course it can work. It worked in Paris, didn't it? So we can make it work again. If I can forgive you for believing the worst of me, if I can believe that you never proposed to me because you secretly wanted to gain control of my money, if I can stop fearing the loss of my independence, then surely you can see that I am not going to try to control you either? I know I wasn't completely frank with you when we first met in Paris, but surely you can see I'm nothing like Lucasta? I want to marry you because I love you. You, Nathan. The man you are. I don't want you to become something else. I don't want to mould you, or push you, or treat you like a puppet by pulling your strings. I just want to make you happy.'

'And what of all your money? What of that?'

'It doesn't matter.'

'Doesn't matter!' He made an angry, impatient gesture. 'I have my pride, you know. In fact, it's about damn near all I do have left.'

'No, it isn't. You have my heart, too. It's yours whether you want it or not. And there's nothing else of any value at all. Without your love, my life is completely empty. Hollow. Money cannot fulfil me.'

She stepped right up to him and grabbed his lapels. 'I made a mistake leaving you behind in Paris. As soon as I got back here, I saw that without you, I will only ever just…exist. I have been so lonely without you. I need you to be…my companion. My soulmate. Nathan, marry me. Make my life worth living again.'

'I am not the man to make any woman's life worth living,' he said bitterly. 'All my life, people have been telling me that. And I've proved it. My first marriage failed—'

'Because you didn't love each other. You married for all the wrong reasons. Marry for the right ones this time. Because you want a companion and a soulmate. Someone to complete you and make *your* life worth living.'

He took a breath as though about to say something. Closed his mouth. Shook his head. 'It's no use. I was just chasing a dream. Paris was—'

'Paris was a taste of what we could have, if we both

trust in the love we found there. When you learned that I hadn't been an unmarried mother, that I hadn't tried to deceive you, I saw the pain etched into your features fade away. And I became a better person when I was with you, too. The anger I'd carried around for so long, like a shield, melted away. I thought that lowering it would make me vulnerable. Instead, it freed me to be myself. And that was the person you loved. The real Amethyst. The one I'd never suspected I could be. It wasn't the girl you knew all those years ago. It was someone I'd become as a result of all I've been through. Just as you'd changed from the boy who swept me off my feet, then broke my heart. You'd grown into a man. A man who'd suffered, and sinned, then finally found a path you could walk with your head held high.

'Money didn't come into it. Reputation didn't matter either. It was who we were when we were together that was important. The fact that we made each other happy.'

'You are right,' he said slowly, 'in that we did make each other happy. But…this is all wrong. A woman doesn't propose to a man.'

'Well, perhaps a woman should, especially if she's been silly enough to turn down a man's proposal so many times it's made him give up hope. Should we both suffer for the rest of our lives because I was too scared to dare believe you really felt something for me? Or because you let my wealth stand between us?'

His hands went to her hips.

'Amy, you are so wealthy you could have any man you wanted. You can't possibly want to throw yourself away on a wretch like me…'

'I don't want any other man. I've never wanted any other man. For some reason, you are the only one who makes me think of kissing and being held, and taking my clothes off and wrapping myself around you.'

'Amy...' He groaned. 'What am I going to do with you?'

'Love me, Nathan. That's all I want from you.'

'I do love you,' he said. 'You're right. It is you...you as you are now that I love, but...'

She didn't let him continue with his protests. She stood on tiptoe, plunged her fingers into his hair and kissed him.

With a groan, he surrendered. He returned the kiss with interest, holding her so tightly that breathing soon became difficult.

Eventually, she had to tear her lips away, just to breathe.

But when she looked into his face, it was to see doubt and misery lingering beneath the passion.

'Very well,' she said. 'I can see that marriage is too big a step for you to take. So I will just have to be content with living with you, as your mistress.'

'No! I won't demean you by making you sink that low. You've already suffered enough on my account. The last thing I want is to embroil you in a scandal.'

'It might be a bit too late to avoid it,' she admitted. 'On the way here I informed the most determined gossip in the county that I'm going to run away with you. If you don't want to ruin my reputation beyond all hope of redemption, you're going to have to marry me. And if,' she said, lifting her chin defiantly, 'you really can't stomach the prospect of having another wealthy wife, then I can give it all away.'

'What? No—I'd never ask you to do that. It wouldn't be right.'

'I would gladly give it away if it would mean winning you. Nathan, can't you see that it doesn't matter? Any more than your reputation matters?'

'You are really ready to give everything away and ally yourself to a man whose reputation is just about as sordid as it can be?'

She nodded, her eyes solemn. 'That's why I've just destroyed my own reputation. So that it makes us even.'

He grabbed her shoulders and shook her. 'Amy, telling one woman, in a small market town in the middle of nowhere, that you're going to run off with what she thinks is a penniless artist hardly compares with the stink I created in society.'

'I will put that picture of me naked up for sale in the auction rooms, then,' she declared defiantly. 'In my father's parish.'

He shook his head ruefully. 'Amy, Amy, how can you want to throw everything away like this? On me of all people? I don't know how you can be so sure I won't break faith with you…'

'I know because your whole life went sour when you thought you'd lost me the first time. When you thought I wasn't the girl you'd fallen in love with, but some mirage conjured up from your fevered imagination. I know because I went through exactly the same process. I know because I've never been so happy as I was in Paris, with you. Even though doubt and fear lingered, I had to take what I could have of you. Just as you snatched at what you thought you could have of me. Even when you still believed I was Monsieur Le Brun's mistress, you came and begged me to leave him and take up with you. You'd been starved of love for so long you were prepared to drink the dregs.

'But, Nathan, you don't have to scrape the dregs of life any longer. We can have the finest vintage. We love each other. What else matters?'

'A great many things,' he said sadly. 'Though you are right about a good deal.' He drew her against his chest, and buried his face in her hair.

'I didn't ever really stop loving you. Even when I thought you the worst kind of woman, when I saw you again, I couldn't prevent myself from wanting you. My body recognised its one true mate.'

She pushed herself away just enough that she could look up into his face.

'It was exactly the same for me. Every time I read some new story about you in the papers, I told myself I was well rid of you. But the moment I saw you again… it was as though there was nobody else in the room. I didn't care what you'd done.'

'I did a great many things of which I'm heartily ashamed now.'

'I know.' Her eyes filled with tears. 'And I also know that if you were as bad as they all say you are, then you wouldn't be ashamed. You wouldn't care.'

'Amy,' he whispered, before lowering his head and kissing her as if she was necessary to his very existence.

She flowed into him, relief rushing through her in a flood.

'They said I was too young to know what I wanted,' he said, breaking off to frame her face with his hands and gaze at her intently. So intently that she knew he was speaking of her.

'Too naïve to know what was good for me. They persuaded me to follow a path that led me to utter misery.'

'I know,' she said. 'They tried to tell me I was too

silly to know truth from wishful thinking, too. But we weren't too young. We knew we'd found the road to happiness. And now we've found it again.'

'Then,' he said and swallowed, 'I will take it.' Then uncertainty clouded his features. 'If you're sure?'

'Oh, yes, Nathan, I'm completely sure. And I promise you,' she said earnestly, 'that this time, marriage won't feel like a prison sentence.'

'I'm not the only one who might think of it like a trap, though, am I? You've been so used to running not only your own life, but also that of hundreds of others, through your manufactories, that it's going to be hard for you to give it all up. Especially when I don't really want any of it.'

'Give it all up? I thought you said you didn't want me to give it all away?'

'Yes, but once we marry, it will all belong to me.'

'Yes, but, Nathan, you don't want to change me, any more than I want you to become something you're not, do you?'

'Of course not. I want you to be happy, too.'

'Well, then, if you don't want me to give it all away and you don't want to be chained to a desk yourself, why don't we do something that nobody would expect? Why don't we just snap our fingers at convention?'

He looked at her with a frown for a few seconds, then his expression cleared.

'We can make our marriage anything we want, you're right. We don't need to let society mould us into being anything we don't want to be. Not either of us.' He drew a deep breath. 'If you want to carry on running your business empire, then I won't try to stop you. I don't want to be the one to clip your wings.'

She beamed at him. 'Any more than I would try to stop you painting. Or…or anything you want to do.'

'I should never have walked out on you, earlier. I just…I got so angry when I heard you had so much money. And that you'd concealed so much from me. It all felt…'

'I know,' she said. 'It all got tangled up in memories of your first marriage. Of getting into it before you really knew what Lucasta was like.'

'You are nothing like her,' he said fervently. 'I'm so sorry for implying that you are.'

'I forgive you. You didn't mean it. I've sometimes said things, when I've been angry, that I've regretted later, haven't I? And you didn't listen to the words I said, but judged what was beneath the surface. The emotions that had made me lash out at you. And then you came after me.'

'Just as you came after me.'

'I feel so sorry for Lucasta,' she said, wrinkling her brow. 'Not only because she had you, and didn't appreciate what she had, but also because she had so many frustrated ambitions. If she wanted to have a voice in Parliament, why shouldn't she?'

'Amy,' he gasped. 'That's…revolutionary talk.'

She grinned up at him impishly. 'And even in France, they don't let women into government, do they?'

'Not legally, no, but behind the scenes…'

'Never mind what goes on behind the scenes in France, Nathan. I'm far more concerned with what is going to go on behind closed doors in Stanton Basset.'

As she spoke, she pulled the pin from his neckcloth, then started to work on the complicated knot with determined, if rather unskilled fingers. When he saw she was getting nowhere, he pushed her hands away and loosed it himself.

'Never let it be said that I disappointed a lady,' he said with a lazy smile.

He led her to the rug before the fire, lowered her down on to it and began to undo her gown, with a great deal more expertise than she'd shown with his neckcloth.

'You won't, Nathan. You couldn't.'

He buried his face in her neck, breathing in as though he was intent on inhaling her.

'I will do my utmost not to, my clever darling. My only love.'

And he didn't disappoint her. Right there on the hearthrug.

* * * * *

LET'S TALK
Romance

For exclusive extracts, competitions
and special offers, find us online:

- **f** facebook.com/millsandboon
- **◉** @millsandboonuk
- **𝕏** @millsandboon

Or get in touch on 0844 844 1351*

For all the latest titles coming soon, visit
millsandboon.co.uk/nextmonth

Want even more
ROMANCE?

Join our bookclub today!

'Mills & Boon books, the perfect way to escape for an hour or so.'

Miss W. Dyer

'Excellent service, promptly delivered and very good subscription choices.'

Miss A. Pearson

'You get fantastic special offers and the chance to get books before they hit the shops'

Mrs V. Hall

Visit millsandbook.co.uk/Bookclub
and save on brand new books.

MILLS & BOON